Sunset Fire

Vikings of Honor, Book One

RENEE VINCENT

SUNSET FIRE
Copyright © 2017, Renee Vincent
Trade Paperback ISBN: 9781944484064

Digital ISBN: 9781944484057
Hardback ISBN: 9781944484156

Cover Art Design by Renee Vincent
Stock Art by BigStock.com
Editor, Linda Ingmanson
Digital Release: May, 2017
Trade Paperback Release: May, 2017
Hardback Release: March, 2022

Publishing History
Originally published by iUniverse.com under the title *Ræliksen,* Copyright © 2008 by Renee Vincent

First Edition of revised work published by Turquoise Morning Press under the title *Ræliksen,* Copyright © 2010 by Renee Vincent

Second Edition of revised work published by Renee Vincent under the title *Ræliksen,* Copyright © 2015 by Renee Vincent

First and foremost, to God, for helping my heart to heal, for the hope of a new tomorrow, and for giving me this wonderful gift of writing.

This novel is dedicated to my youngest sister, Lindsey, whose inspirational words allowed me to finish this love story. I look up to you now.

In Loving Memory of Lindsey
(1984 – 2005)

Praise for SUNSET FIRE

TOP 3 Favorite Viking Romances
—says *USA Today* of *Sunset Fire*

"If you've never heard of the name Renee Vincent then
you're missing out on quality reading that's worth every
second of your undivided attention. It's an escapists dream
and I will most certainly be back for more."
—*Night Owl Reviews*

"A beautifully written story, infused with passion,
surprising plot twists, Ireland, and romance. This series has
become my all-time favorite!"
—*Romance Junkies*

"FAN-FREAKING-TASTIC!"
—*Coffee Beans & Love Scenes*

"A love story that's shaped not only by the land and the
sky, but by the poignancy of a rich and brutal history. And
therein lies the masterpiece. Every word of this story has
meaning. Every moment leads to the next. Every word is
simultaneously natural and brilliant, each one holding an
unmistakable place in history with the telling of this tale."
—*USA Today* bestselling author Sarah Balance

"*Sunset Fire* is a complicated tale of betrayal and deception with a few twists and turns you will really like. However, Daegan and Mara's love is never in doubt. The ending will rip your heart out so that you must buy the sequel to get the full story. Renee Vincent writes with lyrical prose. It's truly beautiful. And she tells a good tale with attention to historic detail that will satisfy lovers of historical romance."
**—Award-winning historical fiction author
Regan Walker**

"The author has done an excellent job of bringing the past back to life with her vivid characters. The story itself is very involving, with vivid characters and an exciting plot!"
—*Coffee Time Romance*

"Let's just make a note that this reader LOVED this book. Every single one of the twists, turns, and Oh. My. Goodness. Moments."
—*Romancing The Book*

"When I read this touching story, I cried! I was overwhelmed with emotions! Ms. Vincent is an amazing writer with captivating words that will leave you wanting more. If you are a fan of historical romances, you will not be disappointed. I highly recommend this book!"
—N. Laverdure, Book Reviewer

"Take a trip with Renee to this amazing world of Viking romance and I can guarantee you won't be disappointed. Without a doubt, this book is 5 STARS (10 if it were possible)."
—R. Lucas, Book Reviewer

SUNSET FIRE
Vikings of Honor, Book 1

Mara, the daughter of an Irish king, was raised to believe the Northmen are murderous pagans without a moral bone in their bodies. Despite warnings of their violent raids and the growing threat of another incursion, Mara is continually drawn to her favorite place - the River Shannon.

Dægan Ræliksen, a wealthy chieftain from Norway's frozen fjords, secretly discovers Mara at the water's edge. Charmed by her beauty and sensuous grace, he decides his search for a wife has ended.

Mara and Dægan come face-to-face in a time when every Irishman is being called up to fight against the Viking foreigners. To acquire the woman he treasures, Dægan must make peace with Mara's father, but can Mara move past her fears and find the noble man within the savage?

*Previously published as *Raeliksen*. (This new edition has been partially rewritten and professionally edited, along with a new title and new cover.)

Chapter One

I shall marry this woman, Dægan Ræliksen decided. It had been over a fortnight since he first followed her through the green meadows to the waters of the River Shannon, watching her with intent. Observing her gave him great pleasure, and every day he anticipated her arrival, secretly longing to hold her in his arms. Only lately did he grow impatient with his desire for her, and this day, he settled on, would finally be the day he'd put his suffering to an end and make her his wife.

She stood amid the knee-high grasses and flowers in a white flowing tunic, hemmed with an embroidery of vibrant gold at the ankles and wrists. The sleeves were long and tapered. The bodice mildly followed the curves of her dainty torso, blooming into a tasteful neckline that allowed just a slight hint of cleavage to show before a single jeweled brooch fastened a matching cloak at her shoulders.

In days past, her tunics included colors of deep crimson, indigo, and sometimes an earthy beige. But today's choice was his favorite. She embodied the very likeness of a beautiful Valkyrie, save for her lack of weapons and fair hair. Her long russet curls were distinctly dark with shades of auburn glistening like radiant sunlight. Her skin was as smooth as fresh buttermilk, and her smile like a cool drink of water. She stood no taller than his shoulders, but she'd easily filled the empty space in his heart and the entire expanse of his mind for the past weeks.

By her attire, Dægan could only guess her to be an

Irish maiden of wealthy descent. This too excited him, for in contrast to her apparent nature, she was rugged and spirited, riding her stallion as well as any of his mounted *birdmen* to this specific place every day, yet still looking elegant upon it.

In the hours she spent alone, no man had ever summoned or demanded her presence. He found this quite odd, for she was old enough for bedding and young enough for bearing healthy sons. She came and went as she pleased, heedless to the fact that she was the object of another's longing. Instead, she'd often sing, tickling his heart with her exuberant voice and an Irish ballad that danced in his soul.

He was unexpectedly mesmerized by her, chained to the very thought that she could be his if he only dared to make his presence known. That in itself would prove to be the most difficult. He dreaded that his countrymen's reputation as savage foreigners would precede any valiant attempt at meeting civilly. He was a handsome man with a persuasive charm, or at least he was told so by other women who had fancied him. Yet he knew an effective *come-hither* approach would not be enough to sway the innocent soul before him.

He'd pondered his options last night over a scanty dinner of roasted rabbit and had come up with the idea of "saving her" from the rampant run of a conveniently spooked steed. It could be done easily enough, assuredly changing her views of a savage foreigner to that of a hero, and quite possibly obtaining the affable encounter for which he so wished.

But now, by midmorning, the idea seemed utterly ridiculous. There were too many opportunities for things to go wrong. The horse might not even spook to begin with.

Or if it did flee, he could have difficulties catching up with it. Or worse, the horse could rear and topple her from its back, gravely injuring her in the process.

Discouraged, Dægan continued to gaze through the trees and brush at his enchanting maiden, wanting desperately to step out and make himself known. Even though he could boast smooth-tonguing a few endearments in the beautiful lilting *Gaeilge*, he knew this woman only had to look at him to know he was not Irish. So how could he show his face without frightening her?

Every idea, no matter how promising it seemed, had its pitfall. He could only close his eyes and pretend to exist in a different world. And how grand a world he could envision behind closed lids; a place where they could meet without apprehension, smile without pause, and converse without falsehoods. What he wouldn't give to make that world a reality…

As Dægan opened his eyes in weary disappointment, he caught his breath to find her walking closer to him. His body became rigid, his heart raced, and only then did he notice just how fiery his blood could run through his veins. The distance between them diminished slowly with each of her steps, and he'd not a plan to remedy this turn of events.

Fleeting ideas swarmed his brain like dancing bees. *'Tis too soon in the day for pilfering and much too foolish to be thinking it.* The only halfway respectable idea that came to mind was to lie down and fake an injury. Perhaps he could say he'd fallen from his own horse, appearing helpless and in dire need of care. But for some reason, he did not drop to his back and put that plan into motion. He sat frozen, only staring as she stopped a few feet from him to peer blindly into the thicket.

"Who's there?"

Her voice was like springtime, genuinely sweet, with a pleasant, melodic tone that could warm a chilled soul after a long daily Erin rain. It was with this thought that he drew in a slow breath, catching her airy spiced scent that sifted between the summer-green leaves of the hedge plant separating them. He wondered if Valkyries smelled as good as she did.

Suddenly, from behind her, Dægan saw several dark figures emerging on the shores of the River Shannon. Although their distance was too far, he managed to make out that they were not alone. Coming closer were three more longboats flaunting red and white sails. He didn't recognize the men, but he knew from the shape and adornments on the prow that they were like him, Norse.

By this time, the first vessel had run aground and the men were descending from each side in large numbers. Sizeable fleets weren't usually merchants, but *hirdmen* who were following their chieftain into a devastating raid for booty or war.

Dægan reacted with lightning speed and pulled the Irish maiden to the ground before she could say another word. Without much effort, he stifled her screams of terror with a simple hardened hand to her mouth and pinned her to the ground as easily as battling a child. But a helpless child she was not.

She threw wide her mouth and bit his palm. When he retracted his hand, she launched her forehead into his nose, jarring him into a dazed state of mind. Everything around him went black and spun.

Despite that, he still felt her thrashing beneath him. He tightened his grasp as if his very will to stay coherent were cinched around her fragile little wrists. The only thing that kept him from passing out was his own agony, for it had now become his only thought. He forgot the woman, her sweet alluring voice, her carefree mornings, and her lighthearted dances amid the tall flowers of the Erin meadow. All he knew now was the pain in his face.

He heard her sudden intake of breath and assumed she finally saw what he'd seen—more men coming ashore. *You shall not die this day,* he wanted to say to her. *You shall not die.* But he hadn't the ability to reassure her or stop the flow of blood from his nostrils now soiling her dress.

Trying to be considerate, he wiped his upper lip on the bear cloak that hung from his shoulders, although it was a prized possession, a trophy from the animal he'd killed in his bygone youth. He wouldn't have that bearskin at all had it not been for his father's words: *a man who slights caution presumes his death.* How foolish he was to dismiss those important words now just because his opponent was a woman and not a growling beast of muscle, claws, and teeth. However innocent her semblance was, his bloodstained fur was a painful reminder of his mistake. He vowed never to underestimate her again, starting with this unusually quiet moment. She was far too passive, and her sudden surrender seemed calculative.

Dægan spoke first. "I know you're frightened. But say not a word. Those men will hear you, and they will kill us both."

She looked at him as though he'd two heads.

"I'll not hurt you," he whispered again. He fixed his gaze on the deep pools of green in hers. And for a moment, time stood still. Even for her, he swore.

He noticed her trembling body and how tightly he held her wrists. He didn't mean to hurt her. It was not his intention to grab her and hold her down like some belligerent thug about to take his pleasures. It was solely to save her life, and if he hadn't forced her to the ground, they would have been seen, probably pursued, and undoubtedly slain.

With kinder eyes, he tried to give her comfort. "You must believe me. I'll not hurt you. I give you my word."

She seemed utterly confused by the viciousness of his actions and the contradiction of his noble words. He could only hope that his pledge meant something to her and that he didn't appear to be just an animal ready to ravage the reward of his successful hunt.

His heart went out to her, and he loosened his hold. But at that very moment, she brought her right elbow up to his nose again, hitting it with such force that it nearly blinded him.

She scrambled out from beneath him, and he could do little about it. The pain was so excruciating, it threatened to split his skull in two. Never before had he taken such abuse from a woman that he actually contemplated the idea of her being a demon from *Hel.*

As blood poured between his fingers and down his wrists, Dægan tried to open his eyes. He saw his lovely hellion on horseback fleeing deeper into the woodlands and shrinking to a distant white blur. He grunted a swift harsh oath. Yet his greatest problem was not the damage done to his face, but the setback of her escape in plain sight. The once-quiet shores of the Shannon were now filled with shouts and commotion from the very men he so desperately tried to elude.

Somehow, Dægan sat up and crawled on all fours to his horse. He took extra care to stay low and out of sight, for it was better that the Northmen not know of his presence. Should she be captured, he'd at least have the element of surprise in his favor. With that in mind, he mounted the animal with dexterity and stealth, then booted his horse into a gallop.

His heart quickened, his body went numb, and his face cooled with the rushing wind. He felt nothing as he tore through the woods, dodging trees and ditches. His only thought was to catch up with her and keep her safe.

What seemed like a ride through eternity ended when Dægan saw the hindquarters of her horse and her white dress flapping like a flag in the wind. He looked over his shoulder to check the other men's advancement and realized they were still far behind as they had not yet come into view.

With the satisfaction of their distance, Dægan contemplated the difficulty of catching her without the others seeing *him*. He was greatly outnumbered, and his injury did not give him any advantage. One more hit to the face and he'd drop like a stone. Nevertheless, he expected the undertaking to be nothing short of arduous, and banished most, if not all, of the strategies that had come to mind, instead relying on the will of the gods.

He gained on her with every stride, and at first chance, he rounded her horse to the left to steal the reins from her hands. But his attempt failed, piloting him straight toward a labyrinth of trees. He barely steered clear of the oaks, teetering in his saddle to avoid crushing his knee, while shifting back to circumvent another. After surviving a few more low-hanging tree limbs, he emerged again, hot on her trail.

Upon seeing a stream in the approaching valley, Dægan drove his heels in and charged his steed forward in hopes of using the water to his advantage. He slipped his feet from the stirrups and pulled them up to squat on the saddle. As he steadied himself on his haunches, he prepared to leap when they crossed the stream so he'd have something other than the hard ground to catch their fall.

She saw him and her eyes widened with a paralyzing fear, failing to see the shallow muddy shore that lined the stream. Her horse fell swiftly to the ground and threw her over its head. She landed hard against the rocky embankment and lay there motionless in a crumpled heap.

Dægan immediately pulled back hard on the reins and cinched his horse's chin to its throat, making every attempt to avoid the same catastrophe. His horse stamped for traction and reared to relieve itself of the bit drawn in its mouth, only to dodge the oncoming path of her fugitive horse that was now running back across the water.

Dægan settled his horse and slid off, running into the flowing stream. He fought the push of rushing water around his knees, and once at her side, he rolled her over. A flash of bright red shocked him as blood had already soaked through her hair and into her eye socket.

Given the force of her fall and the seriousness of her injury, he half expected her to be dead, but was relieved when he laid his hand across her mouth and felt the warmth of her breath. What's more, her flighty horse had given a diversion that kept the other Northmen in the woods.

He looked her over one last time, determining that her wounds were not life-threatening, and picked her up in his arms. He staggered slightly from the current and trudged toward his horse at the stream's edge. Mounting would not be easy, but then again, nothing he'd done this day was. He decided that being moderately careful with her wasn't necessary since she was unconscious, and tossing her over his shoulder was just as good and less troublesome.

Or so he thought.

Her dead weight made him teeter as he put his foot in the stirrup, and the blasted mud beneath him swallowed his other ankle deep in muck. Another harsh oath escaped him before he clutched the horse's mane and threw a heavy leg up over the saddle. As he settled in and lowered her body to his lap, he noticed the return of his own pain. It was a momentary awareness to which he paid little heed, for the woman was now in his possession, draped across his legs, her head cradled in his arms.

He touched her cheek, pleased with his reward—one she'd come to know soon enough.

****

The sun started to set in the western sky above the loping green hills of Ireland. Dægan had been riding all afternoon, trying to reach Limerick before nightfall, where his fellow Northmen awaited him. But having an unconscious rider made it difficult for him to gain any ground. He decided, with dusk fast approaching, he should make camp for the night in the nearby forest, deep enough, though, to escape notice should the men who were after her come as far as he.

It was darker in the woods, and he regretted not finding a spot sooner. The trees stood quiet, absent the scurry of foraging nocturnal animals, and only the crickets were brave enough to proclaim their contentment with the night. Their collective serenade was just enough to convince him that he was being overly cautious.

He slid from his horse with the woman still in his arms

and found a perfect place to lay her down. The soft moss under a tall tree was his first generous offering of many more to come, for he was smitten with the Irish woman. Throughout his life as a merchant, he'd never before been fortunate enough to find such beauty without a high price. Some would argue that a broken nose was too high, but for him, it was a petty fee. He possessed the most valuable of all precious jewels in the world.

Having her was one thing. Having her never awaken again was another. It worried him that she was still unconscious. Even as he rustled around to beat the blackness of night—untying rolled hides from the saddle, tossing food and drink pouches about, and setting up camp—she never moved.

Her unresponsiveness was a quick thought, though, for the aching in his stomach kept the rest of his thoughts on a more primal level. Mostly of how his morning and afternoon meals were both missed, and that what he'd packed wasn't enough for his empty stomach, much less his new guest. A successful hunt and a good night's rest were what he longed for, but on this day, the gods seemed to prefer adversity to victory.

Fixed on turning the tables in his favor, he took some rope from his saddle and confined her to the tree. He hated the idea—detested it, moreover. But after one knot, he reminded himself of her lively spirit and wrapped two more lengths of rope for no other reason than common sense.

He also needed a fire. Not only to cook his meal but for ample warmth throughout the night. Be that as it may, he hesitated, for a fire would no doubt give their location away should the others still be searching for her. The idea that a fire was a necessary evil soon outweighed the risks, and before any more time was wasted, he started gathering wood and kindling for a modest blaze.

Within minutes, he set the kindling afire and proceeded to add wood as the flames reached for more. It was not hard to become entranced by the snapping and popping of the fire. It set the mood as he took in the beautiful sight of purity and grace that lay before him. *Chaste* was the word that contented him.

She had a shapely body, and a rip up the side of her dress bared one leg from mid-thigh to ankle. He envisioned the night she'd finally submit to his touch instead of fighting it so violently.

His own body stirred, and he stood up, trying to extinguish the sudden urges that swept through him like fire. He ached for a woman's touch and the heat of nakedness. They were pleasures he'd done without for many months. His journeys were few, and finding a woman of worth had become more important than his livelihood. And now that she lay only a few feet from him, it was a desire he couldn't just wish away.

As he took notice of the tent pitching beneath his kirtle, he left her alone under the night sky to hunt for a generous meal, lest she'd awaken to two shocking revelations.

****

"M'lord, we couldn't find the girl," Einar said, spilling forth his best excuse. "We retrieved the horse she was riding, but she was not on it. I'd swear by the gods she has disappeared!"

Domaldr continued to stare out over the moonlit River Shannon, his growing irritation keeping him from turning around and facing his *hirdmen*. He was a freeman in the face of Norway's noblemen, but also a man who aspired to gain a noble's title, even if it was through sudden notoriety as opposed to the long road of accruing wealth and support from the local kinsman. Infamy was the shortcut to the title of *Jarl*, and the imminent war for Dubh-Linn was his surefire route to staking that claim—as long as he could survive long enough to get there.

"Believe me, Einar," Domaldr finally said, "women never just disappear. The willowy bitches will haunt you until the day you die. As will I, if you do not find her."

"But—"

"Our purpose here, as you're well aware, is to hold a hidden flank position for Sigtrygg Gale's western front. No one, including a feeble woman, was to know of our presence. And because of your incompetence, you've put me in a very difficult situation, as I'm forced to contemplate the worst with our little woman friend still at large. Surely you've seen that the dress she was wearing was not that of a slave but of a woman of importance. With that said, she's accustomed to others doing for her, therefore lacking the knowledge to take care of herself, much less know how to slip past six full-grown men!"

Einar's silence caused Domaldr to turn on his heels, taking first notice of the dark-haired Irishman among his other unspeaking warriors. "Who is this?"

Soren, a man not easily rattled, spoke for Einar. "We came upon him in the forest. He was hunkered down behind a fallen log, lurking—"

"I was hunting!" the Irishman corrected.

Soren shoved a quick elbow into the man's gut, doubling him over and forcing him to his knees.

Domaldr watched the man cough and retch, and rubbed his own temples fiercely, unwilling to deal with this much chaos so soon after their landing. He stepped forward, eyeing the young man at his feet. Even when the man was shrunk to his knees with his hands tied behind his back, Domaldr could tell he was exceptionally lithe and no stranger to hard work.

"Stand up," Domaldr demanded.

The man did as he was told, looking Domaldr in the eye, despite that he had to lift his chin a bit to do so.

"What is your name?"

"Breandán, son of Liam."

Detesting the pride in the Irishman's voice, Domaldr leaned in close to cut him down. "Sounds much too important a name for just a hunter."

"If I knew *your* name, I wager I too could slight the importance of yours."

Domaldr raised the corner of his mouth in a bristly smile. "You've a sharp tongue, *Éireannach*. Much like myself. But 'tis not enough to spare you. From now on, you best speak as though your very life depends on it, Breandán."

Breandán's jaw clenched. "I swear to you, I was only hunting. I've no interest in the purpose of your gathering."

Domaldr ran his tongue across his teeth. "You don't look like a hunter."

"At first glance, you don't look like a horse's arse. But we are what we are."

Normally, Domaldr would have choked the life from any man who'd make such a remark, but instead, he crossed his arms over his chest. "I actually believe you, hunter, which means there's no reason for me to have you killed. Consider yourself fortunate. However, there's still the matter of *our* discovered presence, and setting you free would not alleviate that. As much as I believe you commonly speak your mind to the fullest of truths, I still don't trust you." Domaldr looked at Soren. "Secure him and guard him well."

"Aye, m'lord." Soren nodded, shoving Breandán forward.

"Einar," Domaldr said, putting a hand on his shoulder. "Let us talk."

Einar said nothing as Domaldr led him away from the group down to the banks of the Shannon. His uneasiness shone like a lantern in the night.

"I'm a patient man, do you not think?"

Einar swallowed hard. "Of course, m'lord."

"And you'd not dare test my patience, would you?"

Einar shook his head adamantly. "Nay. Never."

"Good. Then my burden seems to be lifted. When Sigtrygg asks who is to blame for thwarting his plan, I can say with certainty 'twas you."

Einar's breath caught in his throat. "If you must, m'lord…"

"Yet," Domaldr said, altering his approach, "your idiocy will still be a chink in my armor. The slander of my good name would be a poor representation of my great ability to lead. I cannot have that, Einar. Surely, you understand."

Einar gazed at Domaldr, who feigned both sympathy and regret, yet all too suddenly, a hot pain ripped through his gut. Einar looked down and pressed his hands to the warm blood that saturated his kirtle and breeches. His legs grew weak, and he stumbled forward to grasp his chieftain, but Domaldr stepped aside, shoving him into the river. His body hit the water and floated amongst the red waves that rippled between the floating vessels.

Domaldr glanced up from his bloodied knife at the four men witnessing Einar's death. "Have Soren and two others go with you, and find that girl!"

Chapter Two

Dægan finished his meal of roasted meat and tossed the bones into the fire. Troubled with his inactive dinner guest, he sighed and wished she'd come to on her own. The excessive sleeping made him very nervous and the night far too long.

He rose from the fire, deciding that it was better to encourage her awakening than let any more hours of the night pass in a slow creep. Taking his knife, he cut a piece of hide sparingly and poured water from his skin pouch to soak it. He then knelt beside her, preparing to nurse her wounds.

As he dared to touch her, his eyes drank in the delicateness of her facial features, the fullness of her bottom lip, and the clean cut of her jaw that slipped into a graceful feminine neck. She looked so unlike the other women he'd known, and he found the differences to be quite refreshing.

He reached down and stroked a few locks of her hair that had fallen loosely across her chest, feeling the softness between his fingers. He was doubly pleased that its sweet scent was able to penetrate the swelling within his nostrils. He breathed in deeper this time and savored the fine oils she'd used, similar to the ones he'd sell in the marketplaces.

It took him back to his journeys in the Mediterranean, where silks and oils were plentiful, as well as the number of women who were eager to please the merchant strangers entering their ports. There were many to choose from, he recalled, all different shades of skin, with dark, enchanting eyes and sable, silken hair. Still, none equaled her.

Dægan wiped her brow with the soaked cloth, taking care of the swollen red gash just below her hairline. He pressed the wet cloth to her abrasion and cleaned what blood had dried on her face. Often, he stopped to rinse the cloth, continuing his tedious yet gentle work upon her wounds as she slept.

Although she was unaware of his kindness, he thanked the gods for the opportunity to caress her, even if it was just for a short while. He knew, given the circumstances of their meeting, she'd not be as eager for his touch when she awakened. In fact, he was sure she'd fight twice as hard to escape him once she found herself alone in the dead of night with him. This time, he prepared himself for the worst. No more surprise maneuvers when it came to her.

Soon after he wrung the cloth out again, she began to stir. She moaned and showed signs of awareness, starting with the pain in her head.

"Shh…" Dægan whispered. "You're safe now. You're going to be all right."

Mara moaned again and opened her eyes, finding it hard to focus. She saw the figure of a man before her, calming her with his soothing voice. *Father… It must be Father. I made it home.*

She relaxed as she felt his hands caress her hair and heard his voice reassuring her that no one would hurt her again. It was definitely not her father, but probably a servant of recent hire. She closed her eyes, relishing the warm crackling fire and the strangely familiar scent around her.

She knew that scent.

It was a wonderful smell of masculinity and vigor, one she couldn't get away from. As much as she felt at ease, the strange aroma also surrounded her with a disturbing sense of danger. Trying to make out the figure before her, she blinked away the blurriness and squinted to join the double images into one. His face emerged from the haze, a sharply chiseled face with blond hair and kind eyes.

Blond hair?

Her breath caught, and once again she looked at the man she thought she'd escaped.

Where was she now? Where had he taken her?

Panic shot through her, and she quickly looked around, trying to recognize anything past the light of the fire. The darkness and the thick cover of the trees shading the moon overhead made for a difficult task. She was extremely nervous and dreadfully alone.

Frozen with fear, she watched him stand and walk to the other side of the fire. If he did so as a small act of kindness to make her feel more comfortable, it didn't slow her racing heart. His physical presence, no matter how far away he went, was still enough to terrify her. She couldn't take her eyes off him.

They gawked at each other from across the flames. She'd no idea what he was thinking or what he wanted from her. He simply folded his arms and smiled as if he found pleasure in knowing she'd realized he'd won the chase between them.

The man was a monument of beauty and power, sturdy as the ground beneath him. He had long blond hair, a well-groomed beard, and skin darkened from the sun. His hands showed scars and calluses from years of hard work, yet his clothes presented a different story, one of wealth and importance. His tunic was made of the finest wool, a lovely shade of cerulean with a tablet-woven braid around the neckline and hem. His legs were bare from mid-thigh down, and his lower calves were wrapped in the soft cowhide of his boots. His eyes revealed a sense of maturity and intelligence, yet even the darkness could not hide their color, for they were as blue as the ocean he sailed. Before her stood a being that only one word could suitably describe.

"*Lochlannach*," she breathed.

"*Lochlannach*, aye? I like the sound of that. It means *lake dweller*, does it not?"

She remained quiet.

"'Tis a good name," he said, sitting down. "Better than the ones I've been called before. You needn't fear me, this I swear. I know my word means naught to you. But I assure you, I won't harm you." He then took his dagger, still within its sheath, and tossed it to her.

She was surprised to find her hands tied together as the blade hit her lap, for she was far too engrossed with her captor to have realized it. The knife's hilt was intricately adorned with silver and gold, as was its sheath, and it was quite a substantial piece of weaponry for a barbarian to own.

No doubt stolen.

"Cut yourself free," he stated. "But I wouldn't run away if I were you. You're about a day's distance from home, and your knowledge of tracking landmarks will not help you under this night sky as the clouds are moving in quickly. Getting lost would be the least of your worries, for there are others who search for you. Although their determination may very well match my own, they're truly without care of moral conduct or your well-being. And as much trouble as I've gone through to keep you from these men, I cannot say for certain whether I'd have the might to do it again."

His words were a heavy warning roped with a little strand of humor, like the gentle twine that held her to the tree. She picked up the dagger and began to run the blade carefully across the rope, slowly shredding its binding until it gave way and fell into the folds of her gown. Aggravated, she threw the rope into the fire and watched it twist and ravel. As the rope diminished, so did her hopes for escape.

As a king's daughter, she was sure he'd use her to get what he wanted, and feared just how far he'd go. For that reason, she placed the dagger at her side slightly under her gown, just in case *his* moral conduct warranted drastic measures.

"We have traveled all day. You must be hungry." He pointed to the meat left on the spit. "Go ahead. I've already eaten."

She grabbed the skewer and devoured the meat quickly. She'd no idea how hungry she was until she tasted the roasted hare. It was still warm, and amazingly, the primitive meal was the best she'd ever eaten. Within minutes, the meat was gone, and she wiped her mouth of any residue, only slightly embarrassed to have eaten so voraciously.

"Thirsty?" he asked, reaching for his drinking pouch. He seemed to give thought to throwing it to her, but changed his mind. "May I bring it to you?"

His question spun in her head like a storm. As much as she wanted him to keep his distance, he asked for her consent instead of assuming it. She swallowed her fear and gave a nervous nod, for she was exceedingly parched.

He arose and approached slowly, keeping enough space between them as he sat beside her. He held the pouch in front of her. "Drink it all if you like. I've more."

She accepted it and drank just as quickly as she'd eaten. "How is your head?"

Mara flinched at the approach of his hand, but he stopped short.

"Your head," he pointed out. "You fell from your horse. Do you remember?"

She touched her forehead and winced. "Where *is* my horse?"

"'Twould appear that it gave us a much-needed diversion to keep the men, who were after you, busy in the forest. I'm certain they've secured it back at the river by now. I would have. No sense in letting a perfectly good mount go astray."

"Then why did you?" she snapped.

His lips crept into a smile. "Because I took a beating in its stead."

She gave him a sideways glance. "I should warn you, a broken nose, reminiscent of the one you already have, hurts much worse the third time around."

"Ah, so I *do* have discolored eyes. I was wondering if you'd left any marks upon me."

She frowned. "You speak as though you enjoyed it."

He squeezed his nose gently between his thumb and fingers, which evidently brought a sudden pang between his eyes. "Hardly."

"Who were those men?"

"I know not," he stated with a shrug. "Their presence was as much a surprise to me as it was to you. But if you'd listened to me, they would never have known we were there in the first place, nor would you have that nasty bump on your head."

"So, this is my fault?"

His brows lifted. "I know the means by which I saved you from those men was not as noble as you'd have liked, but nonetheless, you've been saved."

"And I suppose you want compensation from my father worth my weight in silver, aye?"

"I want naught from him. Mayhap a bit of gratitude from *you* would suffice. Need I remind you, if not for my timely presence, you'd be a whore for those men on the River Shannon. Who knows how many would have had you by now. The way I see it, you're indebted to me for saving your life, not to mention your precious maidenhead."

She gasped at his arrogance but could only counter his rude boasts with a gaping mouth and a tied tongue.

He lifted his finger to her chin and closed her mouth for her. "My apologies, my lady. Perhaps we can start over. Say with introductions?"

Mara hardened to stone and crossed her arms. "I don't see how knowing your name will help matters."

"Very well. Then let us begin with yours."

She glared at him. He tilted his head to one side, and his eyes sparkled with benevolence as though he were truly interested in her and only her. His hair had fallen over his shoulder, and several small braids adorned with silver clips flashed in the firelight. They were minute, but incredibly detailed with interlacing designs.

Despite his unmistakably Norse features and what she'd been taught to believe, he was well-groomed and clean. Quite frankly, he was the most beautiful thing she'd ever laid eyes on. He was not at all what she thought the *Fionnghaill* should look like, or act like for that matter, and she assumed that outlandish lies and exaggerated stories existed only because no one had dared to get close enough. By her own understanding, he was surely more than a savage...but no less than a man, who only inquired of her name.

Finally, she gave in, for names were harmless enough. "Mara. My name is Mara."

He smiled and boldly brushed back a lock of her hair. "Are you hurt anywhere else—Lady Mara?"

"Nay."

"Are you certain?" This time he peered closer. "You took quite a fall."

"I'm fine," Mara insisted. "It wasn't the first."

"Do you always make a habit of falling from your horse?"

Mara's mouth curled naturally into a smile, but she forced it away as quickly as it appeared.

"Ah, you find me funny," he pointed out.

"I find you odd and foreign. Nothing more."

"Perhaps I'd be less of those things if you knew my name."

Mara said nothing. Although she was remotely curious, she did not want to give him the satisfaction of thinking she cared. As she expected, he offered it all the same.

"I'm Dægan of Hladir, son of Rælik."

Mara liked the sound of his name, and it fit him well. But she refused to show any regard, acting as if his name were ordinary and, at best, a name that would soon slip from her mind.

But...his name clung to her thoughts, and she found

herself almost brooding over it. Every idling recollection revolved around him: his voice as he spoke his own name, his exceptional generosity, his entrancing blue eyes, and what still seemed to be left unanswered—his reason for risking his life to save her.

Mara felt his hand upon hers, a sudden forwardness she hadn't anticipated. His skin was rather warm compared to the coolness of hers, and his adept fingers found their way around the sensitive underside of her wrist. He held her with a grip demonstrative of his tenacious might and control. But even as the little voice in her head told her to pull away and run, she couldn't. Her hand, he turned over, and in it, he placed the silver-and-gold dagger that once lay at her side.

"You can keep this with you tonight," he said, closing her fingers around it. "I promise you, I won't give you any reason to use it."

How could she doubt those words? Those eyes of dazzling blue? They were the inlet to his soul, where mystery and compassion were harbored, and no matter how hard she tried, she couldn't help but drown in them.

Dægan stood and retreated to the opposite side of the fire, standing massively before her like an old tree rooted in the ground. His arms and legs proved his masculinity and power, and the strength in his jaw accentuated his massive physique. His long golden mane complemented his features well, and his eyes could change like the tides in the sea, stern and intimidating at one glance, and gentle and honest at another.

While she was lost in her thoughts, he suddenly lay down upon the ground and covered himself with his thick bear cloak.

"You're going to sleep?" she asked.

"Aye," he said, shifting on the ground. "Even we *Lochlannaigh* must sleep, my dear."

"But I must get home! My father will be worried sick!"

"I'll get you home, I promise. But not tonight."

Mara's voice rose frantically. "When?"

"When I've an army of men to accompany me. 'Tis not safe for just you and me." He rolled to face her. "And you should put those thoughts of leaving whilst I sleep out of your mind. Even if you left right now, you wouldn't make it back before morn—that is if you didn't lose your way in the night. Let's be smart, Mara, and wait until my men can join us before we go traipsing back through hostile territory."

"I thought your kind always traveled in groups, roving bands of warriors, that sort of thing. Why do *you* not travel with your men?"

"Because for what I was doing, I didn't need their company."

"And what may I ask *were* you doing?"

He sighed. "If you must know, I had chosen a bride and was going to bring her home with me."

"A bride?"

"Aye."

Mara's temperament changed as she gathered the extent of his affections. "You seem quite fond of her."

"I am."

Mara kept watching him, liking the way he held the unknown woman in high regard. She softened a little. "Mayhap I should apologize. Had it not been for me and my untimely need of rescue, you'd likely be in her arms right now."

"Think naught of it," Dægan dismissed, repositioning himself beneath the cloak. "'Twill all work out soon enough."

"How did you acquire this woman to be your bride? An alliance?"

"Not exactly. I've *chosen* her, this is certain, but her father fails to know much about it."

Confused, Mara prodded deeper into his personal affairs. "And how do you plan to persuade this *uninformed* father of hers?"

"Well, I was hoping to offer him a dowry he could not refuse, along with an allotment of seven cows, but it might prove to be unnecessary considering my selfless, heroic measures this fine day."

Realization struck her soundly, and her words stumbled from her mouth. "You speak of me? And my father, Cathal? The King of Connacht?"

Dægan opened his eyes and leaned up on one elbow, stunned by her father's rank. He'd assumed her to be the offspring of some clan nobleman, but never had he given thought to her birth being that of the provincial leader himself. With her father being at the top of such a prominent hierarchy, it would surely be a more difficult situation for him to resolve. Yet, to the best of his ability, he pretended it was frivolous.

"If your father is indeed the King of Connacht, then it looks as if he's certainly the man with whom I must bargain."

Mara stood up, walked over, and kicked him square in his side. "How dare you!"

Dægan took the first strike, but caught her foot with the next attempt. He lifted her heel high enough that she lost her balance and fell to her backside. Still holding firmly to her ankle, he dragged her closer, avoiding her little fists that came like madness. He grabbed both her wrists and pulled them to his chest, forcing her to lean forward in his direction.

"How dare you!" she shouted again, fighting his grip. "You belittle my father with your conniving plan. He'll not fall for it any more than I have."

Dægan drew back in surprise. "You think this whole day has been naught but a conniving plan?"

"Aye, the men at the river, the chase, the rescue. 'Tis all a farce! I know your kind! You're all the same! Cunning thieves who pilfer from the weak and kill others out of greed!"

"I've never done such things!" he defended.

"Nay, you just look for women who will be naught more than your slaves soon after you take them to your marriage bed!"

Dægan's face flamed. "Is that what you think you are? A slave? Odin's blood, woman! I've been beaten, punched, and elbowed in the nose to the extent of bleeding profusely—and not for strategy's sake, my dear, but to truly keep you safe from the foreigners on the riverbank! I've gathered wood for a fire so you'd be warm. Hunted so you could eat. I've even given you a weapon to keep by your side to protect yourself, and all the while declaring to you my honest intentions of not—ever—hurting you!" He threw her hands back at her. "Now tell me again, who is the slave?"

Her sudden silence left him somewhat content that he'd gotten his point across.

He sighed and softened his expression. "I know you're afraid, especially being so far from home with a man preconceived as a savage. If that is all you think of me from this day forth, then so be it. But I'll not let you slander me as being a man without honor or without my kept word. I gave my word I'd take you back home, and I will. Furthermore, you're not my slave, nor do I have hopes of it later. I'm a chieftain who already has his fill of *thralls*, and I simply want a wife."

"You cannot be serious!"

Dægan snickered. "After what I went through today, I'd think there'd be no question."

Mara's breath drained from her lungs. "This cannot happen."

"Why not?" he asked, leaning in.

"My father simply won't allow it."

He took her into his arms. "Would *you* allow it?"

At first, Mara was shocked at how daring he chose to be by taking away the little comfort of space between them. She fought the effects of his sultry eyes, his rugged aroma, and his breath upon her cheek with all she had. But all in all, she could do little about it. She was torn between the spoonful of endearment he shoved down her throat, and the inviting warmth of his arms.

"You've not answered me, princess," he teased, drawing her closer to smell the oils upon her skin beneath her jaw.

"H-how *can* I answer you?" she shuddered as she felt the slight tickle of his beard.

"Just open your mouth and speak."

Before she could utter one word of resistance, he skimmed his lips over her chin and covered her mouth with a kiss. She couldn't move, for it was the first time she'd ever experienced one in all her nineteen years. The world around her ceased to exist as the heat and red-blooded strength of his arms molded her tightly to his chest.

She fell limp in his arms and welcomed the gentle caresses of his tongue parting her lips. He went deeper, tasting her, but was never rough or demanding. He only eased his tongue in as much as she'd allow. He played with her, pulled away, then delved back in, taking every sweetened gasp from her like a thief.

She couldn't help but respond to his every touch, and her virgin tongue dared to dance with his. He moaned softly in her mouth, a noise hardly to be heard, but it was enough to make her open her eyes and find his swirling in drunken lustfulness.

His unashamed forwardness would've sent her fleeing, but his embrace enveloped her with a passion she'd never felt before. A strange heat burned low in her stomach, and a rush of cool shivers trickled down her spine as his kiss fed both of those glorious feelings at once.

She froze, barely able to breathe as he dwelled near her lips. He was a mountain of strength and an endless vision of beauty, two things that both lured her and scared her to death. Caught in the very clutches of his hungry gaze, it was hard to discern what held her motionless. The pull of her own attraction to this man, or the dreadful fear of it?

Dægan drew backward. "You look frightened."

Chapter Three

What might have been a depraved reaction to a simple kiss soon became a pretentious rant of shame. Dægan put his finger to Mara's lips, silencing her. "Say no more. I don't want to hear that you made a mistake."

"But I did."

"You cannot tell me that you didn't want it. I felt it in your kiss, in your body as you fell against me." He reached up with both hands and cradled her face. "What you suffered was a desire that matched my own."

Again, she tried to defend herself, but with a flagrant lie. "What if I'm already betrothed to another man? A man who is far braver than you."

"Then I'd have to say, all bravery aside, he's not very attentive to you. He leaves you to fend for yourself in a cruel, dangerous world on a daily basis. But then again, why should he care what perils await you? He doesn't exist."

Mara harrumphed and substituted her perjury with simple honesty. "I cannot marry you. My father will not allow it."

"You've said that once already. But your father doesn't concern me. Besides, I've come to learn that most everyone has a price."

"You're foolish to think he'll care more for cattle and silver than his own daughter," she added.

"You're foolish for thinking that he won't."

"He'd never submit to such an arrangement, especially

with you being a Northman. He'd more likely kill you."

"And this distresses you?"

"Aye," she returned quickly. "I don't want to see you die. If your death was my true intention, I would have already used the dagger."

"So, you trust me, then."

Mara hesitated. "*Should* I trust you?"

Dægan whispered his answer. "Aye."

"Should my father?"

"As well."

"But if you do not take me back to him as early as tomorrow, there will be no trust from which to build. He'll already deem you a thief, and no amount of heroism or grand marks of silver will be enough to exonerate you from your crimes. He'd take immense pleasure in hanging you."

Dægan measured her, but she remained undeterred, steady in her posture. Her bravery was astounding, and it convinced him that his choice of wife was a good one.

"Enough talk about your father. Let's forget about him for just one moment and get back to the way you accepted me. You resisted me much more at the river than you did just now. Why?"

"Because there's no use in fighting you. I know you're stronger."

Dægan shook his head and grinned. "Try again. Tell me why you let me touch you and kiss you so deeply. If that is not trust, I know not what is." He watched her posture melt and waited.

"I cannot explain to you why I allowed such inappropriateness. I assure you, 'tis not what I wanted."

"You didn't want me to kiss you? I could swear by the gods you wanted me the moment you opened your mouth to the caresses of my tongue."

Mara closed her eyes, trying her hardest to be angry at his insinuating comment, to be disgusted at the thought of his lips on hers. But she couldn't. His kiss was a sweet punishment, which taught her nothing except that his mouth was warm, compulsive, and truly pleasurable.

Entangled in her own confusing thoughts, she stood to leave. She tried to distance herself from the charismatic ogre, but he grabbed her wrist.

"You do realize that my hands are tied, Mara. If not for those men on the river, I'd have had you home by now and your father would be lifting his cup to me, whilst bequeathing your hand in marriage. You and I would not be arguing about this and 'twould already be done. Nevertheless, I'm expected home soon. And upon my return do my people expect a wedding. I'll not fail them."

"You'd marry me without my father's consent?"

"As long as I had yours, aye."

"And what makes you think you'll ever acquire my consent?"

Dægan sported a wry grin. "Anything is possible, my dear."

Mara ripped her hand away, crossing back over to the other side of the fire, not amused by his keen-witted absurdities. She sat there stewing over how much she hated being trapped by the night, dependent upon someone else's ability to get her home, *and* that he was confident anything was possible.

She heard him stir across the dying fire, but refused to look. While her thoughts ran red, he returned to her on bended knee and staked his dagger in the ground. Across his arm lay the thick bear cloak he'd been using to keep warm.

"What is this?" she asked coldly.

"The nights get cool under the shade of the trees."

"And the knife? Are you begging me to cut you?"

"Nay. I'm begging you to trust me."

Mara knew this gesture was more than just a crafty attempt to ease her mind. It was an endowment given to prove he cared about her, sensitive to the fact she'd be cold and miserable if he didn't give away half his bed. For the moment, she put her frustration aside and allowed her concern to come forward.

"What will keep you warm?"

"Worry not. I've two deer hides as well."

"But they're not as big as this cloak."

"Hm…I cannot understand how you can worry about me and kiss me as a wife would, yet you cannot conceive a marriage between us. Is it truly that hard to see?"

Mara refused to answer him.

"No matter," he replied. "I'll gain that consent, first by trust and then by love. Count on it, Lady Mara." He bowed his head and left to return to his makeshift bed.

Mara was speechless. In less than one day, she received a multitude of kindhearted acts from a man sworn to be her enemy. And why should he be an enemy? Because his height put him there? Or the fair hair that grows from his head made for a disreputable character?

Each unfounded reason was but a stone stacked high and wide to protect her, and she believed he'd somehow scale those walls of suspicion, mortared with doubt, to reach her heart on the other side.

Dægan spoke to her from across the fire. "Try to sleep, princess. We leave for Hlymrekr in the morning."

The place he referred to was strange to Mara's ears in pronunciation, but she assumed it was likely the recent Northman trading port of Limerick. She reluctantly lay down, curling beneath the cloak of bear fur. It was soft and warm and smelled just like him. Ironically, it calmed the restlessness of being somewhere lost between the near sweet rapture of Dægan's kiss and her father's far-off sheltering embrace.

****

The light from daybreak had barely stretched above the horizon before dark, steely clouds covered the sky. Mara awoke first and sat up. The wind at her back thieved the morning sun's warmth, and the smell of moisture settled in the air. The fire between her and Dægan emitted a straggling line of smoke, and its ashes drifted on the breeze in hopes to escape the common fall of rain.

Before Mara could announce the approaching storm, she found Dægan already on his feet, saddling his horse. After he gathered his things and fastened them down, he discarded the rocks around the fire and poured the last of the water from his pouch over the embers. They hissed and smoked, and when all was cool and wet, he used a fallen tree branch to dust the ground, removing any evidence of their presence. Moreover, he took some brush from the forest floor and scattered it over the pit, carefully covering every footprint and indentation on the ground so as to recreate the land as it once was. Not even a single bone from last night's meal could be found.

She stood, clutching the bear cloak around her shoulders, and moved out of his way as he took a look for himself.

"You're thorough, I see."

"Need I remind you of the scores of men who gave chase the moment they'd run aground? I'd be a stupid man to think they gave up their pursuit so easily." With reluctance in Dægan's eyes, he glanced at his bear cloak and held out his hand. "You'll thank me later when we are soaked to the skin, and 'tis the only thing kept dry."

Mara gave it up, and he rolled it around his forearm, cramming it into a pouch on the saddle. In one swift motion, he mounted and called her by name as if it were commonplace to summon her. She looked up, amazed by his handsome features. His golden hair blew in the wind, and his horse shifted and stamped. He was stunning, imperious as he sat upon the animal.

"Come, Mara. We must go." Dægan extended his arm as he rode around her, and she grabbed hold, leaping behind him on the horse. She pulled herself against him as they rode away, and soon they burst from the woods.

Mara saw the gleaming silver Shannon before her, a familiar sight that only taunted her with the knowledge she could very well have escaped her Norse captor and followed it north toward home. She watched it wind back into the hills as they headed in the opposite direction, fearing that, despite Dægan's promise, she'd never see home again.

Chapter Four

The thunder rolled like hundreds of heavy horses across a battlefield, shaking the ground as it passed above. The heavens opened and dumped its water in sheets without mercy. Within minutes, the bitter cold rain had seeped through their clothing and bled deep enough to chill the marrow in their bones.

To keep from shivering, Dægan directed his attention to the feel of Mara huddled against his back. She'd found a refuge beneath his wet hair, pressing as close to him as humanly possible. He couldn't ignore the warmth of her breath between his shoulder blades or the softness of her body. The thought of her naked stuck with him as readily as the thin wet tunic and shift clinging to her own body.

He cursed his crude musings. This was certainly not the time for indecency. If Mara only knew what had crossed his mind, she'd never trust him again. He willed depravity away and clutched her arms at his waist in silent reassurance. The shelter he promised was something he'd seen only once, near the river on his way to Connacht several days before. He hoped that his memory served him correctly—even prayed to the gods that it had, for the onslaught of needlelike rain in his face was wearing on his good sense.

Even his horse struggled to cope. The heavy downfall shrouded loose rocks upon the black slated ground beneath its hooves, and the animal slipped several times during their descent. It was a slope much steeper than Dægan had expected, but at least he didn't have to worry about Mara's ability to ride. She proved as competent in this jaunt as she had in yesterday's sprint. With that in mind, he lunged his horse off the incline and drove it faster to where he thought he'd seen the cavern.

Like a gift from Odin, it emerged from the thick gray fog. Although farther from the river than he'd remembered, the overhang was hospitable and tall enough even for his horse. Upon entering the shallow depths of the cave, Dægan relished the sudden end of the chastising rain. Tiny echoes of dripping water crooned an appeasing welcome as his horse's slick black body steamed.

"Are you all right?" Dægan's voice resonated within the cavern walls. Mara nodded as she shuddered, trying to absorb the warmth from his back.

"We must get you warm." He slid from his horse, landing on both feet, and reached for her. Without hesitation, she wrapped her arms around his neck, evidently too cold to care whose protective arms enveloped her. He smiled, for she'd morphed into a little child, burying her head against his neck, contrary to the fiery vixen from yesterday's affair. He cradled her close and savored the petal-soft lips upon his neck. If not for her shivering, he would've held her all day.

He shifted her weight to one arm and untied the hide from his saddle with the other. Giving it a good, hard shake, he covered her body and whispered, "Take off your wet clothes. I'll give you my cloak."

Mara reacted as if his words seared through her like a red-hot brand, and she clutched her arms in protest. "I most certainly will not."

"Then how do you expect to gain warmth in sodden

clothing?"

"If you think I'll remove my clothes simply because you ordered it, you're sorely mistaken. I'll do no such thing." She jumped from his arms and kept the hide for herself.

"Listen, princess," Dægan said as he pulled off his boots and unbuckled his belt. "You, above all, should know this rain will hold us here for many hours, if not days. I'm not going to sit in wet, uncomfortable clothes when I've perfectly dry furs at my disposal. And I suggest you follow my lead."

Mara hadn't long to contemplate Dægan's candid advice before he'd completely disrobed. She gasped and turned her head.

He laughed. "You might as well get used to it, my lady. Soon you'll be seeing me this way every night."

"I will not," Mara argued over her shoulder.

"Will you close your eyes to me, even on our wedding night?"

"You're a stupid heathen of a man! How can you possibly think that I'll *want* to marry you?"

"I felt the tides turn last night—and so did you."

"Nonsense."

"Do you know what your problem is?" he asked, staring at the back of her head. "You don't trust *yourself*. You despise that you gave in to me so quickly, and for that, you question your own good sense. Your heart is talking to you, but you won't listen. You're denying yourself the chance to find love, a love that is different, foreign, and well beyond your dreams. I saw how you'd gaze upon the river waters in Connacht, farther than its shores, wishing for something greater. And now 'tis here in front of you, yet you fear the possibility of its wonder because 'tis not what your father wants. Tell me, Mara, what do *you* want?"

His poetic words coursed a path straight to her chest, almost knocking the wind from her. "You watched me?" The tone of her voice rose with shock and anger. If he wasn't standing behind her completely naked, she would've turned around and slapped his face. All she could do was repeat herself. "You *watched* me? For how long?"

"For many days," he admitted.

"Days?"

"Weeks, actually. I came upon your singing one morning, and 'twas the most beautiful sound I'd ever heard. Your voice was like the sweetness of honey on my tongue. It lingered, and I couldn't rid its hold on me. I took pleasure in watching the simple life you lived and found myself wanting to offer you more. And each afternoon when you'd ride away, I was left with a feeling of utter sadness. I despised that feeling and decided I couldn't walk away from you any longer."

Mara gritted her teeth and tightened the hide at her shoulders. "No matter how charming a tale you tell, you're still a thief if you don't take me to my father!"

She heard him rustling behind her and prayed he'd grabbed the other hide from the saddle for himself.

"If I do that," he replied, "I'll put both our lives at risk. You know this. And by the gods, woman, turn around!"

Mara peeked over her shoulder, fully expecting to see him naked. But he stood with his hands on hips, his eyes tapered to slits, and his lower half covered with a reddish hide. It hung low at his waist, exposing his entire torso. His body was longer than she imagined, but just as well, for she'd never seen an unclothed man before. He was large and magnificent. His chest, his shoulders, his arms. Even the thin layer of dark blond curls running from his navel and beyond the obscurity of the animal skin was a beautiful sight.

"I'll take full responsibility for my theft if the time arises," Dægan said gruffly. "But until then, I'll keep you safe, first and foremost."

Mara tore her gaze from Dægan's body, realizing she'd been staring. She blinked and swallowed hard, trying to remember why he'd become so frustrated with her. Oh aye. She'd accused him of being a thief. At least he admitted doing so, which proved even beautiful men could be criminals.

On the other hand, she knew how the Irish didn't take kindly to lawlessness, especially when carried out by pagan intruders. She didn't want to see him punished for a misunderstanding and worried what her father might do to him.

"You must understand, Dægan, the longer we wait, the harder 'twill be to explain all this. Let us return to my father before he judges you harshly."

Dægan looked her up and down. "Are you made of iron? Or is it your skull that bears the thickness? Not even I'd want to come face-to-face with those men on the river again. I trust they've come for bigger things, and even your faithful steed is not enough to satisfy them."

"We can go around them."

He laughed. "Ireland is only so big. It won't be long before there's an additional group of greedy Northmen making their advancement up another body of water. If you haven't yet heard, your Ireland is a prized piece of land.

Your days of venturing to the Shannon alone are over."

"They're over because of men like you."

His brows lifted. "Better me than those on the four ships numbering in the hundreds, aye?"

Mara shrugged the frightening image from her mind and kept to the subject. "My father is not a man to keep to the Brehon Law when it pertains to the judgment of *Fionnghaill.* He'll not accept your atonement in the form of an honor price, nor will he hang you quickly. He'll more likely throw you in chains and cast you into an open pit where you'll die a slow death of starvation and exposure. Can't you see your death will be a heavy weight upon my shoulders? Why have you done this to yourself?"

"There's no sign of your father thus far. And I doubt this soon in his search, he'd look as distantly as Hlymrekr. By the time he does, I'll have rejoined my men and started our course for bringing you back home. Now, let's put this aside and get you warm. As much as you hate to admit it, you know you'll never get comfortable in those wet clothes you're wearing. Mayhap even catch your death of cold, which I'd rather keep from the list of things your father could hold against me. I can turn around if 'twould suit you."

Every moral bone in Mara's body told her this was wrong, but she was too miserably cold to care any longer. She'd have to discard morality, if just for a little while, and what would it hurt? Who would know?

"I promise," Dægan pledged, turning around to face the rain outside the cavern. "I'll not look."

"Are you giving your word?"

"If that is what it takes…"

Mara flipped the hide from her shoulders and lifted her gown up as quickly as she could. "All right, but if you so much as peek at me..."

"Hm...for the sake of curiosity, what *will* you do if I peek?" he taunted. "I always like to know what I'm up against. And the gods know I've underestimated your vigor in the past. Countless times, I might add."

She imagined Dægan had a big smile across his face. Since she'd never done anything like this before, she found herself constantly adjusting the fur hide around her body. Even with it, she still felt as nude as the day she was born.

Dægan tapped his foot. "Are you finished yet?"

She checked herself one last time. "I suppose so."

He whirled around and froze in his place. "I realize that 'tis not the finest of silk, but you look lovely."

Mara frowned. "You *are* a stupid heathen."

He neared her, pulling his rolled bear cloak from the saddle and wrapping it kindly around her shoulders. "Do you not think I know what beauty is? I've been on many voyages in search of iron, silver, gold, beaded jewels, silk, and the most desired scented oils. Many men have died to acquire these riches. I've even met fathers who've offered their daughters in exchange for such things. I've seen lands lush with green fields and wildflowers, mountains reaching higher than the air we breathe, and waterfalls cascading to the bluest of riverbeds below. And none of these come close to the beauty I see before me right now."

His words sank in swiftly. His description of her in a common animal hide was more than she could imagine any man ever saying. "I thank you for your kindness, although I'm still not sure what you're seeing."

"I see as a heathen sees," he reminded her.

"Hardly. If anything, you've proved yourself..."

"Worthy of you?"

"'Tis not what I meant to say," she insisted.

"But what you were thinking."

Mara hung her head. "What I meant to say is that you've proved yourself to be a man of great mystery."

"I suppose that is a compliment."

"Aye, 'tis. Most men I know can be as easily seen through as the streams that flow toward the rivers, and just as predictable."

"You've proven yourself to be just as mysterious."

He'd taken her words of subtle flattery and fed them back to her. "How so?"

"I never would've thought a woman would gain an upper hand in a struggle with me—twice you did that. Nor would I've guessed you to return a kiss."

Mara's face reddened. She'd tried many times to forget about it since it happened. Even as he spoke, it was difficult not to look at his lips and relive it.

"If memory serves me...I'd say you kissed me deeply."

"I was coerced," she defended.

"It didn't take much."

He grabbed the cloak from under her neck and pulled her closer. She shied from his intrusive eyes, the heat of his stare setting her ablaze.

"I know you're avoiding me because you feel 'tis right. 'Tis moral. 'Tis safer. But you needn't fear me."

Mara took a deep breath. "I do not fear you, Dægan. I simply do not know enough about you."

He drew back his face as if her choice of words stunned him. He released her and crossed his arms. "What would you like to know?"

Mara swallowed first before giving thought to his question. "Where do you make your home?"

Dægan's gaze deepened, and his posture softened.

After a few moments' thought, he made himself comfortable on the ground and patted the place beside him.

Mara had always thought of herself as strong willed, impregnable in the face of temptation, but Dægan always seemed to find a way to push his way through with very little effort and carve his name on her rock-solid principles. Trust had now become a complicated virtue for her, a thin line between faith and fortitude. If she could help it, she'd not let him lure her across that line. Accordingly, she chose her own place to sit—away from him.

Dægan flashed his teeth in a grin. "Very well," he said, crossing his ankles. "Perhaps you've heard of my home. Inishmore?"

Unbeknownst to Mara, her jaw had dropped, and Dægan quickly made her aware of her reaction. "Baffling, isn't it? I suppose I've given you too much credit in thinking you didn't share the same feeble mind as the rest of your Erin neighbors."

Mara straightened at his blunt insult. "What is that supposed to mean?"

"It means you think your land is yours and no one else's. You think your Ireland cannot and will not be shared with others. But I assure you there're those, even with the noblest of Irish blood, who already share their lands equally with foreigners like me. Indeed, it may only be to keep peace, but nonetheless, they share. And why shouldn't they? 'Tis not as if we'd just landed here yesterday. My Northern forefathers have been here for more than a century. As any man wishes to find a more suitable place to call home, I too, am here, but—without the need to murder and steal, as you're so inclined to believe. So will many more after me. We are sooner your husbands and brothers than we are barbarous passersby."

"Indeed, you've landed here, but 'tis only a matter of time before your kind are rid from our shores. Even the mighty Romans were kept at bay."

Dægan laughed aloud. "The mighty Romans were only deterred because they feared the savagery of the Celts, and that savagery is what brought my forefathers here in the first place. But mind you, 'tis the rich land and the beautiful kings' daughters that keep the rest of us here."

"Does that include you?"

He raised his brow. "More or less, but it has never been enough to ground me. I'm still a seaman at heart, and if I could live upon a ship, I would."

The flutter in her stomach bit deep to the bone as she imagined sailing on an open sea. "Not I. I couldn't begin to fathom life upon a ship."

"What is it you fear? I know 'tis not water. I've seen you swim."

Mara saw the heat in his eyes with that statement and tried to hide her embarrassment in knowing he'd probably seen more than a woman treading water. "I suppose I'm like my mother in that respect. I've never known her to step foot off solid ground, or want to."

"What age were you when she died?"

Mara sat stunned by his question. "How did you know my mother had passed?"

"You've never spoken of her before, and usually a girl holds her mother in high regard. In my experience, women tend to follow their mothers' advice in most everything they do. You however, worry only about your father. Am I wrong?"

"Nay, you're not. I was only nine years old when my mother became ill and died. It seemed all too sudden at the time, but I came to learn that she suffered for months. My father sheltered me then, as he still does now."

Dægan fell quiet, as if to reflect on the sensitive subject, then said, "You spend your days by the Shannon because that is where you feel closest to her, aye? You go there alone because you want to be, and not because there's no one else to accompany you. And you sing the songs your mother taught you because you feel comforted by them."

Those memories and more danced around in Mara's head, harmonized by her mother's joyous laughter floating in sweet song. She was amazed at Dægan's careful yet poignant perception of things, and wondered how a pagan could have such an incredible outlook on life while taking notice of its tiny rewards.

"Now that I know your mother is no longer with you," he said kindly, "the days I spent watching you by the river feel quite intrusive. For that, I'm sorry." As the awful silence between them dragged on, Dægan spoke again. "Mara, I believe I've trampled on something I shouldn't have, and I'd be more than willing to speak of other things."

Mara was not so willing. "Do you still have your mother?"

Dægan took a deep breath. "I do. And I know she looks forward to meeting you."

"Your mother knows about me?"

"My mother is eager for grandchildren, and she's encouraged me to find a bride. She fears her age, but I swear she still has an iron fist and a stare that would send Thor running with his hammer between his legs."

Mara couldn't help but laugh with him, despite the

reference to his pagan god. His laughter was delightful, and it was quite fascinating to learn so much about a man who'd been deemed heartless and murderous by everyone she knew. So much so that she decided to walk on the eggshells of religion. "Your god, Thor... He controls the storms in your world?"

Dægan's grin never left. "Aye, among other things. For the traveler, he's believed to protect, and for the warrior in battle, he instills bravery without fear."

"You believe in many gods. Is it not absurd to think there's a god for each detail of your life?"

"Is it not absurd to think one god can do it all?"

"Nay."

"Then your god is a very busy god."

"Do not mock Him."

"Ah, you misunderstand," Dægan said, raising his hands to cut short her incrimination. "I'm sure 'tis a belief passed to you by your mother, as was mine, and I'm well reminded to never forget what she has taught me, including when to politely change the subject."

"Being a man, I'd think you would learn most from your father."

"Being a son, I've learned that mothers are oftentimes smarter than their hard-nosed partners and more aware of things around them. Where my mother is concerned, I'm not ashamed to admit that many of the skills I've learned are from her."

"Tell me one."

"All right." He lifted his chin in thought. "How about making you smile?"

"I'd hardly regard that as a skill."

"If I haven't the skill to make you smile, then it means you're truly enjoying yourself. Either way, I think the odds are in my favor."

"Possibly."

"Are you still cold?"

"Nay." Mara dismissed his question quickly, despite the goose bumps pimpling her skin.

Dægan leaned across the cavern floor and reached beneath the cloak, pulling out her leg. "You lie."

She jerked her leg back. "So what if I do?"

"Considering I aim to take you as a wife, I'd think you'd speak only truths to me. A husband doesn't take kindly to a wife's fibs, no matter how innocent they may be."

"Then you've more than proved my point. Men such as yourself always want things they cannot have."

"If you're going to group me with the likes of other Northmen, then you should remember we're quite able to take things we want. Hence, your Baile Átha Cliath, or as I call it, Dubh-Linn."

She stiffened, knowing he cared little for the port and more for the things he could acquire, like her affections.

He reached farther and slid his hand past her neck, into the mass of tangled hair that hung above her shoulders. He grasped a hold and brought her close enough that his lips were but a hair's breadth from hers. "You're correct in saying that desires often come from things we cannot easily gain—mine being that of your love. By all accounts, I do wish I could steal it. But I'm not that sort of man. I'll wait. Forever and a day…I'll wait."

Chapter Five

The rain was relentless. Its never-ending downpour played out a monotonous rhythm on the ground, putting Mara in trances that led into daydreams about Dægan. She relived the moments his arms had wrapped tightly around her, how he'd kissed her, and what it would be like to hear him whisper his love for her. It was a fantasy at best, but one that somehow found its way into her every thought.

How could it possibly be love? She barely knew him and he barely knew her. Yet as little as she knew of him, she trusted him as though he were a friend of many years. She was going with him to a place far from her own familiarity, simply because he deemed it so, to avoid danger.

Of course, he never used his brute strength, his dagger, or any other weapon to convince her. If he used anything at all, it was his sensuous kiss and his heated touch. Hardly a plausible excuse should her father find her and demand an answer. It was ridiculous. Utterly embarrassing to think she'd been manipulated by a man's kiss—and then again, quite amazing.

Dægan, on the other hand, had been more constructive with his time. He was inspecting his horse's hooves one by one and sweeping through its coat with a carved bone comb. She watched him tend the equine with gentleness and patience, regarding his actions as meticulous. His hands traced over every inch of the horse's back and legs, care that by anyone else's viewing would have seemed overzealous. But to her, it was charming.

When he spoke to the animal, he shattered her stupor. His voice was low as he conveyed some secret words with the animal.

"You speak 'horse'?" Mara asked in jest. "Is that another one of the skills you were referring to earlier?"

"If 'twould change your thoughts of me, then aye." Dægan stroked the horse's back one last time before he sat beside her. "I've others that are far more impressive."

Mara pointed to the long scar across the inside of his upper arm. "Such as surviving the man who did this to you?"

He looked at himself as if he'd forgotten about the lengthy scar. "Ah, this one...I did battle with a man who drew his sword like his insults...very carelessly. He aimed for my heart. And missed."

"And you did not?"

"I missed on purpose, only to maim him instead. He now bears the mark of my sword across his face. A scar just about as big as this one."

Dægan's restraint amazed her. As the king's daughter, she was all too familiar with the male ego. Between her father and his multitude of guards, nothing would stop them from retaliating if anyone made an attempt on their lives. "Anyone would say you were justified. Why did you not kill him?"

"He insulted my brother, Gustaf, not me. Killing him would have been an easy punishment for his offenses. Now whoever looks upon him will see that he was given a warning and doesn't need another, should he speak ill once more."

Mara admired his interpretation of the dispute. "What

did he say about your brother?"

"'Twas a long time ago," he dismissed.

"Please tell me. I want to know more about you...and your family."

Dægan found Mara's inquisition groundless, considering she'd recently lumped him with thugs and savages. "Why? Why know me at all?"

"We have naught else to do," she proclaimed, glancing at the rain behind him.

Of course, she'd say that. Heaven forbid she'd admit to caring about him. But looking into her green eyes, he saw a safe place within them, a peaceful sanctuary with rippling waves of tenderness, and before he knew it, he was spilling his mind like a *skald*.

"He called Gustaf a fool for trying to avenge my father's death, which in turn led Gustaf to his own."

"Your father was killed? By whom?"

"Harald the Fairhair, or the Blond Bastard, as I like to call him. He was a greedy man, a man who wanted all Norway for himself and gave everyone the choice to either give up their titles and serve him, or leave the country. My father, Rælik, chose neither. He'd been a respected chieftain of Hladir for many years, and he was known for his great words in council. He had most of the support of the neighboring clans, so he didn't fear Harald's threats as the others in the south had. I was a man of eighteen with my nose in many other things, but I can still remember the way the people trusted and supported my father."

He paused, taking a few breaths to prepare himself for the next part of the story that was always difficult to think about, much less speak of.

"One day, Harald sent ten men to kill him. Unfortunately, my brothers and I were away on a merchant journey when it happened. When we returned home, we were told the news, and Gustaf became enraged. He left the next morn to find the men who had done this to our father…never to be seen again."

Dægan cleared his throat, determined to keep that blasted lump from hardening. "Nevertheless, I suppose the man who threw the insult was correct. My brother *was* a fool to think he could take on ten men single-handedly."

"Nay," Mara said softly, touching his hand. "Gustaf simply loved his father. The insult would've been if he'd done nothing at all."

Dægan felt the bitterness of resentment leave his body as her hand lingered upon his. For the first time, she stood with him on common ground. Not only had she sympathized with his brother's hasty vengeance, but she reaffirmed it with a touch. She smiled back at him with a kindness so warm and true that he felt it like rays of sunlight on his face.

"I'm sorry I'll never get to meet your brother or your father. But I'm certain when I look at you, I see them in other fashions. Mayhap you've your father's eyes, or your brother's courage. Either way, they're still a part of you, and no one can take that away."

Mara suddenly seemed aware that her hand was still upon his, and, to Dægan's disappointment, she pulled it away. She tried to hide whatever it was that had made her feel uneasy, and quickly modified the conversation. "I suppose your love of traveling came from your father?"

"Aye."

"Where have you gone?"

He raised his brow. "Where have I not gone?"

"Have you a favorite place?"

"Not really."

"Oh, come now," Mara persuaded. "Surely there's one your mind cannot forget."

Dægan reflected for a moment, then moved closer to her. "I suppose there's one. A place, very recently."

"What was it like?"

Dægan sank deep into a reverie and revisited the tender haven within Mara's arms. "'Twas very warm, and the sun seemed to always shine even through the threat of rain."

Mara's gaze drifted past him, as if she were imagining such a place. "Was there a meadow?"

He thought of her eyes. "Naught but green, as far as my eyes could see. And yet, as I stood amid its vastness, I felt the intimate welcome of a delicate embrace as if nature had a lover, and I, its only desire. I too reached out to hold it. I felt the whisper of the wind from a bird's wings on my lips and the thunderous rejoice of the gods in my ears."

"It sounds absolutely beautiful! How did you find it?"

Dægan couldn't hold back his grin. "I'd like to say I happened upon it by accident, but I'd be lying."

"So you've been there before?"

He almost laughed at how easily he'd drawn her in with his metaphorical description. "I've been to similar places, but none have caught my eye or my senses so profoundly."

She inched closer to him. "Were you ever afraid?"

"Afraid of what?"

"Afraid," she repeated, trying to find the right words, "of going beyond the horizon and..."

"Falling off?"

"I suppose that is what I mean."

Dægan tried to rub a growing smile from his lips. "There're not any edges to fall from, at least not on this earth."

"Are you trying to say the earth is round?"

"That is exactly what I'm saying."

She narrowed her eyes in disbelief. "Up until now, I'd thought your intelligence unsurpassed."

"'Tis round, I assure you."

Mara giggled. "I'd not boast that to too many people if I were you."

Dægan let his mouth fall open. "You don't believe me?"

She crossed her arms and smiled emphatically. "Indeed not."

Dægan stood up and searched the ground. "Very well, I shall prove it to you."

"How?"

"Patience, princess. Here. This will do." He picked up a round stone as large as his head and held it up proudly.

Mara turned her mouth under and smoothed the ground beside her. "Sorry, still flat."

"I'm not finished. Next I shall need a fire."

"That should prove even more difficult in this weather."

"What little faith you have, love." And because she'd continued to doubt him, he tore the hide from his waist and retrieved his wet kirtle in the nude. He heard her gasp, but reasoned a tit-for-tat logic for the sarcasm she'd chosen to spit forth.

"You could've at least told me you were going to do that!"

"Why? And miss that look upon your face?"

After dressing and securing his belt and sword at his waist, he resaddled the horse, then stuffed her wet gown in a pouch on the side.

"What are you doing with my clothes?" Mara asked.

"I'm going to get us something to eat, something for which to build a fire, and before the night is over, prove to you the earth is round."

"With my gown?"

He smiled. "I'm making certain you stay here. Is that enough? Or must I take the hide and cloak from your possession as well?"

"You wouldn't."

Dægan pulled a battle-ax from his cantle and raised his brow. "I'm going to ignore that you just dared me. Tell me you'll be here when I return. Remember that I'm taking the horse and weapons, as well. You'll have naught but the hide on your back. And if you leave, I cannot protect you. Tell me I've nothing to worry about, woman. I beg you."

Mara truly had no desire to venture outside the cave in that downpour or to try to escape from his company as he so feared. Strangely enough, she too was looking forward to his return. And not just to bear witness to his unlikely proof of a round earth. She was enjoying him to the fullest and desired more of the Northman's company. "You needn't worry. I promise."

Dægan came to her on bended knee, reached up into the hide for her hand, and placed a kiss upon the top of it. His lips were warm and soft as they pressed gently at her knuckles, and they lingered there even after he left.

****

Dægan returned, much quicker than Mara had expected, with a line of pike in his hand and two great logs dragging behind his horse. Despite that the rain had completely saturated him from head to toe, it hadn't doused the smile on his face once he learned she was still in the cavern.

She stood to help him with the astonishing amount of provisions he'd been able to acquire. "How did you—"

"I doubt your servants in your father's great keep ever failed to bring forth your dinner on account of rain. And neither do I." Dægan dismounted and extended both an ax and a dagger for her choosing. "But don't think for one moment that I'm your *thrall*. Which would you prefer to do? Fillet the fish, or cut the wood for kindling?"

She looked at him with widened eyes. "I've never done either."

"Then today is your most fortunate day." Dægan buried the battle-ax in one of the logs and then grabbed her left hand, slapping the handle of the knife in it.

"But I—"

"Are you afraid of getting your hands a little dirty?"

"Nay, but—"

"Hush, girl," he said as he spun her into his arms with her back against his chest. "I'll teach you." He snaked his arms around her body and slid his hands down her forearms to the blade. He gently pried her constricted fingers from the handle and took the dagger into his own hands.

"Beautiful, is it not? My uncle made it for me. Look how the gold and silver intertwine together. See how they twist and turn, drawing your eyes first to the contrast of their colors, but then eventually on the partnership they serve as they wrap around each other in blended beauty. And not to say that silver and gold are best only together, but there's also nothing distasteful or frightening about their congruent existence. 'Tis a stunning piece of artisan talent, wouldn't you say?"

It was hard to breathe cradled against his chest, and for such a long time. His wet hair tickled her bare shoulders, and his breath upon her neck seared through her as easily as hot coals in butter. It wasn't the kind of instruction she'd think necessary to learn the skills of filleting a fish, but she liked the lesson.

"Now to begin, you must forget all you think you know about weapons and how to wield them. Hold the knife with a gentle yet steady hand, as opposed to the steel grip you had before. Then find a good smooth rock to lay the fish upon, hold it by the tail, and skim the blade just below the layer of scales with one long stroke. Do so until all the scales are removed, but be careful not to go too deep or you'll cut away the meat. Understand?"

"I think so. But what about its head?" She scrunched her nose in disgust.

Dægan released her and gave her backside one solid swat as he walked away. "Chop it off."

Chapter Six

Mara sat at the fire and shared a meal with her most unlikely dinner companion. Not only because of who Dægan was, but for what he'd resorted to wearing. Sure, she too wore nothing but an animal pelt, but at least hers covered the majority of her torso. His concealed only his lower half, laying bare that beautiful, well-toned chest. Though not the most proper attire, he was certainly a sight to behold.

"How is your fish?" he asked.

"'Tis edible," Mara joked.

"Only edible?"

"'Tis missing something…"

"Oh, that hurts!" Dægan held his hand to his heart and pretended to feel an agonizing pain from her heckling. "She not only throws a wicked dagger but pours salt into the wound as well."

"Ah, yes, 'tis salt that's missing," she quickly added.

He playfully threw a fish bone at her. "You ungrateful woman. And you think you deserve to know what knowledge I have of a round earth?"

Mara took her last bite of fish and gave a halfhearted apology.

Dægan sighed. "I'm afraid you'll have to do better than that, my dear."

Mara steepled her hands and dragged her words in a pitiful whine. "Please tell me what you know. Don't let me go another day foolishly thinking the earth is flat."

He rolled his eyes at her whimsical ridiculing and stood. "That will be quite enough. Your behavior here does not merit my knowledge, but I shall give it just the same." He collected the things he needed for his lesson, using a stick and a cut piece of hide to form a makeshift torch, then returned, saying, "I need you to open your mind."

"Open my mind," Mara repeated.

"Aye. Open your mind to things beyond your eyes. We oftentimes only believe in things we can see, and since we cannot fly on bird's wings and reach a height high enough to verify the possibility of a round earth, we must use what we have and what we already know." Dægan rolled the round rock with the bottom of his boot until it rested beside her. "As I'm sure you've already guessed, the rock will serve as the earth, and this," he said, lighting the stick in the fire, "will be the sun. You follow me so far?"

Mara was filled with eagerness and excitement. "I do."

"Good. Now I want you to imagine the purpose of the sun. As you know, it gives us both warmth and light just as our fires do, but obviously on a grander scale." He knelt in front of her and handed her the small torch. "You be the sun."

She took the stick from his hand. "And you're going to be the absurdly round earth, I presume."

Dægan's eyes sparkled with color as he smiled. "Aye, I am." He lifted the rock to her eye level, balancing its heavy weight with one hand. "All right, now bring the torch closer to the rock. Good. Right there." He looked at her deeply. "What do you see?"

She fluttered her lashes. "What should I see?"

"Look at the rock. Where is the light concentrated?"

Mara examined the firelight's path on the stone. "The

light seems brighter in the center."

"Which explains why in the north 'tis colder. In my homeland of Hladir, the winters are very harsh and our summers are cool. But in our journeys, the farther south we sailed, the warmer the heat of the sun."

"Changing seasons do warrant a change in temperature, Dægan."

"You're correct. But we've traveled many a distance, more than most men can sum in their lifetime, and we've found southern lands where the change of seasonal temperature is minimal. And the air is hot almost every day, no matter what season."

"Every day?"

Dægan tapped her forehead with his finger. "Your mind is closed. Open it and listen to me. I've been there myself. I've seen the strange terrain and the native people of the land who wear not much clothing because of the immense heat. The rains are scarce and the ground is dry. There isn't much that can propagate there and thus no reason for me to have stayed much more than a sennight. But I assure you, my father did. For more than five years, he traded with these people for spices, silks, and wines. So when he said the temperature hardly changed, no matter what day it was, I believed him. He explained it all to me in this very same manner, except he used an apple in place of the stone."

Mara became intrigued. "If the earth is truly round, where are we right now in relationship to the rock?"

Dægan seemed to like her question. With his free hand, he pointed several inches above the middle. "Perhaps here."

"And your homeland?"

He pointed farther up the rock. "Here."

Mara pondered the actual distances he'd traveled in his life and couldn't imagine such adventures, nor the dangers that went along with sailing a vulnerable ship on possibly volatile seas. Not to mention the risks in embarking upon a likely hostile front of local natives? It wasn't bravery. It was ludicrous.

But wasn't she doing the same thing? Wasn't she braving the elements of danger without knowing what lay ahead? Despite their amiable relationship, Dægan was *still* a stranger. A man she was putting full faith in to get her home, only by the covenant of his word.

Dægan set the stone down. "What's wrong?"

Mara sighed and tossed the torch into the fire. "I know my fears may seem diminished, especially because of the way I've behaved here lately—laughing, smiling, conversing with you as if you're a friend. But I'm afraid. Not necessarily of you," she amended, "but of the unknown. Of never returning. Of never seeing my father again. Surely you can understand that."

Dægan sat upon the rock and took his time replying. "I can."

"Then can you not sympathize with what you're putting me through? I want to be home. Regardless that I've enjoyed the last few hours with you, I want to go home. I want to be within the confines of my father's keep, where danger cannot lurk."

"Then you surely have a strange way of showing it by sneaking out of that confining keep and riding half a league away down the River Shannon on sprinting horseback."

"I enjoy the river."

"You enjoy the freedom. The sun on your face and the wind in your hair. You cannot get that behind fortified walls of earth and wood. I'd say even your mother knew that."

Mara's heart sank. "Do not speak as though you know her."

"I know enough about kings to know your father was unaware of her travels so far from the security of his palisade. And until yesterday, he knew not of yours. I can understand your reasons for going to the river, but what were your mother's?"

"Why must you speak ill of her?"

"I've not spoken ill of anyone. I only inquired about your mother's reasons for venturing from safety. Perhaps she was waiting for someone...a distant friend? A lover?"

Mara's eyes flared with anger. "There was no one else. My father loved her very much."

"I don't doubt his love. But did she love him?"

Mara slapped his face. "Now you speak ill of her."

Dægan touched his cheek where the sting of her hand still tingled. "Conceivably, that *was* ill. Forgive me." He'd struck a chord, but he wasn't ready to give up entirely. His point had not yet been made. "Mara, I still believe your mother wanted something more than just a passing moment at the water's edge. And I know there's a large part of you, no matter how much you deny it, that longs for the same. I saw it in your eyes. And I can give you that. I *want* to give you that. If you like the river as much as you say you do, then you'll love the sea. You'll love seeing your homeland from the distant bows of a ship where the meadow's flowery arms wave in polite parting and the hills stand up to bid you farewell. 'Tis like nothing you've ever seen. Come with me. Let me take you on the sea and show you what true freedom is."

"But...my father—"

"Mara, listen to me," he said, cupping her face with his hands. "I'm not trying to avoid taking you home or making amends with your father. I promised you I would, and I've never broken a promise in my life. But I need a great number of men, just in case we're confronted by the others, and it takes a while to move a sizable army. So, while we wait in Hlymrekr, let me share with you what has been my whole life. I've seen your world, Mara. Let me show you mine. If only for one day, please let me. One time on the ocean. One time to step into another's shoes."

"But I don't know the first thing about voyages, and sails, and..."

"You'll be a guest upon my *langskip*. Not a finger shall you raise. Your presence will be a blessing to me, if not a welcome sight for all my men." As soon as he said those words, he saw panic strip the color from her face. "Fret not, love. These men follow *my* commands. Some have bled for me, and I trust them with my life. You'll be fine amongst them. 'Tis my brother you should be wary of," he joked. "He's quite the charmer."

Mara challenged his claim with a curious lift of her brow. "More so than you?"

"Aye, but not as good-looking." Dægan stood and stretched out both a big smile and a hand to her. "So what say you? When the rain ceases, will you grant me one day? One day in my world?"

Mara looked first at the spread of fingers from his sturdy palm before finally placing her hand in his. "One day, is it? And then we go to my father?"

Dægan lifted her to stand and humbly bowed before

her. "With not a moment to spare."

Chapter Seven

The day passed long into the night, and the rain continued to fall from the sky. Dægan had kept the fire going with the large pile of wood he'd split earlier, and by the time they settled down for the night, the blazing heat had dried their clothes.

Mara had never felt happier than when she traded the animal pelts for her dirty tunic. Though it was tattered and wrinkled, wearing a noble's garment helped her regain the sense of decency she'd lost since meeting the Northman. If it wasn't for decorum, she might even have sneaked a glance while he dressed behind his horse.

Instead, she lay with her back to the fire, thinking of her father and the pain and anguish she knew he suffered. Would he forgive her for putting him through this, and by the same token, would he condemn Dægan? Surely her father would listen to her and not punish her rescuer. He wasn't that merciless. Was he?

She squeezed her eyes shut and blocked out the images of her father's temper and his swift retribution. She replaced the shouting and anger with the pleasure of other things, like Dægan himself. He lay a close distance from her, awake. If she rolled over, she'd have another chance to gaze into his wondrous eyes.

Ah...those eyes... Albeit mildly black-and-blue, they were as mesmerizing as a falling star in the noon of night. But it wasn't right to think of him that way. She shouldn't have the slightest yearning for him, for she knew her father would surely step between them. It was best to put whatever joy and fondness she had for him out of her mind.

In her vain efforts to forget, she heard a sound—a distant rustling from outside the cavern. *Just a scavenger animal,* she told herself. *But in this rain?*

A hardened palm rolled her to her back and another covered her mouth. It was Dægan, his dagger in hand. The blade reflected an evil shine from the fire, and his eyes expressed a gravity as heavily as the day they saw the four ships with red and white sails. He brought a finger to his lips, demanding her absolute silence, and then pointed outside.

"We have company," he whispered. "Stay here."

Mara sat up to object, but he pushed her back down and brought his face so close to hers that his lips touched her cheek as he spoke. "I said lie still. They don't know I'm with you. Let them think that."

"What will you do?"

Dægan grabbed her trembling hand and placed the dagger she'd used just hours before to scale a fish within it, but didn't answer her. He unsheathed his sword in the very slowest of ways and quietly backed up with the same careful stealth, putting his finger to his lips one last time before the shadows of the cavern swallowed him whole.

Panic gripped her. Disturbing images of foreigners numbering in the hundreds, fully clad in armor and helmets, flashed before her. Pictures of heathen men wielding bloody swords and mighty battle-axes drained the blood from her body like a sieve.

The rustling came again, but closer now as if they were

just outside the opening. She held her breath and searched the darkness, trying to see through the teeming rain. It was useless. How could Dægan leave her like this?

Two men suddenly emerged, their swords drawn, their steps cautious. They dripped from head to toe, and their warm breath emitted like dragon's fire into the cool air.

Mara concealed the dagger she'd been given and waited as Dægan had told her. It was evident now that they believed her to be alone, for they lowered their weapons and stalked toward the fire.

"Well, well," one said resignedly. "Look what we have here. A sly little fox who's not so sly after all."

Mara sat deathly still, looking from one to the other.

"She's in here!" the man called over his shoulder. His voice echoed against the damp rock walls, and at that instant, Dægan came out of the shadows. He slashed fatally across the one man's back and turned about to take on the other. The second man barely got his sword raised before Dægan thrust his blade so deep into the man's stomach that it exited his back. Dægan held his forearms extended until the man slid from the blade and fell to the ground. Dægan glanced at Mara, then slipped back into the shadows.

Dægan's horse shifted about inside the cavern, and Mara jumped up to calm the nervous animal. As she stroked its muzzle and neck, three more men ran into the cavern.

They stopped in their tracks and found their comrades dead at their feet with only Mara in the firelight, her little weapon in hand. Their eyes widened in astonishment and their expressions turned angry and callous.

"You want to play rough, aye?"

She turned to face them head-on and kept one hand on the horse's back. She prepared herself for yet another brutal attack, only this time Dægan came from the opposite side of the cavern.

He slew the first unsuspecting victim with ease and ducked to avoid the coming of a high sword at his head. As he stood up, he spun and cut the second man deeply across the thighs, making ready to take on the third. He let the Northman initiate the duel. Their irons clanged in the night, until Dægan forced the man's sword tip into the ground and stepped on it. He came up swiftly to cut the unguarded throat of the Northman. As that man dropped like a sack of wheat, Dægan revisited the wounded man, double-fisted the hilt above his head, and staked his sword deep into his foe's chest.

Mara stood frozen, awestruck, as Dægan eliminated each man one by one. So much so that she nearly failed to notice two others who were about to strike Dægan from behind. She threw her dagger into the closest man before she even realized what she'd done.

Only wounded in the shoulder, he dropped to his knees and clutched the knife before pulling it out. The man beside him bravely shielded his friend and stood with his sword primed for the imminent fight ahead. As he waited, he watched Dægan rip the broad blade from his friend's body and turn to face him. The light from the fire revealed Dægan's stone-cold eyes.

The man took a step back, and not out of fright, but in bewilderment. He mumbled something and rubbed his eyes, as if he recognized the warrior staring at him.

Dægan pressed forward, measuring the man frozen in his boots. He double-grasped his sword, opening and closing his fingers in succession on the tang to adjust his grip. The act nearly sent the two men out of their own skins. Like bugs beneath a raised rock, they tripped over themselves to get away and scurried back into the night rain.

He followed them to the edge of the cavern and peered out just in time to see them mount and ride off. He remained there for quite some time in case they decided to return. In those moments, his heart settled and the rush of frenzied excitement passed.

He'd been in battles before. Too many for his liking, but it had been a long time since he last killed another. As a merchant, there wasn't much need for drawing his father's sword, except to intimidate the occasional wayward thief from his fully loaded ships. The sound of its unsheathing was usually enough to send any man running. This day was different. There was no forewarning given, no compromise, no point of return, and no mercy in his brandished weapon. Only a warrior's vehemence, given conceivably by the thunder god himself, that knew no end until every last man had fallen.

Dægan exhaled at length, as if to rid the spirit of the *berserker* from his body. It was a feeling of immense power and immortality, but one he'd rather do without. He took no pride in this quiet aftermath.

Turning to Mara, he gazed at her with as much amazement as she had for him. "Where did you learn to throw a knife like that?"

Mara let out a breath as if she were holding it the entire time. "My father."

He shook his head in disbelief. "And I suppose he taught you how to break a man's nose as well."

Mara rushed to Dægan's side, looking him up and

down. "You're hurt!"

He glanced at himself, surprised to see that his upper thigh had been sliced open. "Naught but a flesh wound."

She didn't seem to appreciate his lighthearted humor, as a few tears escaped her.

"Are you all right?"

"Nay, I'm not all right," she sobbed. "You could have been killed."

Dægan wrapped his free arm around her and attempted to make light of the situation. "Not likely with you on my side."

He half expected her to slither from his reach, but she didn't. She stayed where he'd drawn her, and her willing body felt good in his embrace. Natural. As if the small of her back was made just for the crook of his arm.

He felt her body tremble, and sheathed his sword. "Come by the fire and warm yourself. Come, now."

He guided her far beyond the fallen men and made sure to hide the gruesomeness, tucking her into the concave space beneath his shoulder.

She sat where he deemed so and stared about the dancing flames, still in shock at the carnage. "Did you know those men?"

Dægan circled the fire and fetched his bear cloak from the ground, draping it around her shoulders. "Aside from assuming they were the men we encountered on the banks of the River Shannon, I cannot say I know them at all."

"Did you see how they looked at you? 'Twas as if they knew you or—had seen you before."

"I saw it in their eyes as well. But I tell you in truth, I knew them not."

He sat beside her and pulled the bearskin cloak tighter

around her shoulders to keep out the cold of the night and the chill of death around her. His adjustment beside her only prompted a concern for his bleeding wound.

Blood had already seeped into the hem of his kirtle, a red so dark, it looked black in the shadows of the cavern. It trailed a wide path down toward his knee and around his outer thigh.

"You're bleeding," Mara said. "A great deal…"

Before Dægan could argue differently, she took the hem of her gown and dabbed at the blood oozing from his leg. Gingerly at first, as if she were nervous to even touch him, but more ardently as he continued to bleed. Soon, she employed both hands.

He watched her, her hands especially, as they touched his bare skin, that sensitive area on the inside of his thigh. He knew it was oftentimes an erogenous place on a woman, but until he felt the slender fingers of Mara's kind nursing, he had no idea it existed equally for a man.

"You don't wear breeches like the other men."

"In Hladir, 'tis a necessity, for the winds are cold enough to turn a man's skin black. But here, the weather is tolerable. I've grown accustomed to the way the men of the Erin dress. I prefer it, actually."

By the time he finished his explanation, she'd become so absorbed in cleaning his wound that she didn't even realize how high she'd wiped up his leg, just short of grazing him. He couldn't take any more and gathered her hands in his.

She glanced up with eyes of polished emerald. A well of near-falling tears pooled in the reddened corners. "Did I hurt you?"

"Of course not."

"But you stopped me."

Her innocence and naïvety were like healing elixirs for his somber heart. "Only because I've more than recovered. Thank you." He only wished there was something he could say to make her forget about the five corpses lying behind her. Something he could do that would keep her from reliving this night.

This time, he clasped her face and prohibited her from any more wayward glances. "Do not look upon them. Your eyes needn't see what wickedness I've done." He drew her closer and cradled her head on his shoulder. "When the rain dies, I shall remove them from here. Just sleep. I'll stay awake and keep watch. By my guess, they'll not be back without the help of reinforcements, and by that time, I hope to be gone. At first light, rain or shine, we'll be gone."

****

Domaldr barely finished breaking his fast with stale bread and dried meat, both hardly fit for a human, when he heard the sudden rush of horses nearing and sliding to a halt outside his temporary encampment. He heard Soren's voice, and hoped his men would have better news for him. What was left of his pitiful meal he tossed aside, and picked up his cup. He drank heavily, filling his stomach with sour ale.

Soren and Thorbjörn entered, their expressions urgent. They remained subservient as they stood abreast and waited for permission to speak.

"Well?" Domaldr snapped. "Did you find her?"

"Aye, m'lord. We did, but—"

Domaldr threw his men a look that ricocheted between them. "You did but…what?"

"Sh-she was not alone. There was a man with her."

Domaldr rolled his eyes. "A man. I assume you dealt with the matter swiftly."

"I assure you, we tried, but he was not just any man—"

Again, Domaldr cut Soren off. "A man is a man is a man! And there were seven of you! Tell me you two aren't all who're left!"

Soren bowed in reticence. "We were no match for him. His ability with the sword proved he was no stranger to war."

Domaldr scrutinized the appearance of his men. They were soaked to the skin by the all-night rain and ashen in color as they'd been without food or warmth. Aside from the meager wound in Thorbjörn's shoulder, they were relatively unscathed. "By the looks of you both, you didn't put up the fight I would've expected from two well-armed men."

"My lord, we would have…but…he looked exactly like you!"

"What are you talking about?"

"This man was you! Granted, he was dressed differently, without the cover of breeches, and what kirtle he sported was of a finer wool with the trouble of embroidery all over it. But save the manner of his clothing, he was your twin!"

The image of a twin smacked Domaldr square in the face. Unbeknownst to anyone else, he *was* the product of a double birth, but he hadn't seen that brother in about eighteen years as he'd left his family without a kind farewell.

Domaldr was the third son born of Rælik. Gustaf was the first, an elder brother of one year, and then Dægan, born about two minutes before Domaldr. Two years later,

Eirik came into the world, knocking him out of his place as the precious baby of the family. Between that and his twin constantly mastering skills ahead of his time, Domaldr became the overlooked son. He resented his family, knowing full well that any of his father's wealth upon his death would first pass to the oldest, and then the rest would be divvied up between the sons. That bitterness only grew as he aged—until one day, he'd had his fill.

His father had brought home an exquisite sword, handcrafted by the Halfdan Highleg's blacksmith himself. Made of gold and silver inlay, bejeweled with rubies and masterful patterns of filigree, it was the very prick that burst Domaldr's festering blister.

That night, he'd gathered a select few of his friends, took one of his father's ships, and stolen away into the night. He'd been blessed by the gods twofold that day, for the boat he chose wasn't empty. It contained the treasures and wares from his father's recent voyage. Domaldr both escaped the shadow of his ever-gifted identical brother, Dægan, and robbed his family of their much-needed winter supplies.

Domaldr pondered his men's encounter. He doubted that the man they described could be the warrior they claimed, for the brother he shared a womb with was nothing more than a merchant.

He paced as he spoke. "'Tis true, I've a twin. And I don't discount the fact that he could be here, for he's a traveler and a seaman. But for him to slaughter five of my men is quite a tale, Soren."

"I speak not of exaggeration, but of a man proficient with his weapon. There be no doubt he and that sword were one."

Domaldr frowned, hearing the inflated words coming from his own friend. It was as if he were standing amid his father's supporters in Hladir again, and their praises fell like rain upon the beloved Dægan. "Enough of him! Tell me more of the sword he wielded."

"A *jarl's* sword," Soren described. "Of gold and silver and precious stones… There's none like it."

"Do you recall the color of the stones?" Domaldr still wasn't ready to accept the warrior as his twin. "What was their color?"

Thorbjörn piped up. "They were as red as blood."

"Are you certain?"

Thorbjörn hung his head. "Aye. I was wounded, and as Soren stood in front of me, I saw my fill of the man. More so than I actually cared to. I remember his eyes, the way he looked at me as he pulled his sword from Oskar's chest, and the reflection of the fire on his blade. The tiny red stones on the hilt matched the color of the blood that ran from his leg."

A small upsurge of glee bubbled inside Domaldr. "So, he's injured, you say?"

"Aye."

Domaldr smiled, but all too briefly. He was no closer to resolving this predicament. The girl was still roaming about, and his blasted brother was now in the picture. He stalked toward the table and poured himself a full tankard of ale. Again, he drank heavily, then slammed the cup down. "Where did you find them, Soren?"

"In a cavern, m'lord. South of here."

"Good. Amass the men and take me there."

"But, m'lord," Soren interjected. "We cannot possibly find it again. The rain has washed away their tracks."

"You found them before! Do it again!"

"We only found them because we saw the light of their fire. Had it not been for that, we'd still be searching."

Domaldr threw his tankard and growled. "I want that girl! And I want my brother to pay through the nose for what he has done!"

****

Breandán watched Domaldr storm through the camp like a maddened bull on the charge. He knew the reason for the man's anger. He'd heard it easily through the cheap, thin wool of the tent. He also knew that the girl Domaldr wanted in his charge was the fancy-free daughter of the Connacht king. Breandán had often come across her many times while hunting. She often frittered away her time on a white stallion, and since he'd been hauled in with that very horse, it confirmed her identity without a doubt.

Breandán thought about the girl at length and worried over her. She was of a good stomach, but even he knew bravery would not help an innocent, defenseless woman when it came to the merciless Northmen. If they ever found her, she was as good as dead.

He felt his stomach turn with that horrible thought and directed his mind toward things more helpful to her rescue. It would take more than courage to bring her back. He'd also have to deceive Domaldr and countless others in the process. At this point, he had nothing to lose and more to gain.

Breandán might have been only a farmer's son, a mere tenant to the clan lord who served her father, but Mara's rescue could help Breandán on many accounts. He could get the respect he so wished from his fellow clansman. He could help to improve the life of his father, and he could attain the love he craved from the dark-haired lass just by bringing her home. And how hard could that be for a hunter who spent his life tracking the hidden?

No more difficult than tracking the cunning fox.

As Domaldr returned, a swarm of men followed him. Breandán yelled out, gaining the sour Northman's attention, and stood despite the ropes around his ankles and wrists. "If you want to find that brother of yours, I can help you."

Domaldr stopped just before entering his tent. He turned around and stroked his chin as he looked at the fierce, able-bodied group of men before him. All were hungry for battle and fully armored in mail and conical helmets. Then he gazed at Breandán, the single, blunt-spoken prisoner, with only muscled arms to boast in his favor.

Domaldr uttered something to his men and motioned for Soren to bring Breandán forward. Once shoved into Domaldr's tent, Breandán saw the extent of the leader's madness by the toppled table and mess of food scraps scattered on the ground.

"Leave us, Soren," Domaldr commanded without taking his eyes from Breandán. "Sit."

"I've been sitting for hours against the trunk of a tree. I'd rather stand."

Domaldr grinned. "'Twas not a request."

"You'll have me killed for not sitting?" Breandán dared.

"I'll have your tongue cut out for wagging it."

"Then without my tongue, you'll know not how to find the girl or your brother."

Domaldr breathed like a bear on the kill. "Of what do

you claim to know? Speak fast before I have you killed for no other reason than my own pleasure."

Breandán weighed his options. He could probably escape Domaldr and his men now that he'd been cut from the confines of the tree, and he could no doubt track Mara within a few days. But as he contemplated Domaldr's twin and the skill the man had in thwarting seven men single-handedly, he thought it best to use Domaldr's army to his advantage. Perhaps while the two brothers were distracted with fighting each other, he and Mara could steal away without anyone's notice.

He fabricated his story. "I'm a hunter and a trapper. I know the lie of the land better than anyone. I know of the cavern of which your men speak, and I can hunt down any man or beast, rain or shine. But then again, this is Ireland, for God's sake. There's always rain. This task would be effortless for me."

"You're awfully certain of yourself," Domaldr said as he sneered. "How do I know you're not about to send me on a hopeless chase for something that isn't even my brother?"

"I'll wager my own life on it. Kill me if you think I am."

Domaldr looked as if he suspected a wily plan taking shape. "Why would you do all this for me?"

Breandán raised his cinched wrists. "My freedom, of course."

Domaldr cocked his head. "I'll have you know I don't enjoy being deceived."

"Is that a yes?"

Domaldr bit his tongue and removed a dagger from his hip. He held it at Breandán's throat and leaned in for emphasis. "If I so much as *think* I'm being toyed with, I'll sooner cut my losses than be made a fool. You understand me?"

"Clearly."

Domaldr eased the knife between Breandán's wrists and sliced him free. "We leave right now."

Rubbing his wrists, Breandán couldn't help but needle Domaldr one more time. "You're giving up the grand fight on Baile Átha Cliath to settle a petty score with your brother?"

"Given the confidence you have in your abilities, I should be rubbing my brother's face in his losses well before the start of that war. See that I do, Breandán. See that I do."

Chapter Eight

The intensity of the high noon sun pushed through the dense cloud cover. It marked the end of the rainfall, at least for the moment. This was late July, and another storm was sure to blow in. For that reason, Dægan resumed as fast a pace to Limerick as his horse could endure.

When he finally saw the break of the port settlement on the shoreline of the estuary, he slowed the horse's gait and felt the first wave of security since he and Mara had left Connacht.

Not much had been said between them in their final journey. He was sure a beastly battle of sword and flesh filled Mara's mind with horrific images of slain men, a sight no woman need see. Despite having done away with the bodies before she'd awakened that morning, he knew the memories of those killed were still at the forefront of her thoughts.

As they crossed the threshold of the high-mounded earth ring that protected the settlement, Dægan felt Mara's apprehension in her arms wrapped tightly around his waist. Even as they were welcomed by many of his kinsmen who ran to greet them, her feigned smile couldn't hide the fear in her eyes.

Dægan descended from his horse first, then helped Mara do the same. He gave her hands a reassuring squeeze and announced her name. "This is Lady Mara."

The two elders of the group, Vegard and Ottarr,

bowed their heads in humble greeting. Like everyone else who wasn't blind, they seemed to have difficulty accepting that the much-anticipated affianced girl was unexpectedly dirt-ridden, cut, bruised, and dressed in a soiled gown.

The younger man bringing up the rear was not so politely reserved. "By the gods, Dægan, the two of you look like the bottom of a sow's trough."

Dægan forced a smile for Mara. "And this would be my brother, Eirik. I told you he was charming."

Mara noticed that Eirik was just as rugged as Dægan, but a bit shorter in stature. He made up for the disadvantage with rude aggression. His hair was darker and mildly tousled from the day's labors, but he was no less handsome than his older brother.

"Eirik, please. 'Tis obvious they have been through an ordeal," a woman said as she pushed him aside.

She was of tall stature, nearly matching the height of the men, with golden hair and crystalline eyes. Her clothes hung loosely around her waist, but she possessed enough womanly curves that even her cloak couldn't hide them. A figure that Mara imagined most men fancied.

"Look at you, Dægan. Your leg is wounded, and your nose is broken."

Mara stiffened, as she was the one who broke it. To her relief, Dægan dismissed it and embraced the woman warmly. "All minor scrapes, Lillemor, dear."

"So what happened to you?" Eirik asked, taking the reins of Dægan's horse. "Did you try your charm on the lady a little too soon and she got the best of you?"

Lillemor turned her gaze in Mara's direction. "You'll have to excuse my husband. He's been stuck in the hull of the ship for too long, tarring with lingering fumes."

"Which brings me to a question," Dægan added as he ushered Mara and the group toward the longhouses. "How is the *knarr* coming along? Finished, I hope?"

"Ah, the *knarr*..." Eirik said. "It seems we have run into some complications."

"And what would those complications be?"

"Lack of men."

Dægan raised his hands, insinuating his confusion. "I left a whole fleet of men for you, Eirik."

Vegard approached. "Aye, but I sent them to Veigsfjordr to trade the pelts we've acquired. The furs are in high demand, and no one in these ports has as many as we. Delaying the trip would've only resulted in losing the highest-offered coin."

Dægan stopped in his tracks, his irritation as evident as his broken nose. "How many men did you send?"

"Nearly fifty. We had four *knarrs* heavily loaded, and to send any less would have made for a tiresome journey for those at the oars." Vegard narrowed his eyes. "I thought you'd be pleased at the number, m'lord. Not often do we fill more than three vessels at a time."

Dægan sighed. "I am pleased, Vegard, but the timing is what piques me. I need those men. Desperately..."

"For what?" Ottarr asked as Dægan dragged his hands through his hair.

"Lillemor, would you be so kind as to show Lady Mara to my longhouse. Fetch her some clean clothes as well."

"Of course, Dægan."

"Thank you." He turned to Mara. "Will you excuse me for a moment?"

Mara nodded respectfully toward everyone and

followed Lillemor into the spread of longhouses, symmetrically arranged within the semicircular stronghold. It was evident to Mara that the fortification was entirely the work of the Northmen. Their houses were the longest she'd ever seen, with grass strangely growing atop the roofs. A central wooden pathway divided the settlement into two equal halves and connected both the north and south gates. This, she surmised, was not only for convenience, but for aiding in the defense of the stronghold against an attack. Those two gates were the sole means of entering the protected port. The only alternative was through the harbor on the west side. Despite the protective enclosure of the settlement, it wasn't an exclusive community. Mara saw a mixed populace of busy craftsmen, common farmers, bartering merchants, a few smiths, and a slew of others in between. She might still have been in Ireland, but this was definitely not the Ireland to which she was accustomed.

Dægan waited until Mara was farther than earshot before addressing his brother and his two advisors. "I need as many men as I can gather, because I have to take the girl back to her father."

"What?" Eirik barked. "You just got here."

"Bear with me, brother. This is quite a tale." Dægan took a deep breath before he began. "It so happens that my plan of gaining my Irish bride with a flattering amount of silver has been thwarted. There were men who'd just disembarked on the shores of the Shannon and, from my guess, they were Danes set on the spoils to be gained from Dubh-Linn's impending war. We barely escaped with our lives, but in doing so, I was unable to meet with Mara's father. We left Connacht without his consent or knowledge."

Ottarr straightened his stance. "In other words, you took her, m'lord?"

"I had no choice," Dægan spat. "They were not after me and the silver in my keeping. They were after Lady Mara. They would've killed her to silence what news she'd bring of their landing. What else could I have done?"

"I told you going alone was foolish!" Ottarr scolded.

Eirik jumped in with his own complaints. "And what am *I* supposed to do with the seven heifers you were going to offer as a bride price?"

"Feed them." Sarcasm feathered Dægan's words as he snatched the reins from his brother's hands and walked off.

Ottarr followed him on his heels. "Now where are you going?"

"At this moment, I plan to bathe, eat, and rest my mind until morn when my thoughts run fresh. Inform the few men that are left in my command to make ready when I need them." Dægan glanced over his shoulder at Eirik lagging behind. "And finish that blasted *knarr*, brother."

****

The large rectangular room was cool and dim, and absent a fire in the pit centrally located in the longhouse. Mats covered a dirt-packed floor, where parallel boxbeds, filled with fleece, fur hides, and woolen blankets lined the perimeter. At each end of the beds sat wooden chests carved with strange figures and designs. Mara also noticed a bare table with a few chairs for sitting.

The house and its contents were simple and unimpressive, suggesting that Dægan lived merely on necessity. The only things in the room worth a second look were the chests themselves.

Mara tried to dispel the urge to look inside, but the wings of curiosity carried away her determination. And what would it hurt? She only wanted to see what Dægan thought valuable enough to stow away.

She knelt closer to one of the chests and placed her hands on top of its lid. The wood was even more beautiful than she expected. Although the patterns of connecting circles and intertwining serpents were truly pagan, she could still appreciate the intricate art put into the wood.

The lid was heavy, sturdy on its hinges as she opened it. Inside were men's clothing made from expensive linens and fancy embroidered hems, several cloaks of wool and fur, and jeweled brooches of many sizes. All were finely detailed and just as complex as the chest itself.

Her interest for the contents of the other chest in the room was piqued, and she hurried to open it as well. She found mail armor, armor plates, quite a few daggers, silver coins, and one sturdy helmet with a beautiful bronze inlay. The collection of items was very valuable and likely to be the assets of many mercantile journeys.

Between the numerous ships in Dægan's possession and the worth of his belongings, she soon realized the extent of his wealth. Feeling guilty for prying, she promptly stood and found Lillemor in the doorway, watching her.

Mara immediately offered an apology, but the woman entered, unsympathetic of her efforts. She dropped an armful of small logs and kindling for the fire, then gazed at her with cold gray eyes.

"You'll not find anything in here to wear. This is where Dægan stays between his voyages, and, as you can see, there's nothing by way of a woman's influence here. Come with me, and I'll find you something suitable."

Lillemor left the fire pit, leading the way to the next adjacent house. It was similar to the twenty other longhouses made of turf and timber, but larger in size than Dægan's. The hearth, boxbeds, and chests were all in the same locations, but they boasted a greater capacity. In the distant corner stood a large weaving loom, and a table set with wooden bowls. Over the fire in the central hearth, a pot of roasted meat simmered. Looking up, Mara noticed dried meat and herbs hanging from the rafters for future dinners.

Lillemor went straight to her chest and pulled out a simple linen shift, a green woolen cloak, and two silver brooches rattling against a fine linked chain. "'Tis not what nobles are used to, but 'tis clean."

Mara took the clothes, slowly grasping the strange new world she'd stepped into. "Does everyone here know of who I am?"

"Of course," Lillemor replied without hesitation. "'Tis not every day that a man like Dægan finds something worth holding on to. Considering he's a merchant, he's more apt to trade his finds than keep them. But the heart is a different matter. I've not seen him this restless, nor this content all at the same time. I must say he fell in love with you the first time he saw you."

"Fell in love?" Mara repeated.

"Well, of course. Did he not tell you?"

"He told me nothing of the sort."

Lillemor drew back in astonishment. "I'm surprised he kept it to himself. Dægan is usually full of words. A good skald's curse is also his blessing."

****

Mara returned to Dægan's longhouse and found him and his brother sitting on a boxbed. A swath of linen bandages now lay across Dægan's thigh, and a warm fire crackled in the hearth. His lips drew up in a smile at the sight of her. "Did Lillemor have any clothes to fit you?"

Mara envisioned herself swimming in the curvaceous woman's tunic. "She had clothes to offer, but…"

"Worry not," Dægan reassured her. "Tomorrow I shall go down to the harbor and pay a visit to Torvald. He always has a good selection of tunics on his ship. I've heard that his wife makes them from the brocade he acquires in Byzantium."

"Truly?" Mara asked in surprise. "I've never worn silk before."

"Well, I suppose we must remedy that. Come, have a seat beside me."

Mara entered the main room and sat beside Dægan, still wary of Eirik, who sat closely at Dægan's left. For some reason, she found it difficult to feel at ease with the brother's company, a wariness she presumed would fade once she got to know him better.

"How is your leg, Dægan?"

"I'm better now." Strong sincerity gleamed in his eyes. His voice proved deep and rich, indications that both his wounds were on the mend.

"Quit suckling the good woman for attention, Dægan," Eirik ridiculed. "I lost more blood cutting teeth as a child than you did on that scratch. I regret to say, Lady Mara, that my brother will milk a goat 'til her teats are bloody before he's finished nursing."

Dægan hit his brother in the back of the head. "Your

manners, Eirik."

"I'm sorry, m'lady." Eirik chuckled. "Allow me to put that another way."

"Oh no, you won't." Dægan grabbed his brother's tunic by the fist and jerked him close. "Say your farewell, Eirik."

Eirik strained to exchange glances with Mara from the position Dægan held him in. He nodded his parting to his best ability and signed off with a quick peck on Dægan's lips.

Dægan called out in disgust and shoved him away. "Damnation, Eirik, you clod! Leave!" Eirik laughed and tripped as he ran for the door, but Dægan remained taciturn until it slammed shut. He wiped his mouth crossly. "I apologize for Eirik's behavior. He's rather repulsive at times, and he's completely oblivious to when he's worn out his welcome."

"I don't mind. He seems to have quite a way of being the instigator."

"He's quite the horse's arse," Dægan corrected.

"Nonetheless, the two of you seem very close."

"I suppose."

Mara considered the thought of a sibling. "I reckon 'tis nice to have a brother."

"I reckon 'tis doubly nice to be without one."

"You don't mean that," she chided. "I imagine deep down you're fond of his jests, particularly the kiss he gave you."

"'Twas not a kiss," Dægan pointed out.

"It certainly looked like one from where I was sitting."

"To the untrained eye, I suppose 'twould. But I'd be more than willing to show you what a real kiss entails."

Mara froze as he drew near. He lingered just short of her mouth and parted his lips. Butterfly wings fluttered inside her stomach as his nose nudged hers. He tipped her chin upward and took her lips in a tender, gradual kiss, a sweet compromise of patience and passion.

Dægan pulled away and saw the slow burn of amber flames reflecting in Mara's eyes from the hearth beside him. She was a beautiful woman, but too young to know the effect she had on him. All he had to do was remotely think of her and she'd arouse him. And it didn't have to be sexual. A passing image of her face or her angelic voice in his ear. Nothing was too fleeting for him.

A rapping at the door disrupted his thoughts, and a line of servants entered the longhouse. Each one carried different items: a stack of white linens, a small chest, and a tray of food. As the male servants brought in four buckets of water and a large bronze cauldron, the women sorted the items on the table. When finished, they bowed before Dægan and Mara, and departed as quickly as they came.

"What is all this?" Mara asked.

"Your bath."

A final servant entered, and he added the water from the fire pit to the cauldron. "Is there anything else, m'lord?"

"Aye, one last thing. I gave Eirik an item for safekeeping. Bring it to me, please."

The servant bowed and exited in a rush.

Dægan took Mara's hand in his before he spoke. "I know this may seem sudden and a bit forward, but I want to give you a gift—one that would seem more fitting had I had a chance to offer your father a sufficient bride price."

He studied her, holding fast to the innocence of her

face. Like a child, her eyes sparkled with anticipation. He began with a story.

"There once was a king blessed with power, wealth, and dignity. He fell in love with a woman, and she loved him. For a time, they'd sneak out to meet each other. Sometimes to steal a kiss in the thickets of the garden. But always in brevity, for each was all too often called upon. Eventually, the king proposed an arrangement of marriage, but her father wouldn't allow it. He had other intentions of offering her to someone else—someone whose rising authority had threatened his holdings. By means of his daughter, he could secure favor and gain an ally instead of an enemy.

"One day it was done. Her father married her to another, and not just any man, but coincidently, her own lover's sworn enemy. The king's heart broke in two, and he sank in deep despair. Rightly, he could've fought for her if he so chose, and won, for the size of his army was twice that of her husband's. But instead, he traveled as far away as he could from the woman who could no longer be his. He searched the ends of the world for the sweetest of oils, the rarest of silk, and the most beautiful of jewels he'd ever laid eyes on, and gathered them all in a wooden chest for his distant unattainable love. Unfortunately, his journey brought him many trials. It took him ten long years to return, but it was too late. His love had died.

"Now some say it was pneumonia, while others say 'twas a broken heart. Nonetheless, she died alone. You see, her husband had a reputation for making enemies everywhere he went, and he was constantly away fighting in battle. While he was frequently gone, she'd sneak out, waiting for her lover king to come back for her, but he never showed. It took all of nine years for her to assume that he'd found the arms of another before she finally gave up.

"After hearing the news of his love's death, the king couldn't keep the chest any longer. He'd traveled and searched for so long to give it to her that keeping it for himself destroyed the true meaning behind it. As he agonized in his own grief, he felt compelled to give the chest of valuables to her husband and end the feud between them, once and for all.

"The husband refused to accept the gift from the king, thinking it was a trick. He was unaware of the extensive value of the items within, and cast it aside. Still suspicious of the king's intentions, he stabbed him and left him for dead.

"In grave desperation, the king retreated south to a group of merchants who were preparing to set sail. He told his story on his deathbed. His exact words were that 'this chest must be given to the one who holds your heart.'"

As if perfectly timed, the servant reentered carrying a wooden chest of fastidious work and value. Mara's eyes widened as he placed it at her feet.

"Inside this chest are those things, and I give them to you."

Mara covered her gaping mouth. "This is *the king's* chest?"

"It is, and I must adhere to his wishes." Dægan took her hand in his. "From the day I laid eyes on you, you had my heart."

Mara hesitated to open it, though her growing excitement was hard to miss.

"Go on," Dægan gestured. "Open it."

She reached down and lifted the lid, finding a stack of

luxurious linens, jewels of various striking colors, silver, and jars of spices and oils just as Dægan had foretold. A deep smile etched her face, but it gradually fell. "I cannot accept this."

"You have no choice. I'm to give this to whoever holds my heart. I may not hold yours as of yet, but I believe I have your trust else you wouldn't be here with me now."

"I've nothing to give you."

"Ah, but you do," Dægan assured her. He traced his hand down her face and around her neck, stopping at the delicate hollow of her throat. "You can give me the pleasure of witnessing your bath, my lady."

Mara swallowed, and he smiled upon hearing it.

"Surely, you jest, Dægan."

He reclined on the boxbed, and linked his hands behind his head. "I rarely jest." When she didn't budge, he encouraged her with a promise. "Rest assured, I'll not move from this spot, nor will my hands. You've my word."

Dægan waited for her to gather the courage she needed to disrobe and slip beneath the steaming water of her prepared bath, but it never happened.

"I-I cannot do what you've asked of me," Mara said aghast. "You may be accustomed to such acts, but I'm not."

Dægan sat up and noted the way she wrung her hands. "Are you afraid of me?"

Mara closed her eyes. "I'm afraid I may be unable to resist you."

"Why resist me at all?" Dægan leaned forward. "Love and intimacy are not dreadful, Mara."

"Nay, but a broken heart is."

He drew back. "Do you think me that cold? Do you

think I'd endure the trouble of saving your life just to cast you aside? Woman, I'd walk through the curses of a thousand gods for you—as many times as you asked of me."

"'Tis not my heart I worry about. I don't want to be the woman who breaks yours."

He snaked his arms around her waist and pulled her to him. "Would you rather return to your father with the intention of never seeing me again?"

She shook her head. "I cannot begin to imagine such a thing. I want to go where you go, to see the oceans, the mountains, and the sunset on the water from the very ships you've built your life upon. I want all those things. Above all, Dægan, I want to be with you."

"Then dread no more. From your lips to my ears, I'm certain my heart will be safe in your hands."

"You're not safe from my father," she exclaimed. "He'll do everything in his power to keep us apart. His own brother died years ago at the hands of the Northmen at Baile Átha Cliath, and he'll not stand for one to wed his daughter no matter how many head of cattle you push in his face. I'm confident he'll even regard your act of heroism as a ploy and naught more. I know this. I'm as sure as the sun rises in the morn."

Dægan scoffed aloud before he could stop himself. "I don't fear your father."

"Then what of his army that he'll surely send to hunt you down?"

"If your father chooses to do battle with me, he'll lose."

"You'd actually fight him?"

"I'd bend any way I could for him because he's your father. But if he decides that war is the only way to resolve this, then he'd better come prepared. I don't take kindly to threats, nor have I ever pretended to. By now, you should know that." Dægan stood and hobbled toward the door. On his way, he swiped his hand through Mara's bathwater and splashed his face. "I'll leave you to bathe in privacy. When I return, I do not wish to speak of your father any more this night."

Chapter Nine

Dægan decided a bath of his own would do wonders for his mood, and he set out toward the bathhouse. Once inside, it didn't surprise him to see his brother sitting against the far wall of the sauna. Eirik often treated himself to a good sweat from the steaming rocks in the open hearth after a long day's work on the ships.

"She must be quite a woman," Eirik remarked upon eyeing the aggravation on Dægan's face. "I just hope she's worth the pain you've already suffered on her behalf."

"She's worth every bit of it."

"Including the ache in your groin?"

Dægan ripped his kirtle over his head and threw it at his brother. "I'm in no mood for your cracks. I've more pressing things on my mind."

"Sure you do, brother." Eirik balled Dægan's tunic and set it aside as he rested his head against the wall. The stone floor and benches were hot to the touch, melting away the soreness and stiffness of muscles. Dægan released a long, loud sigh, drawn from the depths of his gut.

"You know the girl is young," Eirik tried to reason. "Nearly fifteen years your lesser. And she may not feel comfortable yet…with our ways of doing things."

"I know, Eirik. I'm not an idiot."

"Then you know she'll come around. They always do. Besides, I see the way she looks at you. The words may not leave her mouth, but she's rapt by the very sight of you. In no time, she'll be lifting her gown—"

"Again, Eirik, I'm not an idiot. I know in time she'll groan my name."

"Ah-ha," his brother droned in triumphant understanding. "You're afraid her father will dub you a thief even after you take her back. Is that what troubles you?"

"A good portion of my mind worries I'll be punished as a thief, but not as much as coming to terms with what province the man rules over."

Eirik bolted upright. "You took a *king's* daughter? By the gods, Dægan, you said she was a noble's child—a lord's seed at best!"

"I know what I said, and I was mistaken."

"You're more than mistaken. You're buried facedown with your arse in the air!"

Eirik had a way of adding humor to most everything he said, and sometimes it made Dægan laugh. But laughter wasn't an effective remedy for this crisis. "I need a plan. And it has to be a good one."

Eirik sank back against the hot wall. "Don't look at me. I'm just a shipbuilder."

"And a slow one at that," Dægan added.

"Well, if you didn't need one as big as the sun…"

"Hold fast your tongue, Eirik. I do pay for your work."

Eirik sighed. "You speak as though you're the only man in the port with silver to spare in his pockets."

"I've put food on your table and nearly doubled the number of men under your charge. I've asked you to build three *knarrs* in the last four years, with more to follow. So, for all intents and purposes where you're concerned, I'm the most important man in the port."

Eirik grumbled and slouched further along the bench. "You've always an answer for everything. Such a talent brings me to wonder about the counsel Ottarr and Vegard wish to have with you tomorrow morning. Have you an eloquent response to their objection when they find out Mara is a king's daughter?"

Dægan grew restless with the heat of the coals and his brother's constant chatter. "Some things are better left to the imagination." He stood and stretched the muscles of his legs, thinking no more about his advisors, but about the impressionable girl awaiting him in his longhouse.

Dægan picked up a bucket of cold water and dumped it on himself, refreshed by the cool liquid rush on his head and down his back. He wrapped a linen cloth around his waist and turned to find his brother lost in deep thought with a boorish smile across his face. Dægan picked up another bucket and doused Eirik with the cold water.

Eirik gasped from the shock, then scowled. "What was that for?"

"That was for letting your imagination run wild over my Mara. And this..." Dægan added, grabbing the last stack of linens, "is for thinking that you could *ever* get away with kissing me."

"Ah, come now, 'twas only a jest."

"Good night, brother."

****

Mara wasted no time in taking her bath for fear that Dægan would soon return from wherever he went. Had she known his servants would revisit, she might have done so even faster. Nonetheless, they were helpful and kind. They offered smiles and even idle conversation in the course of their chores, pleasantries she needed after the day she'd had. Mara particularly liked the older woman of about forty—Gormlaith, she thought she heard one say.

Gormlaith, though Irish, seemed to be content with her duties, so much in fact, that she breezed through them as if they were her own routines. The other two, who were younger by far, stumbled around the simple tasks. Conceivably, they were fresh off the slave market.

"Pay them no mind, m'lady," Gormlaith said. "I'll be the one to see to your needs whilst you're here. In the meantime, eat and put some much-needed weight on your bones."

Gormlaith didn't say much after that. She stirred the fire in the hearth and began removing the last of the used water from the cauldron. In no time, it was empty, as was the longhouse in which Mara was left to wait.

She sat at the small table, dressed in the oversized tunic that Lillemor had given her, and listened to the crackling cadence of the fire. She worried what kind of mood Dægan would be in when he returned, as this was the first time he'd ever lacked composure in front of her. Having only her father's temper to go by, she wasn't as eager to find out.

It wasn't long before she heard Dægan's heavy footsteps. He entered through the back door, just past the storage, and walked into the main room, carrying a large stack of folded linens. He wore nothing but a white cloth around his waist and a deeply carved grin on his face. Mara breathed a little easier upon seeing the improvement of his disposition.

He set the cloths on the edge of the table and looked at the empty cauldron and the tray of ample food. "Not hungry?"

"I was waiting for you." Mara stood out of politeness, but he waved her back down.

"Fret not over me, love. My bath was good. Eirik, on the other hand, cannot claim such a thing."

Mara quickly derived a conclusion. "Was there a sudden linen shortage, perhaps?"

Dægan beamed with satisfaction. "You're very perceptive."

Mara also took notice of the water droplets resting on his body and the soaked blond hair clinging to his neck and shoulders. It brought back many pleasant memories of the two of them in the cavern, wet from the drenching Erin rain.

She glanced over his perfect physique and admired him from his broad shoulders to the length of his muscular legs. The linen around his waist didn't hide much, for it was thin and tightly drawn across his legs. She wondered if, as in the cavern, he'd choose to eat his meal dressed as he was, or if he'd slip into clothing more suitable for receiving guests. If she had to be honest, she hoped he'd not resort to civilized conduct on her account, as there were some aspects of his heathen ways she rather enjoyed. Most of which she knew she shouldn't encourage.

As he slid into the nearest chair beside her, she quickly tamed her grin and watched him pour a cup of wine. After that, he plucked a piece of fruit from the tray and presented it before her.

"May I?"

The thought of eating from Dægan's hand tickled her no end. As an adult, she'd never been hand-fed before, but then again, there were a great deal of things she'd never done until Dægan came along. She'd broken his nose, knocked herself unconscious, and spent an entire day in a cavern wearing nothing but animal pelts. She'd even filleted a fish and stopped an attacker from killing Dægan with the same said knife. Now she was sitting in a Northmen's longhouse with a near-naked pagan who'd asked to put food in her mouth—an act even she knew was more sensual than innocent.

Eventually, she leaned forward and took a bite, all the while keeping her gaze on Dægan. Seeing his reaction to her mouth closing short of his fingertips tingled in places she'd never felt before.

"'Tis good?" he asked.

Mara nodded as she chewed.

"I've something better I think you'll like," he said as he opened a small glass jar filled with white granules. "'Tis from a faraway place called Alexandria." He wet his little finger in his mouth and dipped it inside, after which he offered her a taste.

She looked at his pinky, finding it hard to believe that he actually expected her to suck on his finger. "What is it?"

"Just taste it."

Mara licked her lips out of nervousness and did as asked. The grainy substance instantly melted on her tongue with a sweetness akin to honey, but better. She hummed with satisfaction as he withdrew his finger from her puckered mouth.

"Sugar," Dægan stated. "Do you like it?"

"Very much."

"I traded an entire chest of furs for it. Some say 'tis worth more than that. Lillemor mixes it with cream to make those tarts there. Go ahead, try one."

Mara picked up a tart and took a bite. The fruit and sugared cream delighted her taste buds like nothing she'd ever eaten before.

Dægan seized a piece of hard bread and tore it in half, giving her the other. "I still prefer honey, though," he admitted. "I desire a lingering flavor as opposed to a quick release of sudden sweetness."

To Mara's virgin ears, his words sounded suggestive. Heat flushed her cheeks as she tried to read the saucy expression on his face. Unable to determine if his irrepressible smile was due to his fondness for tradable sweeteners or something more titillating, she cleared her throat and steered the conversation toward less provocative subjects. "Where will you go next in your journeys?"

He poured himself a tankard of mead and washed down the bread he was chewing. "I'm not sure. I still await Eirik's completion of the *knarr*, and since my other ships have been sent to Veigsfjordr, I cannot go anywhere until either they return or Eirik finishes the new vessel. He should've had it finished by now, but quality comes with a price, I suppose."

"Eirik is good at what he does?"

Dægan swallowed another large gulp. "Building boats? Aye, the best. But anything else he does is ordinary."

Mara barely got a laugh out before Dægan lifted another piece of fruit to her lips.

"I like you here with me," Dægan said, then sucked his finger. The same one she'd put in her mouth. "Everything is better with you here."

Though taken aback by many of the things Dægan had done or said, Mara couldn't have agreed more. Everything was perfect...aside from running from her father. Dægan was everything she wanted in a man. A strong leader. A gentle companion. A handsome rogue. Traits she'd dreamed about since she was a girl.

"What do you find so amusing?"

"Nothing of importance," Mara mumbled, her mouth full of food. She swallowed quickly and tried to explain. "Forgive me. I'm ignorant to such things as courting."

"As am I."

"Dægan," she chided. "I know a man like yourself knows more about the ways of love than I. I'll not pretend to think I'm your first."

He set the last of his bread on the table and leaned out of his chair toward her. "'Tis true. There have been others before you. But none have made me feel the way I do now. Can you not see that you've rendered me a slave to your will? Or that I'm without thought or care for consequences? I'll do whatever you ask of me, whatever you want." He took her hand in his, drawing his finger lightly around her palm. "But I'll not assume to know what you desire. If you want something from me, then you'll have to ask. Until then, I shall not encourage any acts to which you're not accustomed."

Mara saw the edge that Dægan walked on, the narrow line between his committed honor and the need to satisfy that selfish libido entrenched in every man's soul. How difficult it must be to feel the torment of that deep-rooted hunger and not be able to slake the covetous yearning within.

Mara felt it too. She felt it the first time he'd kissed her, and the care for consequence faded with each breath she took.

Every moment she spent with him was like having wings to fly, to soar over the treetops without fences or palisade walls to confine her. For once, she felt free, lightsome, and happy. But oddly, to feel the elated heights of that thrill was not enough. To look in his eyes was not enough.

She wrapped her arms around his neck and kissed him. Deeply. Madly.

"M'lady, you must speak what 'tis you want..." Dægan breathed. "What 'tis you desire."

Mara quivered at the proposition of those words. Desires, needs, and wants were private matters saved for the marriage bed, between husband and wife, not before. Openly discussing such things, or acting upon them, before taking vows was both inappropriate and utterly immoral. She knew this. She believed this. Yet she felt she was three seconds from giving in.

"You know I'll not take from you, what you may regret in giving. Whatever 'tis you want from me, I must hear it from your very lips."

"I shouldn't. I cannot..."

"And I cannot break the bonds of my word," he reminded. "Only you can release me from such a promise. Say what you want from me, Mara. Say it. I beg you."

"God forgive me, but I want you, Dægan," she exhaled. "I want to be yours, body and soul. Show me just how exquisite love and intimacy can be."

Making love to Mara felt better with her than any other woman Dægan had been with. Perhaps it was because the final gift of her surrender hadn't been given as freely or as quickly as the others from his past. There'd been a process with Mara, a slow seduction without greed or shame, that ended in a long, captivating dance of shared sensuality.

Dægan lay upon her bosom and listened to her heart settle one beat at a time.

"You're pleased?" she asked meekly.

He lifted his head, amazed that she'd even think otherwise. "There's so much you don't know. And so much I want you to understand." He kissed her lips tenderly before he explained.

"I've believed, from the day I was born, that my death would be glorious, and I'd be chosen among the best to fight each day, arm in arm, with those who have gone before me. If that day should come, it would be an honor to be allied with the gods against the beasts of the underworld, a day that every man envies.

"But the more I'm with you, the more I reject the thought of that life. With you in my arms, I've no wish to die in that manner. Not anymore. You've made me believe that love is stronger than a sword arm and more eternal than the last breath of a dying warrior on the battlefield."

Dægan took her hand and placed her open palm firmly on his chest. "What I say to you is not easy, for I'm a warrior of Thor and a son of Odin. In my youth, I gave an oath, an oath that is stronger than a bond between men. To break it, means I'll not have a share in their glory upon my death.

"But hear me now, Mara. I'd rather die in your arms than die a courageous death for Odin's approval or for Thor's immense pride. I want to be as we are now, together in peaceful arms, waiting the start of each day. I want to wake every morning to the sight of your blessed face, to the feel of your body against mine and your kiss on my lips. I want to be with you forever…in this life and the next. What glory you give my heart is beyond a war god's understanding. I need not Odin or Thor anymore. I could die right now—right here—and be a happy man. Marry me, m'lady, and make me a jubilant man!"

Dægan's declaration brought a joyful noise in Mara's head. It could have been the sound of Odin's thunderous wrath over the bond his warrior had severed. More likely it was her heart pounding in her ears.

She understood the great sacrifice Dægan was making for her, and her heart leapt at the idea of being his wife, his lady, his love. Saying the words "I will" came much more easily than she ever thought possible. Explaining this union to her father and obtaining his blessing, however, would be nigh on impossible.

Chapter Ten

Mara awoke the next morning to the feel of Dægan's kiss on her neck. It was soft and barely there, as gentle as a leaf floating on the water. His arms were still wrapped around her as they were when they'd fallen asleep.

"Good morning, m'lady," he whispered, raining more kisses across her bare shoulders.

She giggled and twisted to face him. "My lord."

Dægan smiled jovially and gazed upon her morning face as if to memorize every aspect, from the warmth that reddened her cheeks, to the innocence of her bashful smile. "Shame looks lovely on you."

"Shame?" Mara asked. "And of what should I be ashamed?"

"That you allowed a heathen to kiss and make love to you—and that you enjoyed it."

"I may be guilty of all offenses, but shame is not one of them," she replied. "Maybe 'tis you who are flooded with shame. Perhaps sharing your bed with an Irish princess is more than you cared to allow."

Dægan laughed and rolled on top of her, holding her hands above her head. "I allowed many things to happen in sharing my bed with you, but 'tis not something I shall ever regret." He enveloped her lips in a long, slow, heated kiss before he broke away with a mournful sigh. "The only regret I have is that morning has come, and I have things that require my utmost attention—like seeing to your safe return."

Mara was glad that getting her back home to her father took precedence over all the things he could be doing, but was terribly disappointed when he crawled out of bed to put the task into action. She stared at his bare backside without remorse as he walked to the stack of linens left on the table from the night before.

He chose one from the top and whipped it against the air, fanning it around his hips with ease. Only then did he turn around and see her green eyes leap from below his waist.

"Careful, love. Those wandering eyes could get you into trouble."

"Could they now?" Mara rose to her feet and sauntered in his direction, leaving behind the warm hides they'd shared. It delighted her to know he was unable to keep his gaze from the curves of her body, though he pretended to remain unruffled by her seductive walk.

He casually picked through last night's meal and ate a piece of fruit from the tray. "Hungry?"

Mara parted her lips, and he fed her what was left of his piece. When her mouth closed around his fingertips, the act generated a low hum from the back of his throat. His arousal came as fiercely as a pack of wolves on a winter kill, and she took great pleasure in knowing she alone had caused such a stir within him.

She skated her fingers down his back and pulled the linen from his waist, dropping it to the floor. Dægan groaned and gave up the fight to resist her, pulling her naked body flush against his.

"I swear you're Loki himself in sweet female form."

"Is that another one of your gods?"

Dægan narrowed his gaze and spoke heatedly. "He's

the god of mischief and deceit."

Mara brought her hands up over his shoulders and interlaced her fingers behind his neck. "Deception, unlike your god, is far from my intention. Should I be more direct in my advances?"

"I cannot speak for my brother," Eirik interrupted. "But I know I'd prefer it if you did." He stood leaning against the doorframe with his arms crossed in front of his chest. A proud grin split his lips.

Dægan jerked Mara aside and shielded her with his own body. "By the gods, Eirik. I insist you knock from now on!"

"I couldn't agree more," Eirik said as Dægan charged forward and slammed the door in his face.

Before Dægan could take a step away from the entrance, Eirik knocked. Dægan ripped open the door and glared at his annoying brother. "What?"

Eirik took one glance at his unclothed brother and raised his hands in defense. "I don't mean to be a bother, Dægan, but I feel 'tis my duty to remind you that tongues wag frivolously at seaports. Henceforth, 'twould be best to rub that out before you venture—"

Again, Dægan slammed the door in his brother's face. "See what I mean, Mara? You should come to thank your parents for their lack of providing you with siblings."

She tamped down the urge to laugh at their constant drollery. "Eirik means well."

"Does he now? I know he means to anger me any chance he gets."

"I think he means to please you," Mara contended. "He may try too hard at times, but I believe he aspires to be just like you."

Dægan shook his head at her observation. "You give him too much credit. He's not but a splinter festering in my arse." He snatched a chunk of stale bread from the tray and filled his mouth to keep from ranting, but nevertheless he spat, "He's like the runt of the litter you know you shouldn't keep, but you do anyway, hoping he'll be worth something someday."

Mara fetched one of the animal hides from the boxbed and wrapped it around her shoulders. "Your life would be quite dull without him."

"My life would be many things without him, but dull...I think not." He turned away to retrieve a thin kirtle from his wooden chest for the day's work and slipped it over his head.

Mara neared him and drew the animal hide she had around both their bodies. "I can't help but think how dull my life had been before meeting you, Dægan. A few days ago, I was but a king's daughter. Today, I'm a Northman's betrothed."

"And this Northman will not forget what you started this morning." Dægan locked his fingers in her hair and soundly kissed her before he left.

****

"I've heard Dægan calls for as many men as possible," Rutland said as he carried another load of hand-hewed planks to the crew working on the *knarr*.

"Aye, he does," Hansen replied, fastening the strakes of the hull with iron rivets. He was the burly master shipbuilder of Dægan's group, the man every aspiring lad wanted to be fostered by, in hopes of becoming as brilliant with the making of sound, swift longships.

"Do you know for what purpose?"

"Nay."

Rutland set the boards down and climbed the side of the ship. "Is that not odd?"

"What's odd is you questioning the man. He's devising a plan, as we speak, with two very capable advisors for a purpose, needless of our input. When the man sees fit to inform us, then we'll *all* be the wiser. Even you."

"But—"

Hansen hammered his last peg in the hull and stood abruptly. "Have you got some better place to be, boy?"

"Nay. But I'm a free man," Rutland reminded. He leaned in, matching Hansen's defiant stance with his own. "I don't see why I should be at Dægan's beck and call whenever he asks."

"You should be at his beck and call *because* he asked you. Not by treaty or by the point of his sword aimed at your scrawny little neck, but because he simply asked. You'd not be alive today if he hadn't taken you in after your father's death. I'd say you owe Dægan at least some respect, wouldn't you agree?"

Rutland dropped his aggressive front, realizing that all the men on the ship stood as Hansen did on the subject. They all huddled shoulder to shoulder and stared at him with contempt. He turned and leapt from the ship.

Hansen shook his head, watching the argumentative teenage boy gather another set of planks before he turned around. With a stiff lip, he cast an oath under his breath and yelled at his crew to get back to work. More curses would fall before the day was over—he was certain of that.

Ottarr smiled fondly at the cantankerous shipbuilder. "Rutland is a young lad who's testing the waters, a leader in the making, perhaps. He'll learn loyalty soon enough."

"He'll learn the back of my hand soon enough," Hansen spat, pushing past his friend. "By the gods, I'd better not hear his voice complain anymore today, or—"

"Forget about him. How soon before Dægan's *knarr* is finished?"

"Judging by the crew I have? Tomorrow."

"Dægan needs it finished no later than sundown."

"Well, if you let me flog the boy, and if Eirik ever shows up, I wager I can have it finished by midday." Not even Hansen's thick facial hair could hide the sarcasm on his face.

Ottarr wasn't amused and replied, "Just make certain 'tis finished by tonight." As he descended from the boat's side, he heard Hansen call after him.

"And where's your son Boden? I sent him long ago to fetch the tar and rope. If I cannot caulk it, Dægan cannot sail it!"

Ottarr waved his hand behind him as he climbed the shore, a sign he'd take care of it himself.

****

As Dægan entered the mead hall, Vegard regarded his leg. "I see you've acquired a slight limp with that gash you call a flesh wound."

The laceration bothered Dægan more than he let on, but he dismissed it in light of his company. "I barely know 'tis there."

Both Ottarr and Vegard had been lifelong friends of his father, Rælik. And given the nature of the close bond between them, Dægan respected their opinions, oftentimes calling upon them for advice.

"Tell me you've good news about the *knarr*, Ottarr."

"I've been assured 'twill be finished tonight, but the tar rope must cure before we sail. Not until tomorrow will it be seaworthy."

Dægan sighed. In the past few days, time and consequence had been his brutal enemy. He hoped that once he was in his familiar port settlement, both would work more in his favor. Not today it seemed. He rubbed the stress from his brow.

"You haven't a plan, have you?" Ottarr asked, pouring his chieftain a curative cup of mead.

Dægan drank to drown his burdens. "Nay, I do not. All I know is I need men—many men. There were nearly two hundred on that river, ready to fight anything in their path, Irish or Northmen alike. They want Dubh-Linn, and they'll do everything to see that nothing interferes." Dægan eyed Vegard, who was oddly quiet. "What about you? You've allies in the Orkneys and the Hebrides. How much would it take to hire a solid group of mercenary warriors?"

"More than you think, m'lord. The need for mercenaries has grown since the Danes took Mercia and East Anglia from the Anglo-Saxons."

"Then offer them what they want. I must have an army at my back, and I need them now. I fear Mara's father will soon send word to all major ports in hopes of retrieving her with a heavy reward. I'm certain he thinks highly enough of his daughter that she'd be worth more to someone in the slave market than just killed outright. Regrettably, gossip spreads like the plague around here, and the longer we stay, the more likely someone will take matters into their own hands."

"My lord," Ottarr began regretfully. "I've already heard

the talk. Both merchants and locals have begun to rattle their tongues with such gossip. There's a heavy price issued, not only for the girl's return but for the capture of those responsible for her disappearance. For the kinsfolk, he's offered seven *cumals,* and for the merchants, he's offered payment in straight silver—fifty-six ounces. Considering what it takes to make issues of those amounts, this father is a nobleman indeed, quite possibly a man whose wealth runs heavy in the pockets of nearby kings."

"Or he's the king himself," Dægan mumbled.

Ottarr froze. "You took a king's daughter?"

Dægan stood and paced frantically. "Aye, I took a king's daughter! But as I told you before, her life was in danger, and I'm not a man to shrink behind a rock and watch her die before my very eyes. I did what I saw fit to save her."

"If you want to spare your own life, you've no choice but to leave this port as soon as possible."

Dægan recalled his vow. "I cannot do that. I gave my word to Mara that I'd take her home."

"What good is your word if you're dead?"

Dægan pondered that thought. As much as he hesitated to break a promise to Mara, he worried more that something terrible might happen to her should he stay for ignorance's sake. With the king affording such a large incentive for his daughter's return, most would sell their own mothers to acquire it. He hated to say it, but Ottarr was right. "So I leave Hlymrekr. Then what?"

"Vegard and I can send word to the north of your need for an army. Between your father's reputation and Vegard's influence, I'm certain they'll come as fast as the wind can carry them."

"If I may, Dægan," Vegard appended. "Let's assume

you'll gain your army and defeat the men on the Shannon. What of the king? How will you convince him not to punish you outright?"

Dægan slumped into his chair and almost laughed. "Sometimes, honesty goes a long way."

"Do not make the same mistake your father made by underestimating the vanity of a king. 'Tis larger than *any* army you lay across Connacht, and words of honesty are leaves in the wind."

"There shall be no more ill talk of my father. He was a man of many words, oftentimes keeping our very brothers and sons from the battlefield. If you want a plan, old man, then know I shall walk in my father's footsteps. I'll offer words of apology, a precious herd of fat cattle, and seven marks of silver to match his own reward—along with a fine barrel of mead." Dægan lifted his cup in a brief silent toast and drank like a fiend, only to slam it down and raise a single curious brow. "If that proves unsuccessful, Vegard...then I shall double the *mundr* and try wine."

The burly man shook his head. "Jest all you want, m'lord, but you're in uncharted waters. I hope for your sake you'll not forget the weight of that anchor fastened to your heart before you set sail."

Dægan grinned as he recalled every weight and curve of that pretty little anchor.

****

Night fell, and Dægan sat in his longhouse without the company of Mara. She'd gone missing, and despite his efforts to search the entire settlement—even the homes of strangers—he couldn't find her. He was assured by many that she'd turn up safe, and encouraged to wait in the most obvious place to which she'd return—his longhouse. While he kept himself busy sharpening his dagger on a sanding stone, Eirik and a few others took to the harbor.

Every time the door opened, Dægan caught his breath, only to be disappointed that it wasn't his Mara. After several long hours of torment, she stepped inside and removed the hood of her cloak. Her bright smile faded the moment she took one look at his face.

"Are you all right?" she asked.

"I'm not all right. I was worried about you. No one knew where you'd gone."

"I'm sorry, Dægan. I didn't mean to stay away so long. I was enjoying a walk around the harbor—"

"What? You went to the harbor?"

Mara swallowed and brushed back a straggling lock of hair from her face. "I did."

"Eirik told me he left you in the stables this afternoon."

"Did you think I'd stay there all the while? I'm not sure if you've noticed, but the entire day has come and gone."

"I should pose the same statement to you!" Dægan slammed his dagger to the table and stood, now towering above her. "You're not to leave here without me. A harbor is not the safest place for a woman like you."

Mara turned defensive. "You mean a woman who resembles the likeness of an ill-gotten Connacht princess?"

"I mean a woman who would make some tightfisted vagrant a dandy profit in the slave trade. This is not the Shannon you're used to swimming in. This is Hlymrekr, dear love, where men oftentimes steal from their right hand to feed the left."

Mara stared at him, undeterred by his angry threats.

"Your distress isn't about my absence, is it? There's a greater burden on your shoulders. Is it my father?"

Dægan took a step back and plopped into the chair behind him, groaning because Mara was as correct as she was perceptive. "Your father has issued a price on my head and a reward for your return."

Mara came forward to kneel in front of him. "What are we to do now?"

Dægan let his head fling to the back of the chair. "I don't know. But we certainly cannot stay here. Make no mistake this is a Northmen's port, and you stand out like a dove in a flock of ravens. We must leave this place and not come back until my reinforcements arrive."

"Where will we go?"

"The only place I know we'll be safe—Inishmore."

"And how soon before your reinforcements come?"

Dægan stared at his roof. "Days...weeks most likely." After feeling the weight of her long silence, he reached for her hands and cupped them in his own. He kissed her knuckles, then staggered on his next words. "I know you want to go home. And I gave my word that I'd get you there. But realize that my promise extends to ensure your return is a safe one. As much as I hate doing this, leaving Hlymrekr is the most important thing I can do to keep you out of harm's way. This port is dangerous enough without your father's warrants, and now 'tis twice as unsafe with a hefty sum of coinage dangling in everyone's faces. I couldn't care less about the price on my head, but your value exceeds mine, making you the easier, more profitable find." Dægan pulled her onto his lap and wrapped his arms around her. "I cannot bear for anything to happen to you. I cannot."

Mara touched his face in woeful sympathy. "I understand."

He knew she had, but it was her disappointment that rocked him to the core. "There's something else you should know. My family on Inishmore is expecting a wedding when I return."

Mara nodded, recalling those words.

"But what you fail to understand," he continued, "is that where I come from, a marriage denied for any reason by the woman's family is considered an insult. I realize in your case lack of consent by your father is the grand dilemma you face, but I should warn you, in the past, blood vengeances have been sought for less. I'm not trying to say we should marry the moment we step off the ship, but we should at least assure them of an agreed proposal. I can stall the festivities until we're able to return to Connacht and gain accord from your father once I pay the appropriate *mundr* to him."

Mara touched his face and smiled in her sweet reassuring way. "Faking a marriage proposal will not be as difficult as persuading my father to agree to one. But even so, I shall do what you ask of me."

"Mara, I'll get you home to your father, and I'll amend what I've ruined," Dægan pledged as he cupped her face. "I'll find a way to make this all work."

Mara kissed him, comforting him from all the torments he faced.

"You must be hungry," he said as he realized she hadn't eaten since morning. He gestured toward the tray of food at the table. "Please, eat your fill." He gave up the chair for her and walked to the hearth, stoking the fire from habit, and then to the door.

"Where are you going?" Mara asked in surprise.

"I have to find Eirik. He and the others are probably still searching for you. And then I need to inform Ottarr that we'll leave first thing in the morn. Worry not, I won't be long. Perhaps, while I'm at Eirik's, I can charm his wife into giving me one of those tarts you're fond of."

When his words didn't bring about the smile he wanted, he cocked his head and altered his statement. "You're right. One tart is never enough. Two, then? Ah, there 'tis," Dægan crooned after she smiled. "That sweet little blessing that fills my heart with hope."

Chapter Eleven

Mara sipped the last of her wine in the near dark, meandering through thoughts of her father and the pain he must be suffering because of her absence. She brought to mind his deep-set eyes, his barely-there smile, and the simple joy of hearing his voice echo within the keep, longing to hear it again sooner rather than later. By no stretch of the imagination was he a man of quiet voice or demeanor. Yet, where she was concerned, there was an unusual gentleness in his tone and appearance. Only she could bring that side of him to light and without much effort. She was his only child, his very pride in the flesh.

Lonely, homesick, and helpless, she earned the right to cry but refused to let her tears fall. Dægan would bring her home; he said he would, and she believed him. There was no other man she'd trust more to do the impossible.

But her faith in his ability came with a price: *patience.* And moreover, a miracle that her father wouldn't see just a lowly *Fionnghall* in Dægan.

Mara stood and paced the dimly lit room. Her dismal state of mind matched the somber shadows cast from the dying fire in the hearth and the solitary flame in the dished stone lantern. She'd brought more undue pain and anguish to her father, and wreaked more havoc in Dægan's life than either deserved. If only she hadn't gone so far from the keep that day…

The lantern on the table suddenly blew out, and two

forceful hands pushed against her back. As she fell over the boxbed, her aggressor dove on top of her and shoved her face down. She screamed and flailed, but the thickness of the fleece bedding muted her shouts. A hard fist rocked her temple, and she lay dazed, unable to fight back any longer.

In one swift jerk, he rolled her to her back and stuffed her mouth with a gag, tying it tight behind her head. Tears fell from her eyes, and her ears rang, though she couldn't feel pain. Only pressure as he bound her wrists with a coarse rope.

She stared in the direction of the shadowy figure hovering above her. It was too dark to see his face, and she was still too stunned to focus her gaze.

His voice came deep and low so only her ears could hear. "Now, sweeting, you make a sound and I'll cut you so deep your unborn children will feel it."

His words were barbaric. The thought of dying by evisceration sickened her to the point of vomiting. She swallowed back her nausea and obeyed her attacker as he tore her from the bed.

She tried not to stumble, but her legs weakened with each step. He had no patience for her feebleness and pulled her harder through the room to the back door. Once outside, where a bright silver moon illuminated their path toward the stables, she tried again to make out her kidnapper. Unfortunately, he had deliberately covered his head with a woolen hood and smacked her face as soon as he caught her staring.

"Remember, girl. Not a sound."

He didn't have to remind her. Her stomach churned as though he'd already gutted her on the way.

Where was Dægan? Where was anyone?

Was this the tightfisted vagrant Dægan had warned her about or someone even more ruthless?

She tripped again and fell to her knees, but it didn't go without punishment. He grabbed her throat and lifted her. "Walk, I say!"

Mara gasped and coughed, trying desperately to keep up. When they finally entered the stable, he kicked open the stall gate and propelled her to the ground.

This was it. She'd be raped and left for dead in the dark of night. She knew it. By the sheer brutality of his actions so far, she knew there'd be no mercy, nor would it matter. She already hated him; his voice, his hands, the stale perspiration from his restlessness as though he'd been sweating the idea all day. She deemed him swift and cruel in his intercourse, one who'd demand the most from her and haul her over the coals when she gave any less.

No, she'd not give less. In fact, she'd give him all she had. One mighty kick between his legs before he'd split hers.

But he never joined her on the ground. All Mara heard was a rustling, almost clumsily as he searched through the darkness. She heard the clatter of small metal and links, and then the hollow pat to a horse's back. Dægan's horse.

She should have known. He wasn't going to have his way with her here. He'd wait until after he stole away into the night.

But where would they go?

She prayed, she cried, she waited. The pain in her wrists emerged as the rope cut deeper with every twist of her hands. Her head began to throb, and perspiration prickled her skin.

Heavy footsteps stopped in front of her. She tensed, ready to send a foot to the air, but he stood his distance.

"Get up! Get up now!"

When she didn't move quickly enough for his liking, he grabbed her ankle and dragged her out of the stall, twisting her leg around to roll her to her stomach. He snatched a wad of her hair and pulled her to her knees. "Is this what you're waiting for, lass?" His hands groped her from behind and shoved her skirt up her back.

Mara crawled forward, clawing at the grooves of the stone floor, but he yanked her back again by the hair.

"I can see now why Dægan fancies you," he coaxed, using repulsive flattery. "You're a fiery little one." He drew his hand around her throat and hissed in her ear. "Let me show you what a real man feels like."

"Who's there?"

Mara froze at the sound of the familiar voice. *Eirik.*

She tried to scream his name, but the gag proved successful. The man cursed and jumped to his feet to deal with Dægan's brother, who stood in the entry, holding a lantern.

Tears burned Mara's eyes as she scrambled on all fours, helpless to warn him of the dangerous man stalking in his direction.

"There's no sense in hiding," Eirik said, blindly peering into the dark. "I can hear you. Come out where I can see you."

"Why don't you leave before you get hurt!" the man shouted, disguising his voice through a raspy tone.

Eirik lifted the lantern higher. "Who is that?"

"You want to die? I swear by the gods, I'll slash your throat."

As he stepped forward, Eirik shone the light toward the ground where he heard rustling. His eyes widened as he saw her gagged and bound. "Mara?"

A fist walloped Eirik's jaw, sending him staggering to his right. Fortunately, Eirik's size kept him from falling, but not from getting another, this one to the side of his head. He braced himself against the stall and set the lantern safely to the ground before lunging at the shadowy figure. The two plowed into the wall, breaking several shelves in the process, and tumbled as one amid the clutter.

Mara scrambled to her feet and kept her distance from the thrashing men. She crept to the security of a stall corner and watched the shadows clash, beating each other with anything they could get their hands on. Both cursed and grunted with each hit, striking harder with the next. The commotion caused a third man to enter the stable.

Dægan.

One of the men dropped to the ground and the other drove past, colliding with Dægan's shoulder. Dægan wrapped his forearm around the man's neck and secured a chokehold. "Eirik? Is that you? Where are you?"

"Over...here..." Eirik called faintly from the floor.

The hooded figure slipped from Dægan grasp and fled out of the stable, but Dægan was more concerned with his brother. He charged forward and slid to his knees, clutching Eirik's shoulders. "Are you hurt?"

With the limited use of her hands, Mara brought the lantern to the spot where Eirik lay. Soft light broke the peril of darkness and revealed Eirik's horrifying injury. A knife protruded from his stomach and blood had already soaked his clothes. He freed the dagger from its fleshy sheath with trembling hands and dropped it beside him.

"Eirik! Who did this to you?" Dægan demanded as he examined the rest of his brother's body. "Who, Eirik?"

"I...don't know. But he had...Mara...on the

ground…"

Instantly, Dægan shot Mara a look of gravity, as if his worst fears had come true. His eyes disclosed more guilt and regret than she'd ever recalled seeing in one man. She wanted to take hold of him, comfort him…tell him she was all right, but the gag restricted her from communicating anything intelligible.

Dægan quickly pulled the gag from her mouth, then Eirik coughed. Blood spattered from his mouth and ran down his chin.

"I tried to…" Eirik said, struggling to explain.

"Sh…brother. You're going to be fine."

Dægan lied, and Mara knew it. The large amount of blood pouring from his wound in such a quick amount of time meant a vessel had been direly severed. Nothing could save Eirik, no matter what they tried.

Dægan pushed his palm firmly against the deep wound and held steady pressure, but the blood oozed between his fingers and seeped around his hand. "Eirik…stay with me. Look at me, brother. Look at me."

Mara touched the side of Eirik's face with her bound wrists. He smiled kindly at her. "Are you…all right…m'lady?"

She nodded but didn't dare speak for fear her voice would crack and give away the dreadfulness of his injury.

Eirik tried to speak again but choked on the blood that now filled his throat.

"Don't leave me, Eirik. Don't. Stay with me." Dægan lifted his brother's head to his lap to draw the blood away from his mouth. "Tell me who did this. Tell me now… I must know, brother!"

Dægan shot a glance at Mara, his eyes pleading for the

hooded man's identity, but she didn't know any more than Eirik. She shrugged and opened her mouth to speak, but nothing came out.

Eirik moaned in pain, then coughed. Dægan pushed his palm harder against the gaping wound. "No, Eirik! No!" He leaned closer to his brother's face and encouraged him to speak. "That's it, Eirik. Tell me. Tell me who did this." As Dægan cradled his brother, Eirik's hand reached for Dægan's forearm, then dropped lifelessly to the ground.

"No!" Dægan cried, clutching his brother in his arms. "No! No! No!" Dægan shook as he sobbed at Eirik's chest. He rocked his brother's body and cursed, shouting at the top of his lungs. "No!"

Mara sat motionless and watched Dægan bawl like a child. She closed her eyes, squeezing out a hapless stream of tears. The sight of her weeping Northman and the sound of his harrowing wail would haunt her forever.

Dægan quieted himself, looked at Mara in disbelief and shock, then slid from his brother's corpse. Reaching for the wall of the stable, he pulled himself to his feet.

"Where are you going?" Mara asked.

On unsteady legs, he lurched toward the exit door and shouted in anger for all to hear. "I'll find you, you coward! I'll hunt you down!"

Mara tried to stop him, but he stormed out and ran after Eirik's killer. He found strength with each step, running faster and faster. The cool night air burned in his chest with every breath he inhaled. He frantically searched the harbor for a fleeing hooded man, regretting that he'd let the bastard go. He worried that too much time had passed, blessing the man with freedom and an escape. But out of the corner of his eye, Dægan saw a figure slip around one of the boats on the shore and disappear into the shadows.

Dægan darted straight to the dock, unsheathing his dagger. He crept between boats, one after another, and trailed the steps of his prey like a skilled hunter in search of game. Satisfaction for finding his brother's murderer climbed up his spine, but he remained calm and observant.

Again the figure moved, but this time he scaled the gangplank of a cargo vessel and jumped into its deep hull.

Dægan smiled at the man's stupidity and followed quietly aboard. He crouched on the wooden-planked deck, regarding the empty boat from beneath the silvery moonlight above. He held his breath and listened, feeling the rhythm of the rocking tide. All was as it should be…except that the empty boat leaned too far to the right.

Dægan spun on his heels just in time to trip the man who charged him. He let the individual stand of his own accord, then punched his fist inside the hood. Delicate nasal bones cracked as he made contact with the hidden face.

The man tried to flee, but Dægan caught him by the arm and threw him against the side of the boat. It rocked and Dægan staggered. As he regained his footing, he seized the man by his cloak and whirled him overboard.

Without hesitation, Dægan jumped in the water after him and hauled him to his feet. They exchanged a stint of punches, most of which landed in Dægan's favor. But every now and again, one slipped past his guard and jarred his world anew.

Now cut across his eye, Dægan dove for the man's legs and knocked him on his back. He pounced on his chest and clutched the skinny throat beneath the hood, holding him below the water. He closed his eyes, tightening his grip as the man splashed around. He could hear him calling beneath the water, begging for his life, but Dægan refused to let go. Refused to let the man breathe the air he so desperately fought for, choked for, thrashed for. Until eventually…slowly…the splashing stopped.

Dægan exhaled and fell from his haunches, collapsing in the wake of the river's tide. Every muscle, every part of his body felt paralyzed by the misery of his revenge. It wasn't at all as satisfying as he'd hoped, for his agony persevered in spite of it all.

Dægan dragged the lifeless body to shore and hesitated to reveal the identity of his brother's murderer. The body was lighter than he anticipated, like that of a small man…or an older lad.

The fury that once ran through him turned to white-hot fear as he dreaded the worst. With a jerk of his hand, Dægan flipped the hood from the body. The familiar face shocked him, jolting him to a level of vivid awareness too ghastly to be true.

It was Rutland.

****

Dægan entered his longhouse dripping wet and heavy with bereavement. He saw Mara sitting alone on the floor, her hands still bound like a petty thrall. It wasn't until then that he realized he'd deserted her to avenge his brother's death.

He dragged his feet as he drew near and fell to his knees before her in silent shame. He couldn't even speak, much less beg for forgiveness, for his words were lost somewhere between the river he'd just crawled from and the cool stone pavers of Eirik's stable floor. As much as he wanted to proffer an apology, all he had left to give her was a dagger's edge between her wrists to sever the binding.

He winced when he saw the horrifying ligature marks, then lifted his gaze to the cuts and bruises on her face. Her lips were chapped and dry, reminding him that the dirty cloth shoved in her mouth had probably absorbed every ounce of spit. Immediately, he rose to retrieve a ewer of water. It was in that instant he noticed his table askew, the ewer and wash basin toppled on the floor, and one chair turned over. By the chaos of the room, he came to understand how the evening had unfolded behind his back, in his own longhouse.

"He was in here?" Dægan's voice fractured under the weight of this realization. He didn't even look at Mara to see her nod in reply as it was obvious she'd given her all to fight off Rutland's attack. It was just hard to swallow that one of his own men would do such a thing.

A deep sound emitted from his own throat, much like a dog's growl, as he proceeded past the disarray. He snatched the ewer from the floor and shook it before handing it to Mara. "If you need more, I'll send for it."

Mara took the pitcher and drank the entire amount of water from its concave bottom. Dægan paced, shedding shame and guilt with each step. In their place, anger and resentment returned, and they climbed like a rampant weed as he replayed the night over and over in his head.

"You knew the man, didn't you?" Mara asked.

Dægan froze and glared at her. "Aye, I knew him. He was a chieftain's son, orphaned after Harald Fairhair had killed his family. I took him in, out of respect for his father and of love for mine. I raised him—Eirik raised him! And yet he does this. Why? Why would he do this to me, Mara?"

Dægan grabbed a chair and threw it wildly across the room. The walls of his longhouse were made of sod and rushes, so the chair fell in one solid piece instead of shattering as he'd so hoped.

He collapsed across the length of the table, pounding it with his fist as he muttered abrasive curses from his native tongue. His tirade lasted only as long as his strength could support him. His legs gave out, and he slid like a limp rag to the floor.

"Stay where you are," Dægan murmured when he heard Mara's careful footsteps. "I don't want your sympathy or your kindness. I'm undeserving of either as my brother's wife has just become widowed."

"'Twas not you who widowed her, Dægan."

He smeared both hands down his face and looked up blankly to the hand-hewn timbers above him. "But 'tis I who must tell her." He took a deep breath and slumped forward on his knees. "How, Mara? How do I break this awful news to her?"

A shaky whisper of a voice barely broke in from the back door. "I already know."

Lillemor stood grasping the wooden column of the entryway, morbidly struck with shock and sorrow. By the look of her sallow appearance, there was no denying she'd seen her husband lying in his own pool of blood on the stable floor.

Dægan jolted to his feet just in time to catch her as she buckled to her knees.

"Who did this, Dægan? Who? Who would want to hurt my Eirik?"

Dægan pulled Lillemor close, feeling for the first time the frailty of the hardy Northern woman in his arms. If he told her the truth, he knew it would break her down to almost nothing, and he wished he could put forth a different name to the crime.

It took another one of her pitiful pleas before Dægan could release the lad's name. "'Twas Rutland who did this."

Lillemor stopped breathing until the name sank deep like a hefty boulder in water. Tears streamed from her eyes and down her cheeks, each racing to beat the first.

"You're wrong, Dægan!" Lillemor shouted finally. "You must be wrong! Rutland wouldn't do this!"

He held her tighter, knowing this was only the beginning of her emotions. What grief she plunged into now would soon lift to anger. And in time, back down to a lonely rock bottom.

"I wish I were wrong, Lillemor."

"But why? Why would he do this?"

"I know not that answer," Dægan said sadly. "I suspect that greed can turn the best of men into murderers."

"Greed for what? Eirik hadn't anything worth killing for."

Dægan lowered his head, reluctant to respond. Eirik's death was entirely his fault because he'd brought Mara to Limerick, and her father had issued a reward no common man could ignore.

But Lillemor ascertained differently and placed the blame elsewhere. She looked at Mara with cold gray eyes. "'Twas you, wasn't it? 'Twas you Rutland wanted, and Eirik tried to stop him. Is this how it came to pass, Dægan? Is this what my husband died for?"

"It should have been me, I know." Dægan reached up to touch Lillemor's face, but she smacked his hand away.

"But 'tis not *you!*"

Her hateful remark shocked Dægan so much that he didn't know how to comfort her anymore. He dropped what little embrace he had around her.

Lillemor struck his chest with a sound fist. "What am I going to do?" Each time she asked him, she hit him again and again, a little more fervently. "What am I going to do, Dægan!"

He seized her wrists and tugged her into the protection of his arms. "You're going to come home with me. I'll take care of you."

Lillemor softened and began sobbing in his chest. "Oh, Dægan! Eirik was going to be a father…"

His heart stopped. He hoped he'd heard his sister-in-law wrong.

"Aye, I told him this morning after our morning meal. I've never seen him so happy."

Dægan held her head against his chest so she couldn't see the hot tears welling in his eyes. He wanted to scream. To rip the longhouse to shreds with his bare hands. To choke Rutland again even through the cold of death. He wanted the empty, sick feeling in his gut to go away. He wanted Lillemor to stop crying. And most of all, he wanted Eirik to walk through the door and say it was all just a horrible prank. He wouldn't even hold it against Eirik for doing such a thing.

But Eirik never would. Never again.

The thought pounded at Dægan's temples. Vile images flooded his mind with the evening's events; Eirik choking on his own blood. Thick, red warmth seeping between his fingers. Cold murky river water washing his hands clean as he held tight to Rutland's skinny neck. Odin help him, he couldn't wake from this grievous nightmare.

Nausea hit, and he dashed from the room, unable to

keep his rage and stomach contents within him. After vomiting outside his door, he howled and ran through a group of onlookers gathering around the stable where Eirik had breathed his last. His body still lay there in a pool of viscous blood on the stone floor.

Dægan entered quickly and pounced on his brother, shaking him by the shoulders. "Open your eyes, Eirik. Look at me. I'm through with your games." He dropped two fists to Eirik's chest and yelled at him some more. "Get up. Get up, I say. Lillemor needs you. I need you!"

Dægan crumbled over Eirik's body, fisting his brother's clothes, and wept. He was so consumed with the familiar scent and feel of his brother beneath him that he was completely unaware of someone in the stable with him until Vegard touched his shoulder.

"Leave me be," Dægan said without lifting his head.

"'Tis the will of the gods, Dægan."

"There are no gods. They exist simply because we say they do."

"Careful, m'lord. Odin is watching."

"Is he?" Dægan asked, scrambling to his feet. "Then let him strike me down. Let Thor and his mighty hammer strike me dead right now." He stretched out his arms and reached for the heavens. "Come on, you bastards! Do it!"

Vegard stood in uneasy stillness a short distance from Dægan as if waiting for *Mjollnir* to slam through the rafters of the stable upon his friend's head. But the room was deathly silent and undisturbed by Thor's vengeance.

"You see?" Dægan whispered. "There are no gods. Just as there's no more life in my brother's eyes. We all walk blindly, with no one but ourselves as watchmen."

Vegard shook his head. "I'll hear no more of this."

"And I'll not give praise to a plethora of gods who take from me with pleasure."

"Dægan..." Vegard warned, putting his hand up.

"They laugh at the grief my heart is plagued with. So I curse them, and if Odin were here right now, I'd spit in his eye and have a laugh of my own."

Vegard slammed Dægan against the wall and held him there. "If you want to anger them more, so be it. Curse yourself. But I'll not stand here and let Thor's hammer crush my skull along with yours."

Dægan laughed in cynical disinterest. "Whether you stand beside me or an ocean away...we are all cursed, Vegard."

The old man released Dægan with a jerk. "Go ahead. Pity yourself this night if you must. But come morning, you'd better open your eyes and take a look around at the many blessings that befall you. You've a whole fleet of men and more on the way simply because you say so. You've land, riches, and arms, more than any merchant south of the Hebrides. And by the gods, Dægan, you've a woman of gentle birth in your bed. Is that not enough?"

Dægan sighed and leaned his head against the rock wall behind him. "What good are all those things if one day I lie as Eirik?"

"They account for the grand life you lived on earth, worth bragging of in *Valhalla*—if the gods should still welcome you there."

"I'm no less fortunate if they don't."

"Frankly, you're no more the wiser to forsake them," Vegard stated. "The gods see what you cannot, and that includes the manner in which you shall die. I hope for your sake you've not forgotten what it means to die honorably."

"I'd like to believe there's more to this cursed life than

just an honorable death."

"Like what?" Vegard asked.

"Like peace."

"Peace? Peace you say? Dægan, you'll spend a lifetime looking for peace. Where there's man, there's war. 'Tis been that way since the dawn of time."

"Perhaps in this life, Vegard, but what about the next? Are we to spend a lifetime fighting only to die and fight some more? 'Tis absurd!"

"'Tis an honor. Not all of us are called to *Valhalla*. How we die here determines who we are in the eyes of the gods."

"And I tell you 'tis not *how* we die, but *what we die for* that determines who we are. I'm tired, Vegard. I'm tired of fighting. I just killed a boy, a lad barely a man."

"Rutland made a choice."

"And I killed him! To the gods, I'm a hero. But to my heart, I'm wretched! I want to be more than another warrior called to his doom."

"*Valhalla* is not our doom. 'Tis our reward. Keep talking like that, Dægan, and you *will* be doomed, for I'm certain Odin favors an insult about as much as any other proud man. And what of your father? Do you wish to cut him to the quick too? Abandon the hope of one day joining him in the Great Hall?"

Dægan turned his back on Vegard. "Just to fight?"

"And drink," Vegard added. "Forget not the ample supply of ale and mead that shall spill forth from Odin's bottomless barrels. You want peace? I can think of no better peace than dropping like a stone after a long night of raising horns."

Dægan didn't have to look at the old man's face to

know he sported a smile as big as the horizon. He found a small bit of comfort in Vegard's mead-diluted optimism, but it soon faded as his eyes fell over his brother's corpse.

"I've lost the only brother I had left. I should've been here," Dægan confessed. "It should be me on that floor."

"You cannot undo what has been done," Vegard concluded as he grasped Dægan's shoulders. His hands were full of strength despite his age, and remained there upon Dægan, just as a father's would before he spoke of something important. "What you *can* do is honor Eirik by keeping a keen mind. Do not let his death be in vain. Get Lillemor and Mara to safety lest you risk the possibility of others more capable than Rutland trying their hand at treachery. You must leave Hlymrekr as soon as you can. Ottarr and I will take care of Eirik. And Hansen will round up the men and meet you at the harbor. You leave tonight."

Chapter Twelve

Mara walked alongside Dægan down the length of the steep hill leading toward the harbor. She wore the dark green, ill-fitted cloak with the hood drawn over her head. It was too warm even for the cool night, but she dared not protest given Dægan's sullen temperament. He hadn't said much while packing his belongings and armor, and even as they walked, he remained silent.

She noticed when Dægan had filled each of the two chests, he did so to the brim, emptying the entire contents of his longhouse as if he had no intention of ever returning. His sword, shield, and assortment of bows, arrows, and spears had also been gathered and loaded on the warship. Mara, however, had little to pack. Her only possessions were Dægan's exquisite gifts of silks, spices, jewels, and oils from the king's chest. No matter how diminutive her baggage was compared to Dægan's, she knew she was bringing a world of trouble with her.

Rutland had heard of the substantial reward offered by her father, and tried his hand at bettering his life of fealty through the prospect of obtaining easy coinage. Though Dægan had never been cruel or unjust in his mastership, Rutland's life was not truly his own. This meant there was little at stake for the lad. All he had to overcome was the weight of betrayal, and given how quickly he'd taken to the plan, he obviously had no concern for Dægan, or the countless others who'd opened their homes to him.

Nourishing his ever-hungry, gluttonous self was more important.

For this reason, she'd been forced to wear the hood over her head, and their pace to the harbor was swift. Dægan trusted no one.

Through the fog, she saw the large wooden prow of Dægan's *drakkar*. It was carved as an openmouthed dragon with teeth and scales, raising its head proudly for all to see, even in the dead of night. Its fiendish, bulging eyes stared at everyone who walked in and out of its hull. The neck was rigid and self-righteous, long and curved as it preceded the rest of the ship and ended with a coiled tail for the sternpost.

As they pushed closer, Mara discerned the rest of the wicked ship's body through the murky fog. Colorfully painted round shields arrayed along the gunwales, each one as striking as the next. Five oars on each side extended into the river like a spindle-legged spider, while the belly brimmed with chests, barrels, and assorted sacks.

The impressive boat provoked a feeling of instinctive fear in her heart. She gathered that the Northmen had built it with that very purpose in mind when landing on virgin soil.

"Dægan, the men are ready when you are," Hansen called from within.

Dægan nodded and walked past the longship to the next one on the shore. Mara looked for its bulging-eyed prow, but to her relief, it lacked the carved head and tail of the *drakkar*. It was wider and deeper than the dragon ship, and less ornamental. Simple and plain were its qualities, and Mara quite honestly preferred it that way.

Ottarr joined them on land.

"Where's Eirik?" Dægan asked without much emotion.

Ottarr hesitated to answer the question, dribbling around motives and respect. "Why take him with you, Dægan? He deserves a proper burial."

Dægan's eyes narrowed. "I intend to give him one."

"This was his home," Ottarr reminded.

"I'll not bury my brother in the same soil that betrayed him. 'Twas done to my father before I had a say, and I'll not agree to it again."

"The island you live on is naught but limestone," Ottarr argued sensibly. "You'll never be able to dig deep enough."

Dægan had his own solution. "The *knarr* will be ready by tomorrow morning, aye? Bring the rest of the men and supplies to the island. I'll meet you come midday to help unload. From there, I want you to take as many men as you need and head east for Galway. Bring me back an entire cargo ship full of soil and seaweed."

"Soil and seaweed," Ottarr repeated.

"Aye. The Gaels have used it for many years to substantiate their crops on the island, and I plan to use the same idea. But I need enough to cover a ship. Understand?"

"Aye, m'lord."

Dægan pulled a medium-sized pouch from his cloak, filled with silver coins, and gave it to Ottarr. "This should be enough."

For the rest of the preparations, Dægan lay down a concise strategy as if it were routine. Mara noticed that his voice held less sentiment, but gaining the raw materials for his brother's burial was still markedly imperative. It was a duty he'd not short because of a minor complication, as minor as a bed of rock could be.

"...if you and the men work fast enough, you should also be back by the next morning. Tell them that they will be rewarded with two cows each for their swift return from Galway."

"My lord, 'tis a high price to offer so many men."

"Which is why I expect the *knarr* to be reloaded and beached within two days. Do not fail me, Ottarr."

"Consider it done."

"Now, where's my brother's body?"

"Over here—"

Dægan had already rushed past Ottarr before he could finish and stalked up the gangplank of the large merchant ship with Mara closely behind. When they entered the hull, she saw Eirik's body tightly wrapped in a tan linen cloth. She noted the care that had been taken to hide his unsightly wound and realized the extent of their love and dedication to their own. Nor did it stop there.

As Dægan and two others carried Eirik to the *drakkar*, the rest of the crew on the shoreline stopped working and hushed their voices in respect. Pity and sorrow, as thick as the harbor fog, filled the hearts of every man for the young expectant widow.

Lillemor was already aboard, dressed with a heavy woolen cloak and a braid that hung down her back like a thick golden rope. Dægan set Eirik at the prow, then reached for Lillemor. With a sympathetic hug, he shielded her from the crew's gawking, but gave an unmistakable look that sent them hurrying to load the rest of the supplies for their departure.

Within minutes, the rigging was seaworthy and the narrow hull was fully loaded, with two men at each oar. The chests upon which each man sat doubled as a seat for rowing.

Once the entire crew was ready, Dægan wasted no time in slipping from Lillemor's grasp and fetched Mara from the harbor. He scooped her up in his arms and carried her across the water, paying no heed to the guilt and misery in her eyes. In fact, it seemed he made a conscious effort not to face her, a type of conduct she'd not been acquainted with until now.

After setting her feet to the deck, he stepped in after her and guided her to the tail of the ship with an icy arm. As glad as Mara was to be far away from the ugly dragon's head, she was a little insulted that Dægan felt the need to separate her from Lillemor. She tried not to be offended, but her face must have said otherwise as Dægan misread it.

"The serpent will not hurt you," he said, judging the beast for himself. "'Twas the first thing I too feared as a boy. But in time you'll grow to love the sight of it, as I have."

Mara thought she saw a smile flit across Dægan's face, but as he stared at the carved wood through the drifting fog, she realized it was a cruel adoration for something dark and menacing, reminiscent of his current mood. It was safer to be like his beastly ship, ominous and unapproachable. At least if he were distant, no one could get close enough to be hurt, and they in turn couldn't hurt him.

"Row, men!" Dægan shouted from the steer board. "Row this *langskip* like you stole it!"

At his command, the dragon ship began to move. The men pushed and pulled at the oars, chanting with each effort like a beating drum until the River Shannon coerced the ship easily downstream. The serpent vessel sliced through the water, holding true to the role it was carved to imitate.

"Dægan," Mara said finally from within her hood. "I must admit I'm very nervous to meet your mother. I fear she'll not be able to stand the sight of me after what has happened."

Dægan turned from his navigating and pulled the hood from her face, his eyes piercing the night. "'Twas not your fault. No one blames you and neither will my mother."

"'Twill be hard to face her. I cannot help but think every time she sees me, she'll no doubt recall the tragedy caused to her son. My face will forever be tainted in her eyes."

"No more tainted than mine," he said, turning away. "At least you'll not have to be the one who tells her. 'Twould be easier for me to slay a dozen men than to tell her she's lost yet another son."

Mara opened her mouth to speak, but he gave her another cold shoulder and left her alone at the sternpost. She watched him walk down the narrow aisle between the rowing men and tap one crew member on the shoulder. Obediently, the man stepped up and took his place at the steer board beside Mara while Dægan attended to Lillemor.

Kindly, the man spoke to her. "Our ships are built for the sake of speed, not comfort, else they'd have benches for seating. But you may rest yourself at my chest if you'd like, m'lady."

Mara glanced at his empty seat and shook her head. "Thank you, but I'd rather stand."

"Very well."

Mara eyed the handsome Northman. He was tall and broad, as most seemed to be, but there was a quality that made him more distinct than the others on the ship. Perhaps it was his dark auburn hair that set him apart, or the blue-green eyes beneath his prominent brow. Either way, he carried himself with dignity and confidence, a valor most men lacked. His beard neatly shadowed his jaw, but not enough to conceal a small cleft at his chin. His lips were narrow, and his nose was perfectly straight. Without really knowing him, Mara assumed he held a high rank, more than just another pair of hands at the oars. "What is your name?" she asked.

He looked at her inquisitively, a bit of a swagger to his glance. "Tait."

Mara repeated his name in her head, liking the simplicity of it. "Tell me, Tait. How is it that you can plot this ship's course in the dark?"

Seeming to enjoy her amiable question, he smiled at her. "On clear nights, 'tis easy to use the stars or the land beside us as our guide. But we've sailed this route many times, so even in the thick of fog, there's no threat of getting lost. Fortunately, the fog tonight is drifting and the moon is bright." Tait paused for a moment and licked his finger, raising it above his head. "Feel that?" he asked.

"Feel what?"

"The wind. Do as I have," Tait instructed. "Feel it now?"

She did. It was a subtle coolness on her finger.

"We are approaching the sea, and the breeze will increase as we get closer, making the conditions better; less fog and more wind. When we reach the ocean, 'tis then we shall raise the sail and our journey will not be so laborious for those rowing."

Suddenly, a hand came down upon her shoulder, and she flinched. She'd been so engrossed in Tait's explanation that she didn't hear Dægan approach.

"M'lord." Tait nodded humbly, then returned to his place at the oars.

Mara regarded Dægan closely, unsure if he was upset that she'd conversed with a member of his crew. She couldn't tell anything about his mood at first glance, but she did notice that he now sported his long-cherished bear cloak at his shoulders.

"I see that Tait is teaching you the ways of the sea."

Mara was thankful that he finally spoke on the matter. "I asked it of him. I hope I didn't offend you."

Dægan simply shook his head. "Tait knows the waters better than I, it seems."

"He's kind," Mara declared, hoping to instill in Dægan a need for idle conversation. Unfortunately, her plan didn't work. He neither commented nor discussed Tait further.

How long was he going to avoid her? And how much could she take of him purposefully alienating himself from her to the point of estrangement?

She wiped away a few burning tears and reached out for his arm. "You can push as hard as you'd like, Dægan. I'll still be here."

Dægan closed his eyes as he felt Mara's hand on his forearm. It felt so good and so tender against the misery that stiffened his body. But it wasn't right. It wasn't appropriate to accept such sweet-hearted warmth in front of Lillemor. Even a simple fraction of it would be for no other reason than self-indulgence, and he couldn't do it.

He retreated from Mara's small token of intimacy and called forth an order that probably could have waited. "The wind is picking up! Rig the sail!"

Five men immediately stood and worked with him to

set the weighty pine mast into its chink hole. They wedged the beam firmly into place and raised the square woolen sail. The wind caught hold and threw it open against four taut corners, tied precisely to the sides and bow of the ship.

Dægan nodded with satisfaction; his crew and *drakkar* worked fluently together as one unit. At least something in his life was still manageably painless and operative. He even thought himself capable of calculating just about every adjustment needed to command his warship in a proficient and dexterous manner. But hell if he couldn't predict the profound effect Mara would have on his senses. No matter how hard he tried, he couldn't stop thinking about her sensuous touch.

Chapter Thirteen

For many hours of the voyage, Dægan and his men sat in quiet rumination, sailing over smooth, unthreatening waters toward the Aran Isles of Galway Bay. Some of the seamen had caught a few hours of sleep during the trip north, but Dægan was unable to succumb to such amiable dreaming. He was still living his own private nightmare as he witnessed Lillemor grieve and pine for her lost husband.

Mara, however, seemed to have found that the hard wooden deck was more tolerable than resting vertically against the sternpost. It didn't take long before she'd fallen fast asleep beneath the carved dragon's tail and Dægan's own mindful eyes.

Through the hours that passed, he sat a distance from her, but close enough to see every rise and fall of her deep, steady breathing and still check his course from time to time. Her subtle stirs and sighs were like a harp's strum, imparting the serenity of her dreams. Dægan knew it would be a long time before his dreams ever played out in harmony again, but it struck him to realize that by watching her, he felt peace of mind.

Her dark hair lay tumbled at her shoulders, cascading in heavy waves around her face until they fell like Turkish silk on the plank deck. Despite the harshly colored abrasions on her wrists, and the purple bruising around her forehead, she was a stunning vision of beauty no nightly dream could come close to touching.

Tait's voice broke in quietly. "Dægan, we're fast approaching."

Dægan stood and looked out into the darkness. The sharp hills of Galway encompassed his right while the flat, rock-infested isles spread out to his left.

He steered due west around the north side of the tri-clustered islands and set his course for the last and largest of the three: Inishmore. The southern shores of the island were nothing but three-hundred-foot cliffs of bedrock, which made a convenient natural guard against any unwelcome intruders who wished to flank the treeless island. The northern shore, by which Dægan's permanent settlement was located, was the only accessible port of entry for man and ship, a sure way to secure his home from piracy and plunder.

As part of the crew dismantled the sail and replaced the mast inside the hull, the others fed the oars through their respective keyholes. In no time, the paddles swept against the water in rhythmic symmetry until the keel of the longboat ran aground. They slid to an abrupt halt on the coarse sandy shore littered with driftwood and stringy seaweed.

Dægan and his men descended from the sides with a loud splash and heaved the longship from the shallows of the sea.

Mara awoke to the sound of splashing water and a flurry of voices. Shouts rang out and feet stamped above the sound of sliding chests and barrels within the hull. But through the commotion, she heard the familiar accent of the Gaelic tongue. She pulled herself from the deck to see a spectacle of men working together to unload the ship's contents, men of light and dark hair. She rubbed her eyes, sure that it was all a dream.

Dægan emerged from the Gaels, reaching out his hands for her. "Did you sleep well?"

Taken aback by the swarm of her countrymen assisting the men of the North, Mara stuttered on her answer.

"Still groggy, I see," Dægan said as he lifted her from the ship and carried her just a few steps across the sand and rocks.

"Is Lillemor all right? Should I go to her perhaps?"

"She wants naught more but to be alone," Dægan answered quickly. "And if she does need anyone, my *thralls* will suffice for the night."

Mara glanced back at the ship where Eirik had lain, but he and the rest of the items were missing. "Where *is* your brother?"

"I had him taken under shelter until morning. I cannot bear to let Mother see him before we've had a chance to clean his body properly. 'Tis late and, as you already know, I'm short of words this night."

Mara tried again to comfort him with a small touch of her hand, but Dægan anticipated the move. He avoided the gesture and bent to pick up the chest at his feet. "I must find sleep. Morning will come too soon for me."

He wearily walked toward a grassy hillside, where a longhouse stood in the forefront. Mara followed, still listening to the familiar voices behind her. Their chatter brought her closer to thoughts of home and the servants who'd crowd her father's keep with their chores. But these Irishmen were more than servants. Their dress and mannerisms clearly showed it, and Dægan seemed more subservient to them, a conduct strange for a man of chieftain status.

A calm, bearded man dressed in a long, deep red cloak with golden tassels and silver brooches came into view as they neared the houses. He appeared dignified without being too brash, and he walked rather proudly, as though the island were all his. He was without an escort, but not without a horse, which followed behind him.

He looked fondly at all the Northmen who'd arrived on his shores like long-lost family, but Mara couldn't help but notice how his gaze lingered more upon her. He gave his reins to a passerby and grasped Dægan's shoulders in greeting.

"Welcome home, my friend. Trouble at sea?"

Between the collection of visible injuries on both her and Dægan's faces, it was no wonder the man assumed they'd endured an eventful journey.

"Nay," Dægan said. "'Twas rather tame."

The man looked confused but moved on. "Is this the woman of whom you spoke?"

"Aye." Dægan stepped aside to give the man more room to impose himself. "This is Mara."

"Mara," he repeated with a slight bow of his head. "My name is Nevan, chieftain of the Uí Bhriain here on Inishmore, and we welcome you with open arms. I trust your journey was pleasant?"

Mara didn't dare contradict Dægan's response. She complied with his opinion and noted his reaction as being one of relief. She wondered why he concerned himself with what Nevan might deduce from the cuts and bruises they'd sustained.

"I'm glad to hear this," Nevan said with a kind smile.

Short of being rude, Dægan cleared his throat. "You're

most gracious for sending your men to help me unload my ship in the middle of the night. And as much as I feel I should allow this time for acquainting you with my betrothed, we're both immensely tired. I hope you understand."

"Of course, Dægan. Please. There will be more time for pleasantries and conversation on the morrow. Is there anything I can send for you and your men? Food or drink, perhaps?"

"'Twould be generous of you."

"The pleasure is all mine." Nevan nodded courteously before Mara, then mounted his horse and left.

Dægan said nothing as the king disappeared into the night. Instead, he readjusted the chest in his arms and resumed the walk to his longhouse. His steps were quicker and more determined than before, leaving Mara several paces behind.

"Is Nevan a good friend of yours?" she called after him.

"I suppose that is a fair enough term for him. Though I suspect the islanders would rather I not be."

"I don't understand."

Dægan opened the front entryway door for her and ushered her inside. He set the chest on the floor and removed his cloak, throwing it to the boxbed. "Though we all get along quite well," he stated with hesitance in his voice, "there's still a sense of indifference between my people and Nevan's. I'm working to resolve this." He lit the cottongrass wick in the stone lamp at the hearth and then sat upon the boxbed. His eyes were weary and fatigued, hardly the look of someone who wished to carry on a lengthy conversation.

Mara smiled sympathetically. "Why don't we wait until

morning? You're exhausted, and you need your sleep."

Dægan shook his head and patted the stuffing of the boxbed beside him. "Please. You need to know."

Mara did as he bid her and accepted the hand he offered, relieved that he actually took the initiative to touch her. His grasp was strong despite his weakened fortitude.

"Nevan and I started a relationship quite by accident," he began. "When I met him, he was gravely hurt, and I took him in. Once his strength returned, I sailed him home—here. After that, he and I traded for many years. He needed timber and I needed wool. Both of us made out quite well, and soon we realized we had more to offer in the market than just necessary wares. In time, word got out that this island was an unprotected, flourishing kingdom. Those who had the courage for piracy succeeded favorably, and in their own right struck many times without much resistance. Nevan called upon me to help protect the island from such vagrants, and in return, he granted unto me a permanent settlement for my family.

"With Harald Fairhair rising in power, I'd no choice but to take Nevan's offer. However, his people thought him too generous, and they demonstrated a fervent distaste to the whole idea of sharing their immensely poor, infertile lands with a circle of Northmen. So to alleviate the burden that weighed heavily upon Nevan, I merely suggested that I should marry an Irish woman."

Mara's heart sank. "But I thought you chose me as your wife because you..." She couldn't finish the rest. Perhaps she'd misunderstood his intentions all along.

He reached up and cupped her chin. "I wanted you as my wife before I made the suggestion to Nevan. The idea of a marriage for the purpose of softening the tempers of these strict Gaels was only incidental."

"But the reason still remains. I'm here to bring peace between two feuding groups. I may not be a king, Dægan, but I know what an alliance is." Mara's thoughts drifted over the trials and joys of the last few days, much on the horrendous journey they'd made together and more on the sweetest of love Dægan had made with her. They were moments in her life she'd never forget, and now the hardest to accept. "And to think, I gave myself to you because I thought you wanted me. That you at least felt some sort of affection toward me."

Dægan gently clasped her face with both of his hands. "I want you more now than I did a fortnight ago."

"You want a place to live," Mara bit back. A painful lump hardened in her throat. "Without me, you cannot live here."

Dægan grabbed her shoulders and pulled her to his chest. "I cannot live *anywhere* without you. I need you, Mara. I love you."

She stiffened. "What did you say?"

"You heard me."

"Yes, but is it true?" Mara searched the raging storm of his blue eyes.

Dægan released her and hung his head as if he'd failed yet again as a man. "How can you question me?"

His honesty shone as clear as the morning sun, and it was in his reaction that Mara found the man she thought she'd lost. She fell against his chest and wrapped him in a hug. "Forgive me, Dægan, but you wouldn't allow me your love. You held me away as if I were the one who had hurt you."

Dægan savored the warmth of Mara's embrace and the smell of her hair cascading down around his arms. He wondered why he'd fought so hard to keep her at a distance, why he even denied himself the pleasure and comfort of her affection.

"Forgive me if I've pushed you away," Dægan apologized, "but there's a darkness in my heart now. I'm a wretched man, Mara. I killed a boy...with my bare hands. He begged for his life beneath the water, but I ignored it. I *chose* to ignore it. I'm not proud of what I did. But sadly, I'd do it again. And again and again. Even now, I still want more. And that is a side of me I don't want you to see, nor should you feel compelled to be married to it."

"Dægan, you're not a wretched man. You've been wronged in the most atrocious way. You were betrayed by your own, by someone who didn't care for the sacrifices you'd made on his behalf, but only for the quick spoil. Indeed, he was but a boy, but certainly old enough to understand exactly what he was doing. He made his decision, and you reacted in defense. He killed your brother over a petty reward. And for that, he's not worthy of your grief and pain." Mara looked deep into his eyes as she cradled his face. "I know the man you are, the man you'll always be. And no matter what you do, I'll always be here for you. As your wife, if you'll still have me."

Dægan closed his eyes. Her gracious words caressed him all the way to his soul. "What about your father?"

"This is not about my father. This is about my love for you. He'll have to learn to understand that. But know this, Dægan. When I marry, I marry all of you. Don't ever push me away. My heart can never endure that again."

A relieved smile crept through the haze of Dægan's

sorrows, and he kissed her to accept her precious demands. It was in this very kiss he found a haven, a love without fear, a love without limits, a love without end. And no one, not even her father, could destroy it.

A rapping at the door, however, shattered the moment and caused the kiss to fall short. Inwardly, he kicked himself for accepting Nevan's gracious offer and allowed his lips to linger at hers. He paused to savor the taste of her sensual mouth, then sighed with heavy reluctance. "I suppose we should eat what Nevan was kind enough to bring."

Mara halted him from leaving her arms and recommenced the kiss he'd brought to an end. Her fingers dug deeply into the back of his neck and pulled him closer than ever before. "Never leave me, Dægan."

He groaned, answering her with a deeper kiss and a tighter grip. He'd never let her go, he vowed. No one would keep him from her…not the gods, not the Irish on Inishmore, or the King of Connacht. He swore with every breath he took, she'd be all his until the day death parted them.

Chapter Fourteen

The next morning, Dægan rose early to meet with Nevan. His main concern was to make sure that the men of the island council were still content with the arrangements chosen to better the relationship between the two groups that inhabited the land. Although the suggestion had been made by Dægan, Nevan assured him that the council would certainly approve. Since that time, almost three weeks had passed, and Dægan knew from experience it didn't take long for men to change their minds. He went to make certain the arrangement remained.

The other concern he needed to address was the appropriate time his family would need to mourn the unforeseen death of his brother, thus putting the wedding off for a few more days. He hoped the unexpected rite of burial wouldn't interfere with the notion of bringing a much-desired treaty of peace with the Irish.

Dægan sat rigidly in his chair inside Nevan's great hall, watching him pace the floor.

"These men that lead the council are a bit rash, I'm afraid. Albeit some are my brothers and uncles, but the majority of these men look for you to fail in your end of the truce. And this temporary delay, Dægan, would only add to it."

"My brother is dead, Nevan. He deserves a proper burial."

"Which I don't dispute. I merely ask that you hold it

after the wedding."

Dægan rose from his seat so quickly, it turned over behind him. "Some of your men are here on pilgrimages, seeking to make amends with their Christian god, are they not? Are you telling me that Christians haven't enough respect to give a man a proper burial because of sheer impatience? Tell me your men are more gracious than that, for I'm starting to question why I came back here."

"You knew how they felt about you before you left," Nevan reminded him. "Naught has changed. They've awaited the coming of this Irish bride with great expectation, and telling them that a pagan burial will precede a Christian wedding is not the first step to proving your amity."

"Your people don't wish for amity. They want sovereignty—over me. Yet without me, they'll never be able to keep their precious dominion. Your so-called kingdom will continue to feel the threat of constant pillaging if they choose to banish me. Is that a risk you're willing to take? Can you stand formidable with only sheepherders and farmers?"

"Nay, I cannot," Nevan admitted. "But these men will never admit that."

"Then make them."

"'Tis not that simple, Dægan."

"You cannot make them, or you won't?"

Nevan sighed. "Look around you. These men have been here for hundreds of years, living the same life as their grandfathers, and their grandfathers before them. Change is something they take with a grain of salt. But don't think for one moment these men aren't willing to fight for what they believe in. You're neither the first foreigners on our beaches, nor will you be the last. For years, they've fought to keep what's theirs. And as long as you or any other fleet of pagans comes to these shores, there'll be sheepherders and farmers waiting in arms. And that, my friend, will *never* change. So, if you think altering their minds about living harmoniously with pagans is as easy as simply proclaiming it, then you'd never have needed an Irish bride in the first place, would you?"

"I'm only asking for a few days," Dægan begged. "If it were your brother, Nevan, I wouldn't think twice about it."

"I know you wouldn't. And I commend your decency."

"Then give me that right. You know my brother, under your god or his, deserves a proper burial."

"Or what?" Nevan asked, raising a single brow.

Dægan stepped daringly into Nevan's space, and Nevan lifted his gaze to his taller comrade. "Or I shall assume that right for him myself."

"Is that a threat?"

"Twist my words if you wish," Dægan said sternly, "but the last thing I want to do is wage a war with you. I came here for peace. I'm willing to wed for peace. But I'll bury my brother first. Tell your people there shall be a wedding in three days. Not a day sooner."

"You know you're making things very difficult for me."

Dægan huffed and tramped around the room to give himself some distance. "You did this yourself. You chose me. You chose to ally with me over the countless other options you had. You needed me to protect this land as if it was my own. And in giving me my own land, your men took offense to it. How is that my fault?"

"I'm not saying 'tis your fault," Nevan said as he

slumped into the chair at the head of the table. "Nor is it your problem."

Dægan watched the belligerence slide from Nevan's face, and he felt the scales tilt a little in his favor. To ensure success, he pushed a little further with careful restatement. "Nevan, I'm not going back on my word. I just need three days."

"Go on. Do what you need to do."

Dægan sighed out of relief and bowed his head to Nevan's change of heart. "Thank you."

"Just go before I change my mind," Nevan mumbled. "Three days?"

"Three days," Dægan echoed.

"One other thing. Your little Irish bride…do I know her?"

Dægan stared a long time at the king, who was casually pouring a cup of wine for himself. The thought that Nevan found a familiarity with Mara sent his mind spinning. He swallowed. "I don't believe so."

Nevan paused in thought. "Really? She looks strangely familiar. Of course I've not been to the mainland in over a decade."

"Had you known her ten years ago, that would have made her barely nine, sire."

Nevan waved his hand as if he brushed the ridiculous thought from his mind. He was gracing close to fifty. "You're right," he said, pushing the full cup far across the table. "Perhaps I've drunk too much this morning."

****

From Nevan's mighty stone ringfort, Dægan rushed on horseback to his mother's longhouse. The morning air was cool, but the sun glared in his eyes, adding to the misery of his next obligation. Not only would his mother have to suffer yet another loss, but he'd have to shoulder the burden as the messenger.

He hoped for the sake of buying more time, she'd not be there, that she'd be anywhere but home. To his disappointment, the smoke streamed from the opening in the roof and confirmed his mother's presence inside. Cooking the meals for the day started as early as sunup and continued throughout the afternoon, especially when there were plenty of mouths to feed. Although his mother had many servants to help with the preparations—and she was well within her rights to bid them to do so—she still assumed most of the work.

A smile surfaced as Dægan thought of her. He missed her. Her tall build that had shrunk with time, the warm smile that gave the lines on her face a purpose, the twinkling of her silver eyes, and, oddly enough, the subtle scolding he'd get when he'd steal a taste from her iron cooking pot; he missed it all. If not for his dreadful news, he would've already stormed through the door to see her.

With a long sigh, Dægan dismounted and felt the weight of his feet as they thumped on the ground. His chest tightened and his legs wobbled. Like a child stalling to admit a mistake for fear of the inevitable punishment, he again hesitated to go inside.

Be a man.

He talked himself into it and opened the door. His mother, Svanhild, was at the pit, just as he'd imagined, stirring stewed meat and onions. Her gasp of welcomed surprise dissolved the valor he tried to feign.

"My son," she cried. "You're home." Leaving the

wooden spoon in the pot, she met him before he cleared the doorway. "When did you get here?"

He hugged her tightly. "Last night while you slept. 'Twas too late to disturb you."

"I wish you would have so I could finally meet the mother of my grandchildren." Svanhild peeked around him and then out the door. "Please tell me you brought her with you."

"She's not with me at this—"

"Trouble with her father? Did you not account for enough silver, Dægan?"

Dægan opened his mouth to explain, but she cut him off again. "What happened to you? Look at your face! What have you gotten into?"

"Mother, please. I'm fine."

"Have you seen yourself?" Svanhild asked, touching what was left of the dark patches under his eyes and his slightly swollen nose. "You know 'tis broken?"

He jerked his face to the side to avoid another pinch at his nose. "Aye, I do." He laughed a little at her maternal fixations and walked to the fire pit to smell the cooking meat.

"You should never have gone alone. 'Twas very foolish. Now look at you," she criticized. "What Irish woman would want you now?"

"Don't worry your pretty little head about that, Mother. Despite what horror you may see, the Irish woman is quite taken by my hardships."

Svanhild narrowed her eyes at his lightheartedness about the bruises and broken bones. "I suppose 'tis easy to see through a hardship that will eventually fade with time."

"Then you shouldn't concern yourself with my leg."

Her eyes flashed open wide. "What happened to your

leg?"

"'Tis naught but a scratch," he contended, smiling deeply as he looked down at her crossed arms. In grabbing her elbows, he warmly greeted her. "I've missed you."

"Don't try to change the subject, Dægan. What happened?"

"What happened is I've been away far too long, and I need to fatten up before winter," he joked, patting his hungry stomach.

"Ah, you've not changed, always begging for a meal. But just a taste. 'Twould be embarrassing for your feast to come up short on meat tonight."

"We're feasting?"

"Aye, why not?" She lifted the spoon to his mouth. "Careful. 'Tis hot."

Dægan savored the meat as he chewed. "Why are we feasting?"

"Do we need a reason?"

"Nay, but usually we wait until after harvest when we've determined how many calves we cannot hay this winter. 'Tis a bit hasty, don't you think?"

"My son is home. That's reason enough for me."

"But you were cooking this before you even knew I was home. What was your reason then?" Svanhild thought for a while but couldn't come up with an answer. It seemed he'd finally caught her in a fib.

"I had a reason," she said finally. "But I can't remember it. I'm getting old, you know."

Dægan's smile faded as he walked aimlessly around the main room, trying to devise a good way to tell her about Eirik. His mother was so happy. How could he think of ruining that?

He took a seat on the bench near the hearth and pulled at his mother's hand. "Come, sit with me."

"I cannot, Dægan. I've much to do."

"Please. I really need to talk with you."

Her eyes softened from the sound of distress in his voice. "Is everything all right?

"Nay, 'tis not," Dægan muttered under his breath. "I'm afraid I don't have good news."

"What is it, son?" Svanhild asked, sitting beside him. She reached up to cradle Dægan's jaw, which was usually stiff and sturdy with confidence. Not today.

He felt guilty as her hands consoled him and pulled them down, clasping them in his own. He studied the fragile bones beneath her vellum-like skin spotted gently with age. "I know not where to begin, Mother."

"The last time you looked like this, we'd just buried your father. What is it?"

Dægan almost choked on his breath from her morbid choice of words. "Mother," he started again, finding it difficult to look her in the eyes. For a lack of resilience, he opted to be blunt. "Eirik is dead."

His words bit like a snake, over and done with before Svanhild knew what hit her. Her eyes narrowed in disbelief, then gradually widened in slow understanding. Still, she questioned him. "Eirik is what?"

Cautiously, Dægan spoke again, but just as straightforwardly. "He was killed, stabbed in his own stable in Hlymrekr."

"'Tis not true," Svanhild protested. "Tell me 'tis not true!"

"I wish I could," he said, tightening his hold on her trembling hands. "I'd do anything not to have to tell you this."

"Why?" Svanhild wheezed. "Who would want to hurt Eirik?"

Dægan watched her eyes fill with tears and spill over in trailing lines down her face. "I fear to tell you the rest. It only gets worse."

"Is Lillemor all right? Was she—"

"Nay," Dægan reassured her. "She was unharmed. But I couldn't leave her or Eirik in Hlymrekr. I brought them both here with me."

"Then what else is there? What could possibly be worse?"

Dægan sighed before revealing Lillemor's condition. "She's with child."

Svanhild's face fell with pity. "I have a grandchild?"

"Aye."

"Eirik is a father?"

As soon as Dægan nodded, she ripped her hand from his grip and slapped his face. "You knew this last night as you slept. How could you? How could you not tell me?"

"You needed your sleep."

"Don't tell me what I need!" Svanhild shouted at him. "I'll decide that." She stood from the bench and drew in long, distinct breaths as if the sudden smallness of the room was closing in around her. "Where were you, Dægan? Why were you not there to protect him? You know he's naught but a craftsman. Where were you? How could you let this happen?" At her last outburst, Svanhild grabbed her chest and fell against the wooden post of the room, gasping for air.

"Mother!" Dægan yelled, catching her around the waist and lowering her to the matted floor. "Mother, what's wrong?"

She could barely breathe.

"Mother, speak to me." Unnerved by her silence, he called for his mother's servant. "Gudrun! Gudrun!"

No answer.

"By the gods, Mother, where is Gudrun?"

"Right here, m'lord!" The young *thrall* appeared from the storage room, wiping her hands on her apron. Dægan hunched over his mother and pleaded with her to hold on. "M'lord, what happened?"

"I think her heart is weak. Help me get her to the bed."

Immediately, the woman worked to reassemble the boxbed with stuffed mattresses and linens while Dægan picked up his mother. Svanhild clutched her chest, looking into Dægan's eyes as he talked. She found safety there, he knew, for she'd often said his eyes resembled his father's. He knew how terribly she longed to have Rælik next to her, protecting her from the gravest of life's allotted perils. Rælik had been good in that way, and as her last living son, Dægan vowed to be the same. She tried to speak, but her voice was as faint as the shimmer of gold in her hair.

"Sh... Mother. I've got you. 'Twill pass soon. Just breathe slowly. Sh... That's it. That's it, Mother."

Dægan gently laid her on the boxbed and watched her close her eyes as the softness of the bedding cradled her body. He stroked the loose white hair from her face and felt the wetness of her fallen tears. "Mother, can you hear me?"

Svanhild simply nodded.

"Gudrun, get her some water," Dægan said, slipping his hands back within the frail fingers of his mother's hands. "What can I do, Mother? Are you hurting? Please speak to me."

But words never came, nor did she have the strength to speak them even if they had. And what would she say? What could possibly be worth saying at this point? Another son was dead and there was nothing she could do to change that. It was the will of the gods, or maybe even a curse upon her household. Either way, it was done, and no amount of crying or blaming could undo it. Odin had made his choice.

Despite the silence, her heart ached and raged within her. The gods had taken her family one by one, leaving only a son and an unborn grandchild she probably wouldn't live to see. Silently she cursed them for the never-ending nightmare she was forced to live through, day after day. In hopelessness, she finally succumbed to a deep sleep.

"Here is the water you asked for, m'lord."

Dægan was at a loss, seeing his mother fall limp and unresponsive. He spoke nothing as his thoughts whirled like the wind in his head. Had he just killed her? His throat hurt as he tried to swallow.

Gudrun touched Svanhild's mouth with her fingers. "'Tis all right, m'lord. She's only sleeping."

Dægan sighed with tremendous relief and held his weakened head in his hands. He confined his emotions deep within his soul and cleared his throat of the cursed lump. "Has my mother done this before?"

"Aye," Gudrun said, placing the ewer on the nearest table. "But only once, m'lord."

"While I've been away, I presume."

"Aye. She didn't want anyone to fret over her." Gudrun rolled her hands in her apron nervously. "I gave my word that I wouldn't tell."

"Then I did not hear it at all," Dægan replied to ease her restlessness. "I'm grateful for your loyalty to her. But I'll need you more than ever now, Gudrun."

"I'll do what I can."

"The reason my mother lies here is because I've brought news of Eirik's death. I ask that you watch over her like you would your own mother."

"Happily, m'lord."

Dægan removed the ring of keys from his mother's brooch chain and stood to present them to the trustworthy *thrall*. "I'm putting you in charge of the servants and the household until Mother is better. I ask that you also tend to Lillemor, for she too is mourning, and I'll not have the time to see to her needs as I'd like. She's with child and must remain that way. If Lillemor loses the babe, 'twill certainly take my mother too. Command the others as you see fit and send for me when Mother awakens." Dægan took one last look at his sleeping mother. "I doubt she'll want to see me, but send for me anyway."

"Worry not, m'lord. Odin will keep his watchful eye upon her."

"If you learn anything from me, Gudrun, 'tis this. There are no gods. If my mother lives, 'twill be by your hand alone."

And with that, he left.

Chapter Fifteen

Dægan entered through the rear entrance of his longhouse and found their morning food and drink on the table, untouched. Mara was still asleep in his chambers, in the same position he'd left her hours before.

He removed his cloak and stood at the double doors, taking pleasure in seeing a woman in his bed. Her presence made the detail of the carved boxbed and the excess of fine silks and linens finally look suitable, that it wasn't just a vanity anymore.

Mara stirred under the blankets and rolled to see him crawling across the narrow bed.

"Are you always this late to rise?" he asked, lying atop her. "I've already seen to my chores for the morning."

Sleepily, Mara smiled and wrapped her arms around his neck. "Forgive me. I've never slept this well before."

He kissed her once on the lips. "I'm pleased my bed is to your liking."

"'Tis not the bed. But perhaps 'tis because I no longer sleep alone." Mara twisted a lock of his hair between her fingers. "How did you sleep?"

"Well enough," Dægan lied.

"You fib as pitifully as I do. 'Tis all right to admit your sleep wasn't well, for I can see that your mind is restless and your back is stiff. I'll not think you less of a man for saying such things."

"I'd hope not."

Her fingers strolled down his spine and back up into his hair before she kissed him. But then she froze as if she'd sensed something inside him that he hadn't yet revealed. "You've already visited your mother."

Dægan looked at her sideways, surprised by her perception. "Aye."

"Need I ask how she has taken it?"

"Nay," he said straightly. "Things are as I expected."

"Don't shield me from the truth, Dægan. Please tell me how she fares."

He held his composure. "She's ill. Her heart is weak, and I don't know how much more she can take."

"I'll see to her," Mara insisted. "I'll make certain she's comfortable and has all she needs while you're busy with Eirik's arrangements."

"I cannot ask you to do that."

"Nor will I wait for you to. I'll go to her, and that is that."

As grateful as he was, a pang of disappointment filled his heart when she attempted to slip from his arms. "Please, not now," he begged lightly. "I want to stay here with you for a little while. When I'm with you, my troubles disappear and my world is temporarily at peace. I'm not ready to endure the day I have ahead of me. I simply want to remain with you, at least for the rest of the morning."

Mara slid back into place alongside him and drew her arms tightly around him. "You can stay here as long as you like."

If it were up to Dægan, he'd stay an eternity. She felt delicate and soft against him, contrary to the harshness of the stress that plagued him. He sat up only to remove his clothing so that he could lie next to her, flesh on flesh. As he slipped beneath the covers, he felt an immense relief in the warmth her naked body emitted. He pulled her hips against his own and, with both touch and sight, he admired the sleek lines of her collarbones, the ideal swell of her breasts, and the smallness of her waist.

Finally, he bent to kiss her, taking great pains to be gentle and compassionate. He nipped the tight bud of her breast, then kissed his way farther down her body, spending time at her navel and hips.

Mara threw herself up on her elbows when he'd made his way to her thighs, spreading her legs gently. "What are you doing?"

Dægan grinned. "What I should've done the first night you shared my bed."

"I don't understand," Mara said in a tone of apprehension and shock. "Do you mean to kiss me...*there*?"

Dægan flicked his gaze over the intimate area he'd aimed to pleasure, then back up at Mara. Looking up at her from between her thighs and into the sparkling jewels of her eyes was as if a thousand spells of enchanting magic had consecrated him. "You're mine, Mara, and I can do with you as I please."

"This is what men do to women?"

"Nay. This is what a husband does to his wife."

She swallowed hard, obviously still alarmed by the notion of allowing him to perform such libidinous acts upon her body. "But I'm not yet your wife."

"In three days, you shall be."

Mara covered her face with her hands in what Dægan assumed to be embarrassment, and then giggled. "Does a husband always have that right? To do whatever he pleases, no matter how sinful?"

"Aye, he does. As does the wife to do whatever she

wishes. But 'tis not sinful between husband and wife."

"Again," she reminded, "I'm not your wife."

"Fair enough. I shall wait until our marriage bed to do so if that's what you wish. Three days," he warned as he crawled back up the length of her body. He aligned his pelvis with hers and nudged her legs apart, capturing her mouth in a slow, deep kiss until her frightened expression took him completely by surprise. "Are you all right, love? Is that fear I see?"

Mara looked as if she didn't know what to say, but denied the fear anyway.

"Then what is it? Do you think I'll hurt you?"

She stammered on her words. "W-well, I know you'll not *mean* to hurt me."

Confusion struck him. "I'll *never* hurt you. Why would you think I could do such a thing?"

Mara held motionless without a word of explanation, but her eyes looked timidly down between their naked bodies. The sizeable column of flesh jutting from his body accounted for her apprehension.

"Ah, I see now." He laughed and caressed her cheek with the back of his hand, adoring her naïvety and innocence. "'Twill not hurt anymore. I promise." He kissed her again slowly, hoping to rekindle the fire in her eyes. "This time 'twill be better, love. Trust me."

Chapter Sixteen

"This is the place," Breandán said with certainty.

Domaldr raised a doubting brow from upon his resting horse. "Are you certain, *Éireannach*?"

Breandán dismounted and walked studiously along the ground, taking in every broken twig, every mashed tuft of meadow grass, and every muddied print, man and horse alike. He followed the signs, those of which were insignificant and most often overlooked, leading him directly into the mouth of the cavern. In seeing the telltale scrapes upon the normally undisturbed cavern floor, he discerned it was quite evident that something had been dragged across it, say several bodies. Breandán then ventured farther and found the remnants of ash from a well-dismantled campfire. To anyone else, those signs would have gone unnoticed, but to Breandán's keen eyes, they were blatant indicative marks.

"Aye, I'm sure."

Domaldr looked at Soren and Thorbjörn, who should've known better than anyone if this was the right cavern. "Well? Does he speak the truth?"

Soren surveyed the area, trying to catch sight of something noteworthy. "This looks like the place, m'lord, but—"

Domaldr shook his head in disappointment. "Imbeciles!"

Breandán strode forward with a smile that boasted a

mighty arrogance. "Without a doubt I've found the place where your brother stayed with the Irish woman, so there's no need to question your men or insult them. Besides, did you honestly think your brother would still be here?"

Domaldr lifted his head and sucked in the morning air as if to cool his rising temper. When that didn't work, he unsheathed his sword and laid its blade against Breandán's throat. "Forgive me if I seem brash, but I need more than your words. I need proof! Give me proof, else you lose your head!"

Breandán stood still as Domaldr circled him on his steed. "How many men did you say you lost?"

"What difference does that make?"

Breandán pointed past Domaldr into the woods. "If 'tis five men your brother killed, I thought you might want to pay your respects."

Domaldr whipped his head around and jerked on the reins, his horse stamping disapprovingly as it was forced to obey a hard bit. Just as he implied, there were five distinct grave mounds tucked nicely into the shade of the woods.

Domaldr snarled, despite the evidence confirming his brother's presence, and Breandán imagined he was both relieved and irritated with the find; relieved that Breandán wasn't leading him on a wild chase, and irritated that the hunt for his brother was far from over.

"Now where?" Domaldr asked, gnashing those words between a vise of yellowing teeth.

"Taking into account that you said your brother was naught but a merchant, my guess would be Limerick. 'Tis the nearest port from here and possibly the best place to gain a quick fortune in selling a beautiful princess in the slave market. On the other hand, he risked his life for her, which leads me to believe he thinks of her as more than just chattel. Parting from her might not be his intention. Perhaps he's fallen in love."

"I couldn't care less about what my brother feels for the woman. I just want to find him. Now, on your horse."

Breandán mounted just as casually as the next words rolled off his tongue. "Tell me, Domaldr. Why do you hate this brother of yours so much? He cannot be as bad as you avow him to be. He had enough decency to bury your men."

"I didn't agree to bring you along for the sake of conversation," Domaldr snapped, sheathing his mottled sword at his side. "You've a task. Keep to it—in silence!"

****

Ottarr and Vegard arrived early that afternoon with five ships full of men, just as Dægan had instructed. Four of them were warships, dragged from the sea to dock upon the shore, and the fifth was the newly finished *knarr*. It remained floating in the distance because of the depth of its keel, and the crew emptied its cavernous hull of cargo with the use of small fishing boats. This gave Ottarr, Vegard, and the twenty others enough time to eat and reload for the next quick journey to Galway.

When the tedious task was finished, Dægan escorted his two friends to board the *knarr* from his boat. While rowing out to sea, Ottarr spoke quietly on the issue of an unexpected stowaway. "My lord, there's something you should know." He seemed to struggle with his next words as he tried to read Dægan's mood before doing so. "We brought Rutland here with us."

Dægan furrowed his brow, but the rhythm in his

rowing was undisturbed by his advisor's startling news. "The last thing I want is to see that traitorous bastard. Why did you bring him here?"

"We thought it best in order to keep rumors at bay. People in Hlymrekr know your brother had been killed, but they don't know by whom. If Rutland's body were found, gossip over his death and Eirik's would've followed you everywhere you went."

Vegard added his thoughts on the matter. "Do what you will with him, but leaving him in Hlymrekr wouldn't have been wise."

"And bringing him here would be?" Dægan barked. "A dead man delivered upon these shores is not the kind of proof I need to sway my Irish neighbors that I wish for peace."

"I realize this may not be what you bargained for," Ottarr said. "But you should've thought about that before you hunted him down and killed him."

Dægan stopped rowing. "If you think I should've let him live for murdering my brother, then curse you both."

"Dægan, we are not condemning you," Ottarr amended. "I would've done the same thing, but you cannot expect this to rectify itself."

"And where do you expect me to hide him?"

"I don't know," Ottarr whispered heatedly. "Throw him out to sea for the fishes for all I care."

Dægan groaned and went back to rowing. "Do the men know he's here?"

Vegard shook his head. "We told them nothing, but..." He then looked at Ottarr before explaining further. "In order to slip a dead man past a shipful of men, we put him in an empty barrel and filled the rest with water so that it bore a likeness to mead when the men loaded it."

"Odin's blood," Dægan cried. "This was the best you could come up with?"

Ottarr shouted his answer at first, then realized he needed to whisper so no one else could hear. "We didn't have the time to come up with something better. Would you've rather we strung him from the mast?"

"I've heard enough!" Dægan said. "What's done is done."

"Should I stay with you?" Vegard offered. "'Twill be easier to get rid of this together."

Dægan aligned the fishing boat beside the *knarr* and rubbed his forehead fiercely. "There's no need. Just make sure you return by tomorrow with that soil."

Ottarr stood and boarded the boat quickly, but Vegard bent down to whisper in his chieftain's ear. "Remember, m'lord, don't be drinking the mead tonight."

Dægan swatted at the man. "Get out of here, you old goat."

****

Mara finished her breakfast in the late hours of the morn. The longhouse proved lonely without Dægan, and he'd given her permission to venture outside should she get bored. Yet it wasn't boredom that compelled her to leave, but curiosity. She was anxious to see the place Dægan called home and the beauty of the island of which he often spoke.

Before he left and without much explanation, he'd laid a stack of clothes, neatly folded, on the table. To her surprise, it wasn't an ugly dark-colored cloak and linens for her to wear, but a silk tunic of light green, with rows of emerald jewels running the length of the neckline. The sleeves were long and flared to jeweled hems from the elbows, matching the pattern of the beautifully decorated bodice.

She held it up, smoothing it over her chest as she imagined what it would look like on herself. But before she could get too attached to the gown, her eyes caught sight of two brooches lying atop the folded cloak. Oval in shape, they shimmered with green and amber glass beads between silver filigree. She noticed the green in the brooches matched the emeralds in the dress, probably the work of an expert artisan, if not the finicky demand of a merchant buyer like her Dægan. No doubt the ensemble took a good number of silver coins from his pockets to acquire—with the gown most likely made from Torvald's Byzantium brocade, a noble lady's apparel indeed.

Mara spun in excitement, wishing Dægan was present so she could thank him for his lovely gifts. She slipped happily into the fine fabrics and braided her hair before leaving the longhouse.

As she opened the wooden door and stepped outside, she caught sight of the crystal-blue ocean crashing and receding along the gray shoreline several yards away. It sparkled in the sun as it lapped at the many warships lining the water's edge. Amazingly, there were more ships here than in Limerick. *Too many to count.*

The dragon beasts stood just as proudly from their perches, but lacked the brutish stare in the daylight hours. She smiled, no longer feeling the threat of their petrified visage.

Mara took a deep breath and closed her eyes. The air was different. Smelled different. It was an aroma unlike any other, but she remembered the scent from when they'd left the ports of Limerick. Again she breathed in the clean air, memorizing its salty fragrance. She liked it, even preferred it to the grassy meadows of Connacht.

When Mara turned around, she saw several rows of longhouses, a strange familiarity of Limerick's harbor, except here, each longhouse was partitioned off by stone walls that sectioned off parcels of land for each house. The rock barriers were everywhere throughout the island, even where houses no longer stood.

As she walked around the settlement, she noticed that the island was quite flat and without the blessing of trees. But what it lacked in trees, it made up for in limestone—rocky terrain that pressed up through her sandals between tufts of turf and wildflowers.

Mara bent and picked a few, as in her days on the Shannon, noting that the flora was very unique to her eyes. With the flowers to her nose, she walked on, eager to see what more the isle had to offer.

A few houses down, there were several people working in their gardens, some tending to sheep in the fields, and some beating floor rugs on the stone walls. They were all dressed very simply, contrary to the fine apparel she was now wearing. But without any resentment, they nodded and smiled, acknowledging their new guest and continuing with their chores. Everyone seemed comfortable with her presence, and it became very apparent that the entire settlement knew of the proposed marriage arrangement, not just Dægan's close friends and family. The thought of such a grand assembly didn't bother her in the least. In fact, it lifted her smile to even higher heights.

Suddenly, a woman servant burst through the front door of a nearby longhouse. She cried and pleaded for the gods to help her, anyone to help her, then ran back to the open door. After a brief altercation with someone inside, she backed away with her head in her hands and sobbed.

Mara ran to her and touched her shoulder tenderly. "Do you need help? What is the matter?"

The woman whirled in surprise. "Please, we must stop her. She has a knife!"

"Who has a knife?" Mara asked, gripping the woman's arms.

"Lillemor! She threatens to take her life. Dægan will have my head on a spit!"

Mara's mouth gaped as she turned toward the longhouse and heard the cries from within. She knew that feeble, woeful cry from Lillemor well, but could hardly think with her servant on the ground in hysterics. "Please, calm yourself. You're not helping Lillemor by panicking."

"'Tis my head he'll want! He'll kill me on the spot! I know it! We must stop her!"

Mara grabbed the woman and shook her. "You must stop this yelling. Naught will happen to you. I give you my word."

The servant continued to bawl, taking no comfort in Mara's promise. Another woman joined her and tried to console the lowly servant crying at her feet.

"What is your name?" Mara asked of the newcomer.

"Gudrun, my lady. I serve Dægan's mother."

Mara knew Gudrun had to be more than capable of assisting her if she were skilled enough to be Svanhild's servant. "Lillemor threatens to take her life, and I need you to keep this woman away."

"What about Lillemor?" Gudrun questioned, her eyes wide with concern.

"I shall care for her," Mara whispered.

Gudrun obediently pulled the young servant woman

away and led her a few houses down, where her cries could no longer be heard. Nervously, Mara stepped toward the door and placed her hand on the wood. The sudden eerie silence frightened her most. Was she too late?

Slowly, she opened the door and peeked inside. Lillemor sat in the chair with her arms wrapped around her barely there stomach, and the silver dagger lay on the table, without the stain of blood on its edge. She hesitated to speak, seeing that the widow was sitting calmly and posed no immediate threat to her unborn child. "Lillemor? It's me, Mara."

At the sound of her voice, Lillemor stood with a jerk and grabbed the knife "Get out! Leave me be!"

Mara ignored her and slowly stepped inside. "You have many people worried about you."

"I care not!" she screamed back.

"But I do," Mara replied. "I cannot let you do this."

"Not another step—or I shall do it right now." Lillemor turned the knife on herself, aiming the point at her heart. "I will. I swear I will."

Mara abandoned the idea of getting close enough to take the weapon from Lillemor's possession. It was too risky for either of them. "I shall sit…and we can talk. All right?"

"I've nothing to say."

Mara gradually lowered herself on the boxbed to her right. "You've much to say, it seems, but don't let your death speak for you."

Lillemor's face twisted. "I've nothing to say to *you*, *Mara*."

The hatred and contempt couldn't be mistaken in the way Lillemor emphasized her name. "Fair enough. I don't deserve any pleasantries from you. And I too know that if it weren't for me, Eirik would still be here. I can look in your eyes and know you see me as the cause of his death. But you must believe me, I wish with all my heart I could turn back the day."

Lillemor's eyes narrowed. "I've lost everything because of you."

"Not everything," Mara corrected.

"Everything!" Lillemor argued as she squeezed tears from her eyes. "I have nothing."

"Is the babe that stirs within you nothing?"

"'Tis a curse. A constant reminder that Eirik is gone." Lillemor gripped the handle of the knife so tightly, her knuckles turned white.

"Lillemor, please, 'tis not a curse and you know it. 'Tis a gift from Eirik. He's given you a child...a part of him that will always be with you." Seeing the small change in Lillemor's eyes, Mara stood and took one step at a time, inching closer with each new reason. "This child is something you can hold in your arms. 'Tis even better than a fleeting memory of Eirik. He lives in you, Lillemor. He lives *in you*."

Lillemor closed her eyes even tighter and sobbed like a child. Mara was close enough to reach for the knife, and she cupped Lillemor's hand with her own while carefully prying out the blade with the other.

"Let me have this, Lillemor. You don't need it anymore. You've Eirik inside you. Hold fast to that."

Lillemor released the dagger and collapsed against Mara, crying even harder. Mara threw the blade to the far wall, and both women dropped to the floor in a tangled heap. Mara rocked Dægan's sister-in-law like a helpless baby and stroked her hair, inwardly thanking God that no harm was done. And just like the broken Northern woman, Mara's tears also spilled down her cheeks in deep sorrow for the loss of Eirik.

Gudrun peeked around the door. "My lady?"

Mara quickly wiped her tears from her face and nodded with great reprieve. "All is well, Gudrun. Could you fetch Lillemor some food and drink and bring it to Dægan's chambers? She'll stay with us from now on."

"As you wish. Should I send for her clothes?"

Again Mara nodded. "And please see to any gossip that may travel to Dægan's mother. She needn't hear of this with her weakened heart."

Mara watched the diligent servant woman leave, and a genuinely good feeling filled her heart. She'd achieved something of great importance while Dægan was away, and without much practice beforehand. Finally, she'd done something good for him.

"Come," Mara whispered to Lillemor. "Let's get you comfortable and fed."

Chapter Seventeen

The rest of the afternoon, Dægan made his brother's grave a priority, though he never strayed too far from the thought of Rutland's corpse in a barrel. It was a sinister vision that surfaced many times throughout his day. Not that digging required much concentration, but he'd rather his thoughts roam into other sweeter places, particularly Mara's embrace.

As sundown fast approached, he and the men returned from their long day's work of preparing his brother's grave and setting the ship. The longship chosen to hold Eirik's body was one that Eirik had constructed himself, and given the grandeur of the vessel, it wasn't an easy task to haul it across the roughened terrain of the isle on rolling timbers.

The chosen place was of strict importance, a site deemed to be hallowed ground. No obstacle large or small would stand in Dægan's way of giving his brother the burial he deserved.

In silence, Dægan and his men marched across the land exhausted and weak, dragging their shovels behind them. They were a hungry, grumpy group, oblivious that a feast had been prepared until they came upon the hustle and bustle of their settlement.

Tables and benches sat around a large fire, and breads, cheeses, and stewed meat lined the trays, close to falling off. Servants rushed from table to table, setting trenchers and filling cups. Behind the display, musicians strummed out their songs, and poets practiced their orations with gestures and dance, all of whom were dressed in their finest apparel.

Dægan looked around at all the fuss, thinking his mother had become better and resumed her plans for the feast she'd been preparing. Although glad of the possibility of his mother's improved health, he was somewhat disappointed that her plans had been carried out. This meant he'd have to play host for a few more hours before being able to retire to his bed.

"Well, men, I guess we should get cleaned up. It looks as though we have a celebration to attend."

Tait shared the same wide-eyed stare as his chieftain. "I'm certainly agreeable to that, but there's no sense in getting cleaned up when I plan on getting dirt drunk."

"Some of us more than others," Steinar said enthusiastically before making a beeline for his longhouse.

Dægan rushed straight to his as well, thinking he'd find his mother with Mara, doing what mothers do best—cooking a fine meal. It didn't take him long to hurdle a few rock walls and burst through the back door. Upon his entering, he stopped dead in his tracks.

Mara stood at the hearth in the green dress he'd given her, jeweled from head to toe, with her hair braided down her back. She took his breath away, stunning him with her transformation. He swelled with pride at his choice of color in both the dress and the beads that enhanced the green in her eyes gleaming in the firelight. Without realizing, he'd forgotten all about his mother and flashed a toothy smile. "You look absolutely beautiful."

"Shh…" Mara shushed. "You'll wake her."

Dægan couldn't hide his surprise when he saw Lillemor sleeping in their enclosed private bed-closet.

"What is she doing in there?"

Mara closed the doors of their chamber and motioned for him to follow her deeper into the living quarters of the main hall so as not to wake their guest.

"Lillemor is mourning her husband, and the last thing she needs is to be left alone, or to think no one cares about her grief. I thought it best to let her stay with us."

Dægan looked over his shoulder, still discontented about Lillemor sleeping in his bed—a place he fully intended to occupy after he played host. "How is the babe?"

"Hungry," Mara said. "Lillemor ate as if she were feeding twins."

Dægan's voice rattled a bit as he repeated her. "Twins?"

"Ah, Dægan, 'tis too early to tell. I was only jesting."

He half smiled. "Right."

"Now don't dawdle. Your mother wanted a feast, and a feast she shall have." Mara crinkled her nose in disgust and stepped back. "But I dare say even your mother would prefer you to bathe first."

Dægan's mood lifted again. "My mother is well?"

Mara hesitated. "I went to her, but she didn't awaken. Gudrun says her condition should improve by tomorrow."

"Then who, may I ask, prepared the feast?"

"I did," Mara stated with a smile. "Gudrun also told me your mother had cooked so much meat this morning, 'twould be a waste for it not to be eaten. So we finished what she started. I hope you don't mind. I thought since the men had been working all day, a festive meal would do everyone some good."

Dægan's face lit up. "You did all this?"

"Why does it surprise you? Do you think my father

never feasts as you?"

"I'm sure your father could host an even bigger feast, but I doubt he'd make *you* prepare it. How would you come to know of such things?"

Mara saw both admiration and astonishment twinkling in his eyes. "Perhaps 'tis my little secret."

"Secret or not, 'tis a bit daring to host such a celebration out of doors."

"You should take what small blessings are given you, Dægan. I know I do."

He snagged her around the waist and nuzzled her nose with his. "Speaking of blessings, where shall I sleep this night if you gave my bed to Lillemor?"

Mara sniffed in repulsion. "I've not thought of that yet."

"I suggest you make those arrangements and make them well, dear love. I refuse to lie without you tonight." Dægan released her from his arms, and before he could stop himself, a lustful thought emerged inside his head as he glanced over Mara's body one last time. He grunted and walked out the back door to the bathhouse.

****

Dægan had taken his place at the middle of the table, with Mara at his right and Tait and Steinar at his left. He looked around at the festivities and noticed that everything was better than he could've imagined. Everyone had eaten their fill and was still drinking and laughing as if the mead had already gone to their heads.

Mara had petitioned for a group of musicians with lutes, drums, and flutes, poets painted to mimic their part, acrobats flipped and juggled, and ladies danced in a circle to the cheerful melody. Even the servants took to their duties with grace and organization instead of running around like headless chickens.

Everything was perfect. A little too perfect, Dægan thought, for no one seemed to remember they'd just prepared a grave for his brother.

Dægan looked to his left, and although the seat was not empty, it still didn't seem right to see Steinar seated in it. Normally, Eirik would be the one to fill it during feasts and gatherings, and it suddenly became real that he'd have to get used to it.

Lately, he tried to dismiss any thoughts of his brother, for with Eirik came the thought of Rutland and his betrayal. Oh, how he wished he could rid that memory from his mind. *Nay, sink it to the bottom of the sea.*

And that was when it occurred to him. He still had to rid Rutland from the barrel, and it would have to be done tonight, lest someone else might happen upon him. But how could *he*, the host, get away from the festivities? How could he dispose of Rutland without anyone knowing, for it was a job that would require much of his time and more of a strong stomach, both of which he feared he lacked.

Dægan grabbed the wooden cup in front of him and drank to calm his raging head. After a few large gulps, he stopped and tasted the liquid in his mouth. It was mead, as it always was, but because of Vegard's warning, he suddenly didn't wish to drink any more of the honeyed brew. With much repugnance, he pushed the cup aside.

"Is everything all right, m'lord?" Mara asked, touching his hand. "You look quite disturbed."

Dægan dismissed the urge to explain and used an easy excuse. "I'm merely tired."

"I'll gladly see to the rest of the feast for you if you'd rather retire to your bed."

"I'd prefer to retire to *our* bed, but given that Lillemor now occupies it, I suppose I should become accustomed to this bench. Any other bed you find for me would yield the same degree of discomfort."

Mara rolled her eyes. "Are you truly that fond of it?"

"Hmm... How long did you sleep this morning? Or was it afternoon when you awoke? I cannot be too certain."

Mara seemed humored by his subtle sarcasm. "Enough said, Dægan. I'll see that you regain your bed. Besides, there's more than enough room in your longhouse to accommodate Lillemor and six others if need be. You never know, she just may birth those twins after all."

Dægan grinned and warmly took Mara's hand. "Honestly, I could be anywhere with you, and I'd be a happy man. Your generosity astounds me, and I'm very grateful for the many sacrifices you've made. I know I've not been myself of late, and you've had to take on more than what you probably expected since arriving on this isle. But this feast has helped my people more than you know. I thank you for going to the trouble of making it happen. They're most pleased."

With that, Dægan took a slap to his back. "Here! Drink, you bastard!" Steinar bellowed as if he were far across the table. He stumbled and slammed Dægan's cup of unconsumed mead in front of him.

"As you can see, some are more pleased than others," Dægan said drolly. Without taking his eyes off Mara, he grabbed his cup, threw it up to his cheek and over his right shoulder so that the brew appeared to have been drunk. Once it was emptied upon the ground behind him, he set it on the table, ignoring her look of bewilderment.

Steinar, too drunk to know the difference, raised his hands in praise and went back to his merriment, consuming more mead as he sang and beat the table.

And why shouldn't everyone be happy? It was not their fault Eirik was dead, nor did their celebration mean they weren't saddened by the loss of their friend. A huge feast had been prepared in their honor, so to speak, and it would seem impolite if they didn't enjoy the banquet to its fullest.

Nonetheless, their happiness left an ache in his heart.

Except for Mara's. Her happiness by no means made him hurt inside. He liked her smile and her little laughter that fluttered around him. Even through the drunken shouts and praises, it was like music to his ears. She sparkled like the northern star in the sky, and he felt proud having her seated next to him at his table. He touched her face and drew her chin up. "I too am pleased…to the fullest extent."

Mara raised her cup ever so slightly, offering a private toast. "To small blessings."

Dægan clicked his empty cup with hers, and before he could make good on a kiss, a roar of laughter echoed behind him. Steinar lay flat on his back with his drinking horn still in hand.

"Pour me another!" he ordered.

Tait took Steinar's horn and tossed it aside. "Get to your bed, you dolt. You couldn't drink another drop if you tried."

But Steinar did try. With all his might, he tried—at least to sit up and prove himself capable. No sooner had he lifted his head from the grass than did the world spin around him. He then beckoned for his wife, Etti, who was no more sober than himself.

Tait shoved a heel to Steinar's chest. "Stay down, you fool, before you retch your guts."

"I'll not retch," he cried, raising a pointed finger. "I'm a man. What mead I consume, consumes me, and we do not part—until I have to piss, but then 'tis my choice. I dare any man here to say differently."

Dægan looked at Mara and sighed. "I suppose I should get this drunken sod to his bed before we're forced to carry him. Will you excuse me?"

Mara smiled warmly. "Of course."

Dægan nudged the pitiful man with his boot. "Come on...get up." He helped Steinar to stand, being both a lean pole and a pair of legs, as they teetered and tripped across the way.

Tait laughed as he saw Etti stagger behind them, singing as she'd done all night with her cup raised to the gods. He slid from his seat on the bench, over to Dægan's, and motioned for the cupbearer. Turning to Mara, he said, "You're to be commended, my lady, upon this exquisite feast, *and* for being able to tame the heart of a bear."

Mara studied the man she'd remembered from the ship, an obviously loyal fellow with a striking handsomeness to boot. "I don't understand what you mean."

"Dægan," Tait said flatly. "No woman has ever been able to claim his heart as her own."

"To have claimed anything, I think not."

"Ah, but you have. I've been friends with Dægan since we were boys with sticks for swords. At no time has there been someone who's ever occupied his every living thought. You're the purpose for every breath he takes. He does nothing that is not firstly for you. This I know, as I too have been tamed."

Mara gave him a sideways glance. "So, where is she...this tamer of your heart?"

Tait's admiration for the unknown girl crept into a smile. "Oh, I wish she were here, but she lives in Hlymrekr with her mother. She's young like yourself, but not as quick to learn. I suppose that's what I fancy most about her. She's shameless to—" Tait stopped abruptly, as if his words lacked appropriateness. He changed them accordingly. "Let's just say she's shameless to certain unspeakable pleasures in life...and with that comes this profound purity that I cannot wait to claim as my own. Ottarr's dowry and my bride price have already been determined between us, and we've made the arrangement binding with the shaking of hands before witnesses."

Mara watched Tait melt into the thought of his woman's presence. Without seeing Tait's change in posture, she would've doubted that he even knew what love felt like, much less know how to recognize it in others. But clearly, she was wrong. Gladly wrong. She enjoyed seeing Tait mesmerized by the notion of one woman.

"What is her name?"

"Thordia," Tait uttered romantically. "We are to marry as soon as we return from—" He stopped. "Well, from..."

Mara finished for him. "From making peace with my father?"

Tait nodded.

"May I ask you something? And I want only the truth, not a rhetoric of fanciful words spoken to keep me from worrying."

"All right."

"Do you think that peace can be made between Dægan and my father?"

"Lady Mara," Tait said, adjusting himself closer, "if Dægan can bring the Irish natives of this isle to welcome pagans on their Christian lands through only words and a wedding, then aye, he can make peace with anyone. Including your father."

"You truly believe that?"

Tait's smile turned wry. "If I didn't, I'd not be here. I'd be with Thordia, partaking in those unspeakable pleasures I mentioned before. But that is between you and me. Now, if you'll excuse me, I should see how Dægan fares with Steinar."

Chapter Eighteen

Tait looked everywhere for Dægan. After seeing that Steinar and Etti were both sound asleep in their beds, he tried Dægan's longhouse. Then his mother's, the bathhouse, and finally the barn without success, until he noticed a dark shadowy figure entering the storage house at the far end of the settlement.

Tait sneaked from home to home and made his way to the building, thinking he'd found a thief, or maybe even an opportunistic Irishman stealing dried meat and dairy from their stock while everyone was occupied by the feast.

The figure went in and never came back out.

Cautiously, Tait crept closer and slipped to the back of the storage building. He waited patiently for the thief to exit the door, readying himself for a fight.

Suddenly a tall man emerged from the opening, rocking a full barrel of mead across the ground from the storage house to the wagon. He struggled with the weight of its contents, and no one else exited to help him.

Glad that the thief was a loner, Tait drew in two quick breaths and lunged at the man. They both fell to the ground and Tait threw the first punch before the thief could get up. The man rolled and tried to stand, but Tait kicked him in the stomach, dropping him like a stone.

The thief coughed and groaned, and jumped to his feet, unsheathing his dagger. "I demand you make yourself known!"

Tait gasped, realizing the voice was Dægan's. "Wait!"

"Tait?" Dægan squinted through the darkness, trying to see if his attacker really was his best friend. "Are you mad? I nearly killed you."

"I think I nearly killed you," Tait corrected. "You never laid one hand on me."

Dægan rubbed his side, not at all happy about the pain spasming his gut. He sheathed his dagger and immediately threw a quick punch at his friend's face, knocking him to the ground. "How about now?"

Tait held his chin in his hand. "You bastard. I only struck you because I thought you were thieving."

"And I struck you because you were gloating," Dægan mocked. "Now help me load this barrel, you *kerling*."

"I'm not an old woman, and I wasn't gloating," Tait defended, joining him at the barrel. "I was simply making a point."

"I think my point was better made."

"Now *you're* gloating," Tait indicated. "Does that mean I'm well within my right to strike you back?"

"Try it," Dægan dared. He knew Tait was smart enough not to challenge him, and together, they lifted the barrel to the back of the cart.

"Did Steinar drink all the mead?"

Tate laughed aloud, but Dægan kept to the task unamused. "Nay."

"Then why another barrel?" Tait sniffed the air, then grimaced. "And by the gods, what is that smell?"

Dægan smelled it too. "That would be Rutland."

Tait patted his shoulder. "'Twill be difficult for

everyone to rid that stench from our memories. You shouldn't be so hard on yourself, Dægan. No one, not even Hansen, who wanted to force his fist down the lad's throat, thought him capable of doing such a thing."

"That is not what I mean," Dægan said, incensed. "I mean Rutland is in the barrel, and the smell is literally coming from his corpse."

Tait's eyes widened. "In here?"

"Aye."

"But why in bloody Hel would you do this?"

"I didn't. Ottarr and Vegard—"

Tait staggered backward. "*They* did this?"

Dægan could feel his patience thinning. "I don't like it any more than you, Tait."

"Why even bring him here? In this—this—way?"

"They did what they thought best."

"Best?" Tait snapped, pacing. "This was the best those clever advisors could come up with? Odin's blood, their minds are gone."

"'Tis not as if Rutland truly deserves better. He killed my brother."

"I've not forgotten." Tait spread open his right hand and pointed at the long scar marking his palm. He then jerked Dægan's wrist up to remind him of his own. "Eirik was like my brother too, you know."

Dægan remembered the day as if it were yesterday. He, Eirik, and Tait were a trio of ambitious minds, standing in a great forest of oaks about to be felled for the making of their first ship. They stood shoulder to shoulder, proud as cocks, as each one cut the palm of his own hand to proclaim and secure a lifelong blood oath with each other. On a single iron ring they'd clasped their lacerated hands and let their blood run together where it dripped onto the ground at their feet. In mixing both earth and blood, each of the three men gathered a handful of soil and shook on it, swearing to protect and avenge the others as brothers would.

Dægan hung his head. "Indeed he was your brother. Forgive me, Tait."

"There's no need to be sorry. You avenged Eirik, an oath unbroken. Thor would be proud."

"Could we just get this over with?" Dægan asked.

Tait followed Dægan to the front of the cart, where the hitched horse grazed. Subdued by sorrow, both stood on either side of the animal and led it across Inishmore's harsh terrain toward the ocean. For a long time, nothing more was said between the men, until they arrived at the shore. After they lifted the well-agitated barrel from the cart, Tait stepped back from the rancid wooden drum, cursing.

Dægan rolled the barrel to its side and kicked it down into the lapping surf. He stared at it, dreading with all that was in him to see Rutland again, much less endure the stench that had been fermenting for more than a day.

"I hope you're not too fond of the meal you had tonight," Tait said. "I wager you're about to lose it."

Dægan looked over his shoulder. "I wager you sooner than me."

"Why's that?"

"Because you're going to fetch the rope from the wagon and tie it around Rutland's waist as soon as I open the lid."

"How come I have to tie it?"

"Would you rather stick the rock in his breeches, then?"

Tait cringed. "By the gods, I draw the line at putting

my hands down any man's breeches, especially the breeches of a rotting corpse."

"I shall take that as a nay." Dægan put one foot on the barrel, one hand on the lid, and jerked with all his might, releasing the liquid contents within. The stagnant water gushed from the barrel and filled all the breathable air around him with an unforgiving odor. He gagged, trying to get away from the stench, but it was everywhere. Eventually, after much resistance, he gave in to throwing up his evening meal, just as Tait had predicted.

The ocean broke at his feet, carrying away the vomit along with his desire to continue. The irony of Rutland and him once again in the dark water propelled an unwanted vision of his wretched past, one he didn't want to relive.

He took a deep breath over his shoulder and grabbed Rutland by the back of his tunic, pulling his body all the way out of the drum. The smell of decaying flesh filtered up through his nose—intolerable and relentless as it was—and again, he felt the muscles of his stomach jerk and tighten. He ran from the putrid smell of the shallow waters and up to the wagon, where he vomited anew.

While doubled over on the shore, and cursing several subsequent oaths for no other reason than to make himself feel better, he looked over and saw Tait on all fours, heaving his meal as well.

"What are you laughing at?" Tait growled, spitting the remnants of disgorged matter from his mouth.

"The fact that you're already vomiting and you've yet to tie the rope."

Tait glared at him, then crawled to the small fishing boat on the shore. He tied one end of the rope to the vessel and hesitated before doing the same to Rutland. Dægan knew Tait was hoping for a better idea than this one, but he was already on his feet, choosing a hefty rock for the sinking stone.

****

After Tait and Dægan rowed out to sea and sank the body into the depths of its nadir, they made haste for the bathhouse to scrub themselves of their hideous filth, both what was left on their bodies, as well as what afflicted their minds.

During their fierce cleansing, they heard shouts and praises coming from the remainder of those still celebrating. Tait, aiming to join them in their drunken fun so as to forget what his sober mind could not, rushed from the building and left his chieftain to brood within the steam.

Dægan needed this time for himself, to gather his thoughts and his bearings on the swiftly turning world in which he existed. In a matter of a week, he'd gained a brag-worthy price on his head, killed one of his own men, and all too suddenly lost his brother because he'd fallen in love with a woman. It wasn't like him to mull over something that was already done, but if given the chance to do it all over, he wished his brother's death hadn't been a direct result of it.

Most would say his bad luck was a curse, a punishment for the oath he'd broken with his war god. Mayhap it was. But Dægan refused to believe that a man's path was laid out by the gods, whereby it could also improve or worsen depending on how pleased they were. To him, a man's path to glory should only be blazed by the righteousness of his actions. And that was where Dægan's struggle lay. Adding up his own misdeeds, he was no less corrupt.

He could've done something else with Rutland's body. Perhaps a proper burial would've been a better choice, but he couldn't bring himself to that level of decency. No matter how hard he tried, he couldn't think of one reason why Rutland deserved *anything* moderately honorable. The cold black water was a fitting burial for a man who thought so little of those who raised him before doing the unthinkable. At least that was what Dægan tried to tell himself as he rested his pounding head against the warmth of the bathhouse wall behind him.

****

"I thought I'd find you in here," Mara said through the thickening mist. She entered and gave Dægan a pitying smile as she closed the door behind her. Sitting on a wooden bench along the far wall, he looked as if he hadn't the strength to speak, or rather, the mind to. She knew something terrible had happened after he and Tait helped Steinar to bed, but couldn't begin to fathom a logical explanation.

She stepped farther inside and felt the warm air pervade her lungs. She'd never been in such a peculiar enclosure, nor could she fully understand the real purpose for the heated building. Dægan often spoke of the bathhouse, but it wasn't akin to anything she was used to. There was a hearth—hardly large enough to heat a cauldron for bathing—and only a few buckets of water on the floor. Impressed with the effectiveness of the steaming rocks that heated the entire space and the contents within it, she was more interested in how a sweat-induced bath made anyone feel clean.

As beads of perspiration had already begun to settle across her upper lip, she looked at Dægan and realized the particulars of this strange ablutionary method weren't as important as what had distressed him enough to make him want to hide away in solitude.

"When I saw Tait drinking like a fish, I assumed he was exceptionally thirsty. But now that I see you with the very same look upon your face, I'm convinced you're both plagued by something you wished you hadn't seen or done." She came closer and sat beside him on the hot bench. A fleeting thought of stripping down to nothing, like Dægan, crossed her mind. If she stayed in here much longer, she just might have to. Absently, she fanned her face. "I can't help you if you won't talk to me. Sometimes, talking is the best way to cleanse your soul, rather than bathing, or whatever this is."

Dægan's expression changed as if her words sparked some amusement within him. He stood, letting the small linen cloth that had covered his lap fall to the floor, and dumped a bucket of water over his head. At that point, all her questions about the bathhouse had been answered, and she'd gotten a great view of his bare backside to boot.

After fully dressing and slipping on his boots, he took her by the hand. "I believe we both could use some fresh air. Shall we?"

Chapter Nineteen

On horseback, Dægan took Mara to the end of the island, a place that bore the closest resemblance to his home in Hladir, of sheer rock cliffs, foaming white sea, and a vast plain of tranquil water under a midnight sky. It was just how Dægan liked it. A place of solitary peace with the constant shuffle of the ocean below drowning out the rest of the world's clamor.

Many times, it was just him and the silvery moon, his silent, ever-watchful friend. But tonight, after what he'd endured, he needed Mara with him. She was his best instrument for gaining serenity.

Dægan dismounted and carried her from the horse to the cliff's edge. The air was cool and refreshing compared to the still denseness of the bathhouse, though he feared the approaching cloud cover would soon bring a torrential storm.

He set Mara down and, like most people who come upon a daunting edge, she first peeked over the side. She gasped upon seeing the violent water churn and crash into the blunt face of the isle, leaving an airy froth floating in the aftermath.

As she stepped back, she took in what he'd been boasting of since he met her: a door to another world far from the mundane one in which she lived. There was no limit to the sea, no boundaries to the horizon, no brink from which to fall. One could seemingly sail forever...

"Do you like it?" Dægan asked, watching her gaze off into nothingness.

"I feel so small. So unimportant."

Dægan put his hands upon her shoulders. "Yet part of it all, nonetheless. For me, this place puts everything into perspective. No matter how significant I feel or how proud I get, I look out and know there's something even bigger than my haughty self. Something wiser than I could ever conjure up. Something greater than I could ever hold in my hand. Something beyond words or imagination. I come here often, hoping to discover what that is. Hoping to find what my mind thinks is lost, what my heart thinks is missing." Dægan sat down and casually tossed pebbles over the side. "I've yet to find those answers, Mara."

She knelt in front of him. "Has anyone?"

"You seem to have."

"What do you mean?"

"You're confident in your god. Unwavering as you believe in the things he does for you. Even when you endure a hardship like losing your mother as a child, you don't find blame in the god who stood by and watched."

"I don't believe He simply stands by and watches."

"What do you believe, then?"

"Well, I think He's more active in our lives than we know and…that He intervenes using others around us."

Dægan narrowed his eyes. "Like puppets?"

"Nay, like messengers or heralds. People who do His work without even knowing. They do so because that is who they are. The humble of heart, I suppose."

Dægan sat thinking. His heart was far from humble and that wasn't the man he was brought up to be. He was taught to be a proud, strong man, who wouldn't gain anything unless by the sweat of his brow. His father, Rælik, was that kind of man, and to be humble meant to forget who he was, to deny his father's own sweat and blood that came with the name he passed on. To be humble... It almost seemed impossible.

Until he took one look at Mara.

She was the one thing he'd gladly give up everything for—his name, his wealth, his very pride. But did he have to give up a brother as well?

"Dægan," Mara said, her tone as gentle as the breeze. "Are you all right? You seem so distant tonight."

He pulled her into his arms. "Forgive me. I'm just..." He had no words to describe his thoughts. He'd only a painful perspective in holding her, a tangible sense of irony. "Why does everything have to come with a high price? Can I not have you without...?"

He couldn't finish for fear he'd break down in sorrow again like he had on the cold floor of Eirik's stable. He'd shed many tears upon his brother's very face that night. More of his manhood than he cared to part with.

Mara touched his face. "I'm so sorry, Dægan. If I could take this burden from you, I would."

He sighed and looked away. "If you could truly take this burden, I'd not give it to you. Never would I want you to feel this pain. This empty, hollow, helpless feeling as those around you lay blame upon you. 'Tis only natural for people to find fault elsewhere. 'Tis what makes their hearts feel less heavy in their own chests. And what can I do but live with it and hope that I never heal from this wound, for to heal means to forget my brother."

"Nay, Dægan," Mara crooned sympathetically.

"Aye, I'm to suffer. I'm to feel this pain."

"With your gods, perhaps," Mara corrected. "But not

with mine. What you suffer, He suffers. What you ask, He gives. What you need, He provides. This is God, should you just believe."

A cold splatter of raindrops hit their faces and Dægan removed his bear cloak, wrapping it around Mara. Still holding fast to its fur, he asked, "Are you certain he's all those things, even for a man like me?"

Mara pressed her forehead to his. "In the eyes of God, we are all His children, even you."

Dægan took in a breath, slowly drifting from the virtuous man he should be to the blatantly covetous man he was. He couldn't help it. He wanted her, every part of her in his avaricious hands no matter where they were. They could be sitting in the middle of a Christian church and he'd still want her. "God wants a stronger man than I, a man who doesn't yield so easily to temptation."

Mara stroked his face. "You *are* that man."

He wanted to believe her. He wanted to think he could very well overcome anything he put his mind to. But he knew better, especially when he was drawn to the falling rain that settled on Mara's lips. He watched as some slipped inside her mouth, proving that his weakness was as clear as water. He cupped her face and shook his head at her blindness. "I've many weaknesses, Mara, and *you are* all of them. You and you alone."

She softened in his arms. "Me?"

"How can you not see that? From the moment the word *Lochlannach* slipped poetically from your mouth, I've been struggling to get back just a shred of resilience. You've taken it, and I'm all that is left. If you want a formidable man, you'll not find one here."

She pulled herself close, barely touching his lips with

her own. "What is left is all I want."

Dægan tried to ignore that she pressed her body against him, or that her lips almost touched his, hardly feeling the rain dampening his clothes to his back. "And what does your Christian god want of me?"

"No more than I. No more than the strength of your heart and the depth of your love."

He couldn't resist her anymore and kissed her hard, harder than he intended. Like him, the heavens couldn't hold back either and opened upon them without remorse. He tasted the rain on her lips and deemed this moment another small blessing. There seemed to be no end to them when she was around. She was his only need and his only desire. His entire world somehow fit within her arms.

Was she a gift from the very god he struggled to accept? Was he the answer Dægan had been searching for all along?

With outstretched arms, he looked up into the sky and relished the spatter of rain against his face. It was as if the cascading water were a baptism, a beginning…and conceivably an end; a final farewell to his pagan gods.

Liberated from his burdens, Dægan clasped her face in his strong, wet hands. His eyes fixed on her through rain-soaked lashes. "I love you. Like the relentless rain from the Erin sky, my love will always be. For you, Mara, and no other."

Chapter Twenty

The Erin rain continued to fall, as it did most of the late summer season. The ground was saturated, and every step Dægan took, a muddy hole was left behind him. His boots were soaked through and his feet were cold, an uncomfortable dampness that worsened with each laborious stride.

A lightning strike illuminated the barn up ahead, and he quickened his pace to a trot. When he reached the entrance, he opened the door and stared into the darkness, his senses deadened to the driving rain that beat against his face. He didn't feel cold anymore, just a numbing of body and soul, for he stood at the place where they'd kept Eirik until the burial in the morning.

Dægan meandered past the stalls, his heart skipping in his chest. Without the blessing of a lighted lamp, the aisleway seemed longer and more ominous as the shadows draped like fabric over the dirt ground and into the corners. He found the last few steps toward his brother were the longest by far.

Finally, he came upon the table on which Eirik lay. The wrappings of linen had been removed from his face, and it was a haunting sight that even Dægan wished he'd not seen. His brother's skin was an unforgettable color of gray, and his eyes were a sunken crater of flesh, depressed in the bony sockets of his skull.

Dægan turned away from the hideous sight, but even

behind tightly closed lids, it was an unmerciful lingering image. He felt his throat constrict, trapping the thick, heavy air deeper into his burning chest. His heart pounded against his ribs, and it gave rise to the throb in his temples. His stomach turned and flipped as it had hours before.

He turned to leave, but a hideous laughter erupted from behind him and echoed against the empty stalls. Eirik's hand grabbed his wrist with long, cold fingers, and his sunken eyes opened wide.

Dægan sat straight up in a cold sweat, gasping for breath.

"Dægan, what's wrong?" Mara asked, clutching his shoulders.

He searched his surroundings and started to distinguish every detail of his slowly recognizable bedchamber. Without the laughter, the shadowy corners, and the memory of his brother's ghastly expression, he was safe in his own longhouse. The rain was a light pitter-patter on his roof, and the only grasp that snared him was the loving, tender hands of his fair princess.

He sighed in tremendous relief, thankful that it was all in his mind.

"You're shaking. Are you all right?"

Dægan smiled and kissed her forehead. "Aye, love. 'Twas only a bad dream."

She comforted him with a tight hug around his neck. "Want to tell me about it?"

"Indeed not," he dismissed quickly. He held her close and smelled the clean scent of her hair, finding reassurance in the familiar warmth of her arms. "'Twas nonsense, I assure you. Go back to sleep."

Pushing her gently down to his bed, Dægan curled up beside her. He reflected for a long time on the events of his nightmare, recalling the broken silence from the harrowing laughter within the barn walls.

"Does your god laugh at me?" he finally asked.

Mara spun within his arms and touched his face. "Why do you ask this?"

"I thought perhaps he laughs at anyone who drowns in his own misery."

Mara looked at him sympathetically. "If anything, m'lord, He cries for you."

"Cries for me?" Dægan asked, doubtful.

"Aye, He does. You're but a lost sheep," she explained, "wandering alone in the night, and He, as the shepherd, will search for you until He finds you because He knows of the wolves on your heels. But never does He laugh at you."

Dægan brushed the back of his knuckles against her cheek. He found her words too good to be true, for in all his life, he'd never known a god to be compassionate or gracious. His gods' happiness oftentimes lay in someone else's tragedy, and that was something he was growing quite weary of, not to mention the absurd thought of pleasing his gods with a brutal death. Surely there was a better way to die, and a greater reason to live. Looking into Mara's eyes was where he seemed to always find it.

He tugged her closer, then mused over the comparison she'd made of him with docile barnyard animals. "I'm a sheep, you say. Truly?"

She gazed up at him and kissed him good night. "Truly, m'lord."

****

The next morning, the same threatening clouds

remained from the night before. Luckily, the wind was swift enough to make a difference elsewhere, for it carried Ottarr and Vegard's ship from Galway's impressive walled city port with impeccable speed. By high noon, Dægan's men had emptied the soil and seaweed and transported the fill to the open burial site on the east side of the isle.

The rites began soon after and without incident. Every one of Dægan's people attended, save Mara. She declined to be the presence of bitter reality, and instead, tended to Dægan's sick mother, which allowed Gudrun to attend the ceremony.

By early evening, Eirik was laid to rest in his ship, with the stem and sternposts cut off and buried with him. A perimeter of large stones depicted its shape and boasted a burial fit for a king. Pride was the strength in Dægan's arms as he dropped the last stone in place.

Some men and women lingered at the sight, telling boastful stories of their fallen comrade while others stayed to hear and pass on any gossip related to him. Of those slow to leave, Dægan was the last, trying to find the initiative to see his mother. She wasn't of conscious mind to give him a piece of hers when he'd enter, but he dreaded it all the same as her silence added more guilt to the weight on his shoulders.

Knowing he needed to face her sometime, he lumbered toward her longhouse with every intention of rousing her from her sleep. Variably, it became Dægan's motivation to get to her as soon as possible. In no time, he slipped through her door as quietly as he could and stood at the foot of her boxbed.

Mara was stoking the fire when he'd entered, and she stared at him as if she expected him to say something. Instead, he planted his hands on his hips and calmly summoned her with a jerk of his head. He then whispered, "I wish to have a moment alone with my mother. When you leave, see that you do so quietly. Understand?"

Mara obliged, stopping only to run a sympathetic hand down his arm before she left. He barely felt it as he eyed his crafty mother lying in the very wool she'd drawn over everyone else's eyes.

For a long time, he watched her, hoping she'd soon grow tired of lying still or even forget that he was in the room and move slightly. But she was smarter than that, or mayhap, even more stubborn than he.

Trying something different, he captured the nearest chair and dragged it to her bedside, straddling it with his forehead resting on the back. He stared at the matted floor at his feet and attempted to revive her with emotion. "Mother," he said bleakly. "'Tis done. Eirik is laid to rest. I buried him in a ship. Just as you had done with Father. A ship of equal size."

Dægan hoped she'd stir, but his wish went unanswered. Perhaps she wasn't faking. He tried again. "Mother, I know you're disappointed in me. My heart aches to know I'm the cause of Eirik's death, and to think I could very well be the cause of yours too is killing me by degrees. Damnation, open your eyes! Open your eyes and tell me you forgive me. Or tell me you hate me, I care not. I just need to hear your voice and know you're all right. As much as I want your forgiveness, I need your mercy."

Dægan's tears fell to the floor, and in the long silence that followed, he watched them evaporate from the warm heat of the fire close by. He had tried to bring her to, and even felt a bit guilty for the words he'd chosen, but he failed. So what was he to do now? Pray?

Pray to whom? The gods she believed in, or the God he was learning about?

A hand touched Dægan's knee, and he saw the frail fingers of his mother. He lifted his head from the chair and eagerly warmed her hand in his own. "Mother."

She looked relieved and accepted his touch. "I don't hate you, nor do I blame you, Dægan. You're my son. The last one left. You have all my love. All of it. Always."

****

The following evening, Nevan set out to find Dægan, going instinctively to the cliffs near his ringfort. As expected, the warrior chieftain was there, staring blankly at the crimson sunset. He rode casually up beside Dægan and measured him as he let his horse graze. When Dægan didn't acknowledge even that, Nevan finally spoke. "What is this I hear, you're leaving in a few days?"

"I am."

Nevan nodded in thought, eyeing the full battle gear Dægan wore. "One can only assume the worst when all the iron on this isle has been purchased by *your* blacksmiths, and every available man is being suited for armor. Tell me I shouldn't worry."

"You shouldn't worry," Dægan repeated serenely.

"I'm not a fool, Dægan."

"I never said you were."

Nevan sighed. He knew Dægan's mood all too well. On many occasions in the past, he'd found the Northman in the same spot, with the same reflective stare and morose tone. If Nevan wanted to have a worthwhile conversation, this was surely not going to be the day.

Dismounting, he looked out into the distance, just as

Dægan was doing, trying to see what held the Northman's attention. The only thing he saw was the evening sky and the calmness of the vast ocean, the same things as yesterday and the day before that.

"Why do you come here?" Nevan asked.

Dægan remained silent for a time as if contemplating the king's question. "This place is the closest thing I have to home. The sea. This cliff. The smell of the mist in the air. It reminds me of the fjords in Hladir."

Nevan watched Dægan close his eyes and take a deep breath. "I thought your home was in turmoil."

"My home *was* in turmoil. But the land itself was not. Have you ever noticed that trees do not fight against the very ground that holds them? And the rocks of the mountains do not crumble to the rising rivers below. Only men do that. Only men fight for things beyond their power. We place men on higher ground because of the number of battles they've won or the number of silver coins in their pockets. When in fact, greatness comes from things we cannot hold in our greedy hands. Things that are beyond our destructive reach. Like this place. The sun will always set right there," Dægan said, pointing. "And the water will always meet the sun without resistance or suspicion. Neither the sun nor the water expects more from each other. And neither gives more than what is possible. And the fact that they have done this, each and every night since the dawn of time…that is greatness."

Nevan narrowed his gaze and looked at the setting sun almost fully submerged in its watery bed. "Ah, the sun and water are the best of unlikely allies, but the sun sets in the west because it has been told to. And the water welcomes the sun because it too has been instructed. Obedience is not as great as the command, Dægan. Anyone can obey. And every great man has followed one command or another in his life. But 'tis where the command comes from, that determines just how great he'll be, should he listen—like the sun and the water."

Dægan removed his helmet and held it under his arm. "Who commands you, Nevan?"

"The only one who has determined my birth years ago, and whose greatness will hopefully slow the years to my death."

Dægan thought hard on the reference that Nevan made of his Christian god. He valued the faith Nevan had—and the faith Mara had—for it was certainly what he longed for. An unwavering faith that a god would look upon you, instead of down on you. A god who would protect instead of condemn, and lead instead of forsake. "How do you know if he's giving you a command?"

Nevan tossed a surprised look to Dægan. "God speaks to men in different ways. Perhaps through the perils of a mighty storm or a dream. Or like this sunset, which has caught your eye on many nights. I cannot tell you how God will choose to speak to you. But the best place to hear Him," Nevan said, poking Dægan's armored chest, "is in here."

Twice now, Dægan had been enlightened of the possibility of God beckoning him, and he had to know more. He needed to know all he could of this great opportunity. "Would he really be calling to me?"

"God speaks to everyone. But not everyone hears."

"What would make a man..." Dægan chose his words carefully. Calling their god by name felt inappropriate, but he said it anyway. "What would make a man suddenly hear God?"

Nevan smiled and held his hand out toward the sunken sun and the vibrant colorful sky surrounding it. "Greatness, my friend."

****

Two rows of torches lined the path from the tall wooden gates of Nevan's stone fort to the raised platform inside the spacious bailey. The altar was beautifully decorated with island flowers, a large wooden crucifix, and four panels of flowing white cloths made of the finest linen.

Everyone, Irish and Scandinavian alike, gathered to witness the unorthodox wedding of the Northern chieftain to the Irish princess. Some congregated in small groups in the back, quietly making wagers that the chieftain wouldn't show to collaborate in the union. With their swords and dirks at their sides, the islanders anticipated their cause for rebellion would soon be a reality.

A horse approached from outside the fort, and a man in a full-length cloak dismounted. The light of the torches brightened his face to that of the Irish king, and a murmur of hushed voices erupted over the crowd.

Nevan took his place in front of the altar, standing on the left to represent the Gaels of the alliance. Tait sidestepped across the aisle and approached the king, whispering in his ear, "Where is Dægan?"

"Watching the sun set."

Tait sighed. "Again? He thinks too much."

"Perhaps you think too little. He'll be here, Tait. Worry not."

"Should I hurry him along?"

Nevan eyed the impatience of his people and their suspicious whispers. "I'm afraid that's what my people are waiting for. Besides, I think Mara needs more company than Dægan at this moment."

Tait glanced at Mara and noticed the nervous expression on her face. "What should I tell her?"

"Tell her Dægan is coming," Nevan insisted.

Suddenly, a horse came to a halt at the entrance of the fort and every head turned in surprise, finding Dægan walking up the aisle, his father's great sword at his side.

He was smiling, Nevan noticed, and staring straight at Mara. Nevan and Tait finally breathed a little easier.

****

The only thing Dægan heard was the priest, who started the Christian ceremony by saying, "*In nomine Patris, et Filii, et Spiritus Sancti, Amen.*" After that, he was lost in his own world, staring at the most beautiful woman he'd ever seen. Her hair was let down from the usual braid, cascading in ringlet curls from a crown of island flowers. Her dress was a fine gown of simple white cotton, plunging low at the neckline. Her forehead, once stricken by bruises and cuts, was now healed, and her face shone like polished ivory, her lips the color of summer roses.

Dægan tried to concentrate on the ceremony itself and took a deep breath to calm his wondering mind, but that only made it worse. He could now smell her as remarkably as if she were right in his arms.

Again, he tried to listen to the priest's words. The cursed Latin gibberish. Nothing.

Not a single word did Dægan understand, or

recognize, for that matter. He wasn't even convinced he was getting married. For all he knew, he'd been condemned to the gallows and the priest was saying his last rites before he'd be dropped to his death.

Nay, I am getting married. Certainly, Mara wouldn't be smiling if a hanging were in his course. Her eyes danced and twinkled in the firelight, a shade of darker green this night. He concluded, after much consideration, that by reflecting the gold flames of the many torches, they adopted an air of seduction, shining like crystal jade through the dark of the night.

Looking at her gave him the strength and the will to be a better man. A man who had a reason to cast aside his many demons so as to stand worthy of her. She made him believe that peace wasn't just a hard wave to row, but a destination. A place where love comes as easily as the sunlight falling on one's face.

It was in her eyes at that moment when he saw his children—*many children.* An image he'd never thought of before, but how proud he felt to know that Mara would be the woman to birth them. All of them. *Five,* he thought. *No, six!* All of them strapping boys. *Well, maybe one girl,* he reconsidered.

Suddenly, Mara reached out to him and took his hands in hers, interrupting his thoughts of future family plans. He looked down at her hands so small, tucked within his. They felt good and right, just like everything else when she was in his arms. It was as if everything at this moment was where it should be, and rest of the world, for all he cared, could fall apart at his feet.

For a fleeting moment, he was utterly content. He'd forgotten all about the suspicious Irish watching him, or

Mara's father he'd yet to make amends with. There was nothing in his thoughts right now but his bride. She was one thing good in his life. The one thing in his world that didn't need another man's binding word or the strength of a sword arm to keep.

Lady Mara was finally his, and it was so.

Chapter Twenty-one

Mara was as content as she could be. Her husband lay naked beside her, his arm tightly woven around her body as her head lay on his chest. The rhythmic thumping of his heart was a trancelike drumming in her ears. The fire crackled in the hearth and the quiet whisper of his breathing added to the peaceful song of the room. There was no place she'd rather be.

She strummed her fingers across his chest and sighed. "I don't want this night to end."

Dægan kissed the top of her head. "Nor I. Especially now that Lillemor is staying with Mother. I can have you and my bed all to myself, as it should be."

His jest didn't erase the concerns she had in the back of her mind. "What scares me is as each day passes, it brings your reinforcements that much closer to landing here, and that only means—"

"Shh..." Dægan consoled. "'Twill be all right. You shouldn't fear men simply talking."

"If 'twere truly just simple talk, you'd not need five hundred men."

"Those men are for *your* protection, not mine."

Mara adjusted herself in his arms, short of climbing atop. "You can lie all you want. But I know why those men are coming."

Dægan reached up for the strand of hair tickling his chest and idly twisted it about. "Do you believe in fate,

Mara?"

"Not really.

"Well then, you may not believe the story I have to tell."

Mara couldn't help but be interested. "I could open my mind a bit," she jested. "Although I cannot imagine you proving the existence of fate as well as you did a round earth."

Dægan smiled. "Opening your mind would be helpful, but if you can read, 'twould be better."

"I can read a little, I suppose."

"Good," Dægan said with excitement in his voice. He rolled out of bed and pulled back the mats on his dirt-packed floor, exposing a hidden trapdoor beneath.

"No one knows of this space, Mara, save you. I built this after my longhouse was erected, so I could dig a hole in the floor without anyone knowing. 'Twas what my father did to protect this book, and it proved to be the best way of keeping it a secret."

"Why would a book need be kept in secret?"

"Because of its value," Dægan said. "In sentiment as well as its weight in silver." He reached low inside the dark hole and pulled up an old leather satchel weathered by time. He held it as though it were a fragile newborn babe and blew the dust from its top. "This, love, is what saved my family years ago—twice even."

"Saved your family from what?"

Dægan carried it over to the edge of the boxbed and sat down, staring at its sacred packaging. "From starvation."

Mara sat up straighter. "How does a book keep anyone from starving?"

"Before I tell you how, you should first know that I

used to have another brother. A twin brother named Domaldr."

Those words struck Mara oddly. "Why would you not tell me this before?"

"Because as far as I'm concerned, he doesn't exist to me anymore. He betrayed my father in the worst way and left his own family to die."

"Your own brother? What did he do?"

"What did he *not* do? All his life, he harbored a jealous heart within him, always resenting his family for one reason or another. Despite that Gustaf was the natural seaman and most likely to gain father's inheritance, we were all treated the same. Father wanted his wealth spread evenly amongst his sons, for he was a man of fairness and generosity. We all loved the sea as Father did, going out on explorations as often as he'd let us, except Domaldr. He loved only himself. He truly believed he deserved a better life, a life where his name would precede him, a life where his pockets would spill over and pave the ground in silver before his feet stepped forth. Mother loved him in spite of his envy, and said he'd soon grow out of it. But after sixteen summers, he proved her wrong.

"Father had come home from a long journey that kept him away for nearly three months, and he and his men were exhausted from fighting many treacherous storms. My father ordered the men to leave the *knarr* at its dock fully loaded so they could get a good night's rest and empty it at dawn. Fortunately, Father carried an armful of valuables from his vessel to show us before we took to our beds: a silver brooch for Mother, this book, and the sword I now carry at my side. Father loved that sword. We all did. He let us take turns slicing it into the wind. But not Domaldr. He took one look at its worth and ran from the house in a childish rage. Father thought it was best to let him go. Little did we know he'd bribed a few of his friends into helping him steal the *knarr* with all its contents.

"That night, as we all slept, Domaldr stole away with every piece of fur, every bundle of wool, every crate of spice, and all Father's silver. Everything gone. And 'twasn't as though Father could get more, for you see 'twas the last journey of the year. Winter was quickly approaching, and to go on another voyage would have been madness. Domaldr had made a fortune in one night and we all suffered dearly for his greed. That winter was the hardest we'd ever had. My father sold many cattle and sheep to gain his footing on his losses, and rationed the rest amongst his people for wool and meat. The cold northern winds were harsh, killing the last of the animals just when we needed them most. Some of our people died too, despite my father's effort. There was a mother with a babe still in her womb and several of the elderly. We even buried Vegard's wife." Dægan paused respectfully. "We buried far too many that year. And by the end of the season, food was so scarce, we had soon grown accustomed to the taste of tree bark."

"I cannot believe your brother would do such a thing. And you never heard from him again?"

"Nay. 'Tis been eighteen years since I've seen him, and I doubt he survived much more than a year before someone else, not obligated by kinship, took to slitting his throat in vengeance."

"So please, tell me. How did you all survive?"

Dægan enjoyed seeing Mara's keen interest in the story and continued. "One day, my father awoke to a warm, sunny morning. He looked out over the fjords and the ice on the sea was beginning to melt, far sooner than usual. To father, 'twas a sign. And fortunately for all of us, he took a chance. He ventured out onto the crusted sea, braving freezing winds and floating ice. He journeyed alone in a small fishing boat around the entire southern perimeter of Norway until he could sail northeast toward Gokstad. There, he traded his last possession: this book."

"He traded it?" Mara asked. "To whom?"

"A holy man. My father had heard of his conversion to your Christian religion and knew he was probably the only one who would know its worth."

"Did he?"

"And then some. My father came back with a new crew of men, a bigger boat, and enough food and wool for three winters."

"One book did all that?"

"Ah, but 'tis not just any book, love," Dægan said, scooting closer. "This book is said to have survived both a downpour of rain and a watery grave in the Lough Ree, yet its pages remain as dry as the day it was written."

"And you believe that?"

"I should be asking why you don't. 'Twas your Saint Ciarán who first possessed the book. If I remember correctly, the story goes that he was sitting on a bench outside the monastery of Clonmacnoise reading from this very book, when visitors came. Like a good host, he fed and gave rooms to his traveling friends and forgot all about the open book he'd left on the bench. That night, it rained like never before, but in the morning when he rushed out to retrieve the book he thought ruined, all the pages were dry, even the place in the grass beneath the bench where the book had lain."

"You and your stories, Dægan."

"Do you not like them?"

"I do, but you're so well versed in telling them that 'tis hard to differentiate *tales* from the *truth*."

"Fine. I shall stop."

"You cannot stop now. What about the watery grave you spoke of?" Mara asked skeptically.

"'Tis also said that this man was on a boat on the Lough Ree with many other dedicated followers. The book was still in its satchel, but one of the monks was careless and dropped it over the side of the boat, where it sank to the bottom of the gray lake. To Ciarán's disappointment, he left the water that day empty-handed. Time passed, and one afternoon, the cattle, being hot from the summer sun, waded in the cool water of the Lough Ree. As one of the cows came out, the satchel was tangled around its leg. When Ciarán saw this, he rushed toward the cow and unhooked it, finding the book untouched by the water."

Mara gave Dægan a sideways glance. "As a child, my mother told me that story, but I thought 'twas just a good fireside tale. Surely that couldn't really have happened."

"How is it that you doubt the existence of a magical book, but not of your Christ rising from the dead after three days?"

"Because Christ's rising was called forth by God Himself. With all due respect, Dægan, this book is just legend, and your father was fortunate enough that someone believed in that foolishness."

"Foolishness, aye?"

"I'm afraid so," Mara said, nodding.

"Then open it."

Mara scoffed. "Well, of course it shall be dry. You had

it stored beneath your floor for many years. My opening it after all this time will prove nothing."

"Open it," Dægan said again. "If you can read, then open it."

Mara sighed and took the satchel from his hands, laying it in her lap. He watched her, knowing the smell of aged leather filled her nostrils, as did the faint smell of rain. She paused, taking in another breath, and furrowed her brow.

Dægan's grin smeared to one side. "Cannot imagine why anyone would smell rain on a starry night like tonight."

"I never said that I smelled rain."

"You didn't have to. I know you smell it. Everyone does when they hold the book."

Mara ripped open the satchel and pulled it out. "You must be out of your mind, Dægan. I—I..." Her mouth dropped slightly. "I do smell rain."

"Now open it," Dægan commanded.

She flipped through the pages quickly and found that every page was dry, unsmeared, and perfectly legible. She read a few lines from the middle of the page. "This is a book of the Gospels, Dægan."

"And aren't the Gospels written about your Christ, whose rising was called forth by the hand of God Himself?"

"Aye," Mara said, trying to swallow it all.

"Then tell me why 'tis easier to believe Christ can rise from the dead than his own life's story withstanding a little water?"

Mara couldn't answer. She sat there searching the book for just one mark, one slight stain of lake water, one smudge between words. Her efforts grew in frustration as she flipped faster through the thin, vellum-like pages.

Dægan placed a firm hand upon her wrist. "I've already searched with a thorough eye. You'll not find one blemish upon any of the pages."

"How can that be? Are you certain this is Ciarán's Gospels?"

"All I know is that this book saved my family years ago. Whether this book is truly imperishable, I know not. I've not the nerve to try to destroy it solely for the sake of spite."

"But if your father traded it, then how did *you* get it back?"

Dægan lifted his finger. "Another great story, if I may. My father and brother, Gustaf, were killed some two years later, and I knew we had to leave Hladir soon. Their deaths may have saved many men from going to war, but I wasn't about to pay taxes to support the man who had them killed, nor did I want to bring about my own death. I hadn't enough resources to pack up and leave, because favor with my father had grown in multitudes, which in turn nearly doubled the size of our clan. But I promised our people we would all leave, or no one would.

"One fateful autumn morning, I woke up to a sunny sky. I looked out over the fjords just as my father had two years before, and like him, I took it as a sign. I gathered a few men and left to find the book. I know not why, but I swear I heard my father's voice call to me from across the sea.

"I first went to Gokstad to find the holy man with whom Father had traded. But after questioning the locals, they told me he'd been killed in his sleep because some didn't like his preaching around the ports. I was fortuitous in meeting his daughter, for she told me she knew of the book, but had sold it cheaply to buy food for her bastard son. After finding the man who had bought it from her, and another who stole it from him, and another, and another, and so forth—my journey took me to the Isle of Man.

"When we arrived on the shore, I had realized that a battle was being fought and we were literally caught in the middle. Before we could retreat, several arrows darted passed me and struck the hull, setting it afire."

Mara eyes grew wide. "What did you do?"

"I did what any sane chieftain would do—I commanded we abandon ship and run for our lives to the nearest shelter. We hid inside. Unfortunately, it too was set afire. I waited as long as I could, and just before passing out, I crawled from the burning hut and collapsed. When I awoke, everything was burnt to the ground including my only means of getting off the isle."

"And those who came with you?"

He shook his head.

"What then?"

"I believe I sat for a while on the shore, cursing everything I could. I think I even cursed my father. But night came quickly, and so did my desperation. By morning, I had pulled every salvageable piece of wood from the smoking fires and began to reconstruct a seaworthy raft, albeit very crude with what I had to work with. As I went back in search for one last piece of wood, I caught sight of a leather strap sticking out from under the ashes. My first thought was that 'twould make a fine rope if cut in thin strips, but then I remembered my purpose for going to the isle. And wouldn't you know, it was the satchel's strap. I found the book just as I had remembered it, and how you're seeing it now."

Mara seemed to forget all about the amazing compilation of Gospels. "So? Come, come, tell me," she said impatiently. "How did you get off the island?"

Dægan laughed. "Did you not hear me? I pulled the book from the fire. 'Twas unharmed, just as you see it now."

"I heard you. But how did you ever return home?"

"All right," Dægan said, adjusting himself on the bed. "But I warn you, 'tis not as exciting as the book in the fire. I set back to work on my boat, and within four days, I sailed west for Dubh-Linn. I bought a horse there—the one I have now—and rode to Hlymrekr. From there, I bargained with a young widow I knew who still owned her late husband's *langskip*."

Mara narrowed her eyes at him. "With what?"

Dægan rubbed his chin between his thumb and fingers, sizing Mara up for the answer. "Don't be quick to judge. It had been eight long years since her husband had died, and she was quite lonely."

Mara smacked him across the arm. "Dægan, you didn't."

"I had to get home to my family."

"And you couldn't give the woman your horse?"

"I liked the horse."

Mara scoffed. "Evidently more than your self-respect."

"You asked," Dægan said as he reclined across the boxbed and lugged her on top of him. "I was perfectly content to end the story with the unburned book."

Dægan tried to kiss her, but she resisted for as long as she could until he tickled her. She giggled, then said, "You think you're quite the nobleman."

Dægan rolled over, catching her head in his palm.

"More importantly, what do *you* think of me?"

Mara measured him. "I think you need new stories to tell."

"Is that so?"

"Aye, 'tis."

Dægan successfully kissed her this time and cradled her against him. "Then would you be so kind as to help me make up new tales? You know...the kind I should never tell my children."

A smile crept across Mara's lips. "Your children? And what makes you think you'll have any?"

Dægan nudged her knees apart and settled himself between her thighs. "Perhaps, you're right. We should try again."

Chapter Twenty-two

"Dægan! Ships are approaching!" Tait's voice called through the front door of Dægan's longhouse.

No answer.

Tait pounded on the door. "Dægan! Do you hear me? Ships, m'lord!"

"Aye, I hear you," Dægan groaned from his bed. "I suspect they're my mercenaries, Tait. Grant them permission to come ashore, and I'll meet you soon enough."

"They're not your mercenaries. These ships come from the south. Four ships, red and white sails."

Dægan sat up in a jolt, repeating Tait's words. "Four ships, red and white sails....four ships, red and white sails... Mara, get up!" Dægan scrambled from his chamber almost tripping over his own feet. "Tait?"

"Still here, m'lord."

"Get my horse ready. Now!"

"Already thought of that. I even have one for Mara."

"Dægan, what are you shouting about?" Mara asked. She watched him slip his clothes over his head and his boots to his heels.

"Get up, Mara. Ships approach, and we haven't much time before they're here."

"Who will be here?"

"Those men. Those Northmen from the Shannon. Get up and get dressed!"

Dægan dressed himself in his shirt of mail and then slapped his armor to his chest. "You must ride with me to the cliffs. If 'tis truly them, you'll stay at Nevan's fort."

"And what of you?" Mara asked, her panic rising as she threw her tunic over her head and shoved her arms into the sleeves.

"I'll protect the fort," Dægan said matter-of-factly.

Mara ran into his arms and gripped his neck. "Who will protect you?"

Dægan beat the armor upon his chest twice and pushed her away in a hurry to get his sword.

"That's it? Your armor?"

Dægan grabbed his belt with his scabbard and secured it at his hip. "What do you want me to say, woman? I'm the chieftain on this isle."

"But you're without enough men. You'll be outnumbered more than twice."

"What else am I supposed to do?" Dægan asked. "This is my home, and you're my wife. I'll protect both, with or without men."

"Dægan," Tait called again. "We're losing time."

Dægan grabbed Mara's wrist, rushed past the hearth, and burst through his front door, dragging her behind him. He lifted her to her horse and mounted his with lightning speed, leading the way to the south side of the isle. The three rode as quickly as their horses could carry them, through the settlement and past the long, rock-lined pastures to the lookout point upon the cliffs.

Mara's heart thumped in her chest, matching the speed of her horse's hooves. She kept her eyes forward, never drifting from Dægan's big black beast charging across the field of wildflowers. It almost felt like the day she first met him, their horses running, their hair whipping, their thoughts wildly on each other. But this time, she chased him. Her husband. Her very own heathen warrior and protector. There was no second-guessing, no questioning, no doubt. She'd follow him anywhere.

After a long run, the cliff's edge and the ocean's blanket of blue came into view. Dægan yanked his horse to a stop and slid from its back, then ran to the island's rocky rim. Tait did the same. The two halted and stared at the four oncoming ships.

Mara watched Dægan's shoulders rise and fall with his rapid intake of breath. His hands came to his hips and his head dropped to his chest. He didn't have to say a word. Mara knew that what Dægan feared the worst, was about to happen—was about to land on his shores.

She remained on her horse, reverently quiet.

Dægan, however, cursed and kicked at the ground, clenching his fists into tight balls of rage. His horse sidestepped to distance itself from Dægan's fit, but remained within arm's reach. Dægan closed his eyes and leaned face-first against his loyal steed, mumbling to himself.

Tait finally spoke. "Are you sure these are the same men, Dægan?"

"Aye."

Tait glanced back at Mara before speaking again. "What do you think they want?"

Dægan looked up but didn't answer. He didn't want to answer. The very thought made him sick, made him sweat with fear. He walked away from Tait and came to Mara, her horse nervous from his presence.

Dægan patted its neck and put his other hand on Mara's knee. "Forgive me, Mara. I thought you'd be safe here. I never thought—"

"I know, Dægan," Mara comforted, brushing his hair from his brow. "I don't think anyone could've known."

"I'll not let them get to you," Dægan promised, leaning his forehead against her leg. "I won't."

"They outnumber you."

"Worry not about me," Dægan dismissed.

Mara lifted his face. "How can I not? I love you."

Nevan came galloping from the right of the field, dressed rightfully in his hauberk and armor as well. Dægan sighed and looked at Mara, catching a glimpse of a single fallen tear. He caught it with his thumb and wiped it away. "Cry not for me. I've archers and higher ground. Most will not make it off their ships."

Mara's voice cracked. "And those who do?"

He spoke with conviction. "They'll wish they never did."

"Dægan," Nevan probed as he circled his horse around them. "What is this? My people are frantic. My men are upset! I hope you've better news than what your face tells me."

Dægan briefly turned his back on the king to remount his horse. "I've not the words you'd like to hear, Nevan. Tait, get every woman and child to the fort. No one comes out until I say so. I need every available man and servant fully dressed for battle and in lines thirteen paces from the shore. Archers in the rear, cavalry in the front."

Tait nodded and lifted himself on his horse, but

Dægan trotted near him, grabbing his armor by the shoulder plate. "You see that my mother and Lillemor get to the fort. They're both stubborn females, and 'twill not offend me if you drag them by their hair. See that they get there. I'll meet you at the beach. Now go."

Nevan watched Tait leave before he found his tongue again. "Who are these men, Dægan? What do they want?"

Dægan ignored the king again and trotted over toward Mara. "Go with Nevan to the fort, and under no circumstances do you leave. Do you understand me? No matter what you see, or what you hear. You stay with Nevan. Only I will send for you. No one else. Do you hear me?"

"Aye," Mara said reluctantly.

"No one but me. Say it," Dægan demanded.

"No one but you."

Dægan leaned across her horse and pulled her into a hard kiss. "Only me," he reminded her. He then jerked his horse to the left and faced the surprisingly patient king. "Nevan, I ask that you take my wife to your fort and keep her in your sight. Let no one in. No matter what."

Nevan grew frustrated as orders were directed at him. "I thought you said your troubles remained in Limerick, Dægan."

"You think I want this? You think I want a war?"

"I know not what you want!" Nevan yelled back. "You never speak to me. You never give me more than the vaguest of your thoughts. Damnation, Dægan, I'm your friend. We go too far back not to be. For years we've shared this isle. But never together. We could be so much more, if you'd let it. If you'd just trust me. Can you not look into my eyes and see my loyalty?"

Dægan clenched his jaw. He didn't have time for this.

At this moment, he couldn't care less about what kind of relationship he had with the Irish king. All he wanted was to rid these intruders from his shores, to end this threat once and for all, and if that meant killing every last one of them, then so be it. If he didn't, he feared they would be like rabid dogs coming back without cause or reason, again and again.

"I've not the time to mend your bleeding heart, Nevan."

Nevan sat still, taken aback by Dægan's sarcasm. "With all that I've given to you through blind trust, you dare insult me. You dare treat me like an enemy. I never thought it would ever come to this. To knowing, like a slap in the face, that the one person I hold in high regard thinks naught more of me than the dirt on his own heel. Nonetheless, I'll protect your bride with my life. May God keep you safe."

At that, Nevan turned his horse with a jerk and approached Mara, designating with his hand the way toward his ancient fort.

Dægan rode up quickly and embraced her one last time. "Go, love. Go with him."

"But Dægan—"

"Don't do this," he whispered in her ear. "Be strong. I need you to be strong. I cannot think of your pain right now. Please, do not do this to me."

Mara sucked in a breath of strength and nodded.

"I love you," Dægan whispered and kissed her again. "Now go."

Dægan felt the heat of Nevan's stare and returned the gaze with just as much intensity. He didn't mean to be rash with Nevan, but it just came out. An apology right now would seem almost insincere, and Dægan held his regret in check, hoping he'd be given a chance to reconcile with the loyal king. "Do not forget what I told you, Nevan. Only I will come for her."

Nevan never blinked, never nodded, never spoke. He just trotted away with Mara close behind.

Dægan felt his mistake as heavy as a thousand coats of mail on his back. He cursed and fled toward the shoreline.

****

Tait, Steinar, Dægan, and his army of a hundred sat abreast from each other, waiting silently in their saddles, spears and shields in hand. The only sounds Dægan and his men could hear were the distant chants of the seamen rowing their hardest and the ocean waves lapping before them.

"How many are there, Dægan?" Tait asked.

"Two hundred, perhaps." Dægan assumed his words settled like thorns in Tait's breeches, for he saw his friend shift in his saddle.

"Is it too soon to ask for your orders?"

Dægan cleared his throat. "I've only one. Let no man step foot on this isle."

Steinar looked at Tait with an unquestionable sneer of satisfaction. "Simple enough, is it not?"

Tait shook his head, knowing Steinar was probably aroused with the notion of a bloodthirsty fight. "You enjoy battle way too much, my friend."

Dægan ignored Steinar's raw laughter and raised his hand in the air, commanding the archers behind him to make ready and take aim. The sound of stretching horsehair, drawn to its limits, was a noise that unnerved him above all else, for he knew in time that with an irreversible drop of his hand, the calm shores of his home would be quiet no more, and the shouts and screams of pain and death would soon fill his ears.

Oh, how he hated that sound, that unsettling shriek of agony and desperation. And his hand would be the very start of it all. He alone had the power to commence the misery, or suspend it. But something told Dægan to keep his hand in the air. To hold havoc at bay just a bit longer.

"What are you waiting for?" Tait asked. "The ships will soon be too close for the archers. Give the word now."

"Not yet."

"If you wait much longer, our archers will be useless."

"Just a little longer," Dægan murmured.

"What are you doing? Give the word!"

Suddenly, Dægan heard his name called from the closest ship, faint at first, then stronger with each shout. He craned his neck and jutted his ear forward, determining that the voice belonged to a woman. Astonished that anyone aboard those ships knew him at all, he squinted at the person waving her arms in crazy desperation at the prow.

Tait grabbed Dægan's wrist and tried to force him to give the command to the many archers in position. Dægan gave Tait a fierce look. "Someone aboard is calling me by name."

"So…"

"'Tis a woman, you oaf!"

Tait's eyes widened as he caught sight of a woman's golden hair blowing in the wind. The woman called again, this time, for him. "Thordia," Tait exhaled in a panic. "They have my Thordia."

Dægan quickly signaled the archers to lower their

weapons as he dismounted from his horse. "Stay," he ordered Tait. "Hold your position and wait for my signal."

Tait squirmed in his saddle and gripped his bow. A bead of sweat trickled from his temple. He was likely going out of his mind wondering what they'd done to Thordia.

Dægan reconsidered. "Fine, you can come with me. But don't make me regret this."

Tait practically fell from his horse as he dismounted. "I'll kill them if they've touched her."

"Easy, Tait. This is an obvious trap. Keep your wits about you."

Dægan looked over his shoulder at the lines of brave men staring back at him. They seemed more eager now, more ready to make a stand. He was pleased. "Steinar, keep the archers at bay. Once Thordia is safe, I may give the signal. Be ready."

Steinar growled from behind his wooden shield, anxious to start the fight. "Aye, just say the word, Dægan. Just say the word."

Dægan turned and caught up with Tait, who was already at the water's edge. Waves lapped at their ankles as one ship ran aground, full of men armed to the teeth. A large smile marked Thordia's face as she saw Tait wading in the water for her.

"Stop," Dægan said, drawing him back. "Let her come to you." By his judgment, Thordia was fully clothed, her dress unmarked or torn, and her face was clean and bright, not a woman who'd withstood a forceful taking. "Are you hurt, Thordia?" he asked anyway.

"Of course not, Dægan. Why would I be—"

"Then step off the boat."

She looked over the side at the water. "Are you not going to help me?"

"Get off the ship!" Dægan ordered again.

"Do as he says, Thordia," Tait insisted, his face as straight as pounded iron.

A man stepped up from behind Thordia and put his hand on her shoulder. "We've quite a welcome here. Perhaps you should wait until 'tis safer, Thordia."

"Take your hands off her!" Tait barked as he drew his sword.

Dægan threw his arm across Tait's chest.

"I'll kill him," Tait protested.

"Do you want Thordia alive or dead?"

"What do *you* think?"

Dægan grabbed Tait by his chest armor and hauled him aside. "Then hold your bloody tongue. One more outburst from you, and I'll have you dragged from this shore. You understand me? Hold your tongue." He slowly released Tait when he'd clearly submitted and glared back at the man who no doubt enjoyed the little commotion. "What is your name?"

"His name is Soren," came a familiar voice from somewhere on the ship.

When the man who spoke stepped forward, Dægan could hardly believe his eyes. There in front of him stood his twin brother, Domaldr. He'd thought him dead, almost wished it on several occasions, and wondered how someone hadn't killed him by now. As kindly as Dægan could force it, he said, "Hello, brother. 'Tis good to see you."

Domaldr joined Soren and Thordia at the bow. "I never thought I'd ever hear those words from you, Dægan."

"All right, Domaldr. Enough with the games. Let the

girl go."

"You first."

"What are you talking about?"

"Your archers. Make them put their weapons down, and you can have the girl."

Dægan peered over his shoulder at his archers' positions. "They are lowered."

"I said down, on the ground, not lowered. I'm well aware of how little time it takes for you to give an order and for me to be impaled." Domaldr jerked a dagger under Thordia's chin and held her close against his chest. "On the ground, or she dies."

Dægan immediately yelled to his men, and the archers set their bows on the ground. Domaldr held his position until the distant clatter of wood ceased. Like a heartless snake, he retracted his dagger and kissed Thordia's slim white neck. "There you go, dear. Your Tait awaits you."

Dægan half expected Tait to climb aboard and slash Domaldr's throat. At this point, he wouldn't have blamed Tait, nor did he even think he could stop him if he tried. But Tait waited for his Thordia to jump from the side of the ship before running to her. He wrapped his arms around her and shielded her with his own body, dragging her to the safety of Dægan's men.

Dægan glowered at his twin. "What do you want?"

"Only to see my long-lost brother," Domaldr said warmly.

"I know better," Dægan disputed. "You want something more. You always do."

Domaldr tried descending from the ship, but Dægan drew his sword. "I think not."

Domaldr lifted his leg back inside the hull. "A little harsh, are we not? I've come to see you, and this is the welcome I get? A sword pointed at my gullet?"

"Your presence is certainly a surprise, and although you may not believe it, it does please me that I can actually tell Mother you still live. But that is the most I care to give, for my heart cannot afford much more. You've my word no arrow shall be cast your way as you leave this island. Know, however, that you're not welcome here. If you dare venture toward my shores again, I cannot promise you my reserve."

Domaldr taunted him. "*I cannot promise you my reserve.* That sounds like something Father would say. Where is the old bastard anyway?"

"Leave, Domaldr."

"What? No food or drink? What kind of brother are you? And I even boasted to my men of your generosity."

Dægan recalled those who'd tracked him down and found him in the cavern. "Was that before or after you sent seven men to kill me?"

"Well, you did steal something of mine. The girl?"

Dægan fumed. "She was never yours, Domaldr. And you wanted only to kill her, just as you want to kill *me* right now."

"You're my brother, Dægan. I don't want to kill you."

"But you'd have to, to get what is mine. And I know 'tis not beneath you. Don't waste your breath trying to make me believe otherwise."

Domaldr leaned over the bow as if to challenge his brother's decision. "So, this is how it ends between us?"

Dægan double-fisted his sword and drew it over his shoulder. "You ended *us* a long time ago—you—all by yourself. And I'll not tell you again. Leave this isle and never return. Ever. Else you'll force my hand, and you'll know well my wrath as it has festered for eighteen long years. This is not a threat, Domaldr. 'Tis your last and final warning."

"Dægan…"

"Archers!" Dægan yelled over his shoulder, raising his hand.

Even through the sound of waves breaking upon the shore, the sound of stretching bows could not be mistaken, nor the glare in Domaldr's eyes. "Soren, command the men to retreat."

"Aye, m'lord."

Dægan was never so glad to see his brother leave. But deep down, he knew Domaldr probably wouldn't stay away long, especially since he'd made him look like a fool in front of his own crew.

Chapter Twenty-three

Darkness fell, and Domaldr's ships had circled the isle with stealth to secretly harbor in the distant sea near the high jagged rocks of Inishmore's forbidding western shores. His men sat quiet within the hull, waiting for Domaldr's next orders.

Soren approached the bow. "The men have been instructed as you wished. Half of them to take the isle, and half to stay back and man the ships. All are ready and waiting, m'lord."

"Good. Bring me the *Éireannach*."

"Aye."

Within moments, Soren brought Breandán about. "Am I truly necessary? Have I not already upheld my end of the bargain?"

"Aye, you've tracked my brother as you promised, but…I've yet to see the girl. I wanted both, remember?"

Breandán sighed. "What must I do?"

"What you do best," Domaldr said sardonically. "Scout this island and bring me the whereabouts of my brother and the girl. Soren, you and Thorbjörn go with him. See that he does what he's been told." Domaldr stepped from the bow and leaned in close to Breandán. "You make one move outside this plan, one little mistake—just one—and you'll regret it, *Éireannach*." Both exchanged looks of disdain and suspicion, until Domaldr handed Breandán a bow and a quiver. "You might need these."

Breandán pushed them back and shook his head. "I'm a hunter, not a murderer."

****

It was long after two hours when Breandán and his pair of escorts finally descended the rocks that concealed the four *langskips*. When they climbed aboard, their faces were painted with mud and their clothes likewise soiled, which camouflaged them well into the black of night.

Breandán didn't like the idea of snooping around the isle for Domaldr's benefit, but he liked less the idea of being seen, caught, and killed.

"Well?" Domaldr challenged.

Breandán dreaded giving up what he knew, arming Domaldr with an arsenal of information just for the sake of getting even. It wasn't as if he were actually betraying Dægan and his men. He never knew them, nor did he think they'd ever be allies if he did. But it didn't seem right. It didn't sit well in his gut knowing he'd be the reason for all their deaths.

Domaldr grabbed him and shook him. "Out with it!" When his demand didn't produce results, he shoved a persuasive dagger beneath Breandán's chin. "I said out with it, or I'll cut you from ear to ear."

Breandán knew eventually that was bound to happen. Domaldr wasn't a man to hold fast to a bargain, and he wasn't afraid to die in order to save the princess. But his premature death now wouldn't help her in the least. He was more important to Mara alive rather than filleted like a fish and dumped overboard. He only hoped he could survive long enough to see her home. And for that to happen, he'd have to give Domaldr what he wanted.

Wearily, he spoke, "There are five men standing post as scouts. The rest are in one place, some sort of long hall. I couldn't get close enough to see what they were doing inside."

"The girl?"

"I never saw her or any females. But there's a fort. A stone fort in the distance. I assume your brother has her protected there. I would."

"And my brother?"

"He walks about. The last time I saw him, he left the company of his men and went into the nearest house from the shore."

Domaldr looked at Soren. "Does he speak the truth?"

"Aye, m'lord."

Immediately, Domaldr retracted his knife and patted Breandán on the back. "Now that wasn't so hard, was it?"

"What are you going to do?"

"You know well what I'm going to do, Breandán. We all reap what we sow, and sometimes that means our hands get a little dirty—even yours. I saw the way you looked when we learned of the reward granted by her father. There's no denying you gave it thought. That reward is quite large, and it would go a long way to improving your miserable life to that of a noble clansman. I don't blame you for contemplating it. Any man would. But don't think that it's gone unnoticed. I'm on to you, hunter." Domaldr eyed the tip of his sharp dagger as he twisted it about. "You do realize I need not your services anymore. I could easily dump your carcass over the side of my ship, wash my hands, and never look back, gaining the girl and the reward for myself. But—I want bigger things. I want Connacht, and you're just the man who can help me gain it."

"And why would I do that? As I recall, Connacht was not part of our deal."

Domaldr put his arm around Breandán and leaned on the ship's side, casually waving the dagger as he talked. "Firstly, I suppose I should have told you that I don't consider a deal with an *Éireannach* binding. I only hold pacts with men who are of my caliber. And you...are no better to me than a pathetic *thrall*.

"Secondly...helping me obtain Connacht would benefit you as well. From what I hear, the great High King of Tara has rounded up twelve other sovereignties to fight against us Northmen, but your Connacht king has yet to join. He stalls, he hesitates...and all for good reason. But you, my good friend, could convince him that 'twould be his duty to fight against us for Dubh-Linn, especially since the Northmen were the filthy savages who took his daughter in the first place. Aye?"

Breandán said nothing. He knew well the one-way path down which he was being led.

"Do you see where I'm going with this?" Domaldr asked, his voice as dark as the Atlantic water lapping against the ship. "I'm willing to be generous and let you have the girl the king will no doubt grant you when you bring her back relatively unscathed. As long as you make certain to slander me and my men into the ground, so the king will set off to fight for a campaign sure to lose, leaving his lands vulnerable and unprotected. I'll have my Connacht...you'll have the girl...everyone is happy."

"Why should I think that you'll uphold your end of *this* pact? If you've not noticed, I'm still the *Éireannach* who you find unworthy of a binding agreement."

"Ah, but once you convince your king to leave his lands and fight for Dubh-Linn, you'll have proved yourself to be a traitor to your own countrymen. How could I not glorify that with a reward?"

Breandán saw the shine of the moon bounce off the edge of Domaldr's dagger several times throughout his oration and knew this was the end of the road for him. It was either agree with the devil or sink to the bottom of the sea in death. And the sea looked exceptionally cold this night.

"I get the girl?" Breandán asked, pretending to favor Domaldr's plan.

"As long as I get Connacht."

Breandán made sure to sell the look and fabricated a believable lie. "A woman of gentle birth in my bed would be a nice spoil. And I'm not all that fond of the king anyway. Consider me in."

It wasn't long after Breandán agreed that Domaldr tucked his dagger back into its sheath and unbuckled the belt at his waist. Most everyone lifted their brows in confusion as they watched Domaldr remove his breeches, but Breandán was the only one brave enough to question him. "What in God's name are you doing?"

"Did you happen to notice that Dægan doesn't wear breeches?"

"Aye. So?"

"Well, if I aim to lure the princess from the fort, being Dægan's twin is not enough. I should at least dress like him too."

Breandán swallowed hard. *What have I done?*

****

"Any word from my husband?" Mara asked from the

doorway of Nevan's great hall.

He looked up from his trance amid the fire as if surprised by her presence as well as the servant who obediently tagged along. "My dear, 'tis late."

"All the more reason for my concern."

Nevan offered her a comforting smile and stood from his chair. As he approached, his russet cloak dragged behind him. "Dægan is fine. He's sent word that the fleet of men have moved on, but for lack of trust, he wants everyone to wait out the night here. Please, come in."

Mara followed him deeper into the spacious room. "Does he suspect they'll return another day?"

"You know your husband. He gives me word in piecemeal."

She twisted her hands in front of her, dreading to think what could happen if the men from the north did return. She also hated to be caged like an animal. Nevan must have noticed the knots she mangled her hands into because he poured her a drink as well as one for himself. She gladly accepted the wine and gulped it down.

Nevan smiled and swirled the dark liquid with his wrist, thinking. "You really love Dægan, don't you?"

Mara held the cup with both hands now, a small bit of wine left to sway in the bottom. "Aye."

"That's good. 'Tis good for everyone who lives on Inishmore. And good for your father as well to be allied with a man like Dægan, considering the rising threat that surrounds Baile Átha Cliath. Tell me, who is your father? I've traveled a bit, and I might know him."

Mara thought of her father and the fact that no alliance had ever been made between him and Dægan, or that they'd ever met. It was a conversation she couldn't very well have without damaging Nevan's faith in Dægan. She stared into the cup, feeling the heat of the downed alcohol flushing her face.

"Sire." A servant barged in. "'Tis Dægan. He's come and asks for the lady."

"Well," Nevan said, drinking the last of his wine. "It seems Dægan cannot stay away from you any more than you can from him. It must be love."

****

Mara ran as quickly as she could along the stone terrace and down the steps to the bailey. Her heart leapt upon seeing Dægan standing proudly alongside his great black horse, his sword still drawn like a cautious warrior. She wanted to run into his arms and hold him tight, to feel his heart pound at a speed that would no doubt match her own.

Nevan watched from the wall walk as Mara descended the last set of stairs. "I thought you'd never come, Dægan."

He caught her in his arms and jerked her to the side as if to protect her from those around him.

"What are you doing?" Mara asked.

He looked around suspiciously at everyone along the wall walk, a strange nervousness about him. But before she could ask again, he looked at her. And not deep within her eyes as he normally would have, but down the entire length of her body, gawking even at her cleavage. He pulled her violently to his chest, grinning and licking his lips like some gluttonous pig, then dove to her mouth without the care for tenderness.

Mara whimpered in his mouth, unready for the severity of his kiss and the rape of his tongue. She pushed away, never knowing that kind of mad passion from Dægan before. She wiped the pain and wetness from her lips, looking at him as though he were a total stranger. She tried to dismiss it, to forget the grotesqueness of his kiss, to convince herself he was just overjoyed in seeing her and she should be glad for such fervor.

"I was worried about you," she said at last.

She brought her hands to his face and threaded her fingers into his hair, looking into his eyes, more deeply this time. He stared right back at her, and not with the gentle sea of blue she was accustomed to, but a wicked cobalt that shone as black as midnight on death's hour.

Mara dropped her hands, for they felt as heavy as stones, and stepped back from his hateful grin. She glanced at the sword in his right hand and noticed it wasn't the distinctive weapon of gold, silver, and rubies that Dægan kept at his side. It was one of plainness and tarnished metal.

"Come here, little lass. I've missed you."

Mara's head spun, and her thoughts converged on the oddity of Dægan's visage, especially once he spoke to her in a fashion quite unfamiliar to her ears. Dægan had never called her *little lass* before, and it was strange that he'd take this moment to use it. His unusual conduct was most unlike him, so eccentric, it was almost as if he were someone else entirely, yet identical to the eyes.

Then it hit her. A different sword...a different endearment... It had to be a different man altogether.

Dægan's twin brother.

But she thought him dead. Dægan thought him dead. If he were truly alive, what would bring him here? Then she remembered the four ships with red and white sails, the men who had come upon them in the cavern, and their profound reaction to Dægan when they'd seen him. It all made sense to her now. Domaldr must have been one of their own, tracked his brother down, and conjured a plan to be Dægan himself, even stealing both his steed and a husband's kiss.

Mara's stomach turned, and fear stirred a wave of shivers in her soul. *What has he done to Dægan?*

"Dægan," Nevan called as he was descending the stairs to meet with the chieftain in the courtyard. Behind the king were hordes of men and guards following him as he neared the bottom, his face straight and concerned. "If you've the time, now would be a fine occasion to let me in on the matter of those who have landed on my shores. I've mead to spare…if you can spare the insults."

Domaldr panicked. He hadn't planned on much confrontation, just amiably slipping the princess from the fort. But with so many gathering around him, the truth would be harder to hide, and eventually, as obvious as the bright moon above him.

He twisted Mara about to face the approaching king, shielding his own body with hers. "Open the gate!" he demanded fiercely, taking a few steps backward.

Nevan stopped at the middle of the stairs, looking at the astonishment on Mara's face, her mouth agape in horror. "Dægan, what are you doing?"

"I said open the gate!"

At that point, every Irish guard unsheathed their swords, and every random archer on the wall walk drew back their bows. Nevan, however, commanded otherwise. "Lower your weapons! Do it now!" He gawked at what he believed was Dægan. "What has come over you? Can you not see you're frightening your wife?"

Wife, Domaldr thought. He could barely contain his shock and lowered his mouth to Mara's ear. "My, my, little lass. My brother doesn't waste time, does he?" He tightened his arms around Mara and again yelled to the guard, his insistence now marked by a long sword blade drawn against her throat. "Open them now, or she dies."

Nevan quickly gave the order to the gateman and stared between Mara and the harrowing sword across her chest. "Why do you do this, Dægan? Why do you threaten her? Put down your sword, I beg you."

Domaldr enjoyed the man's pleas while the gates slowly opened behind him. He tossed Mara like a sack of wheat over the nervously shifting horse and leapt behind her, kicking it into a run. He cut down every guard that stood in the way of the gate, and turned around just in time to hear Nevan's frantic voice roar in desperation. "Shoot the horse!"

But Domaldr was quicker and hurled his dagger at the king. Nevan staggered on the steps and fell backward.

Chapter Twenty-four

Mara could see a single man awaiting them at Dægan's longhouse as she and Domaldr approached on the galloping horse. When they skidded to an abrupt halt, Domaldr shoved her to the ground, still punishing the animal with the cruel bit laid sorely across its mouth.

He slid off at her feet and pulled her to a stand by her hair, then coldly shoved her into the man's arms. "Behold your princess, Breandán. You and Soren have Dægan?"

"We do," Breandán replied. He gently pushed Mara's hair from her face and looked at her with such surprise.

"Well?"

Breandán dragged his eyes from Mara's face. "He's in his longhouse. Soren awaits you."

"And Dægan's men?"

"They're still anticipating his arrival at the mead hall. Some are drunk and don't realize the length of his absence. Thirty of your men are posted there, and the rest guard your flank as you've ordered."

"Good. Tell the men to set the mead hall afire. Let no man escape. Burn them all." Domaldr slapped the horse's rear and grabbed Mara from Breandán's arms. She squirmed and screamed, fighting against his grip. "Do you not want to say farewell to your *husband*?"

Breandán's face shot up with those words. "H-husband? She married him?"

"It seems my brother beat you to it, *Éireannach*. But no

matter, she'll soon be widowed."

Domaldr's words were as frigid as the ice in his grip. His fingers dug into Mara's arms short of puncturing her skin. She called for Dægan. But he never came. She called again, this time unable to hold back her sobbing.

"Enough!" Domaldr kicked the back door of Dægan's longhouse open and propelled her inside.

****

"Steinar," Tait spoke from behind his tankard, sniffing the air. "Do you smell that? Smoke."

Steinar and the others lifted their noses and walked around to find the source, but Thordia's desperate cry for help from the back door confirmed something worse. "We are locked in! I cannot open it!"

Tait ran to the front door and discovered the same. He shoved harder, using his shoulder and his hip. "Steinar, help me!"

The two men heaved and grunted, trying with all their might to break the door. The other men scattered and tried the same, but smoke had already started filtering in.

"Tait, what's happening?" Thordia cried.

Tait ripped his sword from his side. "Quick! Cut holes in the roof so the smoke can escape!"

Thordia grabbed Tait's arm and began panicking. "Why would Dægan do this, Tait?"

"'Tis not Dægan!" Tait affirmed.

Steinar's eyes widened in fierce hatred. "'Tis Domaldr! He must have returned and made it past Vegard!" He too unleashed his weapon—a fierce battle-ax for battering the door.

"How will we get out?" Thordia asked.

Tait tore his kirtle from his chest and handed it to her. "Here, soak it with water. All of you. Remove your kirtles and soak them down. Wrap it around your nose and mouth. Do it!"

As instructed, Thordia took everyone's tunics and dunked them in the iron cooking pot at the hearth, then handed them back to the others. "But what about you?"

Tait stood on the table and pierced the roof, cutting the start of a hole. "I said wrap it around your face, Thordia." He began coughing and gagging, as did the others in their fight. "Do not give up!" he called. "Thordia, get on the floor!"

Tait's mind raced as he frantically kept to the roof. He feared for their lives, his Thordia's life…Dægan's life. *Where is he?*

He swallowed the rising bile in his throat and jabbed a bigger hole above him. He pulled at the hay, soil, and grass, ripping the well-constructed roof to shreds until he established an opening as wide as his shoulders. "I have a way out!" he yelled, waving for the men to climb the table as he had. "Come on, Thordia. You first."

"Wait!" Steinar shouted, pulling her back down. "It could be an ambush. I'll go first."

Steinar jumped onto the table, and Tait hoisted him to the opening, struggling to balance his hefty friend on the rickety furniture.

Steinar peered out into the night and saw no one. He squeezed his shoulders through the narrow hole and pushed himself the rest of the way up, standing on the mildly slanted roof. "'Tis clear," he said just before an arrow pierced his back. He fell forward, partly dangling inside the hole.

Tait tried to yank him back in, but Steinar jerked his arm away. He somehow found the strength to push himself to his knees, and like a crazed *berserker*, slid from the rooftop, growling. Tait could only assume his friend had attempted to take on their enemies single-handedly. As he listened, he heard a host of arrows impale Steinar's body from all directions.

"Steinar, no!" Tait jumped from the table and ran to the back door, banging his shoulder and hip into it. An incredible surge pulsated throughout his body and he felt no pain, no bitter smoke sieving into his lungs. His shoulder started bleeding against the wood grain of the door and his chest constricted as he heaved and coughed. But he didn't give up. He wouldn't give up. He'd die pummeling the door.

****

Domaldr entered the main room of Dægan's longhouse, where Soren stood guard over Dægan. He was out cold and tied to a chair. Mara saw him and ran to his side, crying as she wrapped her arms around his seemingly lifeless body. "Dægan, are you all right? What have they done to you? Please wake up."

"You heard the princess," Domaldr said to Soren. "Wake him up."

Soren grabbed Dægan by his hair and slapped his face repeatedly.

"Stop!" Mara shouted, pushing Soren away with meager punches. "Please stop." She glared at Domaldr now. "How can you do this to your own brother?"

"Quite easily," Domaldr snipped as he grabbed an iron pot of water from the unlit hearth. "Dægan never once let himself think of me. Nor would he now, for that matter. He'd just as soon forget me as look at me."

"You're wrong."

"Am I?" Domaldr asked, his question more of a jeering remark. "He killed five of my men."

"He didn't know they were *your* men."

"He wouldn't have cared otherwise. And just like him, I can do *all* this and look the other way." Domaldr dumped the water over Dægan's head, bringing him to a waking jolt.

Dægan shouted and cursed, his eyes failing him as a fierce pain throbbed in his head. He blinked and squinted, trying to free his hands and feet from the rope that bound him to the chair. Failing that, he then saw Domaldr laughing in his face, Mara held captive before him.

"I'll kill you for this, Domaldr. Mark my words. I'll hunt you down and kill you."

"I see your hospitality hasn't improved much." Domaldr chose another chair and placed it a distance from Dægan. "Sit," he told Mara, indicating where with his dagger. "Now." Soren put a firm hand to Mara's shoulder and slammed her into the seat.

Dægan watched his brother closely. "What have you done to my men?"

Domaldr smiled as if happy to hear the question. "The gleam in your eye is most endearing, brother. I almost hate to upset you."

Revulsion and dread rose up like a two-headed dragon. "What did you do to my men?"

"I burned them—every last one. Wait... Shh...you might be able to hear the screams of the last few who refuse to give up."

Dægan roared and thrashed in the chair, trying like mad to pull his hands and ankles loose. The rope wore his skin, cutting him deep. He cried out in anguish, his inner pain greater than the cords to his flesh.

He thought of Tait, of Steinar, of Ottarr, of Hansen... He imagined their horror, their gagging, and their slow, agonizing deaths.

"How could you do this? They were once your family, Domaldr. Your people."

Domaldr shook his head. "They're not my people, Dægan. They never were." He strolled across the room and picked up the sword he'd long hated. The sword of his father. "But this, however, is mine."

"You've no right to even hold it."

Domaldr ignored him. "You know what this sword is to me? This is my redemption from all I suffered being born a son of Rælik, and I shall take it along with Connacht."

"You cannot begin to know what real suffering is, you bastard!"

"Obviously, that's a matter of opinion. But I think we both can agree that your Irish wife is a tasty little morsel," Domaldr replied darkly. He neared Mara and caressed her cheek with his dagger blade. "She's a smart one, though, Dægan. A little too smart. Even the likeness of my clothes didn't fool her."

"Leave her alone."

"I think she discovered I wasn't you the moment my tongue filled her mouth. Is that not right, lass?"

Dægan was helpless as Domaldr hectored him with every stroke of his knife against Mara's skin. He watched in misery as his brother pressed the blade deep along her windpipe and brushed his knuckles across the tops of her breasts. His face burned so hot, he could practically feel his tears evaporate as his own brother defiled his wife.

"Imagine that, Dægan," Domaldr baited as he straddled Mara on the chair. "We look exactly alike, and yet she can still distinguish your kiss from mine." He leaned in, attempting to kiss her again, but she kept her lips sealed— until he simply pricked her throat with the dagger. The moment she cried out, his tongue filled her mouth.

Dægan vigorously assaulted the chair beneath him. "Get off her! She has done naught to you! You wish to humiliate someone, then do it to me! Leave her be, you poor excuse of a man."

Domaldr rose from Mara's lap and lifted her chin, forcing her to look at him. "I did no harm to you, did I? 'Twas just a kiss. I wouldn't think of hurting you." Domaldr looked her over, then after some thought, he grimaced in disgust. "Although…you're married and you lack the innocence of a virgin. But I doubt my men would care."

Mara spat in his face.

Domaldr grinned and casually wiped his upper lip of her saliva before he seized her by the throat and lifted her from the chair. She clawed at his hand, trying to pull free, but he only laughed more.

"Let her go, you bastard! I'll cut your heart out and—"

"Shut him up!" Domaldr shouted over his shoulder.

Soren's boot came swiftly at Dægan's chest, crushing his ribs. He and the chair fell backward at the same time that a man burst through the door.

"Let her go, Domaldr! Let her go, I say!" The man ran to Domaldr and jerked his grasp from Mara's throat, allowing her to collapse in a choking heap on the floor.

Dægan—breathless and red-faced as he tried to draw air within his broken rib cage—regarded the dark-haired man who had entered his home and demanded the princess's life. He thought it strange an Irishman would give demands so freely to his brother, and likewise that Domaldr would stand for it.

"You nearly killed her," the man stated, kneeling at Mara's side.

Dægan listened as the Irish intruder suddenly amended his compassionate voice to that of a nefarious man, more similar to the kind of company Domaldr kept. "Don't forget the bigger spoil. If she's dead, you'll have nothing with which to gain Connacht. And we cannot hold back the islanders much longer. We've got to get to the ships."

Domaldr growled. "Very well, Breandán."

Stranger still, Domaldr obeyed the man's order and walked over to Dægan, still confined to the chair like an overturned turtle. "I'm sorry my visit must come to an end. See you on the other side, brother." And with that, he brought the pommel of his father's sword down hard on Dægan's head, knocking him unconscious again.

Domaldr slapped his dagger to Soren's chest. "I'll take the girl with me to the ship. Slit Dægan's throat and take what you want before it all burns."

Breandán stood dumbfounded as Domaldr ripped Mara to her feet. He struggled to swallow everything at once—Mara crying, Dægan beaten and tied, and Soren about to kill him in cold blood.

Domaldr's eyes darkened. "Are you coming, *Éireannach*?"

Breandán blinked his way back into reality. "Nay," he said steadily. "I mean, I'll do it. I'll kill him."

Domaldr stepped forward, clearly skeptical of his sudden interest in murder, and bounced Dægan's sword blade on his shoulder. "Now is not the time to try me with games. There'd better be blood on that knife when you're through."

Domaldr didn't wait for a response and left, dragging Mara behind him. Soren followed after he relinquished the dagger to Breandán's hands.

He didn't have much time. He could hear the distant shouts of the local Irishmen outside and the chaos of Domaldr's men retreating. He looked at the weapon and then at Dægan, knowing he couldn't kill this man any more than he could kill himself. He exhaled heatedly, trying to find the nerve, of all things, and then hopefully the clarity of an ingenious mind with which to fool Domaldr.

He knelt at the warrior's side and cut the chair from each of Dægan's four limbs, taking heed of their weight as they dropped heavily to the ground. Even in his vulnerable state, Dægan still looked like a man not to be meddled with.

He slapped Dægan's face to try to awaken him. "Dægan. Come on, wake up. Your brother is taking your wife from you. Are you going to just lie here and let that happen? Wake up! I cannot save Mara on my own. Come on, she needs you." Breandán shook him this time. "Wake up, you fool!"

The commotion outside the longhouse grew stronger, and Breandán panicked as Dægan lay still on the floor. If he wanted to ensure Mara's safety, he had to leave and get on Domaldr's longship...but not before the knife was covered in blood.

In total desperation, he decided to cut himself in a place hidden from Domaldr's eyes. He pulled his boot from his own foot and laid the knife assuredly at his heel...

Chapter Twenty-five

Mara sat at the stern of Domaldr's warship, watching the men heave and ho to a rhythm she soon fell in trance to. She'd cried in her solitary place for what seemed like hours, reliving over and over again the sight of Dægan's blood on the Irishman's dagger. Yet, her sobbing fell upon deaf ears, for the men cared only to please Domaldr. And Domaldr cared only for the speed of his ships.

How could his vengeance be more important than the life of his own brother? It was a question she kept asking and an image she kept replaying in her head. She remembered how Dægan howled as his ribs cracked, how he wheezed in laborious gasps, and how Domaldr enjoyed his brother's torment.

No matter how much it haunted her, no man on this ship would condole with her in her loss. These men would celebrate it, tell stories of it, and proudly drink to it. And never, in all their time of reliving their adventure, would they come to speak of her sorrow. To them, Dægan's defeat was glorious.

"Gentle lady," a voice spoke to her. "May I sit?"

Mara slowly looked up and stared into the eyes of the man who had killed her husband. *Breandán*, she remembered they called him. His eyes were kind and sympathetic as he awaited her response.

"Nay, you may not," Mara said as firmly as she could. "And how dare you look at me with pity. How dare you speak to me as if you're worthy, as if your hands are clean of Dægan's blood. May God have mercy on your soul, because I will not."

Breandán took a humble step backward and dropped to his knee. "I wish only to tell you to look to your right, beneath the cover."

"Why would I want to do that?"

"Because if you do not, the item will fall into Domaldr's hands."

"So what if it does? There's not much more he can take from me. Leave me be."

"I insist you cast your eyes in the direction I speak. Dægan would want you to."

Mara slapped his face. It wasn't hard enough. She aimed to do it again, but he caught her wrist and pulled her close to whisper in her ear. "Your husband lives. I didn't slit his throat."

She wanted to believe him, but she'd seen the blood on his dagger. "I saw your dagger. I saw the blood, you despicable—"

"What you saw was not his blood but my own. I swear to you, he lives."

Mara caught her breath. It was too good to be true. "Why do you tell me this?"

"Because just as you've fallen victim to Domaldr's plans, I too am caught up in all this. My name is Breandán, son of Liam. My father is a clansman serving under the overlord of the Uí Briúin Aí, and your father is chieftain. Henceforth, I serve you." Breandán hesitated and looked over his shoulder. "These men think I'll help them take Connacht, but I've only pretended to agree in order to save you. I've no part in their scheme, but I still have a role to play amongst them. My words may very well turn your stomach, but please realize they're not *my* words. I mean you no harm. Do not speak of this to anyone, else it means my death…and yours as well. To solidify your trust in me, I do hope that you'll look under the cover as I've requested. What I bring you is from Dægan's home. 'Twas the only thing I could find worthy of proving my fealty to you. Your Dægan lives, gentle lady. Pray he comes soon."

Breandán stood and walked down the narrow aisle of the ship, taking his place beside Domaldr at the steer board.

Mara watched Breandán whisper to him, and Domaldr turned to look at her, his eyes lustful and greedy. It must have been something crude, for he laughed and patted Breandán on the back.

She cringed at the thought of what vulgarity Breandán and Domaldr had shared about her—and how men could talk so, was beyond her. But that was not important anymore. Dægan was alive. She could breathe again, and it was all because of one man—a stranger, as far as she was concerned—but a man who risked everything to keep her and Dægan from harm.

Who was this man? And why did he care enough to put his life on the line for her? He said he was a clansman of the Uí Bhriúin Aí, but she'd never met him before in her life. And to add another log to the fire, Breandán brought her a token of his loyalty.

Mara waited a few moments more, making certain she was once again an insignificant passenger, and that no eyes, especially those of Domaldr's, gazed in her direction. She lifted the corner of the woolen blanket and there, at her side, was the carved wooden king's chest that Dægan had given her.

****

"I'm sorry my visit must come to an end. See you on the other side, brother."

Dægan jerked and pulled at his wrists bound to the legs of the chair. He watched in helpless agony as Domaldr raised his sword above his head and brought it down hard and swift.

Skull-splitting pain sliced his temple, then...

Dægan's eyes shot open, his hands and ankles unbound. His head pounded unforgivably and his ribs ached. He looked around the large room and saw Nevan sleeping in a chair at the foot of the bed, his right shoulder and chest wrapped in blood-stained linens. Dægan shifted beneath the blankets and groaned as his many aches became more obvious. "Where am I?"

Nevan opened his eyes. "My chambers. I thought it best for you to be here."

Dægan tried to sit up, but his unstable ribs kept him from doing so. He winced and held his side. "What happened?"

"I really don't know myself. From what I've gathered, you and your men cheated death."

Dægan barely remembered the fire. "My men...the mead hall... Did they *all* make it out?"

Nevan hesitated. "Most of them."

Dægan closed his eyes and hung his head. "Tell me, Nevan."

"It seems that Steinar came out first, holding the archers' attentions while the others had a chance to escape. We burst through their flank in time to save the rest from the fire, but—we could only do so much against a well-organized fleet. Your men were retching and gasping for their lives, and by the time they could tell us anything, *your twin brother* Domaldr and his men had already taken to their ships and left."

Nevan watched the change in Dægan's face. "That's right, Dægan. I know you have a twin. Amazing that I know such a thing, since you certainly felt no need to inform me yourself. I had the pleasure of meeting him face-to-face." He glanced at his wounded shoulder with resentment. "And had I known you had a twin, I wouldn't have been so free in giving him your wife."

"You gave her to him?"

"He said he was you. He said he was Dægan, and I had no reason to doubt my own eyes. Mara ran to him, and he kissed her. But until he held her at sword point, we had no reason to suspect otherwise. And even then, we all were reserved in stopping him, for he was *you*! We tried to shoot the horse out from under him, but as you can plainly see, he's well skilled in sabotage."

Dægan voice rose to match his escalating anger. "You gave her to him?"

"I did as I was told."

Dægan sprang from the bed as if he was without any injury. He fisted Nevan's tunic and jerked him erect, shoving him against the back wall. "I told you to guard her with your life! With your very life!"

"I tried, Dægan. I truly did. But I couldn't very well kill you. Or who I thought was you. Some things give me pause, and slaying a man I thought was a friend is a bit unsettling for me."

Dægan released the king, and his memory whirled about him, like slivers of time, broken and random in his mind. He tried to piece it all together, from the time he left the peaceful mead hall to the final moment Domaldr struck him in the head. Little by little, the shattered fragments of his memory slowly came back to him, starting with the two men who burst into his longhouse, the fierce struggle, and then his awakening to Mara crying, with Domaldr at the forefront of it all.

"You know what this sword is to me? This is my redemption from all I suffered being born a son of Rælik, and I shall take it along with Connacht."

Dægan almost fell backward in recollecting Domaldr's words, his motive like a slap in the face. He made haste for the door.

"Where are you going?" Nevan asked, a slight sense of pity suffusing his voice.

"Is it not obvious? I have to save Mara."

"'Tis impossible."

"What do you mean *impossible*?"

Dægan's heart filled with more dread as he watched Nevan struggle to divulge the rest of the devastating truth. "Your brother made sure you couldn't follow him. He looted and burned everything—your homes, your ships. There's nothing left. Even your livestock have been slaughtered."

Dægan gripped the frame of the door with both hands for support as if he'd been kicked in the groin. He squeezed his eyes shut and clenched his fists. He'd make it his life's mission to find Domaldr, even if it took him the rest of his life. He'd find a way to get off this isle and see that his twin would pay for this. *Tenfold.*

He bellowed like a mighty bear and bolted.

****

Dægan raced on horseback to see firsthand the damage done to his home, and inspect the condition of the wood from his burned settlement. Just as he'd done on the Isle of Man years ago, he hoped he could salvage what was left to build at least one ship, one raft, whatever it took to make it to the mainland.

He drove his heels into the horse's flank, urging the animal to run as fast as it could. He suffered through the pain of his cracked ribs moving independently between his skin and muscles until he caught sight of the burnt landscape. Smoke streamed upward where buildings and homes once stood. Embers and ash veiled what was once lush green pasture; now it was black and desolate. No grass, no flowers, no green meadow between the rock wall perimeters, just a barren strip of what used to be his beautiful home.

He slowed the horse to a stop and carefully dismounted, holding his side as he walked across the scorched ground. In the distance, he could see his men gathered around several bodies that lay in respectful lines. He remembered how Domaldr had spoken so dismissively of his men, those who fought with their lives to protect this beach.

Dægan grew sick, knowing his good friends Steinar and Vegard were amongst the many who'd died for him. His mouth watered, his eyes pooled, and his knees gave out. He stared in silence, his dolor at a depth he'd never known.

Tears streamed from his eyes, and he fell to the dusty ground, looking at the sky above him. If not for the taste of his salty tears and ash in his mouth, he'd swear by the color of the clear sky that he'd been dropped into a cruel dream, and the gods were glad of his despair. They painted their pleasure in a sea of blue amongst warm golden sunrays.

He closed his eyes, for the ironic beauty above him was like listening to the gods chatter and mock him. He swore he heard their joyous glee in rolling echoes.

But he heard a voice. A low voice, calling him by name. At first he thought it taunted him, but then it drifted into a sweet whisper.

Mara?

He called back, but she didn't come. Just her voice saying, *"You're but a lost sheep...wandering alone in the night, and He, as the shepherd, will search for you until He finds you because He knows of the wolves on your heels. But never does He laugh at you. Never..."*

"What do I do, Mara? What does He want me to do?"

"Dægan." Tait's voice filtered in. "Dægan, wake up. Are you all right? You must have fallen from your horse."

Dægan opened his eyes, and the sun burst through. He tried to sit but was immediately racked with pain. He grabbed his side and searched the desolation for his wife. "Where's Mara?"

Tait shook his head. "Didn't Nevan tell you?"

"I heard her. She's here, Tait. She talked to me. She's still here."

"I wish she were, Dægan, but—"

"I heard her!"

"And I'm telling you, you must have hit your head in the fall, because I assure you, she's not here. I saw her with my own eyes. Domaldr dragged her to his ship. I tried to swim to her, everyone did, but without our ships..."

Dægan slumped over in disappointment and heartache, reliving every terrible moment over and over again. His wife gone, his men wounded and some dead, his home burned to the ground, and his longships destroyed.

"What do we do now, m'lord?" Tait asked.

Dægan looked at his friend, and somewhere amid his pointless grief, he found a straggling gleam of hope. "Take me to the church on the hill."

****

"Of all the things that need be done, you want to do this?"

Tait eyed Dægan with antipathy as he helped to support his chieftain's weight at the doorway of the small stone church. Dægan nodded, though he too questioned his own actions.

"Dægan, the gods possess powers beyond our understanding, but I've never known one to build a *langskip*. I doubt this Christian one will either, for I've heard he only endows measurements for an ark."

"I'm not here to ask for a *langskip*, Tait."

"Then why *are* you here?"

"I know not that answer. The idea came to me, and so here I stand."

"What are you expecting? The mighty hand of the Christian god to reach down from the sky and—"

The church door opened, and a monk in the common brown garb stepped forward, closing the door behind him. "I can assure you, it does not work that way." He first eyed the Northman who spoke the nonsense, and then to the one with whom he was better acquainted. "Hello, Dægan. You've survived, I see."

Dægan stepped back and nervously dropped to one knee, recognizing the monk who had married him the night before.

"Stand up, son. We are equals in the eyes of God. Now, what is it you want from me?"

Dægan stood slowly, cradling his ribs. "I don't know. When I came here, I merely thought I'd be able to enter without..."

"You want to come into God's house?"

Dægan swallowed hard at the crazy thought. "Aye, I do. Am I not permitted?"

"God welcomes all—even you and your friend, but I've known what desecration your kind are capable of. I saw firsthand that very destructive nature last night, and I'll not let it happen at this place of worship."

Tait instantly drew his sword, but Dægan threw out his arm to halt him. "Put it away."

Tait spoke defensively. "You know we've never done such things to any church, Christian or not, and I resent the suggestion that I'm grouped with scoundrels like your brother."

"You're right. We've been judged and insulted in the same breath, but realize that in drawing your sword, you've justified this man's premature notion. Put it away." Dægan turned to face the brave cleric. "I did not come to desecrate this house, nor do I wish to fight a man of the cloth to get inside. A voice told me to come here—a sweet, kind voice—one that I thought was Mara's. Perhaps, I'm losing my mind...but I just...I thought..." He sighed. "I know not what I thought in coming here." Weary and disillusioned, Dægan gradually fell to his knees. "I wish I knew what God wants of me."

The holy man put a careful hand on Dægan's shoulder, pitying him in his humbled state. "Perhaps He just wants less of you."

Dægan tried to understand the monk, but couldn't decipher the simplistic riddle. "Less of me?"

The monk grinned smugly. "There wasn't much room for a mighty and wealthy warrior chieftain in His house...but perhaps there is now." The priest pushed the door of the church open and walked away, leaving Tait and Dægan to themselves.

"He's right," Dægan muttered. "I was too proud to walk through this door."

"What?" Tait asked, pulling Dægan to his feet. "Are you listening to yourself? You've gone mad. You've lost all sense of reality. Mara is not going to magically appear because you crawl on all fours to this Christian god. Do not lower yourself to this, Dægan. You're greater than that. You're Dægan, son of Rælik."

Dægan lifted his heavy lids to gaze upon his friend. "I'm no one without her."

"You're no one with this Christian god!"

"And with all our gods, too numerous to count? What am I, then?"

"You're a chieftain, Dægan."

Dægan shook his head. "I'm lost."

"Fine. You're a lost chieftain, but a chieftain, nonetheless."

"Something tells me I should be here. It feels right. So what if I'm wrong, Tait? Look around. What else do I have to lose?"

"Your dignity."

Dægan scoffed. "There's nothing left of it either. I'm the weakest I've ever been."

Tait boldly stepped between Dægan and the church door. "Nothing is going to happen. You know this. You can walk in and out of this church a thousand times over, and your home will still be in ashes."

"I'm not asking you to come in with me."

Tait threw his head back and grunted. "Do what you have to do, m'lord. Find what you think you need. But while you're in there, see if you can find Dægan. His people need him."

Tait walked away and sheathed his weapon, his sword taking the brunt of his anger. Dægan knew exactly where his friend stood on the matter, and by all accounts, it ran a bit deeper than just disappointment. But he had to do this, despite Tait's well-founded objection.

He slowly entered the church. It was quiet, dark, and peaceful. There was a table at the altar just as in his place of worship in Hladir. There were wooden benches in straight rows, a large wooden cross with the familiar crucified carving, a few lit torches on the stone walls, and a single small window just below the east steeple. The air inside smelled of old wood and spiced incense, a scent he quickly grew to like as he took a seat in one of the neatly rowed pews.

Dægan closed his eyes and listened. The silence was consuming and yet unnatural, as if he wasn't alone. *"You're but a lost sheep…"*

Dægan wanted to smile at hearing her voice so clearly in his head. At the same time, it made him utterly aware of the reason he was here all alone in an empty church, waiting for a miracle. Waiting for something.

Aye, a miracle.

As miracles went, it was a wonder he'd kept Mara for as long as he had. Everyone seemed determined to keep them apart. If it wasn't Rutland or the Irish themselves, it was his own twin adding a hand in the treachery. His own flesh and blood.

Dægan held his head and felt the hammering pulse of his heartbeat in his temples. He now preferred the unnatural quiet to the rhythmic beat of his heart, for it proved cruelly that he was still very much alive in this nightmare.

Dægan groaned and leaned forward, resting his head on the bench in front of him. "I need my wife back," he whispered feebly. "Help me get her back. Please. I know I'm not a good man, and I don't deserve her. But right now, she needs me. I know well what my brother is capable of doing. I know he'll hurt her. I know he will. Maybe I'm not the man you intended her to be with. I can accept that. Strangely enough, I can even understand it. I'm a wretched man. I've killed many men in my past, and truthfully, I'll kill more to make my brother pay. But I'll do anything to get her back. I'll gladly trade my life for hers if that is what you want. I'll lay down my life for her. Please, let no harm come to her. Please, please, help me…"

His whispers echoed and settled in another deep silence. If he'd felt a presence before, he surely didn't feel it now. Had he spoken heartfelt words in vain?

He wiped the trace of tears left on his face, embarrassed he'd given them up so easily to an empty room of ordinary appeal.

It was in that painfully silent moment that Dægan could hear the scornful words of Tait saying, *"I told you so."* Tait would throw them like stones, not only in judgment but also in hopes of knocking sense into him. This was Tait; a man of obedience, but not without an impetuous tongue in the trade.

Dægan stood to face the inevitable mockery waiting

for him outside the church and shuffled to the door. Upon opening it, he endured the sharp, brutal sun beaming in his eyes as if it were another well-deserved punishment. He squinted and held his forearm to his brow as he exited the church.

Tait rode his horse in front of Dægan, blocking the intensity of the sun with his back. "So what did the Almighty have to say?"

Dægan ignored Tait's sarcasm and mounted behind him, a feat that left him breathless. "Take me home, Tait. My men need me."

"Ah, I see you found Dægan in there," Tait said without compassion. "So was I right? Was the answer to your prayers like that of a sigh on a blustery day? Of course it was. Believe me, you're better off praying to our numerous gods than their single Christian one, for I assure you the odds of someone hearing you is far greater."

"M'lord! M'lord!" a servant called from a sprinting horse. "Your mercenaries are here! They're here!"

Tait whipped his head around at Dægan and then up to the clear blue sky above. "What did you say in there?"

Chapter Twenty-six

Shallow ditches large enough for kindling and wide enough for a man were dug. There was no time for building pyres, no time for sentiment, or ceremony. Time enough only to bury the dead in the sole interest of sending them speedily to the afterlife.

Dægan spoke words of sentiment over each man, pausing longer at Vegard's and Steinar's bodies, before lighting the site with a torch. And not the words of Odin, as his men had chanted, but of his seemingly newfound faith. He prayed that each brave man would be forgiven their sins and granted the peace he so wished for them.

"I'll not forget the sacrifices you all have made for me," he whispered as the smoke billowed into the air. "There's no greater love than what you've done for me this day. May God have mercy on all of you, my brothers-in-arms."

Dægan bowed his head humbly and hobbled inland to where the Irish king and his loyal subjects watched from a distance. Tait easily caught up with Dægan.

"Where are you going? Your mercenaries grow impatient."

"I need to speak to Nevan. Tell the men I'll be ready in a moment."

Tait fell behind and did as instructed.

"My king," Dægan said respectfully upon approach. "May I have a word with you? Alone."

Nevan rubbed the corner of his mouth and dismounted silently. When they were farther than earshot, Dægan faced Nevan and paused for a long time before speaking. "I was told that you too lost many men."

"Aye."

"I'll help you with your dead."

"Thank you, but my dead need not your help."

Dægan recognized the tremendous amount of resentment the king held, and rightly so, for he'd truly taken advantage of the monarch's loyalty. He nervously cleared his throat and bared his soul wide open. "I was wrong to expect your friendship when I never returned it myself. I was wrong to put my wife in your charge and not tell you what you were up against. I never lied to you, Nevan. I hope you'll believe that. But mistakenly, I never confided in you either. And even now, I don't know why—pride, perhaps. I never meant to bring all this upon you and your people. You saved my men," Dægan said gratefully. "You saved me. You took a knife for Mara. And all I did was scorn you. I failed you and your people this day. I'll not beg for your forgiveness, as I don't deserve it."

"You're right. You don't deserve such a thing." Nevan averted his gaze beyond Dægan and allowed a few uncomfortable moments to pass. "You may not deserve my forgiveness, but it has already been given you. So who are these men?"

Dægan stumbled on how to explain this one. "Mercenaries from the Hebrides. I sent for them while I was in Hlymrekr so that I may...well, I needed..." He looked away and huffed. "I sent for them in case we came upon trouble in our return journey to the mainland. I still have a debt to pay with Mara's father, Cathal Mac Conor."

Nevan's eyes widened in shock, then narrowed in

anger. "The king of Connacht? The man who stabbed me and left me for dead? You married his daughter?"

Dægan couldn't hide his astonishment. He had no idea that Nevan's enemy and Mara's father were one and the same. "So 'twould seem. But I swear to you, I knew naught of it. You'd never disclosed his name to me. Even after you'd given me the chest as payment for nursing you back to health, you never gave the man who stabbed you a name. How was I to know?"

"I never said his name because I didn't want anyone to seek vengeance on my behalf. After knowing my true love was gone from this earth, I wanted to forget it all. Especially him. For good." Nevan began to pace. "But how can this be? I know Cathal Mac Conor. And I know he'd never marry his daughter to a Northman. Ever! So what in God's name did you offer for his consent?"

"Nothing. There was no consent. He thinks she's been taken."

Nevan halted and spun on his heel, his cloak flaring around him. "No consent? You married her without consent? How could you do this? How could you do this to me? I don't want my people drawn into another war, especially with Cathal."

"Rest easy, sire. This is not your war to be fought. He doesn't know who took her, much less who my allies are. I assure you, your name shall never escape me."

Nevan paced again. "Is this the trouble you had in Limerick?"

"A small part of it, I suppose."

"Does that small part also include the reason for Eirik's death?"

"Aye."

Nevan shook his head. "I cannot begin to imagine the twisted and no doubt inescapable web you're caught in, Dægan. And I'd wager 'tis so grand, you've not even the time to explain it. Frankly, I don't want to know. I think I've heard enough." Nevan turned his back on Dægan and took another look at the wreckage involving the Northman's home. "Actually, there's one thing I must know. Why your twin brother, Domaldr? Where does he fit in with Mara's father? It makes no sense."

Dægan never felt more ashamed than he did right now. "Domaldr wants the princess so he can take Connacht. Making me suffer is just an additional benefit."

"And now you're going to do the same to him."

Dægan grew uncomfortable with the king's judgments and fidgeted as he spoke. "What I'm going to do is get Mara back. I want her safe. That is all I care about."

Nevan took a long breath. "You need five hundred men for that?"

"To be certain? Aye."

"And what of your brother?"

"What of him?"

"What do you plan for him?"

Dægan rubbed his forehead impatiently. "What do you want me to say? That I feel even slightly guilty for wanting him dead? Well, I don't, and there's not a man here who can say Domaldr doesn't deserve death."

"And who will do it? Who amongst these many will do the deed?"

"What difference does it make?"

"The difference is that your brother's blood will not be on *your* hands. Will you sleep better that way?"

"So what if I do? Does that make me so wretched?"

"It makes you just like him."

Dægan clenched his teeth, trying to keep the sarcasm from escaping, but he failed. "I am his twin, am I not?"

"You both may share similar physical features, but you have your own heart and your own mind. Those two things are what separate great men from savage men. Don't let your brother determine the man you are." Nevan took a step closer. "A wise man once told me that men are too often placed on higher ground because of the number of battles they have won or the number of silver coins they have in their pockets. When in fact greatness comes from things we cannot hold in our greedy hands. Things that are beyond our destructive reach. Is that not what you said to me? There's no doubt that Domaldr is well within your destructive reach, especially with the grand numbers you boast now. But 'twill take a greater man to turn the other cheek."

"Are you suggesting I forget all about what he's done? To let him have Mara, her father's kingdom, and everything else he took from me without punishment?"

"Heavens, no," Nevan said. "I'm not denying his crime or the penalty he faces. But he's still your brother. Savage or not."

"I've tried to make myself believe that, even after the shame and hardship he caused my father years ago. But I cannot anymore. He'll pay for what he has done, I assure you. And whether it be by my hand or by one of the five hundred here, he'll die."

Nevan heard the decisiveness in Dægan's voice. "It seems your mind is set. And what of your wife's father? What do you plan for him?"

"As I told Mara, I'll make amends. I have to."

"Don't forget that I once tried as well…and lost."

"I know," Dægan replied sympathetically. "But I've not much choice."

"And what should I tell your mother?"

"She knows of what Domaldr has done?"

Nevan crossed his arms. "It was hard to keep it from her. There were still straggling rumors that 'twas you who did all this. I couldn't let your mother think that, now could I?"

"How did she take it—knowing Domaldr is alive and still as deceitful as ever?"

"Not very well. But better once she knew your good name remained intact. You really should speak with her before you leave."

Dægan glanced at his war-thrilled mercenaries. "I cannot. Not when I possess thoughts of killing her son. She'd take one look at me and know what I aim to do. I know not how long I'll be gone, but she'll need comfort. Will you do that for me?"

"Of course."

What Dægan prepared to do was extremely dangerous given that his twin brother had already made a zealous attempt at killing both him and everyone he loved. He knew Domaldr wouldn't resist trying to kill him again, especially once he found out he failed the first time. "There's a chance I may not return. Will you also tell her that I love her?"

Nevan nodded. "I've sent for a few things you'll need for your journey. Plenty of clean linens, dried meat, breads, that sort of thing. I believe you'll need weaponry since all yours has been taken. I'll send for my best armor and sword, and I'll not listen to any disputes on the matter. Consider it an order."

Dægan felt grateful and guilty all at the same time.

Even through resentment and frustration, the king had bestowed upon him his loyalty and a surplus of generous gifts. Before he could express his gratitude, Nevan fell into another subject.

"Short of being too forward, Dægan, I couldn't help but notice that in the past few years, you and your men, and even some of the women, carry trinkets of your war god on their belts."

"Aye," Dægan said skeptically. "We do."

"I also couldn't help but notice that in the past few days, *yours* is gone."

Dægan looked at the empty belt around his waist. "I've not much use for good-luck charms. As you can see, they do me no good."

Nevan placed his hand on the chieftain's shoulder as he regarded the vast number of men and ships on his beach. "I heard you went to the church today, and 'tis my guess men do not go to churches in search of luck. But whatever the circumstance, it seems to have been a fruitful visit for you."

Dægan pondered the king's insinuation. "I was told your god doesn't work in that way."

"Quite possibly, He does not. Nonetheless, all is not lost for you. You have your ships. You have your army. You have everything you need to get Mara back. But above all that, you may even have found favor with God, for He now commands a swift and strong wind. Feel it, and know He's with you."

Nevan opened his hand and a string of wooden beads and a cross dangled from his fingers. "Keep this with you, Dægan. Perhaps 'twill help you make the right decision once you have your brother at the end of your sword."

****

Dægan sat on a chest aboard the longship denoted specifically for his command by Havelok, one of the two hired mercenary chieftains. The ship was quite a bit larger than any of the *drakkars* he used to own as it boasted at least twelve oars on each side and held as many as forty-eight men for rowing. The sail was twice the size of his, but the ship itself lacked the menacing dragonhead prows Dægan had come to admire. In their stead were carved posts with gold weathervanes decorated with various animals whose arms, legs, and heads conjoined.

Dægan looked back, verifying the presence of the other nine *drakkars* and the six fully loaded *knarrs*. As he expected, they followed right behind him. He called for Tait.

"Aye, m'lord?"

"I've grown weary with my bones moving in my body. Help me wrap my chest before we set foot on Irish soil."

"Dægan, with all due respect, you're in no shape to fight. You can barely move without gasping in pain. I can lead these men."

"I know you can. But this is my wife. My brother. My fight."

"Dægan, we may not even make it in time. What if Domaldr has decided to make war with the Connacht king? We could be walking into the middle of a battle. What, then?"

Dægan didn't want to think about that possibility. He wanted to believe that the timely arrival of his mercenaries was a sign of God's favor. That he was to be with his one true love. That beating Domaldr to the Lough Ree was more than a slim possibility—it was meant to be.

"To make war, one must face one's opponent, and we both know Domaldr prefers to go for the back. He'll avoid confrontation at all costs. We should also make better time given we're heading straight through Galway. Nevan's men said they sighted him heading due south, which means he'll be coming up the long and winding River Shannon. Granted, we'll have to journey clear around the bogs to get to where the Shannon meets the Lough Ree. But if we keep moving, we'll not fail."

"We cannot travel twenty-seven leagues in a day, Dægan. By the gods, 'twould be virtually impossible in two. We have to rest sometime, or none of these men will be able to lift their eyelids, much less a sword arm."

"Don't forget that Domaldr must rest as well."

"Aye, he does. And he should be well rested since his nights will not be cursed with thoughts of his brother hunting him down."

"All the more reason to believe we shall arrive first. Now, help me with my ribs."

Tait knelt before Dægan and wrapped the first layer of linen strips around his chest, pausing each time his chieftain winced and groaned. "You're an easy target for him, you know. Once Domaldr sees your condition, he'll use it in his favor."

"I know."

"Then let me fight him," Tait said, wrapping a second layer.

"Nay," Dægan said shortly. "Pull it tighter."

"Why not?" Tait asked, tightening the next strip of cloth.

Dægan gritted his teeth and moaned against the

pressure. "Because 'tis my wife he has. I've already lost many because of my decisions, and to lose you…well—that is simply not going to happen. Furthermore, you almost lost Thordia in the fire."

"She's hale and hearty," Tait reminded him. "And she'll be safe at Nevan's fort until we return."

"Thordia surviving the fire was a small blessing, and you should start counting them as they don't often fall upon men like us."

"Dægan, this talk of blessings and God is ridiculous. You cannot win this fight with hugs and forgiveness, and you certainly can't do it on your own. You see to your wife, and I'll see to Domaldr."

"Pull it tighter."

"Are you listening to me?"

Dægan huffed through his nostrils. "I am."

"Then let me do this for you. Give me the chance to prove myself."

"I know the man you are, Tait. And 'tis not with you that I have doubts."

"But—"

"Don't make me not say it again."

Tait wrapped the cloth four more times around and then said, "I too can be stubborn, m'lord. Rest assured I'll be right on your heels the whole time."

Dægan half grinned and then inspected his wrapped ribs. "Domaldr has to be killed. Does he not?"

Tait raised his brow. "You're asking me? If you're having second thoughts, then perhaps my opinion is better left unsaid."

"I'm not having second thoughts," Dægan defended. "I want him dead. I just want to know what you think."

Tait put his hands on his hips. "I think there's no other

choice, unless you want to sleep with one eye open for the rest of your life."

Dægan gazed out over the blue sea, seeing the green Erin shores on the horizon. "Do you think he's capable of—well, what if he has already—"

"Don't wear your mind on petty thoughts. The time will come when you'll learn what Domaldr has done to your wife, and perhaps 'twill help to ease the guilt you feel in wanting him dead. But right now, you need to keep your mind set on getting inland before he does. Mara is a strong woman, and Domaldr is well aware she's more valuable alive than dead. He wouldn't have come all this way for her if he thought her not useful."

Dægan's mind flashed back to when Domaldr had hold of Mara's throat in his longhouse. "Wait. There was a man. A dark-haired man, Irish no doubt. I think Domaldr called him…Breandán. Do you recall him?"

"Nay. Why?"

"I vaguely remember him. He came into my house and saved Mara's life. How odd it was to see my brother give in to him."

"What's your point?"

Dægan squeezed his eyes tighter, struggling to recall the rest. "I've the strangest feeling he spared me as well."

Tait laughed. "Those men set your longhouse on fire. They wanted you dead. If anyone spared you, it was Nevan."

"Nay, this man spoke to me. He was trying to tell me something, but I cannot recall what he said."

"Are you sure he wasn't telling you to stick your head between your legs and kiss your hairy arse good-bye?"

Dægan ignored Tait's remark. "I remember there was

urgency in his voice." He shook his head in disappointment. "Ah, you're right. 'Tis probably all in my head. I was knocked unconscious and tied to a chair. I couldn't possibly have heard him."

Tait looked at Dægan strangely. "You weren't bound, my lord."

"I was. I know I was. That's why Domaldr got away, or I assure you, I wouldn't have let him escape."

"But Nevan said he found you on the floor trying to crawl for the door."

Dægan eyes widened. "Then Breandán *did* spare me. He cut me free so that I'd live. But why? Who is this man? And why did he care enough to do such a thing?"

"I know not the answer to any of those questions, but let's hope this Breandán continues to be the lenient foe. We could surely use an ally on the inside."

Chapter Twenty-seven

Twenty-seven leagues and three days later, Dægan and his band of mercenaries finally arrived at the banks of the Lough Ree. All was quiet. All was still. But Dægan couldn't find cause to breathe easy just yet.

"Tait, take four scouts and search down river."

"Aye, m'lord."

Dægan turned his horse and trotted back behind the lines, toward the two leaders. "Havelok. Ingvarr. I believe we've made it. We did well. Tell your men to make camp two furlongs from the river, beyond those trees. If Domaldr and his men come up the waterway, I'd like to have the element of surprise in my favor."

"Should I send a scout?" Ingvarr asked.

"It has already been done," Dægan said, tasting the first small bite of satisfaction. "All we need to do now is sit and wait for him."

Havelok looked over the confident warrior chieftain before saying, "You're definitely Rælik's son."

Dægan gave him a sideways glance. "You knew my father?"

"Aye, I knew him before you were even born. He had a horde of men at his side and a trail of women on his heels wherever he went. I believe that man could have sworn the sky was green and no one would have thought twice on the matter." Havelok paused and nodded with pride. "He was an impressive man, a sight to watch. And not just when he spoke, but when he wielded his sword. 'Twas like muscle and iron were one. I nearly fell over myself to get here when I heard I had the chance to fight alongside his son."

"I assure you, Havelok, I pale in comparison to my father."

Havelok chuckled deeply. "Ah, I see you acquired his modesty too."

Dægan shook his head. "Do not credit me with modesty, for it goes hand in hand with restraint, and I promise you, should anyone herald this day in my life, neither of those words will spill forth."

****

The Norwegian mercenaries grew impatient. In their long journey from the Hebrides, the hope of fighting in a valiant war had taken root. But now as they sat in monotonous boredom for another full day, their anticipation for such a battle had all but vanished.

Havelok approached Dægan as he sat alone at the trees' edge, gazing down river. "My men have hunted well. Come, eat with us."

"I'm not hungry."

Havelok assumed the stolid warrior would say that. "Then may I sit?"

Dægan stared straight ahead, but made no objection to the fellow chieftain's request.

Havelok looked and listened as his steadfast comrade did, watching the tranquil water of the Lough Ree reflecting the tall dark trees and blue sky in its ripples. Despite the peacefulness of the setting, Havelok brought the turmoil of his men's impatience with him and couldn't confine it any longer. "What if Domaldr does not come?"

"He'll come."

"How soon?"

"If I knew, I wouldn't be sitting here."

Havelok bit his lip. "Let me rephrase, Dægan. How long will *you* sit here? How long will you expect *my men* to sit here and wait?"

"Have I not paid you well enough, Havelok? Is that it?"

"Of course not. We have been paid well over expectation."

"Then how is waiting more painful than fighting? Enjoy this small peace while it lasts, for I shall soon bring hell upon this earth the moment my brother's ships heave into view. There's not much I share in common with him but that of determination. This I know. He'll come."

"Let us assume he does," Havelok tried to bargain. "What is your plan? At least give me something to tell my men."

"A strategy I can give, for there has been naught else on my mind but Domaldr's fall."

Havelok saw Dægan on the verge of madness, and thought that before long, the young warrior might take to the river and drag his itinerant brother back to this very spot, just so revenge wasn't robbed from him.

"I've learned through my own experience that revenge is often too swift and quite unsatisfying. So to thwart my brother before he learns the true identity of his attackers would be far too kind. When the scouts return, I want you and half your men to ride east a bit, turn around and then come back, meeting Domaldr at this lake. Tell him you're part of Sigtrygg Gale's western front and have orders to make camp and wait for his signal. Tell him that a strong flank position is needed, as the Irish will soon be retreating from their fallen Dubh-Linn.

"Make camp with him, befriend him and his men if you must, especially a man named Breandán. He stands out amongst his peers as his hair is as black as midnight. Spare him and keep him from my brother, but above all, find out where Domaldr keeps my wife. Once you send word, we'll strike hard and do unto him that which he's done to me. Every last one of his men will die, and he'll watch, as I did, everything being ripped from him and burned to the ground. I want to see him beg. I want to see him grovel for my mercy, and only then will I be satisfied."

Tait suddenly appeared through the thick of the forest on his galloping horse, leading his scouts. "Dægan! He's here! Domaldr has come!"

Dægan looked at Havelok and offered the start of a smug yet well-composed smile. "Bring to me the news of my wife, and I shall give your men the bloodthirsty battle they want."

****

"You might as well make yourself comfortable, m'lady," Domaldr spat as he and Breandán entered her tent. "It seems Connacht will have to wait a few more days for its new sovereign. And Breandán, just to show you how grateful I am that you've brought me this much closer to my fame, I offer you the girl you wanted, in advance, if you will. Consider it a gift for your loyalty."

Breandán grew uncomfortably hot with playing this charade. He kept his eyes on Domaldr as it was easier than facing the princess.

"When you're finished having your way with her, I

want at least ten men guarding her outside. Can you see to that for me?"

Breandán steadied his voice as best he could. "Of course."

Domaldr untied a ring of rope from his belt. "See that she's securely tied up, gagged, and blindfolded before you leave too. I'd rather Sigtrygg not know of her, for I'm certain he wouldn't think twice about stealing Connacht right out from under me. And you know how I hate to share my spoils with others."

Unfortunately, Breandán knew more about him than he cared to admit.

"Ease up, *Éireannach*," Domaldr said, slapping his back. "You act as though you've never been with a woman before. I assure you, 'tis even better when there's no husband to yield to." Domaldr took one last look at Mara, who had already begun to inch backward toward the far corner of the tent. "Be kind, princess."

Breandán released a long breath the second Domaldr left, then addressed Mara with eyes that demanded her forgiveness. "Please rest easy. I could never do such things to you."

He sat upon the ground and raised his knees, hanging his head between them. He massaged his scalp and racked his brain for an escape plan that didn't risk Mara's life. He then heard Mara approach and kneel before him. She timidly pulled his hands from his head and lifted his chin.

For the first time, he was able to return her gaze without the threat of someone else noticing. He fixed his eyes on the green of hers, the daintiness of her nose, and the way she parted her lips to utter his name.

"Breandán, why are you doing this? You don't even

know me."

He offered her a kind smile. "But I do. I've seen you many times in the meadow, on the River Shannon, as I was hunting. I thought I could save you and bring you back to your father. Had I known you were married, I wouldn't have interfered."

"Even if I weren't married, why risk death to save me?"

"Because I hoped maybe then you'd notice me. 'Tis all right, though. I don't expect you to, even now. I'm but a commoner." He lowered his gaze. "I should go."

Mara reached out for his arm. "Please, do not leave me. What if Domaldr returns and he wants…"

Breandán saw the sheer terror in her eyes and instantly, he wanted to embrace her. To comfort her. But he forced himself not to, pinning his arms at his sides. "He'll not lay a hand on you."

"How can you be so certain? You heard what he said. Perhaps, after he's drunk with ale, he'll want the pleasures he's awarded you."

"To him, Dægan is dead. The need to take more from your husband…is gone. 'Tis taking from your father that spurs him now. And—" He stopped, realizing his next reason was not suitable for a lady's ears. He struggled to mend the choice of vulgarity Domaldr had used in front of the men. "Domaldr is repulsed by you because he knows his brother had you first."

Contrary to what he thought, Mara didn't seem the least bit offended. Instead, she looked utterly saddened by it. "How many days has it been, Breandán?"

"Four."

She covered her face now, hiding her tears. "Dægan has to come. He has to."

Breandán felt the weight of blame heavy on his shoulders. "Right now, I have to assume he can't because he's without ships, and I must find a way to get you home on my own. Be ready, Mara. When everyone sleeps, I'll come for you." Breandán defied his better judgment and allowed himself to touch her face, wiping a tear from her eye. "Domaldr will not hurt you anymore. I'll die first."

****

Dægan, Tait, Hansen, Ingvarr, and a few other choice men eagerly gathered around Ottarr.

"M'lord, you'll be pleased to know that Havelok and his men have been very successful tonight. Your brother believes wholeheartedly that they're, in fact, Sigtrygg's troops from the east and he's welcomed them to stay. Havelok says that he himself has made camp on the east side, just short of the Lough Ree, far enough away from our archers' reach. This way, they have both created a protected flank and a barricade for those who wish to retreat once the charge has commenced."

Dægan shook his head impatiently. "I want to know of my wife."

Ottarr drew a square in the dirt with his finger. "This is Havelok and his group. Over here, just a bit north is where Domaldr has made his camp, and he's drinking like a fish." He then drew an X in the dirt on the southwest corner of the square. "Your wife is here. But she cannot escape on her own. She's bound, blindfolded, and gagged."

"Is she alone?"

"Nay. There are ten guards that surround her camp."

"And how is it we know all these minute details?"

Dægan interjected.

"From the *Éireannach*. Havelok says he but mentioned your name to Breandán, and he was very forthcoming. Astonishingly though, he's found the gall to make demands—one being that he goes wherever the princess goes."

Dægan thought for a moment. "Fine. I'll allow it. In fact, I think it best I send them both back to the king."

"Send her back?" Tait asked. "Are you mad? Listen to what you're saying."

"I cannot possibly protect her while I engage in battle. Besides, I have to deal with her father regardless."

"You only give the king the upper hand in doing this," Tait argued.

"What I give him is his sanity, knowing his daughter is all right. I've been fortunate enough to have been given that blessing tonight, and he deserves the same."

"And what will keep him from suiting up for war against *us*?"

"Hopefully my wife and my new Irish ally," Dægan said plainly. "I don't think Breandán spared me because he lacked a backbone, Tait."

Dægan scanned the makeshift map in the dirt before giving his orders to the rest of the men. "Tait and I will take a small group of twenty and rid the princess's camp of her guards. Once I've seen to Breandán's and Mara's safety, I'll launch an arrow to signal the archers. I want the entire camp lit afire, including Domaldr's ships. Ingvarr and Ottarr will lead their men in a full frontal attack, Havelok from the east, and I'll meet you all in the middle from the south."

Chapter Twenty-eight

The night air was still and the moon was a faithful, silent ally perched high in the sky, lighting Dægan's path around the Lough Ree. Regardless of its vivid brightness, the lunar light cast many shadows amid the cover of the trees, which also gave Dægan and his men the shaded camouflage they needed to invisibly press forward into position.

They rode as far as they could without detection and descended from their horses like liquid silhouettes, sneaking within the forest around oaks and birches, crawling amid brush and boulders, until they came to the princess's tent.

It was dark and quiet, a little too quiet for Dægan's taste. He had hoped to hear Mara's voice, possibly a song she might be humming in an effort to calm herself to sleep. At this point, he'd even take the sad sound of crying. At least he'd know she was all right, that Domaldr hadn't grown weary of her and taken her life.

Nay, she has to be alive. Domaldr wouldn't waste ten men on a dead woman. It was only to his benefit that Mara remain more than just a returnable item lest he not acquire Connacht. The last thing Domaldr would want to bring upon himself was a war with her father. War was too difficult for him, too dangerous, too risky—as everything could be lost in a matter of seconds. Or worse, his own life could be snuffed amongst those who might otherwise neglect to protect him. She was there, and Domaldr's excessive armada, with a ten-to-one ratio, more than proved it.

He surveyed the land surrounding them and discerned that no one else walked about in the night. It was just as Havelok described...everyone sleeping, save ten.

Gesturing with a series of fingers in a circular motion, Dægan signaled for two groups of five to split up and surround the camp, giving cover should Domaldr's men stir and wander out.

Tait and the ten others followed Dægan as he advanced, each taking cover behind whatever was blessed them, directly in arrow's line of the guards. Dægan checked his men's placement with a casual glance, pleased that the guards were still unaware of their presence. He motioned for the archers to proceed as planned.

Each archer removed an arrow from his shoulder quiver and fitted it slowly and quietly to his bow, taking aim at the corresponding man in front of him. Dægan and Tait crouched into position and white-knuckled their sword hilts, ready to lunge forward. Ready to kill.

Tait nodded first, indicating he was ready.

Dægan nodded back and whistled once, commencing a simultaneous barrage of ten whizzing arrows. Bodies dropped, then he and Tait sprang forward, bringing an end to whatever agony the guards suffered.

****

Mara jumped.

She heard a frenzied rustling in the leaves outside, a ruckus of simultaneous thuds, then complete silence. Through the ghastly stillness that followed, panic crawled beneath her skin like a thousand willowy spiders.

Domaldr.

She knew it. For despite Breandán's insistence, Domaldr was likely intoxicated and stumbling around, while the thought of Dægan having her first was no longer a foul pretense. And who'd know? Who would dare stop him, for what he said was law. He had probably waited for Breandán and everyone else to fall sound asleep before wandering about.

She twisted her wrists and tried to squeeze her hands from the rope. Breandán's cursed extra knots, the ones he placed with the hope that no one would insinuate her part in it all, were too tight to slip out of.

Now she heard footsteps, determined ones, steps that were long and dire as they grew closer to her tent. She frantically rubbed her shoulder against the side of her face, uncovering one eye from her blindfold. Perhaps, it wasn't Domaldr. Maybe Breandán was coming for her, attempting a daring escape.

Aye, it could be done. They were only a few leagues from home, and being this close to her father and safety, she swore she could run forever without tiring.

Mara rubbed the other side of her face, completely ridding the blindfold from both eyes and working like mad on her wrists. She pulled, stretched, twisted, and jerked.

At that fateful moment, a man much too brawny to be Breandán briskly entered her tent. He stood with legs spread, his shining sword marked with the color of violent death, and his flaxen hair curling from under his helmet. He removed it with one jerking motion and dropped it at his feet. Her stomach coiled and turned over. Her breath stopped in her chest. Her eyes fixed on Domaldr's awful face.

And he smiled.

The bastard smiled as if he'd just won her after a fierce tournament. As if he'd seen through Breandán's ruse and was showing her what was left of Breandán dripping from his blade. He snapped his wrist to remove the blood from the weapon, then wiped the residual on his sleeve before sheathing it. Once he yanked a dagger from his belt, Mara had already begun to crawl away.

He came down on top of her and rolled her over, holding her tightly in his arms. Mara screamed and writhed against his body, jerking sharply in hopes her knees would catch his groin.

He called her name and ordered her to be quiet, but she continued to thrash. His hard, cold armor and mail pushed sharply through her gown and against her legs as he sat upon her.

"Mara, 'tis me," he whispered forcibly. "Dægan."

Oh God, she thought. He was callous enough to use that trick again. *How dare he. How dare he think me that stupid!*

She cursed him behind the gag, a long slur of words quite unbefitting a woman, and if she could have spit at him, she would've done that too. Instead, she made doubly certain his effort to procure her was nothing short of difficult.

He grabbed her wrists now, yanking them up to the level of his eyes. Mara braced herself for his swift punishment and even welcomed the possibility of death before he could have his way with her.

"Hold still!" he commanded as he held the blade between her wrists. He paused only for a moment, then put the knife directly on the rope and pulled. Her hands dropped free, and instantly she fought for all she was worth. She tried throwing her forehead into his nose, but missed. She tried gouging out his eyes, but he defended himself at every turn.

"Mara, please listen to me. 'Tis I, Dægan. I swear it. Look at me."

She clenched her hand into an embittered fist and struck him solidly, snapping his head to the right. He groaned and gripped both her hands, forcing them above her head as he pinned her to the ground.

"Look at me," he said again, but she squeezed her eyes shut on purpose. "Damnation, woman!" He plummeted to her ear and spoke in a gentled tone. "Shh…listen to my voice, love. Listen to it. I beg you."

Mara stilled for a brief moment, nauseated by the heated whisper upon her skin and cringing at the thought of Domaldr's putrid breath upon her. He made no effort to maul her neck as she thought he would. Through her desperate heavy panting, she smelled a hint of expensive oils, the familiar scent of his hair, and the faint masculine aura of his leather armor.

She stared as he sat up. She wanted to believe with everything in her that this man was Dægan. That, through the impossible, her tried-and-true husband had found a way to travel across the sea and rescue her.

She studied his chest and broad shoulders, eyeing the thick shell of metal plates, leather, and ringlets around his torso and arms. His armor looked nothing like Dægan's. She feared it was a trick. Almost felt in her heart that it was, and sucked in a breath for screaming, but he placed a gentle finger to her gagged mouth.

"Look at me," he whispered to her. "Listen closely to what I say to you, for there's not much time. You first gave yourself to me in Hlymrekr. And the next morning, I thought you regretted it, but you didn't. I can describe every part of you if you want me to. I can tell you how sweet your tongue is after you've sucked the sugar from my finger. I can count on one hand the times I made love to you and wish on my very life 'twere more. I can speak of the solitary freckle just beneath your right breast and the birthmark on your inner thigh, for only a husband could know such intimate things. I'm your husband. I want naught more than your love and trust right now and by the great God in Heaven, I wish I could steal it. But I won't. I'll wait forever and a day for you. Listen to my words, Mara, for I speak as a lost sheep. Find me. Find me in your heart...*I just might be there.*"

Mara felt the certainty in his words and the sweet ring of familiarity. No one could know those things save for Dægan himself. Relief and unfettered happiness washed over her like an ocean wave, though her words were trapped behind the gag. As final proof of his true identity, she quickly lifted his kirtle and there, like a brand, was the wound across his left thigh that he'd received ten days ago in the cavern.

He's alive. Dægan is truly alive! She reached for him, and with her fingertips, she traced his face, drawing a shuddering sigh from his lips.

Dægan pulled Mara's gag down over her chin, and her sweet voice filled his ears. His name never sounded as good as it did right then. He pushed her hair from her face and smiled with her—his wife was safe in his arms.

"Shh..." he whispered, then dove tenderly to her mouth, eager to feel the warmth of her supple lips once again. He kissed her passionately, far from the perversity of

Domaldr's kiss. If she had any doubt at all about his true identity, he made sure to resolve it.

"How did you get here?" she asked. "I saw your ships burn, every last one of them. And your men? Are they all right?"

Dægan didn't want to explain. He didn't even want to talk, for it was far too long a story. He just wanted to savor this moment and hold her for an eternity. Unfortunately, he knew this small moment of peace was merely a brief calm before the storm. He only nodded to answer her string of questions and hid the tears of relief pooling in his eyes.

"M'lord, you've suffered, and I cannot begin to imagine your pain. Speak to me."

Dægan couldn't. He didn't even know where to begin. He just closed his eyes and slowly let his head fall to her bosom, finally finding consolation from all his troubles, all his bitterly nagging worries. He exhaled a breath that clung so deep and fierce within his lungs, and lost himself in the soft swell of her body. The feel of her delicate fingertips in his hair and the strength of her dainty arms around him felt so right.

So perfect.

So content he almost forgot about his men waiting outside.

The tent flap lifted, and Tait walked in unannounced. As soon as he realized the intimate positon Dægan and Mara were in, he quickly turned his head. "My apologies, m'lady. I knew well that the two of you would need time to reacquaint yourselves, but I didn't think there was time for much more."

Dægan looked up from his idyllic heaven and stared into the green of Mara's eyes he'd missed so much. "Leave us, Tait."

"But, m'lord—"

"I said leave us. Drag the dead into the woods and replace them with ten of our own."

"You cannot be serious. We have no time for this—"

Dægan finally tore his eyes away from his wife and glared sternly at Tait. "Leave us!"

Tait respectfully stepped backward and exited the tent, but not before fighting with the flap that tangled around his arm. Dægan heard him curse and then give the orders, after which he heard dragging bodies.

He redirected his attention on Mara and stared for such a long time without smiling or speaking.

"Why do you look at me this way?"

"Can a husband not drown in his wife's eyes while she holds him?" He paused for the length of several breaths, looking beyond her beautiful green eyes at the rest of her body. What was first a sensual fixation now became a demanding search for Domaldr's telltale brutality. He nearly trembled as he searched for bruises and marks.

"Did he hurt you?" Dægan examined every inch of her face, neck, and arms. "Tell me now, did he hurt you, Mara?"

"Nay."

"Did he *touch* you?"

Mara shook her head. "M'lord, please. He did naught to me."

Dægan knew better. Domaldr had done plenty to Mara, and the effect it had on her was obvious, since it had taken a battling insistence to convince her that he was who he claimed to be. He retrieved the dagger from the ground beside him, flipped it with a quick toss, and reached down her legs between her ankles. "Hold still," he commanded, and in one swift motion, he cut the rope.

Dægan rubbed the life back into her legs, but hid the sharp pain in his ribs that cruelly reminded him of his cursed brother.

Mara sat up to meet him and stroked his cheek. "I see anger in your eyes."

"Of course you do. I've yet to find a place for this hatred."

"This has to end."

"Oh, it will, Mara. 'Twill all end tonight." He pushed himself up to his knees, and Mara shuffled closer to him.

"Do not do this," she pleaded. "Take what is yours and leave."

"I will do just that, but not before I see Domaldr beg for mercy."

Mara frowned. "Even if he dropped to his knees, you'd not give him that luxury. I know you. I can see it in your eyes. But don't forget what little your wrath will bring you, what little Rutland's death did to comfort your breaking heart over Eirik. And just like Eirik, Domaldr is still your broth—"

"Do not finish that thought, I beg you. I've heard those words one too many times."

Mara cupped his face, peering into eyes that Dægan knew were twisting in turbulent storms. "Can you truly live with killing your own blood?"

"'Twould be far easier to live with his death than yours, Mara. Why can you not understand that?" He gripped her arms tightly, and his voice shook as he spoke. "I cannot live without you. And we'll speak no more of it ever again." He realized the harshness of his grip and eased the grasp of his fingertips, regretting that he'd reacted with such brutality against her. "I've five hundred men awaiting me outside and your father awaits you as well. You'll be safer with him."

Mara stilled in the moment. "My father?"

Dægan nodded. "I've sent for Breandán to see to your return."

Mara's eyes widened. "You know of Breandán?"

"I know of his loyalty to you and his mercy to me. For the latter, I still cannot understand why, but if you know any reason *not* to trust him, now would be the time to tell me."

Mara thought of Breandán's devotion. "He's all that and more."

As if he heard his name called, Breandán burst through the tent, Tait following closely behind. "I tried to stop him, m'lord, but he threatened to wake the entire camp."

Dægan stood with a hitch in his stride and shielded Mara instinctively behind his back. "I told you to wait outside."

"And I was told you'd not be long." Breandán retorted. He eyed Mara. "Are you all right?"

Tait grabbed Breandán by his cloak. "Of course she's all right. Are you blind?"

"Tait," Dægan interrupted, raising his hand. "Release him."

Tait uncurled his fingers from the man's clothing, and Breandán shook his clothes back into place, then reached for Mara's hand. "Time is wasting. We should go."

At first, Dægan found Breandán's command a little out of place, but he let it pass since he couldn't argue differently. He stepped aside, allowing Breandán to come nearer. "He's right, Mara. You must go."

"I want to stay with you, Dægan."

But Dægan marched right up to her and clasped her face in his hands, resting his forehead upon hers. "God in heaven, Mara. This is no place for you. I aim to make war this night and vengeance doesn't come without bloodshed. I'd be a fool to let you stay. Please, I cannot bear to lose you again."

Mara rubbed her nose against his and gave in. Slowly, Dægan turned his attention back to Breandán. "Do you know the way to go from here?"

"I do."

"You'll be escorted for most of the journey, simply as a precaution. I trust my wife's judgment on your loyalty, but don't think for one moment that you should *ever* stray from my plan."

Breandán didn't seem shaken by Dægan's order and stepped forward to grab Mara's arm. "I'll get her home. Of this you can be certain."

Normally, Dægan would admire confidence in any man, especially when it involved taking care of his wife. But for some reason, he didn't care for Breandán's. The fact that he came barging in unannounced and was now grabbing Mara's arm as if he had the authority to do so didn't sit well. To Dægan, the Irishman was throwing more weight around than he had to spare on his thin, youthful frame.

Dægan grabbed Mara's other arm and leaned forward. "Before I let you leave with my wife, there's something you need to do for me."

Breandán held his ground. "What would that be?"

"Keep the king from coming here."

Breandán looked at Mara and then back at Dægan, who never faltered in his steely glare. "'Twould be better to come from her mouth than mine. I'm not one of his army, but a mere commoner. He'll not listen to me."

Dægan didn't buy his sad excuse. "He'll think enough of you when you walk through his gates with his rescued daughter."

"Dægan," Mara butted in. "I can show my father the chest. Then he'll know of your good will for me—"

"What chest?"

"This one," she said, running to its hidden location in the tent. "Your wedding gift to me."

Bewilderment overtook Dægan as he laid his eyes on the precious wooden chest. He walked to it and dropped to his knees, placing his hands upon the lid. "I thought it burned with everything else… I thought it gone…" He opened it, inspecting the contents within. Every single item was there. The folded silks, the oil jars, the jewels, and the silver sparkling in the corner.

Dægan slammed the lid shut and narrowed his gaze on the mysterious Irishman. "Did you take this from my longhouse?"

"Only to give it to Mara. Your house was on fire—"

"Why? Why would you do that?"

"You're welcome," Breandán uttered in response.

"Don't play the nobleman with me," he said, charging forward.

But Tait jumped between them. "Dægan, enough. We haven't the time for this."

Dægan ignored Tait's warning. "Why would you even care to save this from the fire? You had a purpose, and it had naught to do with selflessness. Come on, tell me. Why would you bring this?"

The silent deadly stare between Dægan and Breandán was long and barbed with jealous animosity. Neither blinked nor flinched as they gazed deeply into each other's souls, until realization struck Dægan. "You love Mara. You brought this in hopes to win her heart should I have died. To begin where I left off."

Mara stepped forward and touched Dægan's forearm, his fist clenched at his side. "That is absurd, Dægan. He pulled it from the fire so that I might trust him. Tell him, Breandán."

Dægan scornfully coaxed the Irishman, "Aye, Breandán. Do tell."

"Fine. I love her. But what good does it do to proclaim it? My heart's longing will never be satisfied. At the least, you might find consolation in *that*, Northman. Be that as it may, I'll protect her with every beat of my heart, and there's naught you can do about it."

"You bastard!" Dægan seethed through his teeth as he brought up his hands to choke Breandán.

Tait fought to hold back his chieftain as much as Dægan struggled to control his rage. "Enough! You cannot settle this here, not now. And what does it matter? She's married to you. She loves you—you know this. Hate him if you must, but he's right. Who better to protect your wife than someone who loves her?" Tait grabbed Dægan by the jaw and jerked it in his direction. "He's not the threat here! Send her on her way before 'tis too late. Do it!"

Dægan twisted from Tait's grasp and drilled his palm into his own eye socket, unable to dam the stream of images afflicting his mind. He paced as he came to terms with Breandán's so-called gracious intentions. "I'm going to forget what you just said to me, *Éireannach*. But I order you again to keep your king away from here."

"What if I cannot?" Breandán asked. "What if he

doesn't listen to me? What, then?"

Dægan knew he had to make a decision concerning the Connacht king, a crucial one, as it meant war might surely erupt between them. He looked at Mara now, her green eyes fixed so brilliantly on him. "I'll surrender."

Tait cursed and kicked the ground, but Dægan stood his ground. "I cannot fight this king any more than I could my own father. Mara, you must help me. You have to keep him from coming. I can't win this battle with my brother if your father intervenes."

Mara's answer came in the form of a swift embrace, and his ribs moved under the small weight of her arms. He held back a moan and returned her love with a lasting kiss, one that still fell too short for his liking. He bowed his head, touching his forehead to hers, and smelled the sweet oils of her hair one last time. Memorizing it. "Go, love."

Breandán warily pulled Mara from his arms and led her away. "Dægan," he began, but was cut short by the chieftain's icy, hard gaze.

"What now?" Dægan snarled.

Breandán squared his shoulders. "I cannot stop what my heart feels for Mara, no more than you can. But she loves you, and you, her. My love could never equal that. Nor should you think me a challenge when this is all done. I'll see her home. Trust me, Northman, on both accounts."

Chapter Twenty-nine

Dægan sat upon his great black horse, the only thing Domaldr had not killed, stolen, or burned to ashes before he left the isle. Dægan wasn't sure why he'd spared the horses over the sheep and cattle. An ignorant oversight, he thought, for Domaldr made many in his life, including leaving another man to slit his throat for him.

He patted the horse's neck as it fidgeted to burst from the woods. "Easy, boy," he crooned. *Not much longer.* His mind drifted with idle thoughts of Breandán and Mara, wondering if they'd made it to the keep by now, wondering if Breandán was truly trustworthy, if he dared stray from the plan given him. But even if the answers to his many questions were all nay, what good would regret do now, for his hands were tied with more pressing matters.

He tried to keep his mind on the battle that was soon to come, and the surprise he aimed to give his brother in the end. He devised that he'd be helmeted, as would Tait, Hansen, and Ottarr, and any other man Domaldr would recognize from his childhood. This would keep their identity hidden until the final splendid moment when all was burned to the ground and only Domaldr was left standing.

Dægan smiled in imagining Domaldr's astonishment the moment he'd discover his adversaries. The thought brought him great pleasure, as did the thought of the sure silence to follow, for he knew Domaldr would be beside himself.

Speechless and dumbstruck.

He looked down at the helmet in his lap as the dark, empty eyeholes stared back at him. He thought he heard Nevan's voice echoing from within the riveted metal. *"Don't let your brother determine the man you are."*

Dægan looked away, hoping to restore a cold, dull pulse into his warm-blooded heart. It proved difficult as he sat quietly on his steed, looking out upon the camp of sleeping men. It seemed underhanded to be readying themselves in the night's shadows for an all-out attack. This was no way for any man to die, unprepared and unaware. But in remembering his brother's lack of compassion, the way he killed Steinar and Vegard like dogs, the way he murdered them and countless others so savagely, he quickly set upon *an eye for an eye.*

Tait rode up behind him with an intense expression, and only then did Dægan feel his blood course through his veins.

"Mara's chest is buried as you ordered, and the men are ready." Tait placed his helmet on his head. "Are you?"

Dægan took a deep breath and rehashed his friend's poignant words. Was he ready? Was he prepared to see his own brother at the end of his sword and not think twice about running him through? Would he cower at killing his own flesh and blood, or would that close lineage be the very motivation he needed to come at Domaldr full throated and savage?

Tait asked again, "Are you ready, m'lord?"

Dægan blinked his reeling thoughts away and placed his helmet upon his head, nodding as he took a burning arrow from one of his foot soldiers and laid it across his bow. He paused and stared at the dancing flame, the smoldering color of sunset orange contained in a fiery ball at the tip. He watched it writhe and flicker against the blackness of night as if it were joyous for the flight ahead—that it too had rage and vengeance in its being.

Dægan looked over his shoulder at the many *hirdmen* armed to the teeth with swords, axes, spears, and shields. Their eyes eager for the fight, their hearts pounding for the thrill, their blood racing for the cause, all for righting a tremendous wrong.

He returned their hard, blistering stares and stretched his bow to its limits, taking aim at the distant north. "Remember men, no mercy, no prisoners. Take what you want, and let the rest burn."

"And what of Domaldr?" Tait asked as his horse stamped impatiently.

"Leave him for me."

Suddenly a whisper of chanting filled Dægan's ears just as he let the arrow fly. It echoed low in the night, as if it actually trailed from the hissing arrow across the camp.

Dægan looked at Tait, and saw that his friend's helmet did nothing to conceal the satisfaction on his face, or the low chanting of his name in unison with those who had started it. *Ræliksen...Ræliksen... Ræliksen...*was on every man's lips.

****

Cathal Mac Conor looked up from his goblet of wine as he heard one of his servants calling from the empty inner bailey below. Since his daughter had gone missing, he often found himself locked away in his private chambers to drown in his cups, and this night was no different. At first, he wondered if he'd imagined the voice telling him that riders were approaching. He was just drunk enough to believe it. Then he heard swift footfalls upon the stairs as if someone were taking them two at a time. He stood stoically before the servant entered his room and draped his great cloak over his forearm.

His door burst open and a servant doubled over, panting. "Sire, there are riders approaching. Two...and one looks to be your daughter."

"Mara? Alive?"

The servant tried to regain a stately composure. "Aye, sire. She lives."

Cathal rushed past his servant, almost knocking him over, and ran down the stairs to the great room of the keep. He ran faster than he'd ever run in his life across the bailey, meeting Fergus, his advisor, at the gatehouse. "Is it true? Is it true my daughter lives? She lives?"

Fergus kept a restrained poise about him. "We cannot be certain. I've sent men to ride out and meet them."

"It has to be her," Cathal exclaimed.

"Sire," Fergus said firmly. "It could be a trick. Everyone, slave or freeman, within a hundred leagues of Dún na hAbhann has heard of your daughter's disappearance and the reward for her return. Raising hope at this point would be hasty and reckless."

Cathal felt his heart sink heavily into his stomach. It was the first time he'd heard any news—any good news—and for it all to be slighted by the prospect of someone hoping to benefit from his loss by pretending to be his daughter was more than he could bear. He tasted the foulness of treachery once again, and swallowed back the bitter lump that swelled in his throat. Bleakly, he turned to walk away.

"Sire!" a guard shouted from the top of the arsenal tower. "They ride with the flag high, sire. The flag is high. 'Tis Mara."

Cathal burst with emotion. "Open the gates! Open the gates! Quickly!" He dropped to his knees and thanked God for his daughter's return, crying in his hands like a child. His tears spilled in happiness as the sound of hooves clopped merrily on the old dirt pathway. When the riders came into view, he sprang to his feet and ran from the narrowly opened portcullis to his daughter.

"Mara!" he called, arms outstretched. "Oh, my sweet Mara! You're home!"

Mara slid from the horse and dove into her father's arms. Her joy matched his. "I cannot believe I'm here! I'm home! Oh, Father, I'm home!"

Cathal held her tight, his arms almost crushing her. "Are you all right, my sweet?" He pulled her face from his chest and looked her over. "Where have you been? What happened to you?"

Immediately, Fergus and the guards within the gatehouse unsheathed their swords, and those above them marked their arrows assuredly for Breandán's head through the murder holes in the ceiling.

"Father!" Mara cried. "Breandán is not the enemy. He's my rescuer. He's unarmed."

Cathal spun his daughter around and shielded her with his back. "Fergus, lower your weapons. This man deserves our gratitude, not death. My apologies, Breandán," the king declared. He spread his arms and welcomed his daughter's rescuer to his ringfort. "Please. My home is your home. Becka!"

"Coming, sire!" Becka, a short and plump servant,

tottered from her quarters across the bailey and came running. She threw a cloak around her shoulders and tucked a few loosely bouncing tresses back into her bun.

Cathal barely noticed Becka's bedclothes or the fact that every servant—awakened by his shouts—shared the same night garments as they filtered about the chaotic courtyard. He took his cloak from his shoulders and wrapped it around his daughter. "Becka, draw two hot baths. And food. Get them hot soup and bread, cheese, whatever they want. Make them a feast, for all I care! Let's all eat!"

"Father, I need to talk to you," Mara said, pulling him aside. "So much has happened, and I know not where to begin."

"Let's start with rewarding the brave Breandán," Cathal declared. "Yours is of seven *cumals*. Have you enough land to support that sum of cattle, son?"

"I believe so."

"And who is your father?"

Breandán stumbled to keep up with all the excitement. "Um, Liam, sire."

"Ah, one of my own clansmen. Then Liam shall have seven *cumals* as well." Cathal jerked Breandán into his arms and patted his back in joyous thunder. "From this day forth, everyone shall know of your great name. You'll be amongst the noblest of kinsman with a fine display of cattle in your holding and—take the silver as well. 'Tis yours!"

"But, sire—"

"Enough," Cathal said, raising his hand. "Go, fetch your bath and fill your stomachs. Both of you." He hugged his daughter one more time and kissed her forehead. "This is a great day! Praise be to God!"

The entire keep cheered as their king had, filling the

bailey with laughter and smiles, chatter and busy feet, each one prompted by duty first and then excitement.

"Father," Mara tried again. "Please, you must listen to me. There's a war going on just beyond your gates near the Lough Ree. And I'm a married woman."

Chapter Thirty

Dægan stretched his neck from side to side and pressed a hand to his broken ribs one last time. He'd never fussed so much over an injury before, and he could only hope in the heat of battle that a surging would overtake his body and desensitize everything from his pains to his reluctance in this fight.

Normally, by now he'd be praying, hoping to foster the spirit of his war god in body and mind, in the strokes of his sword, and the drive of his steps. Tonight, he simply asked for victory from any god who'd hear him.

Dægan slipped his dagger from his belt and placed it between his teeth. His bow he brought to his shoulder and leaned forward in his stirrups, preparing for when his horse erupted from its shadowy hiding place. He and his mounted *hirdmen* watched the last shower of lighted arrows from the west land on their targets, setting ablaze each and every tent situated before them.

"Hold," Dægan said to the men behind him. "Let them all come out."

Tait naturally objected to giving Domaldr's men an advantage, but held his position as ordered. Dægan fixed his eyes on the spreading fires and the increasing numbers of men dashing from their burning beds and assembling in the open, confused and distraught.

Dægan brandished his sword high in the air and bellowed for all to hear, commencing the great charge at the south end of the camp. Twenty horses tore from the forest, and their hooves dug into the dirt for traction with clumps of grass and soil spattering behind them. In seconds, they were sprinting at top speed, a thunderous herd of beasts and blades.

They rode in a fervent cluster toward the first group of disoriented men in their way and, without so much as slowing their pace, Dægan and his men cut them down like saplings. Those who still stood shouted warnings of a hell-bent stampede through camp.

A trap! We've been had by Sigtrygg's men! Arm yourselves!

Dægan and his men had already begun to split up, taking on the stragglers who were either too late in gathering their weapons from the blazing tents or in fleeing for their lives. In no time, the southern part of the camp was laden with bodies and blood. No mercy…no prisoners.

Just as the thought of an easy slaughter entered Dægan's mind, a pair of men raced to cut him and his men off. Only a few paces away, they stood abreast from each other and stretched their bows for Dægan.

Unable to stop his horse's gallop, he steered directly toward them. He took the dagger from his mouth and aimed at one while setting to leap upon the other. Before he could release the blade, two well-marked arrows cut across his path from the east. One sank into the archer's open chest and the other found a home in a tender throat.

Dægan wrenched his horse about-face, anticipating rampant enemy fire, but was relieved to see Havelok and his men charging wildly toward him. He smiled, raising his sword in gratitude for the timely assistance, and continued on his virulent crusade.

Finally, from the west, Dægan saw the flurry of

Ottarr's and Ingvarr's *hirdmen* running at full speed, sifting between the flame-consumed tents like seeping water, and sniping the distant men with arrows and spears. They quickly laid waste to the narrow pathways and herded the rest of the fleeing men like aimless cattle toward Dægan's horsemen. Those of Domaldr's men from the north, who had ample time to arm themselves, made like a swarm of angry bees toward the core of the camp, unaware of the tragedy in store for them.

As in any battle, the casualties reigned on both sides, death being an unbiased reaper. But to Dægan's dismay, his brother had not yet reared in any form of retaliation. He should have surrendered by now, for it was obvious his plan of overtaking Connacht was quickly going awry. Without a tent to hide in or a solid place to protect himself, Dægan feared his craven snake of a brother had already slithered away.

Coward, Dægan thought as he hacked his way through the last determined men who clung at his stirrups like meddlesome flies. He spun his horse, searching the turmoil of clanging iron for his gutless brother, only to lock eyes with Tait across the field. "Where's Domaldr?" Dægan shouted, wielding another hard blow to his right. "Find him! Find him now!"

Tait searched through the shadows of the firelight and disorder, but a sturdy brute scaled his horse from behind, wrapped his arm around Tait's throat, and pulled him to the ground. Both fell in a heap, each scrambling to stand before the other. The diligent soldier was the quicker, and he rammed his shoulder into Tait's gut. With the momentum of his charge, he wrapped his arms around the back of Tait's thighs and stood up, flipping him over.

Tait slammed upon the ground and rolled quickly to

his knees, gasping for breath. The large man turned on his heel and saw Tait still on all fours, wheezing for all he was worth.

Dægan watched helplessly as his friend became an easy kill. He was too far away for a broadsword, and a dagger was too light a weapon to throw and make the distance.

Seeing one of Domaldr's men about to throw a spear in the same direction, Dægan charged forward on his horse and snatched it from the man's hands. He took aim and launched it into Tait's adversary before the man could deliver a final blow. The spear sank deep into the man's chest, and he fell to his death, clutching the wooden pole that jutted from his body.

Dægan rode up quickly and circled Tait, using his horse as a shield. He guarded Tait with his sword held high in fury until his friend was able to draw an effortless breath. Tait clasped Dægan's outstretched forearm and mounted behind him. "Are you all right?" Dægan asked, knowing Tait had never been so close to death before.

Tait nodded and rested his head on Dægan's shoulder, until he saw an armed mass invasion heading straight for them. "Odin's blood, m'lord."

Dægan turned his horse one-eighty and made quick to alert the others. "Havelok! Your flank!"

Havelok shouted to his men, and they reined their horses to hold off the oncoming horde. They outnumbered the riotous group, but unfortunately, their horses were no match for the assailing arrows hungry to settle bitter scores. Many steeds reared and dropped like stones, casting their riders to a dreadful fall upon the hard ground. Some met a crushing death underneath.

Dægan joined Havelok and steered his horse back into

the thick of the rampage. He lifted his right leg over the horse's neck and steadied himself over the horn. "Tait, take the reins. Ride around and thin this herd with your bow."

"What in damnation are you doing?" But before Tait could stop his chieftain, he dove off the horse and landed on the enemy's back, tackling him to the ground. Dægan rose up and slit his throat.

There was no time for him to breathe or rest, for the next foe was already swinging a wide sword at him. He rose clumsily to his feet and charged the man head-on, stopping short of his reach. The man lost his balance with the momentum of his swing and fell straight into Dægan's slashing dagger, getting a second dose of punishment in his face from Dægan's knee. As the man fell, Dægan pressed on through the tight huddle of combating men, striking at vulnerable heads and legs in his path.

Another persevering foe trained his sights on Dægan and lunged with a powerful sweep of his iron. Dægan blocked the blow with a downward slash and elbowed an unmasked nose bridge, but not without feeling a slight pull from his ribs. He groaned and shoved the man aside, rounding a hard swing at the man's head.

Dægan took down many men. His strikes and counterblows gave no mercy to anything in his channeled eyesight. He turned and twisted, punched and kicked, clearing his path for a maddened thrust behind him.

Blood covered his weapons now and seeped into the small grooves of mail armor protecting his arms and torso. Even his helmet spoke of his wrath, spattered with red. But in his violent rage, a fist caught him unawares across his face and then again in his already-broken rib cage.

Dægan slumped to his knees. The pain was so excruciating, it took his breath away as well as his sense of reality. He'd no thought of danger, and no will to fight back. He couldn't even determine from where the blow had come. All he could think and feel were the shards of loose bone piercing his side.

Once more, another fist grazed Dægan's face, this time knocking him flat on his back. The jolt of his fall restoked the burning pain that wrapped around his entire chest. Dægan opened his eyes, just in time to see his attacker looming over him with a sword point aimed at his gut. He sent his foot swiftly in between the man's legs, and gladly watched him fall to his knees and cradle his groin.

Still unable to bring strength to his upper body, Dægan smashed the man's windpipe with his booted heel and watched him writhe and gasp for air through the gurgle of blood and splintered cartilage.

Hoping no one else was aiming for him, Dægan gingerly rolled to all fours and crept across the ground. Every inhale and flex of his torso felt as if someone was gouging out his organs through his rib cage.

He wanted to call out and summon Tait's attention amongst the trampling feet of his enemies, but he thought even the slightest cry for help would mark him with an "easy kill" flag above his head.

Alternately, he wormed in silence and exhaled in tattered breaths. His compromising condition rendered him a vulnerable target, and it was only a matter of time before his luck ran out. Dragging himself an inch at a time took more energy than he had to spare, and the lowly act of groveling was an insult to his very being.

He was more than that. More than just another wounded body on the field, withering in defeat. He was Dægan, son of Rælik. A warrior who didn't give up without a fight.

Gnashing his teeth, he used all his might and his sword to push himself to his knees and then to his feet. The simple task was colossal, but he exhaled a breath of relief in feeling the ground beneath his boots. His tiny blessing of liberation was short-lived, for he felt the looming presence of danger behind him.

He turned in an instant and saw the face of another aggressor running straight for him, a horrifying sight of muscular arms extending a blood-dripping battle-ax over his head. With catlike instinct, Dægan knelt to avoid the oncoming blade and thrust his sword deep into the man's gut. He twisted as he pulled his weapon free, and it felt as if his own flesh had torn from his bones.

Unable to hold back this time, he wailed in pain and fell forward, stiff-arming the ground to catch himself. His body shook as he clutched the grass. He refused to succumb to a fate where he crawled along the ground again.

A familiar voice shouted his name. He looked up and saw Tait galloping toward him, his bow stretched tight in marking a target behind him. Dægan closed his eyes and put total faith in his friend's ability, holding as still as he could. The arrow sailed from its counterpart and hissed past Dægan's ear, fatally piercing the intended prey just in time.

He opened his eyes once he heard the body hit the ground and the eruption of boisterous cheers from his *hirdmen*. With weapons raised, they chanted their praises to each other and to Thor for his godly assistance. The battle waged had been won.

Tait trotted up and dismounted alongside his fallen friend. "Are you hurt?" He threw Dægan's arm over his shoulder and helped him to his feet. Despite great care, he still drew a painful moan from his chieftain. "Is it your ribs?"

Dægan nodded, incapable of responding with words.

"Someone help me!" Tait called to the others. "Ottarr!"

Ottarr removed his helmet and came running. Blood and dirt soiled his old gray beard and deep concern etched his face. He steadied Dægan as they walked him toward a large boulder at the edge of the meadow. They eased him to a sitting position and waited for Dægan to settle before they examined his injuries.

Dark red blood oozed from beneath his leather armor, but in truth, it was impossible to determine whose blood it was. Every man on the battlefield had been spattered with blood in one way or another.

Ottarr lifted Dægan's mail and armor, and discovered the source of the flow. Upon further inspection, he determined that the injury was much worse than a couple of broken bones. "M'lord, your ribs have come through the skin."

Dægan waved Ottarr's hands away and groaned. "Where is Domaldr? Tell me you found him." He saw the hesitation in both Ottarr's and Tait's faces, and he grew restless.

Ottarr eventually obliged, "Just say the word and 'twill all be over."

Dægan perused their strange expressions. "What is that supposed to mean?"

"It means that you're in no condition to fight Domaldr," Ottarr explained, "and there are plenty of men here who'd gladly see to it for you."

"Where is he?" Dægan shouted, trying to stand. But

the stabbing pain rippled through him, and he sat back down. He glared through the eyeholes of his helmet, a stark contrast to the scanty whisper of his voice. "Tell me where he is."

Tait sighed. "He's tied to a tree. Ready to hang."

"Nay," Dægan protested, striving to stand again. "He's mine."

"Dægan, sit down."

As soon as Tait forced him to sit, Dægan seized his hand and hyperflexed it, palm up, until Tait fell to his knees. Holding pressure on his friend's wrist, he looked Tait in the eye. "Don't ever try that again."

Tait held very still lest he'd lose his wrist. "If you think tearing my hand from my arm will make a difference where Domaldr is concerned, then you'd better have the heart to do more than that. I'll not let you kill yourself just because you cannot let down your pride. In the end, all that matters is that Domaldr is dead. Say the word, and he hangs. You can still have your revenge if it means that much to you. Let him see your face as he takes his last breaths, while you still live to fight another day."

Live to fight another day...

Dægan heard those words as distinctly as a slap across his face. Had it been a fortnight ago, before he met Mara, he would've gladly glorified the chance to prove himself to Thor on future battlefields. But now, he detested the notion of existing in this world just so he could draw his sword one more time—one more opportunity to die valiantly for a nonexistent god. After he dealt with his brother, Dægan swore he'd hang up his sword and fight no more.

He released Tait's hand and stubbornly stood without assistance. "Ottarr, place your helmet back on your head."

"Dægan, is this really necessary?" Ottarr responded

with reproach. "You've had your enjoyment, and there comes a time when all games must end."

"Enjoyment? You think I'm enjoying this? That I'll take pleasure in killing my own brother? How dare you? How dare you think that little of me, Ottarr?

"I've battled with this, day after day, night after night, moment after cursed moment, and do you know what I see in my thoughts and in my dreams? I see the men I called my brothers, unselfishly devoted kinsmen whom I grew up with—Steinar, Vegard, Sveir—all slain by *his* hand like they were nothing. Domaldr grew up with them just as I did. He shared their homes, their food, their love, and their loyalty. But yet he spat on them, not once, but twice. He's been the reason for so many of our people's deaths. My father's people. And for that, he deserves nothing less than death. But not by a rope," Dægan said, shaking his head. "Nay. Not by a rope. By the very remnants of the family who brought him into this world. By the same flesh and blood he so despises. 'Twill be *my* hand, Ottarr, and no other. Now hide your face and show me where the bastard is."

Ottarr picked up his helmet, replaced it on his head, and led his chieftain to the distant tree where they held Domaldr captive. Many of the others followed closely behind, including Tait, who'd lugged himself from the ground in a hurry. No one was going to miss this epic clash between the brothers.

Havelok met Dægan and his crew halfway into the woods and handed off Domaldr's weapons to Dægan, including the beautiful sword that was once his father's. "He's all yours."

Dægan didn't say a word. With the sentimental sword in his hands once again, he thought of his father and the pain he must have felt years ago after realizing his own son had betrayed him. How difficult it must have been for his father to look his kinsmen in the eyes and see their sorrow, their disappointment, their anger. Or to hear through rumors and whispered scorn that some had put the blame on him. Dægan recalled those spineless men who'd gossiped in the dark corners of the mead hall about his father—how they still had enough gall to disparage Rælik while drinking his mead. Although Dægan was unsure of how many tables he, himself, overturned that night, he knew well he had put an end to the disgraceful criticism of their jarl. He only wished he could've brought justice to his people for the misdeeds Domaldr had committed—deliberate crimes, he reminded himself.

Dægan hated that Domaldr had gotten away with it then, and he hated it now more than ever. With this duel, he'd bring justice to his people and honor back to his father's name.

He fit his hand around the jeweled hilt, tilting the blade down to the ground and rotating it to check its condition.

Flawless.

"You've done well, Havelok. But there's one last thing I must ask of you. I sent Breandán to see that the Connacht king does not strike out in search of us. Right now, I'm a weary man in mind and body, and I cannot afford to assume Breandán's clout with the king, nor my own wife's for that matter. If the Irish come, I must know of their whereabouts before they know of mine. Set up a perimeter of scouts around this area, but under no circumstance does anyone strike out against them. Give that order clearly."

Havelok gripped Dægan's shoulders. "Your father was a great man, and I should've served him better. Perhaps he'd still be alive. But I hope I do him well in continuing to serve under you." Havelok ended his sentimental speech with a good, manly embrace and then left, unaware that he'd adjusted the loose bones of Dægan's ribs.

Dægan took a long and deep breath, as much as his ribs would allow, and held back every oath that came to mind on Havelok's behalf. In redirecting his anger to someone more deserving of curses, he stared at his brother at the base of the large oak.

Domaldr's head hung. His will was crushed. He was not exactly the man Dægan wanted to spit oaths at and punish without mercy. Where was Domaldr's dynamic fire, his ruthlessness, his loudmouthed threats and curses—all the things he wanted to deliver a swift justice to? Where were they?

Dægan called to him as he walked closer. "You there!"

Domaldr looked up and saw a hellishly intimidating warrior approach, his armor and mail tainted with his men's blood. His strides were long and formidable. His voice was deep and certain. Domaldr could only assume a man as notable and powerfully built as this one, was none other than the infamous Sigtrygg Gale.

"What is your name?" the stranger asked.

Domaldr heard the very familiar voice, but thought the ale he drank that night had finally gone to his head. "Domaldr Ræliksen."

"Ah," the stranger said, feigning a slim recollection. "You're the great son of Rælik. Domaldr 'the Long-Winded,' I think I've heard. Word has also spread across the seas that you wronged a great many people in your life, killed more men than Kleng 'the Claw' Thorsson, have you?"

Domaldr squirmed at the man's compliment, knowing it was really a blatantly sarcastic taunt. "That is a bit far-fetched, but I assure you, I've wronged no one. What I've done, I've done with honor."

"Are you certain about that? Are you certain you want to lie to me so boldly?"

"Let the gods strike me dead if I'm lying."

All the men who gathered around that tree simultaneously took a few steps backward, looking into the sky for Thor's hammer. The stranger laughed as he witnessed their genuine fear, then removed his helmet. "Really, Domaldr? You can't recognize your own twin's voice?"

Domaldr eyes widened in utter shock and his mouth went dry, the question of "how" screaming in his mind.

"Your first mistake," Dægan pointed out, "was that you were foolish enough to let another man slit my throat for you. You should've done it yourself. But then again, I've never known you to lift much more than a finger, especially if there were others who could do for you.

"Ah, I can see your thoughts reeling in your head now, Domaldr—and yes, I speak of the *Éireannach*, Breandán. The one you thought you cunningly befriended. That was your second mistake.

"You thought an Irishman couldn't get the better of you. But you'll not find him here amongst your slain men. I spared him just as he spared me on Inishmore. Both he and the princess have been safely led away, and you'll not have Connacht, no more than you'll have your dignity when I'm through with you."

Domaldr jerked and writhed beneath the ropes across his chest and legs. "I'll kill you, Dægan! I'll hang you by your intestines from the mast of your own *langskip*!"

"Now, that's the spirit!" Dægan cheered. He lifted his father's sword high in the air and sliced through the ropes that held his brother prisoner. Domaldr fell facedown into the dirt, for Dægan purposely left the rope at his ankles intact.

"You bastard!" Domaldr shrieked as he sat up in humiliation and tugged at the rope at his feet. He finally freed his legs and jumped up, anticipating Dægan would rush him.

But Dægan didn't.

He simply stood tall and fixed, unaffected by Domaldr's poised fighting stance. Within seconds, Ottarr removed his helmet and brought two spears, staking them solidly into the ground, along with a pair of shields. Domaldr saw his face, and then Tait, who had also removed his helmet. One by one, Dægan's men removed their helmets and tossed them aside.

Domaldr tasted bile, his stomach turning at the sight of all the faces he thought he'd rid himself of days ago. He looked at the tightened circle of men around him and the set of weapons between him and Dægan. "What is this?"

"What does it look like?" Dægan replied calmly, setting both his father's sword and Nevan's next to the shields. "For once in your life, you're going to earn something through sweat, blood, and tears—that being your freedom."

Domaldr gave a nervous chuckle. "You know this is not fair. What do you have, four hundred men?"

Dægan shifted his lips about. "Hmmm...closer to five."

Domaldr shook his head. "I've not a fighting chance, and you know it."

"'Tis only me you have to kill, Domaldr."

"Even if I do, I'm still a dead man."

"Nay," Dægan corrected. "*If*...you kill me, these men will not touch you. You'll have earned your freedom. I give my word."

"And why should I believe you?"

Dægan half grinned. "Have I ever lied to you? I told you before you left the isle that I'd hunt you down. And here I am, making good on every word I said. Now choose your weapons, Domaldr. Take Father's, if you'd like. I care not."

"And if I kill you, I get to walk away with my life *and* Father's sword?"

"If you can still *walk*, aye."

Domaldr quickly chose the sword he valued most, along with one of the shields, keeping a suspicious eye on Dægan who stood much too confident and calm for his liking. He stepped closer to Dægan, hoping to rouse a nervousness within him. "I'm not the frail boy from your childhood, Dægan. I've learned a thing or two since we were lads."

"For your sake, I hope you have."

Domaldr clenched his jaw. "Let's get this over with."

Dægan smiled and leaned in close, his nose just inches from Domaldr's. "Gladly."

If not for Tait splitting the two brothers up, they would have stayed locked in a heinous battle of staring, for neither seemed ready to yield just yet. Tait handed Dægan Nevan's sword and shield and pushed him backward. "Need I remind you of the Irish king who also seeks justice? If you want a fair chance at killing this bastard, then

I suggest you get to it before the king enforces his right of *infangenethef*."

Dægan noticed the peculiar tone of Tait's chosen words and the obvious game of intimidation he tied to instigate by letting Domaldr hear. Likewise, he played along. "Ah, *infangenethef*. I'd nearly forgotten."

Domaldr looked as though he was tossing the strange term in his head. "What is he talking about?"

Dægan checked his weapons instinctively first, letting Domaldr fret a bit longer before explaining the heraldic phrase. It was an English custom not yet adopted by the men of the Erin, but he knew Domaldr was too stupid to realize it. "Basically, brother, if the king gets here first, before I kill you, then he has every right to pursue you and do what he will to you, for the crimes you committed against his daughter were on his land and not mine."

Domaldr looked confused. "But I committed no crime. You did. You stole her from this land and took her to yours. If anything, I could say I rescued her from you."

Dægan nodded. "Aye, you could. But I'm confident Breandán will see to rectifying that part of the account in my favor. I *did* save his life."

Domaldr grew restless with the exchange of battle banter. "Breandán may have forged his way into my life, but I'd wager he did the same to you too."

Dægan took his place, his shield on the left outside position, in order to hide his injury as well as to protect it. He held his sword in plow, ready for the first of many wards. "You'll have to do better than that, Domaldr. Save your tricks and lies for someone who doesn't know you as well."

"Oh, I'd not dare lie now. Not when I'm about to run

you through," Domaldr bragged. He stepped to his left, marking a target at Dægan's head. "As your twin, I feel compelled to warn you of Breandán. He's not the man you think he is."

Dægan matched him step for step as they continued to throw words at each other like sharpened daggers. "What I think of Breandán is irrelevant compared to what I think of you. Hence, the reason *you're* a marked man and he's not."

Dægan took the first opportunity to swing a brutal, heavy blow at Domaldr's shoulder, forcing him to raise his shield in defense and expose his entire left leg. As Dægan's sword pounded into the wood of Domaldr's shield, he quickly retracted and sliced downward, cutting Domaldr's thigh just above the knee.

Domaldr fell and his wound gaped, bleeding from under his breeches. He cried out and dropped his shield to tend his open gash. Dægan sighed, unimpressed with his brother's lack of hand-to-hand tactics. He tried to fathom the idea of not only killing his brother but utterly slaying an unworthy opponent so quickly. So easily.

He stepped backward, giving Domaldr time to regroup and limp back to his place on the field, hoping Domaldr would at least show *some* ability with the sword.

"Come on!" Dægan snapped back, irritated with the delay.

Domaldr angrily looked up from his maimed leg and forced a half smile. "As I was saying…it seems that Breandán is very skilled at putting on a mask. If you didn't know, he has quite the fondness for your wife. And to think I actually gave her to him as a gift for his loyalty. I did," Domaldr insisted. "By the gods, I must have drunk at least six tankards of ale before he ever returned from her tent."

Dægan clenched his jaw and marched forward. "Fight me."

Domaldr backed away, still baring a grin as he heckled Dægan's easily pricked pride. "I would've thought a young man like that wouldn't know the first thing about stamina. He must have learned to pace himself."

"I said fight me, you *hrafnasueltir*!" Dægan lunged and thrust his sword low at Domaldr's gut. Domaldr finally demonstrated his agility and countered a heavy blow for himself. The next two strikes were also that of Domaldr's, and clearly as menacing as a warrior should boast. But Dægan returned the fierceness, his iron smoothly shifting between wards. He charged closer and struck Domaldr's shield with repetitive blows, forcing him to lift it constantly in defense.

Somehow, Domaldr got lucky and thrust his blade into Dægan's open right flank. Dægan felt a hot, blunt pressure as the broad point impaled his armor just under his ribs, then a burning sting as Domaldr withdrew it. He staggered backward and looked down at his bloodied mail, surprised by the lancing of metal and flesh. Domaldr succeeded in wounding him—a gash so deep that, until he checked for himself, he thought it exited out his back.

Domaldr laughed, but only briefly. Dægan retaliated and swung his iron at his brother's head. Domaldr instinctively lifted his shield in defense and stumbled as he absorbed the blows from overhead. In a desperate attempt to escape Dægan's might and speed, Domaldr spun and swept his sword upward to catch an unprotected hip or an extended sword arm. Dægan had already anticipated the move, and turned in the same direction, deflecting Domaldr's sword with his shield. Unfortunately, his broken ribs reminded him that any movement of his left side would always come with a great price. He immediately gave in to the pain and hunched over, staggering away from Domaldr's reach. But of course, Domaldr followed him, lifting his sword in ox-ward position.

Dægan heard Domaldr's sloppy approach and turned just in time to avert a fatal strike to his back, but not enough to avoid Domaldr's shield walloping him square in the face. The blow was hard, but not as painful as when he fell on his left side. He curled into a ball to favor his moving bones, only to gasp and wince in tremors.

Domaldr stood more confidently, seeing that Dægan harbored an injury much like himself—and quite possibly more crippling. Taking advantage of the situation, he was quick to charge in at Dægan, this time his sword in high-ward for taking off his head.

Dægan knew he'd no time to stand. Without hesitation, he gripped the outer rim of his shield and threw it like a disk at Domaldr's legs. The shield caught Domaldr's bad knee and tripped him to the ground. The two men crawled at opposite sides of the circle to catch their breaths while their hatred for each other festered.

Dægan stood up first and threw his sword aside. He jerked one of the two spears from the ground, deciding it was better to keep Domaldr distanced with a long spear than let him have another opportunity at his broken ribs.

As a young boy, he'd often win bets with the cocky older lads who had come to bullying him, by waging a game of spear throwing. He had even learned to catch a spear in flight, turning with the momentum of the spear to launch it right back at his opponent. Fortunately, for the older lads who were not too quick on the uptake, the spears were only that of blunt wood, leaving bruises instead of puncture wounds. And that was at age ten. Each passing year brought Dægan an even better aim, and a stronger, faster release.

Domaldr cringed at seeing Dægan arm himself with a spear, but dished out another insult in defense. "If your wife's womb happens to swell with child, I wonder whose babe she'll carry—yours or Breandán's?"

From years of practice, Dægan concealed his emotions from Domaldr's taunts and habitual lies. He lifted the spear at shoulder height and gently tossed it a couple of times to balance it just so, keeping his attention on his target and not on Breandán, as Domaldr clearly wanted.

"I doubt you'll ever truly know whose child it is until he's birthed. I hope for your sanity's sake the wee one is born with flaxen hair and not that of a raven."

Dægan spread his footing to steady himself and set his aim straight for Domaldr's mouth. All he wanted was one more comment so he could heave the spear right down his brother's throat. But just as Domaldr stepped in front of a large pine, Dægan saw a better target and took it. He hurled the spear with such force that it broke through the top right corner of Domaldr's shield and pierced his brother's shoulder, pinning him to the softwood tree.

Domaldr squawked and yanked on the long stake jutting from his body, but it had lodged itself in the pine too deeply to be budged. He cursed and growled, and then panicked when he realized his sword had fallen to the ground out of his reach. He could do nothing to defend himself, and he couldn't stop Dægan from taking possession of his father's sword.

Dægan double-fisted the grip and extended the point of the blade over his right shoulder, aiming for a swift death across the throat. "Go ahead, brother. I know you'd like to have the last word…you always do."

Domaldr panted through his pain. "There's not much more to say. You've always been the better brother, the better warrior—*the better son*. But before you send me to the underworld, know that with your own wrath comes mine. What you've always loathed in me, you'll possess the moment your sword cuts through my flesh. And just as we had shared the same home in our mother's womb, we too shall share the same home in the afterlife. I'll wait for you, Dægan. I'll wait for you and smile at the glorious irony when one day you shall fall from this earth and rejoin me in Hel. You'll never sever yourself from me. Not even in death."

Dægan stared at his brother, his final words giving him pause. He stood there frozen, unable to follow through with the final swing. For the first time in Dægan's life, it was as if his sword was no longer an exquisite extension of his body, but an unfamiliar piece of metal in his grip. A weapon not fashioned for status, but for the sole purpose of killing another. That was all it was, and all *he'd* ever be, as long as he held it in his hands.

Dægan dropped his arms as if weights were tied to his wrists and then stood erect to wipe the blood from his sword. Once he sheathed the weapon at his side, Domaldr exhaled a sigh of relief and gazed into the sky above him.

"What are you doing?" Tait asked as he trudged up beside Dægan and shoved a wad of cloth, cut from his own tunic, into his chieftain's stomach wound.

"I cannot do it," Dægan said. He allowed Tait to crudely tend to his new injury as he'd almost forgotten about it. But now he definitely felt the throes of it—that pivotal moment when adrenaline recedes and pain resurfaces. Since willing it away was nigh on impossible, he ignored it as best he could and walked onward.

Tait followed. "You do realize that hanging Domaldr has now become doubly difficult since he's speared to a tree."

Unimpressed, Dægan suggested a different outcome. "Then leave him for the Connacht king."

Domaldr jolted his head in attention. "You wouldn't do such a thing, would you?"

Dægan kept walking. "I would."

Tait picked up his pace to mutter his next words in Dægan's ear. "But what if your brother escapes? You know he'll come back for you."

Dægan stopped and looked over his shoulder, regarding his speared brother, who was frantically entreating others for pity and assistance. "He'll have to cut his own arm from his body to escape, and we both know he's not capable of that. He can bleed to death for all I care, but I'll not kill him. I'd rather spend a lifetime looking over my shoulder for Domaldr than spend one more hideous moment like him. I came one fatal swing from being *him*, and thanks to his long-winded sermon, he reminded me that I'm not. I am my father's son. Not my brother's twin."

Suddenly, Havelok and his men came thundering through the forest on galloping horses with Breandán in their company. The look on all their faces foretold of something dreadfully wrong.

The Irishman dismounted and approached Dægan with caution. He was quickly distracted by the bloodied battlefield of littered bodies, and the smoking remnants of tents and warships that lay in waste around the lake's western bank. The bludgeoned skulls, the lanced torsos, and the petrified expressions of the morbidly departed who blanketed the once-beautiful Erin field left a grim sense of what God's forsakenness might look like. Each mutilated body had a story, a mirthless account of their last moments on earth with their final breaths being that of Dægan's name.

"Speak, Breandán," Dægan demanded as he lunged forward. "What's wrong?"

Breandán glanced at the two large hands fisting his cloak and leine. "Mara has been arrested."

"Arrested? Under what charge?"

"The king has accused her of treason."

"For what?"

Breandán hesitated as Dægan lifted him slightly from the ground. "For marrying you."

Dægan's eyes smoldered as he scrutinized the raven-haired messenger. There was not an inkling of dishonesty to be found in the savvy Irishman, and he released him. "'Tis not quite the reaction I would've expected from a father whose only child had been safely returned to him."

"I tried to dispute it and defend your name, but he threatened to clap me in irons as well. I assure you 'twas not an easy decision to leave Mara behind, but I accepted the king's leniency and left to find you."

Dægan stroked his bottom lip with his thumb and index finger. "'Twas not leniency he showed you by letting you leave, Breandán, but a clever tactic. He was hoping you'd come warn me of Mara's arrest to draw me out."

"How can you be so sure?"

"Did anyone follow you here?"

"I would never have compromised your position if someone did," Breandán reassured.

"Then I think you were naught but a pawn. You were

merely cast into the wolves' den with my wife's detainment as bait, hoping I'd bite."

Tait stepped in. "The question is, will you?"

Dægan gave Tait a look as if he'd been offered a dare. "Oh, aye, I'll bite. Quite frankly, I've had enough of coddling this king like a toddler. 'Tis time I meet the man beneath the crown." Dægan glanced at Breandán. "For the sake of Mara, I'm going to need you again. Can you help me breach his walls?"

"As long as you're not afraid to crawl on your hands and knees, Northman, I can get you to the countermine shaft."

"I'm going with you," Tait made sure to say.

"Not this time," Dægan said firmly. "I'll need you to create the diversion. My only companion will be the chest I gave Mara as a wedding gift. I'm afraid it's been buried for far too long."

Chapter Thirty-one

The mighty fortress of Dún na hAbhann stood preeminently in the open space of Connacht's skewed checkerboard fields and plowed pastures. Its earthen walls, built generations ago, had settled durably against the high timbered ramparts that enclosed the stronghold, making the palisade—although weathered with time—a prevailing and prominent first defense. It was both the solid backbone and carapace of the fort, safeguarding those within.

To add to its security, a grand assembly of armed soldiers guarded the wall walk, each with their own replacement should they be sniped by enemy fire. A single square wooden keep rose high from the center of the bailey at a strategic distance from the gatehouse, which boasted two sturdy iron portcullises at its entrance and an arsenal tower above. The tower height itself paled in comparison to the keep's, but the hillside on which Dún na hAbhann resided gave the tower an immense vantage point overlooking any stretch of land in the forefront.

To the west lay shadowed paddocks, vast rolling meadows, and blackened forests. To the east, rested the waters of the Lough Ree mirroring a reflective stripe of the brilliant moon above. As one would expect in the small hours of the night, the territory surrounding Dún na hAbhann seemed undisturbed and tranquil. But with enemies sure to be drawing close, Fergus and Cathal reckoned it downright unnatural.

"It makes no sense," Cathal finally said from atop the arsenal tower. "As much as Breandán upheld that *Fionnghall's* honor, I would've wagered my life that he'd have made a desperate attempt to collaborate with the Northman one last time. Especially when my daughter's freedom was at stake."

Fergus didn't answer, and Cathal noticed his deep circumspection.

"Let me ask you something, Fergus. What kind of man rids an enemy from my lands without expecting some sort of payment in return? Better yet, what kind of man steals a woman of high birth, seduces her into marriage, and then sends her home with another, never to show his face again?"

"A man who is up to something," Fergus murmured into the cool air.

"Then what is he waiting for?"

"He's wearing you down, sire. He's hoping this war will be won before it starts, especially if he can keep you battling with your own thoughts. If it puts you at ease, I would've wagered my life as well that Breandán would have run straight to the *Fionnghall* for help, seeing how the feigned arrest of Mara affected him." Fergus paused over a brief thought. "But we should realize he survived these savage men, and there's no telling what travesties he went through during his capture—or what skills of deception he mastered in order to escape them. Though this chieftain he brags of is still a Northman like his captors, Breandán was smart enough to know who was the better ally. He chose well, as your daughter is safely home. To say that Breandán is fit only to trap animals is quite narrow-minded. I'd even go so far as to say he may have fooled you, moreover."

Cathal looked at his advisor crossly. "Breandán is a commoner by birth and now a noble by luck. If he returns with that wine-bag infidel Northman, he'll have proved my point tenfold—that he's *still* common, and knows naught about mature, noble issues such as plotting waylays and warfare."

"You're right, sire," Fergus stated sarcastically. "War is a very mature undertaking. Wait." He leaned forward and squinted into the dark void of night. "Do you see that?"

Cathal peered out and saw a distant flicker of light at the top of the next rolling hill. It was just a single torch at first, and then there were two. Then three. Four, five, six… Many torches lit in succession, surrounding the area of Dún na hAbhann.

"What is he doing?" Cathal sneered.

Fergus almost smiled at the mental strategy Dægan was creating. "'Tis a head count. He's letting you know how many men he boasts. From the looks of it, his army must be colossal, or I doubt he'd go to this much trouble for only a few hundred."

Cathal was mesmerized by the growing chain of torches illuminating his countryside. Once the entire horizon from southeast to west was lit, another long row behind that one was also lit, doubling the intent to intimidate him. If that were not enough, a third row appeared soon after.

Cathal began to sweat nervously. "He's toying with me. He's just lighting torches staked in the ground to make it look like an enormous army so that I'll grow weary and surrender. Ignorant fool. He can light them all night, for all I care."

Fergus wasn't as willing to dismiss the tactic as just a simple game of intimidation. He estimated three hundred so far and still, the torches illuminated, one by one. "Correct me if I'm wrong, but those torches are moving closer to us."

"Nay, 'tis simply your eyes playing with you now."

Fergus shook his head adamantly. "Watch them. Every so often, they take a step forward, and not one at a time, but as a group. This is no game, sire. He has at least five hundred in his command…maybe more. I've lost count."

"Are you certain?"

Fergus turned toward his king and scoffed. "If you believed this man didn't want a single scrap of payment for annihilating your enemies, think again. He's coming for his due right now…which I'd guess is your daughter."

Cathal fumed. "Then let him try. I'll not bargain with this sea rat."

"Perhaps you should hear his terms," Fergus said wisely. "They may not be as painful as losing Dún na hAbhann over a few silver coins."

Cathal clenched his jaw. "I'll not give this man the hair off my freckled arse. Rally the men and prepare the archers."

"As you wish," Fergus mumbled. "But 'twould be better for all of Dún na hAbhann, myself included, if your presence within the stronghold was undeterminable."

Cathal stared, dismayed with what Fergus wanted. "I'll not hide away in my chambers like a coward, if that's what you had in mind."

"Call it an elusive strategy, if you will. But I suggest you should do to him what he's doing to you," Fergus explained. "Keep him guessing, or at the least force him to use careful consideration in his assault. He wants his wife—pardon…your daughter. And I doubt he's willing to risk her well-being for the sake of bringing you down, especially if he has consummated the marriage and rooted a child within her. As much as you loathe that thought, sire, you should at least use it to your advantage. With the size of his army and the number of torches he flaunts in your face, he can burn this whole timbered fort to the ground in a matter of minutes. But if he doesn't know the exact whereabouts of you or your daughter within, he'll be more apt to scale the walls with precision instead of devastation and chaos. I beg you, sire. Don't make this easy for him. Stay with your daughter in the keep."

****

Cathal was not pleased with the advice Fergus had given him. He was not normally inclined to take shelter while his fort weathered an attack, nor was he ready to put himself near his daughter. In truth, he loved Mara very much and wanted to keep her safe, but he couldn't dismiss what she'd done.

Marrying a Northman, ach!

To ease his mind about her safekeeping without having to dwell in close proximity to her, he'd locked Mara in her own chambers, ordering two guards at her door. For his own security, he'd ordered another two at his, and waited there alone.

The room was quiet, forlorn, and dimly lit by a few torches on corresponding walls, which draped the four corners in shadows. He knew the room by heart and strolled to the table near the unlit hearth to settle his shambled nerves with a good long drink of mead.

He poured the honeyed brew as if his cup were larger, spilling most out of carelessness, and drank in the same reckless manner. He slammed the cup down when it was empty and wiped his bearded chin of the residual droplets, before pouring another.

From beside him in the shadows, a figure of a man stepped forward. Cathal's reaction was not as polished as the intruder's, for he stumbled against the leg of the table to get away.

Cathal unsheathed his sword in fumbling haste, but not quickly enough. The stranger's sword point was already inches from his throat, held in decisive restraint beneath his chin. The king gawked at the man—a statuesque sort of fellow. His face was stern and confident, and his sword arm was assuredly steady.

Cathal's face turned from a reflective stun to a souring grimace. "Ah, I finally get to meet the sea rover himself. I've heard so much about you. How you journeyed for days on end just to save my crown from treachery—from your own twin, I've been told. Dægan, is it?"

"Forgive me if I fail to share in your enthusiasm," Dægan said rather softly, cocking his head. "As you can imagine, I'm a bit tired from all my labors."

"Thieving does that to a man."

A grin befell Dægan's lips. "You should know."

A rush of confusion swept over the king as he examined the sizeable man more closely, still unable to decipher his comment. "How did you get in here?"

"How I got in here is not as important as how I leave. I can leave just as quietly as I came—or we can clash in fierce battle. But before you make a desperate attempt to shout to the two guards outside your door, I encourage you to put these thoughts into your head. Your mighty Dún na hAbhann has been breached without your knowing, and I assure you, I don't make a habit of traveling into hostile territory alone. With that in mind, you should also know that every loyal son of Dún na hAbhann is looking death in the eye as we speak and they're totally unaware of the tragedy they face. With one word, I could have them massacred before their next breath. However, I'd just as soon not give that word, as I'm gravely wounded myself. Keeping this as gentlemanly as possible is in everyone's best interest." Dægan's face was straight and cold as he continued. "Twice, I've been courteous enough to warn you—now—as well as outside your palisade. Surely, your own men deserve the same respect."

"You call hundreds of torches a *respectful* warning?"

"Who would have thought advancing sticks of fire could be so distracting? Now, I'm assuming your response is that of favoring your men's lives. So if you'd be so kind, s*ire*, sheath your sword and give it to me, belt and all."

If the king had any thought of calling the Northman's bluff, the invading tip of his sword was enough to discourage the idea rather quickly, so much so, that a subsequent verbal reminder from Dægan was unnecessary. Cathal reluctantly shoved his weapon back into its casing and removed his belt from his waist.

"You'll never leave here alive," Cathal growled, before slapping his belongings into Dægan's outstretched hand.

Dægan disregarded the king's threat and kept his demeanor tame as he backed up to the double chamber doors. He pulled each lever to the center and shoved the iron bolts into the ceiling and floor boreholes, locking them from the inside. As a double precaution, he also took a remnant slack of chain from his waist that he'd found on his way in, and wrapped it quietly around the door latches.

"Your blacksmith is quite a drunkard. He leaves his goods lying about," Dægan said impassively as he strolled back toward the king. "But I must say, an expert craftsman."

"Spare me the flattery. You didn't come here for ironware. What do you want?"

Dægan took an encroaching step forward and forced the king to back away from his sword point and into the seat behind him. The chair slid slightly as Cathal fell into it. "You know what I want."

"You cannot have her."

"I don't think you're in a position to make that claim."

"I *can* as long as there's breath in me," Cathal snarled hatefully.

"And I didn't come here with the intention of ridding the breath from your noble lungs." Dægan sheathed his sword with so much force that he heard the small clatter of beads from the dangling crucifix at his waist, reminding him of Nevan's careful reflection and patience, and the importance of emulating the same. "So perhaps, we can talk as men. You and I, king and *jarl*, Celt and *Fionnghall*."

"For what purpose?"

Dægan took a seat directly across from the king and laid the man's weapon on the wooden floor at his left. "For amends, of course. I promised Mara I would."

Cathal almost burst into laughter. "Amends? How can you possibly think I'll come to terms with you stealing my daughter and marrying her without my consent?"

"I've done no such thing," Dægan said flatly.

"You deny your crimes, you pompous bastard? Did you not take her from this land and shepherd her to yours?"

"Aye, I did."

"Did you not marry her under Irish witnesses?"

"As well," Dægan said. "I've done all you say, but none of it was done to *your* daughter."

Cathal narrowed his eyes to hateful slits. "What are you talking about?"

"If I wished to gain consent for Mara's hand by her father, 'twould not be gotten from you. I'd need to go elsewhere for that, would I not?" He saw Cathal's throat bob as he swallowed nervously.

"Who are you?"

"No one of relevance, I assure you. But let me remind you who *you are.*"

Dægan put his booted foot under the table and shoved the wooden chest he'd given to Mara forward into the king's view.

Cathal's face dropped as his eyes pored over the familiar carved box. Dægan knew he'd try desperately to evade any emotions affiliated with it, and he concealed them quite well at first, including his knowledge of the peculiar coffer.

"And what would this be, *Fionnghall?* A bribe for my daughter's hand, perhaps?"

"I know you'd like to see me upon my knees, pouring riches over your ankles, but my intentions this night will lack the openhanded endowment you're accustomed to. I know who you are, and I know the man you wronged ten years ago. He was the owner of this chest, the man who wished to end the feud between the two of you—the feud that started over one woman—yet you stabbed him and left him for dead. Nonetheless, I'm curious as to why you raised his daughter as your own. I cannot possibly fathom why a greedy sovereign like yourself would find fulfillment in another king's bastard child, especially a female whose inheritance will stay amongst her own kinsman. What is there to gain?"

Cathal sat frozen, discerning the Northman's purpose for bringing the past to light after more than twenty years. No one, not even his own betrothed's father, knew of his wife's pregnancy before their marriage. With the rising upheaval of the neighboring clans, Cathal thought it in the best interest of his name and his powerful reign to keep her scandalous premarital affair a secret and declare that her growing womb was from his consummated seed. But how could this foreigner know differently, much less know the intricate details of the ill-fated death of his wife's lover?

"Where did you get this chest?" Cathal asked skeptically.

Dægan grabbed the ewer from the table and refilled Cathal's cup with mead for his own nagging thirst. "Your wife's first love gave it to me. The man she gave herself to before she was forced to marry you."

"You lie."

Dægan lifted the cup to his lips and took a long drink before replying. "What you thought to be a fatal injury to his heart turned out to be only a deep flesh wound of his shoulder, giving him enough time to make it back to the ports of Galway with quite an interesting tale to tell on his deathbed."

"He aimed to kill me," Cathal spurted defensively. "I was merely defending myself."

Dægan lifted his brow and poured another full cup for

himself. "Really? From what? Fine silk thread and glass beads?"

"Don't mock me, *Fionnghall*. At the time he offered it, there was no way for me to know the contents of that chest. Threatening words were spoken between us and swords were drawn, his being first."

"Now you lie," Dægan reprimanded. "When he came to me, his *fridbönd* was tightly secured around his sword. Which means he couldn't have drawn his weapon without unfastening the peace-band, and you didn't give him the chance."

Cathal smiled callously as if a flattering compliment had kindly passed his way. "And what summoning of my peerage is going to believe you? Need I remind you that the majority of my kin are all fighting, as we speak, to rid men such as you from our shores. Our Baile Átha Cliath. You've put our Erin lands under your rape for more than a century, and we shall stand for it no longer. Nor will I let you threaten me with wasted stories of the past."

"Care to eat those words?"

"With what?" Cathal provoked. "A spoon made of that fool's bones?"

Dægan snuffed the grisly image from his mind and spoke with a locked jaw. "I hardly find humor in that, and I wouldn't think Mara would either, once she's told who her real father is."

"Yet without those bones, she'll never know, will she?"

Dægan leaned across the table and gripped Cathal by the throat, scowling into the king's smug face. "You truly disgust me. And to think, I thought higher of you for raising a child on your own, albeit a stolen child."

"He had every opportunity to claim Mara, and he never did."

"He never knew!" Dægan shouted, lifting the king from his chair and shoving him back against the wall. "He believed as everyone else had that Mara was yours. I assure you, had he known, he would've stormed this fort like a madman."

"Oh, he knew. But he only came back when it benefited him to take away the child he'd rooted in my wife. He only brought the chest as a means to trade quietly before he could set to ruining me thereafter with gossip."

Dægan shook his head. "He knew naught of a child."

Cathal's mind whirled into the dark depths of his tumultuous past and spoke upon it despite the Northman's iron grip. "If he truly never knew he had a child when he died, how would *you* come to know of it?"

Dægan slowly released the king and stepped back, letting him brood a bit longer. There was no doubt Cathal was on to him, and thus coming apart in the small silence that followed. Dægan was all too satisfied with the king's torment to end it so quickly. He only smiled.

Cathal pounced back into Dægan's space, his fists tightly woven. "Tell me, you worthless thug. How could you know Mara was his?"

Dægan looked down the length of his nose at the tortured Irishman and raised a single derisive brow. "I didn't know. I was baiting you to see if you'd admit it."

Cathal's eyes changed from a hard-sunken realization to a bolstering fire of rage. "You conniving bastard!"

Cathal dove for his sword on the floor, but Dægan, not in any hurry, drew his sword and casually turned it on the kneeling king, who was still fumbling with the leather strap Dægan had purposely made sure to secure around the hilt before he laid it to the floor.

"The taste of irony is close to that of bile, is it not? How does it feel to know you're hopelessly close to death with your peace-band fastened, *sire*?"

Cathal glanced at the shiny broadsword inches from his neck, and then tossed his entangled sword and scabbard across the room. "You'll hang for this. You'll not walk out of here with anyone believing you."

Dægan hauled the king to his feet by his lavishly embroidered leine and slammed him against the wall again. He strung his fingers into Cathal's dark hair and exposed his tender royal throat beneath a well-whetted iron. "I needn't anyone to believe me, save you. And now that you admit Mara isn't yours, these are my terms. You'll release the dear sweet Lady Mara to me. And her father—blood father, who still lives and breathes, by the way—promises never to set foot on your lands ever again. He also vows to keep your despicable secret, a secret. Mara shall never know you are the shrewd weasel you are, and in turn, you get to keep your good name. She shall leave with me a happy, grateful, loving daughter, since you—the generous parent— will have granted me full consent, as her loyal and notably merciful husband. Whereby you also get to keep the respect and admiration she unconditionally and ever so blindly bestows upon you. Should you not agree to these terms," Dægan added with a gentle gruffness, "you'll have surely declared war on me as well as Mara's father, and I should lay emphasis on the term *war*, for if you look out upon your countryside, you'll not find compassion there."

"Your terms are rather slanted, *Fionnghall*."

Dægan jerked Cathal's head farther back and pushed the tip dangerously under his jaw. "My terms are what they are. So what say you?"

"I've not much choice now, do I?"

"In every decision, there's a choice. Make yours well."

"But what about my people? What about the *Ard Rí*, the High King of Tara? As soon as I agree to this outlandish demand, gossip will grace every ear from here to Northumbria of this implausible union of my daughter with a savage. I may not concern myself with the High King's war for Baile Átha Cliath, but I needn't him questioning my loyalties. If I agree to this, I'll have more enemies than you have men outside my gates."

"So you *did* count," Dægan jested. "But shouldn't you ask yourself where Mara's loyalties would lie if she knew the truth about you?"

Cathal quieted under that remark.

"Very well," Dægan allowed. "I'm willing to extend my mercies a bit further and help you keep your intolerant reputation for the men of the north if that contents you. You can lay claim to the massacre of my twin brother's army just west of the River Shannon, boasting your fiendish hatred for my kind, using the slaughter as your proof, and Domaldr's hanging as your testimony."

"I hardly believe you," Cathal sneered. "You'd give up your own brother, your own blood, knowing 'twould mean his death?"

"'Tis hard to fathom, I know. But hostilities between brothers are no more forgiven through blood than you and I through heedless war."

"How endearing," Cathal sneered.

Dægan stepped back and placed the bare tip of his sword at Cathal's heart, double-fisting the hilt in preparation for a good hard thrust through his rib cage.

"Remember, you stubborn fool, Mara is more my wife than she is your daughter. And as much as I hate to bring this pain upon her with your sudden death, I'll take back what is mine—with or without your consent."

Dægan felt a cold shiver ripple through him and his fingertips began to tingle, a feeling he'd never felt before. He supposed it was his body's way of forewarning severe blood loss, and he gritted his teeth against it, holding fast to gaining the king's agreement. "Last chance, sire! What say you to my terms?"

Cathal instinctively braced himself against the wall, held his breath, and closed his eyes. He more than deserved this death for what he'd done. By rights, he shouldn't even have lasted as king as long as he had, considering all the enemies he'd made from conquests and bloody victories, while Mara was too young to remember. Up until his wife died, he continued his reign of cogent kingship, putting men under the sword for refusing to serve. And now, it was brought unto him full circle—to either die or submit.

He thought about Mara and how he'd cursed her for admitting her love for a man he considered *his enemy*. Yet, the heathen before him had truly done nothing to warrant the title. Dægan's was not the hand that killed his brother some twenty-eight years past, a grudge he continued to hold over every Northman. As enemies went, Cathal couldn't forge a single present-day reason for hating the man in his chamber, except that he was annoyingly meticulous, respectfully civil, and highly intellectual. And yes, there was the fact that he took Mara for close to a fortnight, but even that was forgivable in light of the story Mara and Breandán had told. If anything, he knew he should be praising the Northman for his undaunted bravery at saving his very crown. And if that were not enough, the bastard didn't even sink to the level of demanding a preposterous compensation for lost men and arms. All he wanted was to be given back the woman he married—a daughter who was not rightly Cathal's to say otherwise.

He could see Mara's crying face now, tears pouring from her eyes. By just consenting to the terms, he could take away all the pain and anguish she was going through, and above all, avoid her ever knowing the truth behind her conception and the attempt he'd made to kill her real father so many years ago.

Cathal swallowed hard and opened his eyes. "All right," he muttered. "I'll agree to your terms. But not because I fear death by your hand, *Fionnghall*, but because I could not bear to see the look of disappointment on Mara's face if she knew the truth. I'd gladly give all I have to keep her from knowing. Call me a coward, if you must, but I love her too much to hurt her. She may not be my daughter by blood, but from the moment I held her in my arms, I existed. And from the day she first called me Father, I lived. If you take that away from me, I have nothing. One day I know I'll have to face the good Lord above for all the sins I've committed, but I'm not ready to face *her*. Not yet."

Dægan watched as the king's fiery spirit dispersed like a misty fog. Whatever restless fight had consumed Cathal before was now just a bleak rustling amid the settling dust of their dispute. He lowered his weapon, confounded by the king's sudden outpouring, and sheathed it. Doing so sent the tiny beads of his rosary to clatter in joyous exuberance.

"Thank you, wise king," Dægan said.

"For what?"

"For reaffirming why I didn't want to kill you in the first place. I had hopes that a man who raises a daughter into a fine woman, whether his own or someone else's, does so by example and not by chance. You've taught her well. She's of sound mind and good heart, not to mention hardheaded," Dægan added in humor, gripping his nose between his thumb and fingers. "I'd have to say even you took to me better than she did in the beginning. 'Twas not an easy courtship between a fearless woman and an arrogant warrior, I assure you."

"Broke your nose, did she?"

"Aye," Dægan said, giving up some of his pride. "I hope that brings you some comfort."

"Little..." Cathal sighed, still burdened by his surrender, despite the Northman's lighthearted idle talk. "What now?"

"We do what truced men do. We uphold our ends of the bargain and walk away peacefully with our blessings."

"And what blessings do I have as you leave with Mara?"

Dægan walked to the far wall and bent over to pick up the king's scabbard. He felt another tiny current of weakness cut through him and a blackness overtaking his vision. He shook it away so as not to bring it to the king's awareness and focused his attention on the encased weapon in his hands. He twisted it about, admiring the bronzed scabbard and the talent that the Irish artisan had in creating such a piece. "You have a long life ahead of you."

Cathal scoffed. "I'm not too certain of the length of my life with these lands in exasperating conflict."

Dægan handed the scabbard to the king. "You speak of Dubh-Linn. Or rather, your Baile Átha Cliath?"

"Aye," Cathal said, accepting the sword with much skepticism before securing it at his side.

"May I ask why you concern yourself with a port whose control has often wavered like the changing weather?"

"My concern is not for the port itself, but for the unity of Ireland."

"Is that what the High King has used to gather his baker's dozen?"

Cathal eyes widened. "You know of his numbers?"

"I know of his meager numbers. He and these twelve lesser kings, and you giving thought to being the fourteenth, will not make the slightest difference in this war. He could assemble twenty lesser kings and their armies, but 'twill still not be enough. You'll all die. Songs will be sung in your defeat for years to come and stories will emerge from fireside drunkenness. Is that how you want to be remembered? With Mara visiting a makeshift grave of your scattered bones across Connacht's battlefield? Heed well my warning, old king, and Mara shall visit you at your door, for many blessed days to come."

"You speak very assuredly," Cathal noted, "almost as if you've chosen your side and would hate to come across me in your affairs, fighting for Baile Átha Cliath yourself."

"Baile Átha Cliath is not my affair. I'm through fighting—*ours* being the last."

"One can never be too certain, as enemies rise and fall like the sun."

Dægan saw the concern in Cathal's eyes that had long been etched by years of fear and childhood prejudices, fed not only by his elders who had personally clashed with the Northmen of their day, but by witnessing his own brother's bloody death.

"I'm not your enemy. I never was," Dægan said sincerely as he started to remove his own sword and scabbard from his belt. "This was my father's. 'Tis a king's sword, and it belongs in a king's hands. Take it, and may you never doubt that I'm not a threat to you."

Cathal looked at Dægan as if it were a trick, but Dægan insisted, saying, "My father died much like your brother, in the hands of ruthless, greedy men. Let this sword be a reminder that hearts can mend, and even uncommon ties can bind."

Cathal shook his head in disbelief as he held the sumptuous gift in both hands. "Who *are* you?"

"Truth be told, I'm no one. Just a man who bleeds like any other and sins just as much as the next. I cannot change what has happened in the past, but I can surely steer the course to where I'm going. And hopefully, I have your Christian god at my starboard."

Cathal watched Dægan turn and walk toward the barred door. As Dægan started to undo the chains from the levers, Cathal slowly pulled the newly acquired heavy iron from its sheath, letting the high-pitched ring of pounded metal be heard. "You know I could kill you right now, and no one would be the wiser of our truce."

Dægan froze. "You could...but I'm afraid my twin may have beaten you to it..." The chain in his hands fell to the floor. His body trembled. He turned around, fearing his doom was upon him.

Cathal noticed Dægan's injuries and their magnitude now that he stood beneath the torch light at both sides of the door. The deep lacerations he'd suffered finally affected his strength as he stood there, losing blood upon the floor.

Dægan's legs wobbled, and despite his efforts to stay erect, they eventually buckled beneath him. He collapsed in his own blood pool, barely coherent. His eyes fluttered and his head drifted backward, unable to hold the weight of his own head anymore. Finally, he lay down and exhaled a breath of exhaustion.

Cathal came to Dægan, a slight sense of pity on his face. "*Fionnghall*, you're bleeding to death."

Dægan pressed his own hand to his punctured right side, blood oozing between his fingers. "So I am…"

Cathal stared, almost in a trance. "You cannot die here. Not within these walls. I'm no fool. You die in my charge and, truce or not, your men will storm my gates in revenge. Get up. Get up now."

"Believe me, I would if I had the strength."

"Then call your men off," Cathal pleaded. "The ones who've come with you, hiding within Dún na hAbhann, waiting for your word. My men should not die because you failed to say otherwise. Give the word, and I'll see that your wounds are closed. Give it, *Fionnghall*."

Dægan tried hard to stay awake. "There are no men hiding in the shadows of your fort. I breached your walls on my own. I swear it. Search the entire fort if you need to. You'll not find a single man, save your own. But you're right in presuming my men's vengeance should my last breaths be taken inside Dún na hAbhann. Get me out of here, with my wife, and all will be well. This I too swear. Please…I ask of you, sire. Let me go home with my wife."

Cathal heard nothing more from the Northman, save

Mara's name repeatedly on his lips. For the first time in Cathal's life, he believed and trusted in the words of a *Fionnghall.*

There never was a threat of scores of Northmen in his fort, and he needn't search the grounds. He learned that it was only a crafty way to create a necessary hesitation for acquiring a truce between men...two very different men, despite the improbable. Dægan succeeded on all counts, without bloodshed, and Cathal respected that.

He reached out and touched Dægan's arm. "Find your strength and hold on a bit longer. I shall bring you what you want."

Chapter Thirty-two

Through a momentous rocking, an occasional bump brought Dægan from his sleep. Voices carried all around him and the sound of swift horses' hooves, rolling wooden wheels, and slapping leather gave him the interest necessary to open his eyes.

The brilliance of the sun's rays through his eyelids drew a pounding throb across his forehead, and after many times of trying to concede to the intensity of the sun, he gave up and covered his brow with his arm. It was then that he felt the sharp pain in his ribs reminding him of the assault he'd endured and not yet recovered from. He peered down the length of his body and saw that he lacked his bloodstained brown tunic and armor. Instead, he was dressed in a clean white kirtle that hid the stiff bandages across his torso. At his feet lay the notorious king's chest.

"Easy, Dægan," a familiar voice lulled over the cadence of trotting hooves. "Lie still."

Dægan smiled as he knew well the dulcet voice, and tried eagerly to see the lovely face that owned it. He succeeded without much punishment, for Mara sat in front of him, shadowing him from the rays of the fierce afternoon sun.

"Where am I?" he asked, still uncertain of his exact whereabouts aside from lying in a bumpy horse-drawn wagon on a bed of straw, fleece, and animal furs.

"You're on your way home, my lord. Tait and all of

your men are leading the escort to Limerick." She paused, remembering what he'd called the port, and attempted to pronounce it his way. "Or as you say, Hlymrekr."

His lip twitched at the corner, a slight indication that he enjoyed the effort she took to use his language. "But our ships are not in—"

"Shh…" Mara said, soothing Dægan's furrowed brow. "Ottarr led half the men westward to Galway to retrieve the ships, along with Havelok and Ingvarr. They will unite with us in Limerick and sail you home again. I realize 'tis a shorter distance to Galway, but this wagon would not make it through the bogs. My father has arranged everything, and he's even provided his own men for protection."

"More importantly, what did he arrange for Domaldr?"

Mara straightened her face. "He's been hung by the neck. My father declares you the victor and a lifelong ally of the Uí Briúin Ai. With that union, he said he'd brave whatever the *Ard Rí* would accuse him of, just as you braved him. He also asked that I return you this." Mara uncovered the sword of Dægan's father. "My father said it takes a brave man to lift a sword in battle, and an even braver man not to. You made use of a sharp tongue in place of a sharp iron as a stronger, more compelling means of peace, and the reward for your courage should be no less than the withheld iron itself. With it, may you never think of him as a threat."

Dægan couldn't believe his eyes as he held the noble weapon in his hands once again. Perhaps it was weakness that kept him from expressing his joy, but all in all, he was elated to once again hold the sword that had protected him so many times.

"Is something wrong?" Mara asked of Dægan's quiet reserve.

He rested his heavy head back onto the bedding and took hold of Mara's hand. "I've only dreamed of this day— you and I, together at last—with no one trying to come between us. I cannot help but feel that even my own eyes deceive me. Are you certain you're naught more than a vivid dream, sure to disperse as I wake?"

Mara leaned forward, slowly stroking his face from his forehead to jaw. "If you fear your eyes deceive you, then close them and feel for yourself that I'm real."

Dægan closed his eyes as he was told, and was soon rewarded with a kiss from his beautiful wife's lips. He threaded his fingers in her hair and pulled her into a deeper kiss, tasting sweet victory for the first time in his life.

Mara succumbed to the pull of his arms around her and draped herself carefully across his chest, avoiding his many injuries. "There's still strength in your hands and in your kiss. 'Tis good."

Dægan saw the fear hiding behind her eyes. He caressed her cheek. "Your words say one thing, while your eyes tell me another. Don't fret over me, love. I'm a blessed man this day."

****

Days passed.

The journey to Dægan's small port settlement seemed relentless at best as each passing hour proved more difficult for him. Not only did he continue to grow weaker, but an insurmountable fever had taken hold.

Mara had hydrated him often with a thrice-boiled brew of barley, water, and honey and had wiped his entire body down with a cool wet cloth that had been steeped alongside several agate stones. Despite her thorough efforts using remedies, prayer, and even superstition, the fever still clung to him without any sign of breaking.

His next struggle came as he spent the last hours of the night shivering uncontrollably. No matter how many furs Mara wrapped around him, or even how long she used her own body heat for warmth, the trembling continued, and his fever grew to heights beyond her imagination. He tossed his head and straightened his limbs as though chained to a violent nightmare, only a stuporous mumble escaping his pursed lips. By the third day, his dreams had escalated in aggression.

Mara continued to wipe his brow, calling his name. "Dægan, can you hear me?"

He shouted at her, but not in a language she understood. He rambled in his native tongue—swear words, she thought. To her, they seemed like formidable commands as if he were right in the middle of a bloodthirsty battle.

"Dægan, please, open your eyes to me."

He assuredly heard her, for his brows twitched, but his answer came in another fierce bawl.

Mara worried and prayed over his condition, frightened by his obsessive delirium. His long days of fighting the fever were the source, and unless it subsided, she feared he'd soon lose his mind completely.

She touched him again, stroking his puckered brow full of intensity and savage anger. "Dægan, you need to drink. Your body begs for water."

She reached behind her and dipped a wooden ladle into the barrel of herbal water, readying herself to take on her combative husband. She then tucked her arm under his head and lifted it just enough to pour the water between his parted lips without choking him. But it only spilled as he protested it. She readjusted his head and tried again, coaxing him to swallow as she poured, but the liquid sought more of his neck than his open throat.

Desperately, an idea came to her. She drank the water herself, keeping it within her mouth, and stroked him gently to calm him. When he settled, she parted his lips with her finger and bent down to cover his mouth with hers. As she'd hoped, he didn't fight the closeness. In fact, a sound of pleasure hummed from him as she allowed the drink to gradually flow across his tongue and down his throat. His hands unclenched, and he instinctively swallowed. Again and again, she drank and took his lips, successfully giving him the fluids he needed.

"M'lady," Tait interrupted as he trotted up beside the wagon. He saw that Dægan lay motionless, unmoved by the woman's intimate kiss. He stared at her. "What are you doing?"

"Help me, Tait. Dægan's fever rages and he's talking out of his mind. The only way he'll drink is from my lips to his."

Tait thought a moment and smiled. "Interesting... Have you got enough in him?"

"Not enough to matter, I'm afraid."

Dægan suddenly tensed and blurted out, "*Taka þú hvat þín hug fýsa ok brenna þú allan til aurum! Foera mér, mín broðúr!*"

Tait raised a single brow at the familiar words of his Norse language, knowing at that moment, Dægan was quickly losing his grip on reality. He steered his horse closer to the wagon and reached in, feeling Dægan's forehead. "Odin's blood, he's on fire." A thought rushed him, and his eyes widened with hope. "The river. We can submerge him, and mayhap that will shock the fever from him."

****

Piles of mail, armor, swords, kirtles, and helmets all lay in the grass at the shoreline of the River Shannon, as Tait and five other dedicated *hirdmen* stood at the edge, looking down at the cold river water. There were three men on each side, half-brooding and fully naked, holding the makeshift gurney of oak limbs and linen on which their chieftain lay. They all seemed hesitant, not quite ready to take the plunge, while Dægan still lay in oblivious sleep.

With Tait at one side, in the middle, he sighed and looked at the man to his left. "He's not going to like this, Gunnar. There'll be a fight, you know."

Gunnar studied Dægan's injured body. "Aye, but he's right-handed. And you're on his left."

Gunnar's insight caught Tait off guard as he realized he was surely the only one within striking distance.

"There's a brighter side, though," Gunnar added.

"And what would that be?"

"If Dægan gets a hold of you, I'd wager he'd sink like a stone if we let go—given he's tied to this contrived bed."

Tait eyed the man sharply. "If Dægan gets hold of me...you can be certain I'll tell him who came up with the idea of tying him down in the first place."

****

Mara sat amid the forest cover, while the other men, Irish and Northman alike, lay like fallen autumn leaves dispersed on the ground, most already asleep with fatigue. She, however, couldn't sleep. Her mind was far too heavy with worry. And the length of time it was taking for Tait to return from the river was not helping matters.

"Is everything all right?"

"Aye," she said, though her reply was more habitual, than true.

Breandán sat beside her. "You lie pitifully."

"So I've been told."

This time when Breandán spoke, he aimed straight for the heart. "I know you love Dægan and you fear for him. But he's going to be all right. He's a strong man—stubborn, moreover."

Mara brought to mind the show of mulish jealousy that Dægan had exhibited on her behalf. "Stubborn, he is indeed."

"I only hope I served you well."

She looked into Breandán's blue-green eyes, noticing the immense sincerity in them. "Of course you did."

"What I mean is, I hope you know I didn't serve you for the reward and the recognition. I did it—"

"I know," Mara interrupted. "I know why. And I hope you know your kindness and bravery will never be forgotten in my heart."

Breandán simply smiled. "That means a great deal to me."

They held each other's gazes for a long time until Mara ultimately cleared her throat. "So, what will you do first as a noble clansman now?"

"What I've always done. Hunt. I know it seems odd, but 'tis what I love to do. 'Tis all I know how to do."

"Why not come with us?" Mara suggested.

Breandán smiled appreciatively. "Thank you, but I know I'm the last person Dægan wants to see. Besides, my place is here. And I now have cattle to look after. I pray the rest of your journey is safe. And hopefully, I shall see you again one day." He embraced her, saying, "I'll never forget you, Mara. Never."

Mara watched Breandán disappear into the forest like the elusive hunter he was. And only then did she catch sight of Tait. Her heart skipped, and she jumped to her feet, running to meet him.

As she neared him, she saw that his left eye appeared red and slightly purple, the makings of an intense shiner. Mara brought her hand to her mouth and hid her delight. "I see Dægan has not lost *all* his strength."

"Ah, you're a funny little one," Tait retorted. "Dægan asks for you and for water. But not from a wooden ladle." He fashioned a boorish grin. "From your lips."

Mara scolded him with a look. "I did what I had to do to get him to drink."

"I'm only informing you what he sent me to say. Dægan might be charming where you're concerned, but don't forget, he's still a man."

****

"What is this I hear...you thirst for water?" Mara whispered as she climbed back into the wagon beside her husband.

The corner of Dægan's mouth lifted in a smile, but he did nothing else in response. She touched his face, his neck, and then his arms. "The river did you good. Your fever has left you."

Dægan opened his lids just enough see her. "You knew about this?"

"I'm sorry, m'lord, but your fever was madly climbing.

We were only trying to save you."

"By drowning me in a river?"

"Aye, if that is what it takes," Mara jested with him. "Just as it takes a kiss to make a man drink on occasion."

"Hmm, I might just refuse to drink any other way from now on."

Mara took his hand and weaved her fingers between his, before resting her head in the pocket of his right shoulder. She pulled the furs up to his chin and said, "Sleep, m'lord. Our journey home ends soon."

****

Tomorrow came, and by that afternoon, Dægan, Mara, and all his men were loaded on the sixteen ships harbored in Limerick, ready to make sail for Inishmore. The Northmen sat doubled at the oars and rowed for all they were worth in order to vacate the crowded harbor and drift down river. In due course, the sea opened her arms and welcomed them into her enormous waters, kissing their bearded faces with a cool mist.

They withdrew their oars, their arms and backs cramping from the hard repetitive rowing, and happily letting the power of the wind take over for the rest of the trip at sea. The sails ballooned above them and the ropes stretched and strained, the knots twisting tighter. The large wood mast creaked like never before and what first seemed like godly aid from the sky soon turned against them.

A hushed panic plagued every seaman aboard as they watched the storm blow in from the southwest. There was no time to pray to the gods. A menacing curse had been brought down upon the entire multitude of vessels. They were trapped amid their own ships, their very lives at the sea's disposal.

The wind and waves picked up, tossing the warships as if they were mere driftwood. Lightning flashed like fibrous fury, and the sky scourged them with sheets of driving rain.

Tait held fast to the sternpost as the churning water splashed in over the edge and glided swiftly over the planks of the shallow hull, seeping into every man's boots, bags, and chests aboard the ship.

"Drop sail, men!" he yelled as the wind gripped the woolen fabric and almost tore it from its mast. He looked behind him and saw the other ships fast becoming the ocean's prize for undue strength. A few men had already lost their lives to the fish as they fell overboard. "Row, men, row! Or be claimed by the sea!"

Tait looked behind him again. The sails of the other ships came down in succession and they were fighting just as desperately for control as he was. The sea fought back even harder, bitterly swelling and withdrawing beneath them. The seriousness in his eyes was as plain as his grip on the steer board. "Row!"

Mara hovered over Dægan and clung to him, keeping his weak body from sliding across the slick deck. In doing so, she also took the brunt of the ocean's punishment in her face.

Tait looked down at her, his eyes as turbulent as the raging storm above him. His thick bear cloak whipped in the wind. "Hold on!"

Mara needed not his command, for her fingers dug deep into the dragon's mighty breadth, anchored to the faith of the ship's soundness. She squeezed her eyes shut and buried her face against Dægan. She prayed. She prepared for death—either by the vengeful sea or the crushing rocks of the approaching isle.

She cried. Harder now, for the ship jostled against a large wave and its prow lifted high in the air as the water pushed up from underneath. She lost her grip and was thrown against Tait's legs, knocking him from the rudder. He fell against the dense wood post of the stern, with Dægan following. All three lay crumpled against the ship's hull, water pouring in around them.

Finally, the sea withdrew and the ship took a nosedive, shifting the fallen men from the back to the front. Their only hope as they rolled across the hull was to grab hold of something nailed to the floor.

Mara caught hold of the mast chink in the center of the hull, as Tait and Dægan wildly skated past. Tait, being the more coherent, was able to grab one of the crossbeams and still reach out to snag his tumbling chieftain. Dægan moaned, his ribs getting crushed underneath him.

"Hold on, m'lord! I have you!" Tait shouted over the chaos of the wailing crew. He pulled with all his might and dragged Dægan closer to the *keelson*, another wave spilling in over the hull.

Dægan gasped and choked, unable to keep his head above the water filling the hull until the rocking of the ship shifted the water away. He grabbed Tait's cloak, shouting. "Forget me. Man the ship, or we'll all die."

"I'm not giving you up to the sea."

Suddenly, a sharp screech from a woman's voice sounded across the hostile gales. Tait and Dægan both jerked their heads in the direction of the cry, and to their surprise, Mara had crawled to the stern and was taking the steer board into her own hands. Once there, she reached down and grabbed a length of rope from the deplored mast's rigging and tied herself to the sternpost.

"Come on, men! Get back to your post and row!" Mara howled above the sea. "Your jarl needs you!"

Dægan punched Tait's arm to gain his attention. "Get these men to row!"

Tait stood up, fighting the constant splash of water and tug of the winds as he dragged Dægan across the slippery strakes toward the rudder. Like Mara, he secured Dægan to the hull with rope.

Another wave billowed over the edge, and Tait fell at Mara's feet, winded and weak. "Give me the rudder."

"Nay!" Mara shouted back. "I'm no match for the sea. You take the oars. Get the men to row. The other ships are too near us."

Tait quickly looked out through the sleeting rain and saw that one of Havelok's ships was coming dangerously close to colliding with theirs. He sprang toward the larboard side and heaved his way to the closest chest, taking hold of a near-breaking oar.

Waves continued to hurl at him, and his waterlogged cloak yanked him aside, pulling him from his seat. He ripped the cloak from his neck and threw it overboard, his anger becoming his fuel.

"Take your oars, men! Climb this miserable ship and row with me! Now, or we'll die!"

The men started their arduous crawl over the ribs and strakes of the ship's deck, helping each man beside them as they went. Tait reached out his arm and clasped hold of a fellow seaman's forearm. "Come on, men! Climb!"

One by one, the men made harrowing progress toward their posts and finally white-knuckled the oars. In gaining timing and strength in numbers, the oars delved into the merciless waters, as they were made to do, and strode out, a force to be reckoned with.

With jaws locked, arms extended, and backs taut in the might and strain of the rowing, the warrior men propelled their *drakkar* through the tumbling tides, settling an even score with their aquatic foe. The sea had met her match and soon each of the sixteen ships dragged keel and crested on Inishmore's rocky beach.

Tait looked up from his hands, still clasped tightly around the oar, and into Mara's frightened face. She lay draped across the steer board trying to catch her breath. "Well done, m'lady," he said before collapsing over his own oar. "Well done."

Mara glanced over the exhausted and water-beaten men within the ship, and was as proud as she could be of their bravery and fierce resolution in the face of death. If not for their collective hellish determination, the sea would have had a colossal victory this day.

****

"Dægan? Dægan, where are you?" Nevan shouted amid the wreckage of beached longships and scattered men who lay about the shore. He ran from one ship to another, through spitting rain and knee-high waves, searching the dark empty hulls for his friend. "Dægan? Say you're here!"

Tait lifted his head above the gunwale upon hearing Nevan's voice. "Over here. Bring your strongest."

Nevan motioned for a crew of Irishman to follow, and when they got to the correct ship, they climbed in, finding Dægan struggling like the devil to breathe, Mara beside him.

Tait dropped to his knees and ripped open Dægan's white tunic, exposing the tightly woven wrap around his chest that seemed to cause the trouble. The water from the ocean had shrunk the linens, squeezing his ribs so tightly, he was forced to take shallow breaths.

Tait seized his dagger from his belt and cut the constrictive wrap from bottom to top, releasing the pressure around Dægan's body. His relief came quickly, but as he drew in a desperate breath, it pained him more, and he grabbed his side, rolling to favor it.

Tait jerked Dægan's hands away and rolled him to his back. Even through the pouring rain and dark of night, Tait couldn't miss the spurting of blood from his chieftain's ribs. The air that escaped his newly punctured lung was sifting within the vital organs of his chest, crushing his own heart with every breath he took.

Tait panicked. "Get him out of the rain. Come on, help me pick him up!"

Nevan and a horde of able-bodied men swarmed the fraught chieftain and lifted him from the watery hull of the ship, carrying him to the shoreline. Tait led the way, holding firm to Dægan's injured left side, calling out orders to the others who started to loiter in helplessness. "Bring the sails from the *langskips*. Cut them if you must, but hurry!"

Tait looked down at Dægan, and his frantic face spilled the awful truth of his injury, yet he offered a little white lie. "You're going to be all right."

Dægan groaned, each breath being more painful than the last. And each thought being that of dying. He tried to talk, but Tait hushed him.

"Shh...m'lord. Use your strength to breathe."

"Where is Mara?"

"She's right here," Tait replied, setting him gently on the ground.

Nevan immediately removed his long cloak and handed it to Tait. "Here. Cover him with this."

With one hand holding pressure to Dægan's open wound, Tait draped the thick cape over himself and his chieftain's face, forming a small refuge from the rain until the others could dismantle the ship and mount a shelter of heavy pine and raw wool.

Mara slid beneath it too, covering Dægan's shivering body with dry blankets she'd gathered from a warrior's chest aboard the abandoned ship. "I'm right here, Dægan. I'm right here."

Dægan labored to give her a smile and grabbed her hand, fighting through the pain of breathing. He closed his eyes in hopes his lids would keep secret his agony, but neither Mara nor Tait was that naïve.

Tait checked the wound and found his hand thickly covered with blood. The rain dumped upon them now. He tried to rub heat into Dægan's arms and cursed at the men who'd only just started to erect the crude structure above them. "I need a fire! Someone build a fire!"

Tait's voice, no matter how stern and dynamic it sounded, cracked and quivered under the weight and burden of watching Dægan's struggle. He cursed again, this time at Dægan, whose eyes had closed.

"Do not leave me, Dægan. Dare not even think it."

Dægan rolled his eyes open. "I'm still here."

"Aye, that's grand," Tait replied, reaching into nothingness. "You stay with me. You hear?" Tait shot a look toward Nevan. "Send one of your men to the fort and bring me back a mistress's embroidery needle and thread. This wound must be closed right away. Do it!"

Nevan did as he was asked, insisting urgency to the

chosen man. But he knew full well it would never work, even if he returned in time. Although robbed of speech by the magnitude of Dægan's wounds, Nevan wasn't destitute of understanding the gravity of the situation. Denying Tait optimism, though, was pointless, especially since that was clearly all he had a grasp of at the moment.

Mara heard her name from Dægan's lips. "Aye, m'lord?"

"I'm proud of you..." Dægan said finally. "Wife of mine...you sailed a *langskip*...like a great seafaring man...you sailed me home... I'm home."

"Aye, you're home now."

A large woolen sail was tossed into the air and draped over the tightly roped mast poles, forming a much appreciated sanctuary. Its purpose was a blessing as many gathered beneath it, only to watch their chieftain suffer.

Tait threw Nevan's cloak aside, as it was thoroughly drenched. He grabbed Mara's hand and pushed it firmly against Dægan's bloody left side, his eyes terrified. "Keep your hand here. Understand?" He didn't wait for a response and stood in frustration, shouting more commands outside the tent in the rain. "Where's the fire? We need a fire!"

Mara cringed at Tait's harsh, raging voice. She thought she could hear him ordering that several chests be brought from the ship to burn and possibly cursing a few men he deemed stupid for not thinking of it themselves.

"Tait is worried about you, Dægan," Mara softly whispered, feeling the warmth of Dægan's blood oozing between her fingers now.

He nodded. "As are you."

"Aye," she said trembling. "But you're going to be all right. I know it."

Dægan reached up and touched her face, catching a

tear in his palm. "Do you remember...what I told you...after the first time...I made love to you? I said...that my love is stronger...than a sword arm...and more eternal...than the last breaths...of a dying warrior... Do you remember that?"

Mara nodded, and her eyes spilled more tears into his hand.

"I'm dying, love..."

"Nay!"

"Shh..." Dægan comforted, pulling her down to his face. "'Tis all right... Be not afraid... I love you...eternally..." he said, releasing a breath. "You're safe...and I'm in your arms...just as I wanted...just as I prayed... There's nothing left...for me to do. Your Christian god let me...do all that I asked... My days on this earth are done..."

Mara shook her head frantically. Her overwhelming sorrow squeezed so tightly around her aching heart that she couldn't believe this might be the end.

"I made a deal...with your god, Mara... A promise... Forgive me, but I did... I asked Him...to let no harm come to you... That I might see you...one more time...even if it meant my death... He granted...all that I asked of Him... You must understand... No god...has ever done that for me..."

Dægan kissed her, as tenderly and as long as he could until he was incapable of holding back a convulsive shudder. He gritted his teeth, determined to finish what he wanted to say.

"I'm where I want to be...in your arms...waiting the start of another day...whether it be here...or in the next life... I'll wait for you... Forever and a day, I will wait for you…"

Mara held his face with one hand, her forehead gently resting on his. "Dægan, please. Don't give up. Please. Dægan, please!"

"I'm not giving up…" he said, exhaling longer than before. "I'm simply keeping my word…"

"No, no, no!" Mara wept. "Please, stay with me. Please, Dægan, please. I'll be lost without you. I need you." She gently shook him as he became so still. "Please speak to me."

"Hold fast to the small blessings, love…" Dægan took in a deep breath and looked as if to say one more last thing to her, but his eyes closed and the air escaped him, slowly…

Easily…

Painlessly.

Mara's breath caught in her throat, and she crumbled upon him. The harsh reality of his death sank in as she could no longer hear his heart beat in his chest.

Tait dashed inside the shelter upon hearing Mara's pitiful cry. He stopped abruptly at the scene, his arms full of wet and broken ship pieces. One slow step at a time, he walked closer, and his heart dropped like a stone in his stomach as he looked at Nevan and then Ottarr, Havelok, Ingvarr. But no one gave him the look he wished to see.

The face of optimism.

The gleam in one's proud eyes.

The smile of triumphant success against all odds.

There was nothing encouraging about their expressions, only a speechless, grief-ridden sadness.

His last look was to Dægan, and he stared with

disbelief, falling to his knees. He still held the dripping dark wood in his arms, and he squeezed them tight, trying with all he had to hide his emotional wounds. But he wasn't strong enough. His tears trailed in lines down his cheeks, and his heart broke in two.

Tait let the wood tumble from his arms and reached out to touch Dægan's right arm that had slid to the ground, his hand upturned. He noticed the scar on Dægan's palm, the one symbol that marked them permanently and indisputably as brothers, when blood alone could not join them.

"He's cold," Tait muttered. And he began to build a fire with the wood he'd brought.

Ottarr put his hands upon his shoulders. "'Tis done."

Tait pushed him away. "Dægan needs a fire."

Ottarr understood Tait's madness, but hoped to bring sense to him. "Your fire will not bring him back, son."

As if the very words slapped him, Tait jumped to his feet. The peal of his unsheathed sword rang loud into the night despite the crash of thunder overhead, and he began to hack at the unfortunate wood on the ground.

Ottarr let many cyclical swings go by before he came up behind Tait and took the weapon from his hands. It didn't go without its struggle, but with Tait already starting to break down, he soon gave it up and slid at Ottarr's feet. He finally let himself cry.

Ottarr handed Havelok the slightly chinked blade and took notice of everyone gawking. "Do not just stand there. Tait wants a fire. Give the man a damn fire."

Chapter Thirty-three

Tait opened his eyes and looked around him. The morning sun's light came unforgivably through the open sides of the tent, and he was still lying upon the ground, in the same spot where he'd collapsed, yet a good crackling fire was ablaze beside him. His last volatile actions from the night before readily became his first thoughts as he noticed the scattered pieces of Havelok's warship, further damaged from the bludgeon of his sword.

He raised his head and saw that no one, including Dægan, was present—save Nevan. The king sat on the opposite side of the fire, his face miserably aged and tired, for he'd been there all night.

Tait gathered himself from the ground and sat with his knees bent to his chest, arms crossed to hide his face in the cover of his lap. "I suppose everyone is talking about me—and my bout of madness."

"There's no shame in what you did."

Tait scoffed and rolled his head across his forearm, back and forth. "I'm no more of a man for it."

"Nor are you any less," Nevan added kindly. "Tears do not show weakness, Tait. They proudly declare your love, and there's no denying the strength of the loyal bond between you and Dægan."

Tait frowned to keep the embarrassing tears from falling again and stared out into the distant lapping shores. "Where is he?"

"He's being prepared."

"Nothing short of a king's ceremony."

"Of course," Nevan agreed. He drew in a breath. "You know you're still welcome amongst my people. There's much work to be done, but this can be your home again. Your people—"

"Dægan's people," Tait corrected sternly, short of being delusional.

Nevan paused as if he'd realized the eggshells beneath his feet. "All right. Dægan's people...are without a leader. A chieftain, or as his people call him, a *jarl*. There's no heir or brother to take his place. Moreover, his people need a home. 'Tis only fitting they look to you for those answers. What will you do, Tait?"

"I know not. I know not what I'm doing right now. All I know is that I feel like I'm lost in a nightmare, stuck in the remote boundaries of sorrow and pity, where I'm sinking deeper into the bottom of the sea. Cold, black, and heavy is the water above me."

"This burden will pass, my friend. 'Twill not be tomorrow morn, nor will it probably be before the winter solstice. But 'twill pass. I promise."

Tait tried with all he had to find comfort in Nevan's assurance, but none came. "Have you tried those fanciful words on Dægan's mother?"

"Unfortunately, hers is a mother's burden, one that will never pass. If this tragedy does not take her, the winter will."

"How is Mara?" Tait inquired, his tears welling despite his effort to inhibit them.

Nevan crossed his arms. "She mourns as you. Deeply."

"Perhaps Mara should decide where we make our

home, given she's Dægan's wife."

"Given she's widowed, I expect her to soon long for her father. And enemy or not, if she wishes to return home to that man," Nevan muttered, his voice taking a resentful tone, "I'll make those arrangements for her."

Tait looked up at the solemn king, his words triggering a conversation he and Dægan had once had in confidence. "You don't know, do you?"

Nevan's brows lifted just enough to give the impression that he minimally cared to know anything about Mara's father. "Know what?"

Tait took a deep breath, never thinking he'd be the man to say this. "Mara is your daughter."

Nevan froze, looking as if he'd heard Tait wrong or mayhap his grief was toying with his good sense. "What did you say?"

"The widow princess. Mara. She's *your* daughter."

Nevan slowly leaned forward, his expression laden with shock, disbelief, and confusion. "Why would you say something like that?"

"I say only what is true, Nevan. Dægan told me himself."

"But how? How did Dægan come to find this out?"

Tait scoffed and rolled his teary eyes. "You know Dægan. He's the most persuasive man to ever speak words. He breached your enemy's walls as a highly marked man and came out with the king all but kissing the ground where he walked. I swear Dægan could convince a bird its wings are more suitable for swimming in the sea if he so wanted."

Nevan searched the dancing flames of the fire as if the answer would emerge from the flares of red and gold. "Cathal set out to kill me ten years ago, and I doubt he'd knowingly raise my bastard child as his own. 'Twould make more sense if you told me he threw her from the cliffs at birth."

"You both loved the same woman. Is that not how your feud came about?"

"Aye, but—"

"She was your virgin love. *Your* virgin love," Tait persisted, strolling through the secret life of Nevan's past. "Could you imagine how Cathal felt, finding out the woman he was promised had given herself to someone else and that her womb grew with a seed not planted by him? What better way to get back at the man who planted the seed than stealing it right out from under him?"

"What revenge is that if your enemy knows nothing about it?" Nevan questioned. "When I came to Cathal to end the feud, why did he not tell me then? Why just kill me?"

"Because with you alive, you still threatened the one thing he had left. You may have had his wife and all her love to yourself, but he wasn't willing to share Mara with you. With your death came his sweet revenge. He had something of yours, and he wanted to make sure you never got it back."

Nevan rubbed his bearded chin, twisting and turning through the most implausible and yet most heartening change of events. "But why would Cathal, after all these years, finally admit to it?"

Tait actually smiled now. "Rest assured, Cathal didn't want to admit Mara was yours, but with a few carefully chosen words, Dægan had tricked him into doing so. He also made certain to inform Cathal that you still live, his proof being *the chest*."

Nevan's mouth gaped as everything came full circle.

"You mean the one I gave Dægan the night he found me close to death. He actually kept it?"

"Aye—and your wish as well—giving it to Mara, the one who held his heart."

Those very words pulled tears from Nevan's eyes as he remembered the one who held *his* heart twenty years ago. After all the trouble he'd gone through to fill the chest for her, he couldn't help but think that if he hadn't journeyed across the world to fill it, she might very well be alive. He thought of her sensual grace, her long dark hair, and her eyes as green as the emerald sea. But the trails of her distant memory soon led him meandering toward one other person similar in description—their daughter, *Mara*.

"Does Mara know?" Nevan asked.

Tait shook his head.

A gradual change came over Nevan's whole face and he stood with excitement. "I should tell her."

Tait leapt to his feet and blocked the way. "Nay, you cannot."

"Why not?" Nevan asked.

"Did Dægan tell her?" Tait replied. "I ask you, did he tell her? Did he ever say a word about it in his last dying breaths?"

Nevan sank in disappointment. "Nay…"

Tait gripped Nevan's arms and spoke carefully. "I know this is very hard for you, to find out you have a daughter, born of the only woman you've ever loved, and that it must not come to light. But think it through. Right now, Mara has three men who love her. If you tell her, she'll hate you all. She'll hate Cathal for keeping the secret, she'll hate you for bastardizing her, and she'll hate Dægan for knowing the truth and taking it with him to his grave. Do you really want to hurt Dægan that way? Dægan made this all possible. He made it so you can be with your daughter, and he gave his life for it. Do not tarnish his memory over details of little worth. All that matters is Mara is yours, and you know it to be true. Is that not the better revenge?"

That question and more tumbled in Nevan's mind. "Did Dægan know this prior to our arrangement? Is this why he married Mara?"

"He knew nothing of the kind then. Once he found out from you that Mara's father was your sworn enemy, he started to put the pieces together. What prompted him to delve deeper into Cathal Mac Conor's affairs was your familiarity with her appearance and that even timelines could likely mesh. After Dægan had seen for himself that she bore no resemblance to the Connacht king, he lured the truth from him. I know he would've told you himself if—" Tait tested the waters in his mind first before he took that initial step toward Christianity. "If...God...had not taken him so suddenly."

Nevan furrowed his brows at hearing the Northman's choice of words and quickly glanced at Tait's belt for the silver war god trinket he always had in his possession. In place of the pagan amulet hung the wooden rosary he'd given to Dægan.

Tait reached down and removed the beads with care, as though they were made of glass, and closed his fist around them. "Dægan told me during our journey home that peace is only found by way of peace and that obedience is only as good as the command. If we should quiet our warring voices to that of humble men, we will hear God like a trumpet in the night." Tait lowered his voice to that of a quivering whisper and fought the tears that came like a flood. "He truly believed that he could find peace in this wretched world and 'twas within every man's reach should he hear the voice of God. I want to hear it, Nevan. I want to hear it as Dægan heard it."

Nevan smiled with pride. "I believe you already have."

****

And so, at dusk, they laid their chieftain to rest in the hull of a warship. And not as a pagan accompanied by all his material possessions needed for the afterlife, but with perishables of flowers and incense. It was an eclectic sight of Viking inheritance joined with that of the Christian influence, slowly drifting out to sea.

Tait took his bow, that which he restrung with Lady Mara's hair, and stretched it above his head. A single flaming arrow awaited its flight off the cliffs of Inishmore. Everyone of the two diverse groups was present at the place where Dægan had many times gone to ponder his deepest thoughts, or to escape his troubled world to find peace. And now, from the very windswept crag Dægan adored, they gathered to celebrate him finally finding that eternal peace.

Tait released the arrow, and it cut through the dim light of the swiftly setting sun, sinking firmly into the hard oak wood of the *drakkar,* lighting the petal-strewn hull afire. Soon thereafter, his numerous loyal kinsmen cast a wave of flaming arrows in the same direction, each one finding a home within the Norse ship.

There was silence in watching the fire spread and consume the vessel, with Dægan's silhouetted body unable to be seen anymore through the high flames of the blaze. Its beautiful shades of amber and bronze reflected in the surrounding sea, equal to the breathtaking colors of the evening sky.

Mara couldn't recall a more perfect sunset than this day. She took in everything—the coolness of the mist in her face, the gentle breeze in her hair, and the distant firelight of Dægan's drifting longship against a backdrop of golden orange and sunset fire.

She memorized his last words, every single one, and branded his face in her memory, for Dægan Ræliksen's story would be told, if not amongst those who craved a good tale, then to his very child, sure to stir within her womb. It would be spread from ear to ear, and with just as much grandeur and excitement as the warrior-skald himself would've put forth.

Yet Dægan's story does not end here with his body laid to rest, for there's more to be told....

With his settlement lying in burnt ruins and everything taken for which to trade, there was still the heavy burden on his people of how to rebuild their houses of wood and sod when the very land they lived upon could not furnish those materials.

Mara had the perfect idea to remedy this predicament.

Just as Dægan had done, and his father before him, she took the beautiful sunset as a sign, an indication that no other place would be more suited for her and the people Dægan left behind than that of the splendorous Inishmore.

That night as everyone slept, Mara sped her horse across the rocky plain to what was left of Dægan's house. She walked carefully through the ashes and scorched timbers to what would have been the main room of the longhouse and past the central hearth. She imagined where their boxbed chamber would've been and dropped to her knees to search amid the ash-strewn ground for evidence of the trapdoor. She knocked on the floor in several random places and listened for the hollow spot that denoted the empty space below.

Tucking her fingers between the boards, she pried open the badly damaged trapdoor and feared the flames had reached beneath and ruined that for which she so desperately searched. She reached blindly into the dark hole and felt the old leather satchel at her fingertips. She gripped it fervently with both hands and lifted it from its deep earthen home, hugging it tightly against her chest as though it were Dægan himself.

Mara looked up at the dark midnight sky brazen with bright stars and smiled, knowing Saint Ciarán's book would again save Dægan's people.

And…she smelled rain.

THE END

Author's Note

If you enjoyed *Sunset Fire*, I encourage you to read on, as Dægan's epic tale is not yet finished. I know it may seem as though his story ended tragically, but I promise to provide you with one of the most beautiful and moving happily ever afters ever written.

Because I too desire the coveted Happily Ever After ending when reading romance novels, I've provided a memorable, grand finale for all my readers in the continuing books of my Vikings of Honor series. The incredible adventure of timeless, true love awaits you...

Vikings of Honor Series
Sunset Fire, Book 1
Emerald Glory, Book 2
Souls Reborn, Book 3
Tempered Steel, Book 4

****

Are you intrigued enough to read more of my Viking series? For your reading pleasure, I've included the first two chapters of *Emerald Glory*. I hope you enjoy!

Sincerely yours,
Renee Vincent

Emerald Glory

Vikings of Honor, Book Two

Chapter One

Iceland, AD 923

The door of the longhouse burst open, and seven men, outfitted in conical helmets, snow-dusted wolfskin cloaks, and swords, rushed in. They hastened to surround the boxbed where two entangled bodies sat up in complete surprise, the covers drawn to their chins to hide their nakedness.

Before the master of the house could utter a single word of protest about the rude intrusion—not to mention the seven swords now pointed at his heart—an eighth man entered, taller and broader in stature but with more of a casual arrogance than his comrades. He too was helmeted. But as he strolled closer, he removed it, revealing a headful of dark blond hair.

The master of the house swallowed hard and somehow gained his tongue for speaking. "How dare you burst into my home!"

The Norse intruder only stared, as if to collect his thoughts after the long tiresome journey he'd endured before this moment. His breathing was not heavy or labored, and his face showed no signs of emotion. It was difficult to say why his words failed him, but there was no doubt the tension in the room grew as the silence lengthened. Finally, he spoke, but not to the master. He looked at the woman.

"Are you his wife?"

"Of course not! She's but a whore!" the man answered for her. "And what matter is it of yours?"

The red-haired woman's lips pursed tightly, and she slapped her master's face. In the heat of her anger, the linen sheets she'd been holding to her chin dropped and revealed an ample blessing of youthful breasts for all to see.

For the first time since his entering, the Northman smiled. "Be not angered, woman. The insult this man delivered has just saved your life. Get your clothes and leave."

"And where must I go on a cold night like this?" she asked, seemingly unafraid of the eight towering men surrounding her.

"Wherever you choose. But know this, I shall never insult you should you decide to leave with me, *my lady*."

A slight grin eased across her rosy cheeks upon hearing the noble title the bearded stranger flattered her. Likely no one had ever called her by a dignified name. And it seemed enough to convince her that tagging along with the man— whose name she'd yet to learn—was a better idea than wading in knee-high snowdrifts toward the next warm longhouse owned by a man she'd already lain with countless times.

She stood up from the boxbed and approached the handsome Northman. She looked at him with seductive eyes, and he gazed over her firm stark-naked body, blushed pink from the warmth of the room's fire.

The Northman reached out to the nearest wall and swiped her master's fine bear cloak, then wrapped it around her shoulders. "My langskip awaits you outside. Go on," he said with a subtle jerk of his head. "This is no place for a delicate woman."

She slowly walked away, dragging her hand across his armored chest before bending down and gathering the rest of her clothes. The Northman didn't catch sight of her provocative stoop, for his eyes remained fixed on her master, whose face now fumed with rage.

Once the Northman heard the door close behind him, he stepped forward, this time in a quicker fashion. "Get up," he demanded.

The man stood as he was told and locked eyes with his aggressor, the very man who stole his woman property right out from under him with barely an effort. "Who do you think you are?" he growled.

As if thankful the man finally asked, the Northman smiled callously and introduced himself in a monotone voice. "I'm Gustaf, son of Rælik, son of the man you slaughtered in Hladir twenty-three winters ago…in his own home…his wife to watch. I've come to avenge my father. There were ten of you sent by Harald Fairhair. I've traveled through rain, snow, and bone-chilling north winds in search of each one. You're the ninth, Ragnar, son of Thorsteinn."

Gustaf watched as Ragnar's eyes widened. Not only had he burst into this man's home, threatened him with a show of swords, and taken his harlot, he'd also traced Ragnar's lineage and proved that the rumors of Fairhair's involvement in the other eight deaths were all untrue. Fairhair had not paid a group of thugs to eradicate those who knew any of his past treacheries left hanging in the wind. It was one man's vengeance—an avenging son.

Ragnar scoffed. "So 'twould be you who have forced us all to leave our families and homelands to live in exile—"

"Give me the name of the tenth man," Gustaf cut in, "and I swear your death will be swift. Give it not, and you'll die in the same manner which you had once deemed necessary for my father—drawn and hanged by your own entrails."

It did not take long for the man to decide his fate. "I'll not give you his name, as I'm neither a coward nor a traitor. What I did, was by order of the king." He spat at Gustaf's feet. "Long live Harald Fairhair."

"So be it." Gustaf unsheathed his dagger for the punishment at hand.

Chapter Two

Ireland, AD 923
Seven Years After Dægan Ræliksen's Death

Breandán Mac Liam rested his weary bones against a select tree trunk in the forest of the Clan Rourke hunting grounds. He was an adept hunter of both large and small game, and his talent for doing so brought him a considerable amount of wealth in the trade market despite his tender age of twenty-seven years. The livelihood of red deer, hare, and fox fur trading in Galway afforded him much freedom and independence, but he didn't particularly enjoy the solitude. The unfortunate result of loneliness was often having too much time to think. And all he could think about was the Connacht king's daughter.

Though it had been more than seven years since he'd seen Mara, his love for her hadn't lessened. He was chained to her memory and the hope that one day they could be together.

When he'd first laid eyes on Mara, she was a teenage girl, riding her horse through the meadows of his father's land. Had it been anyone else, Breandán would've put a swift stop to it. But with Mara, he didn't mind that she occasionally disturbed his hunting.

Her natural beauty and grace caught his eye first. The more he'd seen her lingering in the fields and lounging near the River Shannon, the more he came to appreciate her freeborn spirit and gentle kindness, traits he assumed she hadn't inherited from her pompous father, Cathal Mac Conor.

Mara was nothing like him. She was lighthearted and nimble as she sang and danced in the wildflowered fields. She was elegant and agile as she raced her horse through brooks and briars. And above all, she hadn't an arrogant bone in her body. She'd greet and welcome anyone who came into her life without ever looking down on them.

Despite her graciousness, Breandán had never felt comfortable enough to approach her. In his eyes, he was naught but a common man with common needs, and—given her noble status—he couldn't give her what he thought she deserved.

When he finally had made himself known to her, she was already in love with and married to a Northman named Dægan Ræliksen. To add to his misfortune, Mara no longer lived near Breandán, but on Inishmore, an island off the west coast of Ireland.

Since that time, Breandán had desperately tried to move on. Tried to forget her. But it proved useless. Each passing summer, when the ports brimmed with gossip, he'd hear tidbits of information regarding her current state of affairs. One summer, it was news about her husband's tragic death. The next year, it was how she'd given birth to the Northman's son the following spring.

While most of the chin wagging was usually hearsay, the thought of Mara being all alone and raising a son on such a harsh island as Inishmore pulled at his heart. Much of his desire to see her again was driven by the deep love he'd always had for her and the sincere need to make certain she was all right. He'd mulled the idea of going to her a thousand times over in his head. But the one time he'd finally convinced himself to visit her, he'd learned there was talk of another marriage between her and another Northman.

Again, he'd missed out on his opportunity to be with Mara.

That was the final stake driven through his heart, and since then, he could hardly bring himself to step foot in Galway. Instead, he relied on his childhood friend and hunting partner, Marcas, to trade his goods. He stayed clear of everything that would or might remind him of Mara. He even went as far as hunting farther north to avoid familiar landmarks she used to frequent.

None of his efforts or the changes he'd made to his routine mattered. Nothing, not even time, could lessen the pain or water down the vivid image of Mara's face. She haunted his thoughts and his dreams.

"I suppose you expect me to build the fire tonight," Marcas grumbled as he dismounted from his horse and found Breandán already relaxing against a tree.

"I snared more rabbits than you this day, did I not?"

"You always do, but I didn't know it meant I had to wait on you hand and foot. Would you like me to cook your dinner as well? Perhaps even draw a hot bath for you?"

The sarcasm in his friend's remark was almost humorous. Almost. "Dinner will suffice."

Marcas scoffed at his reply and unsaddled his horse, tossing the heavy tack on the ground beside Breandán. "When are you going to get Mara out of your head?"

It was bad enough he had to cope with her absence, much less explain the reason why he couldn't let go to someone else. He wanted and needed her as badly as any man could want or need a woman, and trying to put it into words was beyond his capability.

"Or better yet," Marcas added, adjusting the cloak around his shoulders, "why do you not simply go to her. Perhaps her marriage to another was naught more than port gossip."

"The man I spoke to said he heard it directly from Tait's mouth. Why would Dægan's comrade say anything untrue? Besides, I cannot go to her without a relevant reason. Imagine the chatter my unsolicited visit would bring. I don't want that for her, nor do I want to appear desperate in her eyes."

"It's been seven years, *a chara*. I'm certain she's moved on, and you must do the same."

"I've tried."

"Isolating yourself in the hunting grounds is not going to help you forget her. You need to remove her from your mind permanently. And I know the perfect remedy."

Breandán let his head fall back against the tree, knowing his friend's antidote was probably either a drunken stupor or a wild romp with a practiced woman, neither of which interested him.

"What you need," Marcas said joyously as he slid to his knees beside Breandán, "is that fine woman your father has deemed worthy of you. Regan's daughter. What is her name again?"

"Sorcha."

Marcas's smile grew at the sweet sound of her name. He even reached out with both hands in a gesture that resembled mild groping. He shot Breandán a sideways glance. "Can you not see what gifts she has to offer you?"

Breandán cracked a smile at his crude companion. "My eyes have seen, but…"

"But what?"

"She's like a sister to me."

"Ach," Marcas groaned. "Why must you resort to that?"

"Because she is," Breandán confirmed. "I've known her all my life. She used to meet me in the forest when her father and brothers were busy with their chores. She'd often keep me from mine, which in the beginning gained me a swift beating, but I found ways around it. Rising before sunrise to get a head start or simply working faster."

Marcas's interest was suddenly piqued, albeit for suggestive reasons. "Aye…go on."

"Nothing ever happened," Breandán amended. "We were merely children who got along well together. We fished, climbed trees, laughed at each other…"

"Naught more?"

Breandán furrowed his brow. "We were children, Marcas."

"Not forever. She grew up mighty quickly if I recall."

Breandán nodded and swiftly added, "And so lost interest in fishing and climbing trees, as most girls do."

Marcas shook his head in disappointment. "You're truly daft, *a chara*. There are other things you could've done in that forest to keep her interest."

"And have her three brute brothers, not to mention her very large father, after my hide? I think not."

Marcas raised a single finger, denouncing Breandán's logic. "But now you've attained their blessings. You could do anything you wanted with that voluptuous woman and have no ill will from any of her family because you'd be her rightful husband. You'd obtain a heavy dowry along with her, and your father would gain the alliance he desires with Regan. Everyone would win, including me."

Breandán looked at his friend oddly. "*You?* How would *you* benefit from the union?"

"By getting to hear all the naughty details of your conjugal interludes. I relate all my interludes as they happen."

Breandán rolled his eyes. "Well, it's certainly not because I've ever asked you to." He became suspicious of Marcas's motives. "Did my father put you up to this?"

"You'd like to think that, wouldn't you? 'Twould be easier to dismiss altogether if others tried to involve themselves in your private matters. But rest assured, I'm the only one who matters, and I couldn't care less about your privates."

As Marcas walked away into the depths of the dark forest, laughing at his own joke, Breandán gave thought to the arrangement between him and Sorcha. It would be a good match considering they were already friends. Most often a man was married to a woman he barely knew, and love came, hopefully, thereafter. They, however, wouldn't have to endure that awkward part of the relationship.

I could love her, he thought. Sorcha was a beautiful young woman with long ebony hair and ice-blue eyes that looked straight into a man's soul. She was taller than most girls her age, and more endowed than most women who'd birthed three or more children. While she wasn't a promiscuous woman, a man would have to be blind not to notice her.

Aye, I could love her. He already cared deeply for her, given their childhood and the time they'd spent together. Learning to love her as his wife might come easier than he thought…if he tried hard enough.

Breandán pulled his cloak of gray hare tighter around his shoulders as his breath misted the air. He started to feel the chill of the cool night and eventually the cold, harsh reality that even if he could love another the way he loved Mara, did he really want to?

****

Breandán woke to the sound of a twig snapping underfoot and realized he'd fallen asleep sitting up against the tree. The last thing he remembered was thinking about Mara as Marcas left to fetch wood for a fire.

He examined his surroundings with a careful shift of his eyes. Marcas lay a few feet from him, snoring quietly. A fire burned warmly at his feet, and his dinner—that Marcas must have cooked anyway—hung from a spit beside him.

Farther beyond his immediate surroundings, he noticed the horses had their ears perked high as if they too heard the sound. He peered in the direction they stared and unsheathed his dagger. He tried to awaken Marcas with a hard nudge of his foot, but Marcas only grunted and rolled over, muttering something about "get your own wood."

While keeping his eyes on the darkness ahead, Breandán frowned and decided to search the woods alone. He didn't bother with his bow, as it was too dark to make out a distant target. His plan was to sneak up on the intruders in the same manner as they'd sneaked up on him, while hoping he'd not be terribly outnumbered.

He rounded the horses and darted behind a tree. Cautiously, he looked again, allowing his vision to adjust from the bright light of the fire to the dim obscurity of the dense woods. Once his eyesight adapted and he could distinguish woodland objects, he scurried from tree to tree, taking a deliberate wide and circular path until he found refuge behind a vantage point of thick brush and boulders.

He scouted the area as he crept and caught sight of a single dark figure in a hood and cloak, moving closer to where he and Marcas had made camp. The stranger was not close enough to do any harm to Marcas yet, but it was obvious the person was advancing in that direction.

Breandán reached down and picked up a stone. He launched it distantly behind the trespasser and hit a tree to distract him. As planned, the hooded figure walked guardedly away from Marcas, but foolishly in the direction of the ricocheting stone.

The man was quite short in stature and apparently unskilled in stealth or hunting. Breandán could easily take him alone, bearing in mind he wouldn't get much help from his oblivious comrade. Taking a deep breath, he cut a path straight toward the stranger and pounced on him. With one arm around the man's forehead, Breandán stretched the hooded man's neck to meet a well-placed dagger. "Who are you? Speak your name."

"Please," a woman's whimpering voice proclaimed. "Do not kill me. I beg you."

Breandán's heart stopped, and his breath caught. He knew that voice but couldn't believe his ears. He spun the woman around and jerked the hood from her head, gasping at his find. His legs faltered and his steady hunting hands shook until he dropped his knife.

Breandán spoke Mara's name, but it came out so erratically, he sounded more like a stuttering fool.

She smiled after hearing it on his lips. "I feared perhaps you'd forgotten me."

Breandán gawked at her, thinking he was dreaming and she'd soon disappear. But he watched her step forward and heard the sound of the wet autumn leaves beneath her feet. He saw the few wisps of hair blow back from her face. He even swore he felt her light, warm breath on his cheek as she neared.

He swallowed hard, trying to pull himself together, but he failed. He recognized the fragrant oils she used from when they'd first met, like honeysuckle, only sweeter, and it made her presence that much more convincing.

This was no dream. Mara was real and standing before him.

An image of him pressing his dagger against her precious throat flashed in his memory, and his voice returned. "God's teeth, Mara, I could've killed you!" He cradled her jaw and tilted her head. To his relief, her skin hadn't even reddened from his blade.

Mara looked deep into his eyes. "You would never harm me."

Captured by her sensuous stare, he held it with his own. A slight grin tugged at his lips. "Aye, I would never harm you, Mara."

She melted against him and laid her head upon his chest. "I thought I'd never find you."

Reality smacked him in the face, and he gripped her shoulders, holding her from his body. "You came alone? Surely your new husband would not approve of such recklessness." He peered into the forest, searching for a spouse. Surely, not even a neglectful husband would allow her to journey this distance unaided. "Did you come alone?" Breandán demanded, "Answer me, Mara."

"Aye," she replied. "No one is aware of my travels."

Breandán couldn't believe she'd journeyed so far on her own without some sort of escort. Was she mad? "Mara, do you not know the risks you've taken in coming here, let alone the strains you may have placed upon your marriage? Your husband won't take kindly to this. We must get you home."

"Please, do not sent me back there." Mara gripped his arms. "I've come so far to see you. Please, do not send me away."

Breandán read deeper into her pleas. "Has he hurt you? Has anyone hurt you?"

Mara shook her head. "Nay, he is a good man."

"Then why are you here?"

"Because I love—"

"Mara," Breandán interrupted quickly. "Do not say that."

"But 'tis true. For so long, I've held it inside me, and I cannot anymore. I belong with you."

Her words opened a dam, and his emotions came rushing forward. Everything he'd ever felt—ever hoped for.

I belong with you.

But as soon as that little phrase echoed in his ears, he remembered the man who'd taken her as his wife. His heart deflated. "You married again before God and witnesses. What is done is done."

Mara's eyes welled with tears. "Did you not hear me? I said I belong with you."

"I heard you," Breandán replied, adoring those words. "But 'tis not something you should say to me. Do you not know how difficult 'tis to stand here and look at you, and not greedily take what is rightfully another man's?"

"Then you still love me as I've always believed."

"Aye, but my undying love for you does not make this just." She burrowed closer to his chest, looking at him in a way that matched his own lustful feelings. "Please, Mara," Breandán begged halfheartedly. "I cannot resist you in this way."

For years, he'd dreamed of this moment and now, when it was actually upon him, he was pushing her away. Was he out of his mind? Marcas would call him an absolute imbecile.

"Kiss me," Mara encouraged.

And her little request stole his last fiber of strength. "God forgive me," he muttered before he threaded his hands in her hair and took her lips with a slow, hesitant kiss.

"Breandán," was all he heard, but it did not come from Mara. It was male and very stern. As he whirled to face the voice behind him, a solid fist walloped him square in the jaw.

Breandán gasped, and his eyes flashed open to find himself sitting by the fire, against the tree, with Marcas now looking at him oddly. Everything was as it had been before he fell asleep, and the figure of another man was nowhere in sight.

"Are you all right?" Marcas asked. "You were talking in your sleep. At one point, you were asking God Almighty for forgiveness. What were you doing?"

Breandán finally allowed himself to breathe. "I dreamt Mara came to me. And she was there in my arms, in my very possession."

Marcas sighed and rolled back under his warm animal pelt. "And I suppose you're gathering meaning from this now."

Breandán pondered the actual difference between this dream and the ones from his past. He could still feel the remnant sensations of Mara's lips on his, and he could smell the distinct aroma of honeysuckle when it was far too early in the season for blossoms. How could he not gather meaning from this encounter?

Though he had no idea if they were destined to meet again, he prayed that fate, or chance, or even God would somehow bring them together.

About Renee Vincent

RENEE VINCENT is a *USA Today* bestselling author of romance and women's fiction. Her books have earned numerous accolades, including a #1 Bestseller for Viking Romance.

She lives on a secluded hundred-acre horse farm in the rolling hills of Kentucky with her husband, two beautiful daughters, and a few fur babies who've managed to weasel their way into a couple of books. When she's not writing, she loves to decorate (and redecorate) her home, knit cozy blankets, send homemade cards to family and friends, and concoct her own versions of recipes to pass down to her girls.

Through the years, Renee has connected with some of the most dedicated and gracious readers who crave unpredictable plot twists, gripping adventure, and undying love. For that, she is most grateful.

www.ReneeVincent.com

Books By Series

Vikings of Honor Series
Sunset Fire, Book 1
Emerald Glory, Book 2
Souls Reborn, Book 3
Tempered Steel, Book 4

Mavericks of Meeteetse Series
Longing for Langston, Brody & Liv, Book 1
Made for McKinley, Jonas & Ava, Book 2
Falling For Forester, Cole & Crys, Book 3

Jamett & Joseph Series
The Start of Something Good, Book 1
The Road to Something Better, Book 2
The Gift of Something Grand, Book 3
Something's Bound to Happen, Books 1 - 3

Stand Alone Novel
Silent Partner

If you enjoyed this book by Renee Vincent, please consider leaving an honest review at your favorite vendor. Reviews not only give credibility to an author's work, they also help other readers find quality books worth reading.